Judith Wynne

Judith Wynne

Catherine Louisa Pirkis

MINT EDITIONS

Judith Wynne was first published in 1884.

This edition published by Mint Editions 2021.

ISBN 9781513272009 | E-ISBN 9781513277004

Published by Mint Editions®

MINT
EDITIONS

minteditionbooks.com

Publishing Director: Jennifer Newens
Design & Production: Rachel Lopez Metzger
Project Manager: Micaela Clark
Typesetting: Westchester Publishing Services

To
NORAH MARGUERITE CHANDOS CECIL
This Book
Is Dedicated.
NUTFIELD, 1884

Contents

Volume III

VOLUME I

I

It lay in a deep, shadowy hollow, a forlorn, God-forgotten house to look at. Like the Grange of poetic legend, it was surrounded by a moat, but it could not be said of it, as of the ill-fated Mariana's abode, that around "for leagues no tree did mark the waste," for it was backed by a dark, thick wood of most ancient growth. Plas-y-coed the old house was called by the people in the district; The Grange was the name by which it was as a rule distinguished by the Reeces, in whose family, with its acres of park and arable land, it had been for generations, passing in steady, unbroken line from heirs male to heirs male.

Beyond the background of dark wood rose the blue mountains of Llanniswth, peak over peak in all their sharp, lonely grandeur. Down their rough, cleft sides rushed ceaselessly the cataracts, which fertilised the deep-growing trees of the ancient wood. The air was always humid, a grey mist seemed ever hanging about. The lichen on the old walls, the marish mosses which fringed the paths, had reached an almost tropical luxuriance; the stone-paved terrace was absolutely slippery with the minute vegetation which grew in every crevice between the flags.

"I say, old fellow," cried Oscar Reece, coming down the five steps which led from the house with a spring and a bound, "you should turn in an army of gardeners here; our lives are not safe, a coroner's inquest will be the end of it—that's a fact."

Wolfgang Reece, standing on the terrace with a sealed letter in his hand, paid no heed to the speaker. He was elder brother by about a dozen years to Oscar, and is the present master of The Grange.

"Where is my mother?" he asked, and getting Oscar's reply, "In the breakfast-room," he opened a little door leading off the terrace and went into the house.

Within, the house was as desolate as it was without. It abounded in long, winding passages, and small, low-ceiled rooms. The breakfast-room, with the morning sun upon it, was possibly the cheeriest and best lighted of these. When Wolfgang turned the handle and went in, it seemed full of the chequered sunlight which fell through the beech-trees growing close—too close for health one would think—to the casemented window. An elderly lady was seated in a huge armchair with knitting-needles in her hand; a big, brown mastiff lay at her feet, and formed her footstool. Her head was large and well-set, her features good, but too massive to suit conventional ideas of female beauty. Her hair was white as snow, her complexion clear and pale. The least exact of observers might have identified these two as mother and son. Wolfgang had the same large, well-set head, and regular, massive features. Her hair must have been fair as his in her early youth, her eyes possibly as deep a grey, and as clear and bright as his, though now, alas! dim and glazed with premature disease which was slowly but surely ending in total blindness.

When they spoke their voices had the same clear, strong vibration.

"Here is a letter, mother," he said, "with an Indian stamp on it. Shall I read it to you?"

"An Indian stamp!" she repeated. "I only know of one person in India likely to write to me—Colonel Wynne, my mother's third cousin. But it's seven or eight years at least since we last corresponded. Yes, read it, Wolf."

It was from Colonel Wynne. The first page of the letter was given up to congratulations.

"I heard quite by chance," he wrote, "of Wolf coming into the Welsh property. From the bottom of my heart I congratulate you all. It was an odd thing poor Bernard Reece dying so suddenly. Only twenty-seven, wasn't he? That trip to Bermuda was a wild thing for a man to undertake without any rhyme or reason. However, it has brought good fortune to you and yours, so we won't moan over it. Now I am writing to ask a special favour of you, Elizabeth. Will you take my little girl, Judith, under your wing, for the next two years? As you know, she has been brought up in France with her mother's people. When my Mélanie died, Judith went to live with her aunt and uncle at St. André. That was ten years ago, and I have not seen her since. Well, the aunt was a strict Presbyterian, the uncle a Catholic priest, an odd commingling of influence to place a child under, was it not? All I begged of them was not to interfere with her religious opinions. I don't think they have, for she writes to me that she has never failed in her attendance at a Protestant place of worship. The aunt has just died, and as I do not like the idea of her staying on with the priest, I shall be very grateful to you if you will take her into your home, give her an insight, as it were, into an English household, till I can return to England and make one for her. In two years' time I hope to be able to do this, but not before. I know of no one in England but yourself of whom I could ask this favour."

Oscar had come into the room during the reading of this letter. He now burst forth exuberantly:

"A girl coming to stay with us? How awfully jolly! Mother, of course you'll say yes. It would be downright cruel to refuse to take her in. I hope she'll be a good specimen. Of course, Wolf, you'll have the old place made habitable now?"

Mrs. Reece laid down her knitting.

"Let me see, Oscar," she said meditatively: "Judith Wynne is just nineteen, you are just twenty. Ah, you will be safe enough. Nothing under five-and-twenty would suit you at the present moment. Wolf is in the greater danger, he is turned thirty-one, but still thirty-one is an age at which a man ought to be able to take care of himself."

"Yes, if he is ever going to," said Wolf, laying down the letter and walking towards the door.

"I say," shouted Oscar after him, "you'll see about the repairs at once, won't you?"

But to this Wolf made no reply.

II

From whatever cause it might arise, the fact remained that no sound of workman's hammer nor gardener's hoe broke the silence which, like the mountain mist, seemed perpetually to overhang the old Grange.

Judith Wynne, as she drove up the weedy road leading to the old house, thought in all her life she had never set eyes upon a more hopelessly desolate and forlorn-looking habitation.

The neat, pretty French home she had just quitted was still photographed vividly on her brain. She shut her eyes, and once more it rose up before her as on the morning when she had looked her last good-bye to it—a square, white-fronted villa, in the streaming June sunlight, long-windowed, with pretty green veranda which ran the length of its frontage, and was broken here and there by the big orange-trees in tubs, and pink-flowered oleanders. A house, in fact, giving every outward sign of neat housewifery and careful keeping. She opened her eyes, and, lo! there stood before her a long, low, damp-looking building, grey with the lichen that hung about its eaves, green in patches with the smaller-growing mosses, its wood-work bronzed and blistered, its windows uncurtained, its frontage unswept. The contrast between the two homes—the one which her memory held and the one which faced her—was keen. It set her shuddering, and it set her thinking.

WOLF AND OSCAR HAD MET her at Pen-Cwellyn, the little station seven miles from The Grange, and had driven her home. It was a long drive. The June sun was at its highest, and Wolf had apologised for the open carriage he had brought for her.

"We have no other," he had said simply. Oscar's fair, boyish face had flushed crimson as he spoke.

Judith, looking from one to the other, thought she had never seen two brothers more unlike in form and feature.

"He will be handsome in ten years' time," she had said to herself, taking stock of Oscar's bronzed hair, blue eyes, and fine, though slight figure. "And he will be an old man in ten years' time," she had thought as her eye rested on Wolf's stooping shoulders, the grey that showed here and there on his brown hair and beard, the deep, knotted frown which drew his brows together and made his dark eyes seem sunken and dim.

CATHERINE LOUISA PIRKIS

Oscar kept cheerful talk going as they drove along the flinty road. It necessarily had to be talk on general topics, for they were strangers, one to the other, in all but name. Judith knew but little of these distant cousins of hers. She had heard some seven or eight years previously of the death of their father, a hard-working East of London clergyman, who had taken typhus-fever from one of his poor parishioners, and had died at his post. She had heard that his mantle had fallen on his son Wolfgang, and that he had worked as hard as a curate as his father had as a rector. Whispers had also reached her, though she scarcely knew how true they were, of hardship and poverty which the widow had been called upon to endure; of the death by fever of all her children, save the eldest and youngest; of the gradual, though certain loss of her own eyesight. All this Judith had heard in a far-off roundabout sort of way from time to time, and she had listened to it much as she would have listened to anyone telling her of changes in the government of Australia or Japan, a sort of something altogether outside her little circle of living interests. Then, quite unexpectedly, there had come to her news in a more direct fashion from her father, telling her of the change in the fortunes of these people, of their sudden accession to comparative wealth and importance through the death of Bernard Reece. With this news Colonel Wynne had coupled the wish that, for a time at any rate, Judith should make her home with these distant relatives.

It seemed odd to the girl to have her life thus suddenly linked to the family life of these strangers. She could scarcely realise the fact, even as she drove along the lonely Welsh road with the two brothers. It seemed to her almost incredible that her bright, beautiful, tranquil French life was altogether a thing of the past, that for the next two years at any rate her days were to be passed among people of whom she knew little more than the names.

Mrs. Reece gave the young girl a kindly greeting.

"I wish I could see your face, my dear," she said, "that I might see whether there is anything of your father in you."

She had not learnt that quick, light touch which comes naturally to the born-blind, and which conveys to them likeness of feature as well as knowledge of colour. Poor soul! her blindness had struck her too late in life for that. She was obliged to trust to one or other of her sons for her impressions of the outer world.

Later on in the day, when Judith had gone to her room to rest, tired out with her long journey, Mrs. Reece, hearing Oscar over his fishing-tackle, asked him to come and tell her what the new comer was like, and what he thought of her. Oscar gave a low whistle.

"Oh, well, she's—she's just so—nothing more. That's what I think of her."

"Unintelligible, as usual, Oscar," said his mother; "try to put your meaning into plain English, for my special benefit."

"'Pon my life I can't, mother. She's just so—nothing more. I can't say she is what she isn't."

"But you can tell me whether she is tall or short, ugly or pretty, fair or dark, I suppose."

"No; I don't think she's anything of all that; she's what I said, 'just so,' and nothing will make anything else of her."

"So!"—Mrs. Reece had passed her early days in Germany, and had brought back with her a fondness for this monosyllable together with a love for knitting-pins. "Is Wolf there? Ask him to come to me."

And Wolf coming had the questions repeated to him. What was Judith like, and what did he think of her?

He answered slowly and thoughtfully:

"She is small, and slight, with dark hair, pale face, and very dark eyes. She speaks little, but I should imagine thinks a great deal. I should say she was fond of poetry and that sort of thing, not of the realities of life."

"Stop—stop, Wolf; that will do. I didn't ask for a rhapsody. Ah, I can see which of you two boys will want keeping out of harm's way."

If she could have seen the sudden dark cloud that swept over Wolf's face, she would not have hazarded her light words.

Oscar saw it and sought to effect a diversion.

"Why, mother!" he cried, "after seven years of a curate's life, with all the women in the parish shooting at him, do you think Wolf will fall a victim to the first little dark girl who comes into the house?"

The old lady shook her head wisely.

"Ah," she answered, "Cupid takes some with darts, and some with traps. Look to yourself, Wolf, that's all."

III

Next to the keen eye which pierces straight to the heart of things, the clear eye for an outline is perhaps one of the most blessed gifts a man or woman can be dowered with. It keeps the senses unmystified by the small, pressing, multitudinous details of everyday life, the brain free to take in "the situation" whatever it may be, the hand ready and strong for action.

Judith had possessed this clear, true eye for an outline in a remarkable degree from childhood upwards. Wolf, describing her to his mother, had credited her with a poetic temperament; nevertheless, others seeing her from their point of view, had been wont to speak of her as a remarkably practical, matter-of-fact person. Both descriptions were true; the two temperaments are not irreconcilable, whatever some superficial thinkers may say.

Be this as it may, Judith had not been a week in the old Grange before she said to herself as she noted Wolf's gloomy, abstracted ways, the manifest yet unsuccessful efforts he made to be one with the rest of the household: "That man has suffered." Before the end of a second week she had appended a rider to her verdict, which ran thus: "He is suffering now." At the close of three weeks another rider was added to this effect: "And he has a secret locked up in his heart."

With Oscar she speedily became on very good terms. They called each other by their Christian names before the first fortnight was over their heads. Their dispositions, though diverse, harmonised admirably. Oscar was a good talker, Judith a first-rate listener. Oscar loved a free, outdoor life for the sake of sport and plentiful bodily exercise, and Judith loved the fields, the mountains, the woods, because she had an eye for a landscape, and a heart that beat in sympathetic response to every glad sound of bird, beast, or insect.

Thus it came about that most of the bright June mornings were passed in each other's society; and when, June ended, Oscar announced the fact that he was going up to London to stay in the house of a clergyman, who was to coach him for matriculation at Oxford, Judith felt that all the sunshine was leaving Plas-y-Coed, and wondered what other companion would be given her for her morning walks and mountain scrambles.

There was no talk, however, of other companionship.

"Judith will be dull, I fear," said Wolf to his mother, a day or two after Oscar had gone.

He called her Judith behind her back; Miss Wynne always when addressing her.

He had watched the young girl go slowly along the weedy gravel path, and lean over the mossy gate as though she were looking longingly across the green fields to the dark hills beyond.

Mrs. Reece was pursuing her own train of thought.

"No one but a man or an idiot would have sent a girl of that age into a house with two grown-up sons, unless he wanted her to marry one of them," she said slowly.

Wolf started as if struck by some sudden idea.

"Judith will be very rich some day. She is an heiress, is she not?" he asked abruptly.

The mother nodded.

"Her father has coined money, I hear, since he retired from the service. Of course, as she is an only child, it must all go to her. Then, too, her mother's money is settled on her. She was Mélanie MacIvor Dutertre, half Scotch, half French. She and her sister—Judith's aunt, lately dead—were both strict Presbyterians. The brother followed his father's faith, and became a priest. Of course his money will go to the Church, but the aunt's money has been carefully tied up for Judith when she comes of age."

"It's a thousand pities Oscar isn't ten years older," said Wolf dreamily.

The mother laughed outright.

"What, are you turning matchmaker, Wolf? You are coming out in a new character with a vengeance. She would suit you ever so much better than Oscar."

Wolf did not hear her; he had taken his hat and followed Judith down the garden-path.

She was leaning over the gate, half-thinking, half-dreaming, in that disjointed, hazy sort of way girls of nineteen are given to. Her heart at first had been full of sweet, sad memories of the dear dead aunt as she had leaned over the gate, but one by one they had been chased away by the glad, bright realities about her—the flooding sunshine, the gloriously blue sky, the fresh greenness of field and woodland, the summer-scented breeze and soft air.

A shadow fell across her as she stood. She started, and turned to see Wolf at her elbow. She had not heard his footfall on the path. Somehow

CATHERINE LOUISA PIRKIS

the mere approach of this grave, stern man always seemed to send a chill through her. She could never think of him as parish priest, pastor and shepherd of his flock; she could picture him rather as one of the soldier-priests of old time, leading on his host, crozier in one hand, falchion in the other, and crying aloud in his deep, strong voice: "Strike, and smite, and let not one of them escape!"

"Let us go for a walk," he said, opening the gate as he spoke; "it's too hot for climbing, but the woods will be pleasant."

Judith would rather he had said: "Will you like to go for a walk?" His air of command offended her. For one thing, she was not used to it—a gentle, unvarying courtesy had ever been the order of the day in her French home. However, she raised no objection, so to the woods they went.

"You miss Oscar, of course?" he said, going on before her through the rough tangle of briar and long grass so as to make her path a little clear for her.

"The dear bright boy! Yes; of course I do," answered Judith warmly, and with a frankness that scattered the feeble hopes Wolf had conjured up to the four winds of heaven.

Nevertheless he persevered.

"Is he such a boy?" he questioned. "He's nearly twenty. I was a man—I had to be a man when I was but little older than he."

"Ah, you might be a man at twenty, I doubt very much if Oscar will be one much before he's thirty!"

"Yes, circumstances count for something," he said in a tone that had a touch of bitterness in it.

Then for five minutes they walked on together in silence.

It might be he was thinking of the hard times he had lived through as curate on a hundred and fifty pounds a year, and when that sum, added to a hundred pounds annuity of his mother's, was the total from which their household wants had to be supplied.

Judith guessed whither his thoughts were tending. Oscar had been very confidential with her as to the past experiences of his family in the East of London. She hastened to change the subject.

"Oscar will feel strange shut up in London after the open-air life he has led here! Is he a good student?" she asked. She knew in her own heart that the answer must be in the negative, if Wolf answered truly.

"Oscar is not a good student," he said. "But, Miss Wynne, do you think that matters? Do you think a man is any the worse for loving nature better than books? A man's mind we all know can be, and often is, marred by books rather than made by them. Now nothing would make a student of Oscar."

"No," interrupted Judith laughingly; "nothing would make a student of Oscar."

"But," pursued Wolf eagerly, wistfully almost, it seemed to Judith, "I'll undertake to say, in five or six years' time, no one will beat Oscar in honour, in integrity—"

"Or in jumping a five-barred gate, or in fly-fishing, or fox-hunting!" again interrupted Judith.

"In all that goes to make an all-round good man; but—but I want him to be more than this—something over and above all this—"

Judith here came to a standstill in the narrow path they were following. Her dress had caught in the thorns of a low-growing bramble-bush.

Wolf paused in his talk, but stood watching her disengage the hem of her dress without offering assistance.

How surprisingly little there seemed of the Frenchwoman in this young girl, naught, indeed, if one excepted the extreme neatness and daintiness of her personal appearance. What an odd, frank way she had of speaking, as though necessity were laid upon her to speak always the exact truth. Yet she was not fond of talking, never opened her lips, in fact, unless specially addressed. She must have read much, thought more, possibly.

All this passed through Wolf's mind as he stood silently surveying her.

The dress disentangled, Judith went on her way again in silence. Wolf took up his theme once more, but found the difficulties of expression growing upon him.

"As I was saying," he began, "I want him to be something more than all this. Can you guess what I mean? I want him to be happy, contented, at peace."

Judith's dark eyes, lifted to her companion's face, expressed her amazement.

"The dear bright boy!" she cried again. "Why should he not be happy?"

"Why—why," stammered Wolf; "why is it so many of us are not happy? How is it so few of us find real, lasting peace and blessedness?"

He broke off abruptly. His words were hurrying him on, whither he knew not. But it was difficult pleading with a girl for a suitor whom she persisted in calling "a dear bright boy." Besides—and this thought pressed upon him now for the first time—even supposing Judith should be inclined to look upon Oscar as a likely suitor, it might be possible Oscar would not be willing to present himself in that guise. He must give up the idea, as of late he had given up so many other cherished notions.

His next words broke from him with something of a sigh:

"It is evident, Miss Wynne, that your lines have been cast in pleasant places. May God keep your feet always from rough and thorny paths!"

Judith turned to face him in her astonishment. The words seemed somehow wrung from the very depths of his heart. It was as though they had been startled out of him. Yet she could not help feeling sore and a little indignant that he should thus entirely ignore the fact that her crape had not yet lost its freshness, that she had sorrowed and suffered, though she had learnt to bear her pain in silence.

"I loved Aunt Maggie passionately," she said in a low, quiet voice, "and if I had my choice, I would have died sooner than have left Uncle Pierre alone in his sorrow."

Wolf caught her meaning in an instant.

"Forgive me," he exclaimed, taking her hand; "it must have been a terrible wrench for you to leave your old home and come among strangers. But those were outside sorrows, sorrows that came and were not invited. What I meant was—"

Again he broke off and walked on with quick strides. He seemed to have forgotten that he still held Judith's hand, till she gently endeavoured to release it from his grasp. Then he dropped it as though it had stung him.

They had now reached the very heart of the wood. Straight across their path a brisk rivulet sparkled and rippled. It was an offshoot from one of the big cascades, whose rush and tumble of water went on from morning till night. Wolf paused, looking down into the little stream.

"'Wash me,'" he murmured, "'and I shall be clean.' Once I preached a sermon on those words." Then suddenly turning to Judith, he asked her: "Miss Wynne, do you believe in the possibility of repentance, of a man whose whole soul is steeped in sin, ever again becoming pure, white, and clean?"

And Judith, looking up in his face, answered simply:

"I believe in repentance just as I believe in the resurrection of the dead, the remaking of the soul as I believe in the remaking of the body."

"And scientists of the present day will tell you the one thing is as impossible as the other," he said with a short, abrupt laugh. Then he turned to her again. "Child, tell me, where did you get your faith and what is it? Is it Presbyterian or is it Catholic? Did you pick it up by the wayside, or did you hear it thundered from some pulpit by a man professing himself to be a servant of God, but who in heart was the devil's prime minister?"

Judith had no answer ready for him. His words startled and pained her. What did he—could he mean? He, a minister of God, a man of full age, asking her, little more than a child, of her beliefs and how she got them, just as though he were seeking wherewith to bolster up his own!

He did not seem to expect a reply. He turned his back on her and began walking rapidly forwards, following the upward course of the stream.

Judith remained standing where she was.

"He has forgotten me," she thought; and she also thought, "so much the better. I will get back to the house alone; the walk has been long enough."

Suddenly he paused, turned back, and with slow, irregular footsteps came towards her. His head was bowed, his face ashen-white, his brow drawn as though he were in actual bodily pain. He took both her hands in his, looking down in her face.

"'And found no place for repentance,'" he said in hoarse, low tones, "'though he sought it carefully and with tears.' Child, how do you explain those words? Esau was made of better stuff than most of us; he sins once and finds no place for repentance, though he seeks for it carefully—carefully, mark you—and with tears. What have you to say to that?"

He seemed to wait with breath suspended for her answer. He grasped her hands so tightly that they felt crushed, bruised. The wood seemed suddenly to have grown still. From afar came the tap-tap of a lonely woodpecker.

Her reply came clear and distinct enough after a moment's pause.

"I should say," she answered simply, "that his tears blinded him, and prevented him finding what he sought. He should have held out his hand for someone to help him with eyes and hands."

She spoke, well knowing what she was saying, anxious only to be of some little service to one who was so evidently sorrowing and suffering.

For a moment he stood still, looking at her, and Judith could feel that he was trembling from head to foot. His lips parted as though about to speak, then closed resolutely. He let go her hands abruptly; his face grew hard and rigid.

"Come, let us go home," he said in dry, short tones. "My mother will think we have lost ourselves in the wood."

They made their way back to the house almost in perfect silence. Wolf made no further attempt at conversation, and Judith was as disinclined for it as he.

IV

For several days after this Wolf and Judith saw but little of each other. It seemed as though by mutual consent they kept out of each other's way. A large portion of Wolf's mornings were of necessity given to an audience with old Maurice, the land-steward, who had the management of affairs in the old squire's time, and was loth to let them slip through his fingers now. This audience took place in a study, a little den which Wolf had temporarily fitted for his use on the ground-floor.

Here he listened patiently, or at any rate with iron endurance, to the old man's complaints of the late squire's niggardliness in money matters, the miserly fashion in which he had kept up a house that had once been the pride of the county, the terrible outbursts that had invariably attended young Mr. Bernard's applications (numerous it must be confessed) for money. The said complaints, however, generally wound up with a brief doxology to the old master's memory (on the principle, possibly, of giving even Lucifer his due). "For all that, he was a good master to me, and I've no occasion to speak ill of him," and a brief appeal to his present master, made at first as a matter of course, but of late somewhat uncertainly and dubiously: "And I suppose, sir, you'll be setting the repairs going soon; it will take a mint of money to make things as they ought to be."

But at this point Wolf's iron endurance seemed invariably to have reached its limit, for he would rise from his chair and politely give the old man his *congé* with a "That will do this morning, Maurice; I think we have got through enough for today."

An equally large portion, however, of Wolf's time seemed to be passed in the library, a dark, damp, long room, which ran the entire length of the darkest, dampest side of the house.

"Here are the products of some hundreds of dead men's brains, let us make haste to give them decent burial," seems to be the thought in some men's minds, when they construct their libraries, and hurry their volumes as fast as possible out of sight and into oblivion. Anyhow, this library was vault-like enough to have hurried men's bodies as well as their brain-products to corruption.

So at least Judith thought in the one glimpse she had of it. Now a library had ever been to her the one chamber of delights in every house she had ever visited. At Villa Rosa she and Uncle Pierre had passed the greater part of their lives among the books. Her one idea of happiness had been to pull a score or so of volumes on to the floor, seat herself in their midst, and in succession devour or at any rate taste them. She longed to repeat the experiment here, and one day coming in hot and dusty from a long walk, and finding the door ajar, she crept in, thinking she would rest there till the luncheon-bell rang.

Shade of Magliabechi, what a room it was! Coming in from the sunlight it seemed so dark she could scarcely distinguish aught; the small-paned windows were greened with a thin veil of moss, and outside, scratching the very glass with their lusty arms, creaked and groaned cedars and yews, which had kept at least three or four hundred birthdays. Little by little, however, as her eyes grew accustomed to the dimness, she could make out her surroundings. She looked round her in vain for sofa or easy-chair. A large round table stood in the middle of the room, at which were placed, at equal distances, four high-backed chairs, one a little withdrawn, as though some one had just risen from the table.

"That must be where Wolf was sitting," she thought. "But what can make him choose the darkest part of the room? He could neither read nor write there without a lamp. And oh, what an odour!"

The air seemed positively heavy with damp, mildewed dust, and that peculiar "old book smell" which tells of decaying volumes.

It hung about everywhere, to the walls, to the ceiling; the very curtains, dark, thick, heavily-fringed, seemed to exhale it. And no wonder! The massive oak book-shelves were simply inch thick with dust; the volumes scattered here and there on the smaller tables, and one or two, casually left on the high carved mantelpiece, were buried under a solid, clinging, white coating.

Over this mantelpiece hung the portrait, finely painted in oils, of a man about twenty-five years of age. Judith stood for at least five minutes looking up at him. His features were well-shaped, his eyes bright and laughing. Something in the face, though it certainly was not in the expression of the eyes, brought back Wolf's to her mind.

"Was this an ancient Reece," she wondered, noting the sodden and faded appearance alike of canvas and frame, "or a modern Reece? Ten years of this dust and mildew would make any picture antique."

"That is the portrait of my cousin—fourth or fifth cousin, I should say—Bernard Reece," said a voice at her elbow, and turning, she saw

Wolf had come in, and was surveying her and the picture with anything but a pleased expression of countenance.

Judith felt herself an intruder immediately, and began to make apologies.

"It was so hot outside; this room looked so dark and cool," she said.

Wolf went on as though he had not heard her:

"He was the last owner of this place. This was the last room he sat in before he sailed for America. Do you see this round table? It was placed here on the day of his father's funeral, when the will was read. This lamp in the centre must have been lighted then; they could not have read a lawyer's handwriting without it. See, it has not been trimmed since. These four chairs were placed, one for the lawyer, one for the parson, one for the steward—old Maurice, you know, my present steward—and one for Bernard. This was Bernard's chair; it is my seat now," here he gave a short, hard laugh, "and my favourite seat, I may say. I never use any other in the room."

It was all said in the driest and hardest of voices—the sort of voice a man might use in reading an uninteresting parliamentary debate which had to be got through for the benefit of another; or in which a man with a broken heart would tell the story of his darling's death to an unconcerned listener.

Judith's eyes wandered from the living to the dead man's face.

"It is like you and not like you," she said. "The features are the same, but—"

"But the soul that shows through them is different," Wolf interrupted. "No two men could be more unlike than my cousin Bernard and myself."

He paused a moment, then added in slightly sarcastic tones:

"Now, Miss Wynne, that you have scanned the mysteries of the library, don't you think that the sooner you get out of this damp, mildewy air the better? Five minutes more of it will give you ague, or fever, or something equally unpleasant, I am confident."

He held open the door for her. Judith had no choice but to pass out.

Half-way down the corridor she heard the oak door shut heavily, and she fancied, too, she heard the key turned in the lock.

She felt altogether mystified and bewildered. What could he find to do in that dark, mournful room? Why did he not have it cleaned out, and made comfortable and habitable?

What, too, had been the history of this Bernard Reece? Had he belonged to that unlucky and numerous class of individuals described in common parlance as "nobody's enemy but their own," or had his brief life been lived in such sort as to bring upon him the enmity of these his only surviving relatives? Of what kind and strength had been the bond between Wolf and him? She loved old legends of any and every sort, and this one, with its train of attendant mysteries, of which now and again she seemed to catch glimpses, she felt must be worth knowing.

Later on in the day, as she and Mrs. Reece sat alone over their knitting, she hazarded a question or two.

How old was Bernard Reece when he died? What sort of life had he led? Was that frank, handsome picture a good likeness of him?

"Ah, you mean the one in the library where Wolf writes his sermons," answered Mrs. Reece. "Yes, they tell me it is an excellent likeness. He was a handsome young fellow, no doubt; but wild and headstrong to a degree. I don't speak from personal knowledge, however, only from report. None of us ever set eyes on him."

"Not even Wolf?" questioned Judith.

"Not even Wolf, nor Wolf's father either. You see, my husband in a measure cut himself adrift from the Caernarvon Reeces when he went to London as a curate. They were such distant cousins, too. We never expected to come into this property. It was only a rapid succession of deaths gave it to us."

Mrs. Reece was exceptionally frank and plain in her speech. She went on with her confidences, in no wise unwilling to have so interested a listener.

"Then, too, old Bernard Reece—young Bernard's father—was such a disagreeable brute no one cared to have much to do with him. He was a terrible miser, and loved nothing better than hoarding up his money. Young Bernard loved nothing better than to spend it, so you may imagine there were awful rows between the father and son at times. Old Bernard used to threaten his son that if he didn't turn over a new leaf he would leave half his money to the county asylum. Young Bernard did not turn over a new leaf, and when his father's will was read he found that every penny the old man could leave away from the estate was bequeathed to the asylum. Bernard, in disgust, threw up the house and sailed for New York within a week of his father's funeral. Afterwards he went on to Bermuda, where he died about three years after his father. Meantime, this place was left in the hands of servants. Bernard said whoever liked might look after it, and it fell into its present dilapidated state. They tell me—at least Oscar tells me—it is all but a ruin. Of course I can't see for myself what it's like, and Oscar always speaks—well, let us say poetically. Now, tell me, Judith, does it seem to you in a terrible state of dilapidation? I know you are fond of speaking the truth."

But Judith was burning to hear more of Bernard and his careless, headstrong ways. The subject had a strange fascination for her.

"Why did he never marry?" she asked. "It was odd that a man of that sort should never have fallen in love."

"How do I know he never fell in love?" laughed Mrs. Reece. "I know so little about him. I dare say he fell into love and out of love as many times as there are months in the year. Ask old Bryce about him, she can tell you his whole history if she chooses. She was his nurse from babyhood."

"Bryce was his nurse!" repeated Judith in astonishment.

Now Bryce (otherwise Nancy Bryce) was the housekeeper at The Grange, and was a person of whom Judith stood not a little in awe on account of her abrupt manners and rugged countenance. She was a woman close upon seventy years of age, and went about the house in short skirts and mobcap. She acted as interpreter between Mrs. Reece and the other servants of the household, who only spoke Welsh, a language in which Bryce herself invariably indulged when crossed in her wishes or annoyed at any order for which she could see neither rhyme nor reason. She carried her head very high, she used a stick in walking up and down stairs, and had a habit of muttering and talking to herself as she went about her duties.

Judith felt that her hopes of hearing more of Bernard Reece and his erratic career were at an end now. It would, she knew, be of as much use to question the great Egyptian Sphinx itself as Nancy Bryce, unless she volunteered to open her lips.

V

The days went by in an even monotony at the old Grange, a monotony that would have been absolutely insupportable to most girls of Judith's age. Wolf, waking up suddenly one day to the fact that she was a girl of nineteen, a visitor in their house, and had a right to expect some sort of entertainment at their hands, startled his mother with the query whether they ought not to provide her with amusement of some kind.

"She might as well be in a convent at once," he said, "cut off as she is here from all society."

"My dear," answered the shrewd Mrs. Reece, "don't you think this is exactly what her father wished she should have—conventual seclusion without the objectionable religious part? Why did he send her to us if he did not wish her to be cut off from society? He knew perfectly well what he was doing. He must have scores of friends in London who could bring her out and introduce her and all that sort of thing, but no doubt he prefers that she should not make her first appearance in society till he can be by her side, and look after her himself. And he's quite right too. The only mistake he made in the matter was in ignoring the existence of my grown-up sons, but no doubt he thought you must be married by this time, and that Oscar would be well out of her way at college."

"Oughtn't she to have a horse, and keep up her riding?" persisted Wolf, feeling in his own mind that something ought to be done, though altogether dubious what the something should be.

"And who is to ride out with her, I should like to know?" queried Mrs. Reece. "Are you prepared to give up your sermon-writing and go for a two hours' canter over the hills every morning? By-the-bye, my dear, when will that book of sermons be finished? They ought to be something super-excellent from the time you've spent over them."

This question sent back Wolf, silenced, to his lair.

It seemed to be a received theory in the household that the solitary hours he passed in the library were spent in sermon-writing. Judith did not believe it. For one thing, in her brief survey of the large centre-table she had noted that neither books nor manuscripts lay upon it; the pen-tray also was simply buried in dust; in the black-marble inkstand the ink had dried away. Wolf himself had drawn her attention to the fact that the lamp in the centre of the table had not been trimmed since the day of old Bernard's funeral. Candles there were none in the room, and without light at that table anything but the wildest hieroglyphics would have been an impossibility.

The thought pressed upon her intermittently, if not sermon-writing, what could that silent, abstracted man be doing through those long hours in that desolate room? She had set herself to make a collection of Welsh field-flowers, and sometimes as she wandered along some pleasant bowery lane a glance up at those dark windows of the old Grange would set her shuddering and thinking. She would shut her eyes and conjure up a mental picture of that library interior with all its dreary details. The odour of damp and dust would seem to smite her senses once more; the handsome face of Bernard Reece would smile down on her from the wall; and there, seated opposite to it, looking up at it with solemn, lack-lustre eyes, she could picture to herself Wolf, with elbows resting on the table, and upturned, haggard face.

This likeness of Wolf thus seated somehow took possession of her brain, and seemed to haunt her. She had no conscious perception of the monotony of the days that went by, so charged did they seem to her with meaning and mystery. The very air of the place seemed laden with something. What could it be—an untold story—a dismal secret?

She had been brought up in an atmosphere of legend and tradition. From her earliest years her Aunt Maggie had instilled into her brain stories of the MacIvor race. How they had left their highland home and settled among their lowland brethren, an altogether superior, yet nevertheless despised, people, with their hand against every man, and every man's hand against them; how they swore to and bled for the holy Covenant; how they fought for their king and country; what bitter persecutions, starvations, and imprisonments they had endured; how they were despised, afflicted, tormented; what miraculous escapes they had at times from pursuing enemies how at last they had come triumphantly out of all their troubles, settled down peacefully as good money-making citizens, and had bequeathed large fortunes to their children and children's children.

Then also Uncle Pierre's one idea of education had been the laying a solid foundation of church history and legendary lore. Books by the score—infantine, juvenile, or for "those of riper years"—had found their way to her hand, filled with the histories of prophet, saint, and martyr.

Or, in the long summer evenings, as, side by side, he and she had strolled under the trees of the neatly-kept, broad walks of Villa Rosa, with a big yellow moon overhead, and the croak and hum of a hundred thousand twilight creatures growing faint and fainter as darkness crept over the land, he had, in his soft, even monotone, related these sacred stories, explaining here, adding a picturesque, life-giving touch there, till the girl, with strangely-aroused fancy, had imagined herself living and moving among the heroic actors of those bygone tragedies, and would occasionally oddly mix up the doughty deeds of her own lusty Scotch ancestors with those of the early martyrs of the Catholic Church.

It was certainly strange that this oddly-paired brother and sister should each have assailed their young niece on the same side of her nature—the poetic. As might be expected, her imaginative faculties were prematurely developed, and, when the run of the library was granted to her, the works of the great poets, the volumes of ancient myth and legend, were those she fell upon and devoured. They served her in good stead, however; they gave her—or if they did not give, helped to develope in her—that most precious of all gifts—poeic insight.

When she came as a visitor to this old Welsh Grange, the young girl, to a certain extent, brought her atmosphere with her, and saw and judged her surroundings through its medium.

To her the grey old rooms and dim corridors seemed echoing with sad whisperings and mournful voices, or else sullen and heavy with mysteries and unrevealed secrets. Even the room which had been set apart for her on the sunniest side of the house, and which had been— at Oscar's suggestion—slightly furbished up and supplied with some modern furniture in addition to the old, seemed begirt with the same air of significant mystery.

Often and often did Judith lie awake half through the night listening to what seemed to her soft raps against the window-panes, or on one of the many doors the room owned to. Or sometimes, half asleep, she would start up in bed thinking she heard her name called, and expecting to see some weird, misty shape spin itself out by her bedside.

A feeling of intense curiosity took possession of her at times, occasionally so great as almost to compel her to rise from her bed, dress herself, and make the tour of the old house in the dead of night, searching for she knew not what.

All terror of the supernatural seemed to have died in her heart, merged in this one deep longing to get to the bottom of something unfathomable and impenetrable, yet ever at hand.

In the morning, as the warm July sun streamed into her room, fancies, curiosities, and longings fled away together; but none the less as the silence of night fell on the small household, true as the stars themselves would they troop back again and hold sway till dawn once more.

VI

Over and above midnight fancies the noonday realities at the old Grange gave abundant food for thought to a young person fond of wondering and puzzling over mysteries, of conjuring the Possible out of the Actual. Wolf's odd, silent ways, his persistent habits of seclusion, were, however, the things which seemed to niche themselves most firmly in her brain—in fact, were seldom or never out of it. What did it all mean? Had he, a minister of God's Church, committed some heinous sin from whose consequences he found it impossible to free himself? Or had he, all unwittingly, been made the depositary of some guilty secret, and did he, vicariously, endure, the torments of another's stricken soul.

The more she wondered over it, the darker the matter grew to her.

Oscar had, in moments of confidential talk, told her much of the hard-working, hard-living days they had gone through at the East End of London. Specially he had loved to dwell upon Wolf's incessant activity among the poor and sick, his habits of rigid self-denial, his devotion to his mother and brother.

"Where we should have been without him, I don't know," Oscar had exclaimed enthusiastically, after an hour of declamation on the matter. "He denied himself food, and the commonest necessaries of life, to pay for my books and schooling. Why, he lived on turnips and potatoes for nearly six months to pay my mother's doctor's fees when she first grew blind. She did not know it, for he always took care she should have meat on her plate, but he did it all the same. I say, Judith, I should like you just to have seen us all when the news came that the Grange had fallen to Wolf. Wolf stipulated that every penny we had, every article of furniture and clothing, should be given to the poor people in the neighbourhood. I was jolly glad to get rid of my old shiny coats, I can tell you. Then the first money he drew from the estate he put untouched into the offertory-bag. I say, Judith"—this *sotto voce*, with a nervous look towards the door—"you mustn't think Wolf was always the queer, silent fellow he is now. Something like a blight seemed to fall upon him on the very first day we set foot in the Grange. He had given orders for all sorts of repairs to be done here, and we were going in for decoration on a grand scale. Suddenly he puts a stop to everything, packs off the workmen before they've so much as time to get their tools out of their baskets, and from that day to this won't hear a word about painters and glaziers. Isn't it queer?"

Judith certainly thought it was queer, and the more she thought over the whole thing the queerer it seemed to her. It was well-nigh an impossibility for her to link the past life of this man with his life in the present, to identify the hard-working, self-denying benevolent clergyman with the gloomy, taciturn man, who seemed willing to ignore the existence of every living soul in the house, and to have no thought nor desire in life beyond the attainment of complete, unbroken solitude and seclusion.

Mrs. Reece also, as confidence grew between her and Judith, adverted to the change that had taken place in her son.

"He was so bright and cheerful in our hard times; it seems strange he should grow sad and silent now that times are easy," she said.

The alteration in him, however, did not seem to her so marked as it did to Oscar, who, with his keen young eyesight, noted a variety of small details of which she was necessarily ignorant.

Not only did Wolf and his eccentricities occupy Judith's thoughts at this time. After a while a second person came in for a large share of her observation.

This person was old Nancy Bryce, of the rugged countenance and short petticoats.

Judith had felt something of an antipathy to old Nancy from the first day she had set foot in the house. Why it was she could scarcely explain to herself, but she certainly took it into her head that for some purpose of her own Bryce was playing the part of a spy. She felt positive, also, that the old woman bore no good-will towards the Reece family, and was convinced that those soft sibilant Welsh sentences she was perpetually muttering about the house were nothing more nor less than a string of anathemas upon the present master and mistress of the Grange.

Mrs. Reece in no wise shared Judith's feelings towards Bryce; she would speak of her as a faithful old retainer, a good old body, who looked well after her (Mrs. Reece's) interests in the house.

Judith had volunteered to spend an hour or so every morning in reading to Mrs. Reece. The hour was, however, more frequently than otherwise spent in long pleasant chats, in which the elder lady talked freely of her own early married life, of her dead husband, and of her children. Of the former she drew a portrait so graphic and life-like, that Judith felt sure it must be a true one.

CATHERINE LOUISA PIRKIS

"My first Wolf," she said, "was hardworking and self-denying like my second, but he was not so strong a man in will, nor so decisive and abrupt in manner. He was nervous and vacillating at times. It cost him so much to say an unkind or harsh word, that he was frequently silent when he ought to have spoken. I think it was his excessive timidity of giving offence that taught me plain-speaking. Some one has to do the disagreeable part of life, the skirmishing, aggressive and defensive; if the husband gets behind the hedge, depend upon it the wife comes to the front and gets the scars. Now, my second Wolf errs in the opposite direction. Some people used to say he was too harsh on the sins of the poor people who formed his flock, did not make allowance enough for their temptations and ignorances when he told them of their sins. He would call a man a liar to his face. 'Sir,' one man said to him, 'if I had not told that one lie, and said I hadn't been sent to gaol when I had, I should have got no work, and then I and my wife would have starved.' 'Better starve than tell lies,' I heard Wolf reply, and I haven't the least doubt that if he had been in that man's place he would have starved. Ah, well! we were near enough to starvation more than once in those days, but, thank Heaven, our temptations were never greater than we could bear. Thank Heaven we came out of it all unscathed!"

Judith fell to wondering whether Wolf would echo his mother's thanksgiving. Also supposing he could be for one short week restored to his ministry among the poor people, would he be quite so harsh in his judgments on them, quite so confident of his own power of resisting evil?

Her wonderings carried her farther. Should she ever see him in the pulpit preaching the doctrines of repentance and faith? Should she ever hear him reading the beautiful prayers of the Church, pronouncing absolution on the penitents kneeling around him?

She shut her eyes, and tried to picture him kneeling and praying beside the death-bed of some sinner, or standing, white-robed, within the altar rails, speaking words of peace and benediction. No; she cou'd not do it. His vehement, half-defiant words about one who sought, but could not find, repentance, would ring in her ears, out-sounding the gospel-words of peace and blessing; his white, haggard face—a face that seemed to have sin as well as sorrow written upon it—would rise up before her, and make to vanish the calm and holy one she had tried to image. She could picture him in the regal garb of a conscience-stricken Macbeth, in the goatskin even of a red-handed Cain; but in the white robes of a minister of God—no.

It is true she had heard him read the household prayers night and morning ever since her coming to the house, but they were in Welsh, not in English; they touched no chord in her heart, possibly they touched none in Wolf's. At any rate he read them in perfunctory style with voice pitched on one note which neither rose nor fell, and with eyes fixed and expressionless.

His manner of reading these prayers had struck her on the first morning of her arrival.

"They are in Welsh, for the sake of the servants," he had explained to her as he had opened his book.

Then he had seemed to harden and straighten his features, and he had gone through the prayers from beginning to end without so much as an inflection in the dry, hard monotone to which his voice had risen.

All this had flashed through Judith's mind as Mrs. Reece ceased speaking. The elder lady did not remark her silence; indeed, if the truth be told, it was a circumstance she rarely remarked in any one, although the opposite condition of things was apt on occasions to bring forth vehement comment from her lips. Possibly it was Judith's wonderful aptitude for playing the part of listener that had first warmed and opened the old lady's heart towards her.

"She is one of the sweetest girls I ever met," she said very loud, and very often, in Wolf's presence, "and our morning hour together is the pleasantest I have known for many a long day past."

The morning hour was, however, interrupted on this particular morning by Bryce, who came in to ask for some more wool for the stocking-knitting that went on below-stairs. "Those idle girls had scarcely anything to do from morning till night, and would waste their time in gossip and nonsense if they weren't set to work." She grumbled.

"Nothing to do!" thought Judith, "and so many rooms in that undusted, cobwebby condition!"

It always seemed to her that the maids had more on their hands than they knew how to get through; that the house, from top to bottom, suffered from an insufficiency of servants. If Mrs. Reece had but had her eyesight for five minutes, surely she could have found the maids ample employment independently of stocking-knitting.

Mrs. Reece, however, had not her eyesight, so all she did was to pull a heavy skein of yarn from her ample work-basket. Judith took it from her and handed it to Bryce.

The old woman was about to take it when suddenly the ring on Judith's right hand caught her eye. A look of horror overspread her brown wrinkled face. She drew back a step, pointing to the ring, and shaking her head to the skein of wool.

"I take nothing from that hand," she cried, retreating farther and farther. "Take it off—take it off, Miss Judith, if you don't want to bring a curse upon the house!"

The ring was a large bloodstone, in antique setting. It had belonged to an ancient MacIvor, and Judith had worn it for the first time that morning.

She slipped it off her finger immediately. She was accustomed to superstitions. The people of St. André had enough and to spare. She had loved to hear them tell their quaint stories of bird, or tree, or flower. To her they were all wild, beautiful tales, the outcome of some deep human feeling, or founded on the fragments of some ruins of a bygone religion.

"No doubt," she thought, "Bryce has in her mind some fantastic Welsh story of love and blood-shedding, which would be well worth the hearing. Will you take it now, Bryce?" she asked, as she once more proffered the wool, while not even the shadow of a smile showed itself about the corners of her mouth.

Bryce shook her head.

"Your hand must be dipped thrice in the stream that runs through the wood," she said in her harsh, creaking voice, "before it will be as the hand of a Christian again. St. Govan once, wearied with his journey, stopped and bathed his blessed feet in it on his way to the cil in the mountains. It will cleanse your hand as nothing else will. Lay the skein on the floor."

"Very well," said Judith, laying the wool on the floor at the old body's feet. "This afternoon I shall be in the wood, and will make a point of dipping my hand three times in the stream, kneeling, I suppose, with my face to the east; will that be right?"

"What is it all about?" asked Mrs. Reece, dropping her work and adjusting her spectacles on her high nose, just as though they were of real use to her.

Wolf, coming in at that moment, repeated the question.

As he entered, Bryce passed out of the room, giving, what seemed to Judith, one backward look of ill-will at her master as she went.

"What is that about dipping your hand in the stream with your face to the east?" he asked in his usual short, hard tones.

Judith explained Bryce's dread of the bloodstone.

Wolf laughed outright, the harsh, unpleasant laugh of scorn, not that of goodwill and merriment.

"What rubbish can the old body have got into her head?" he exclaimed. "I know nearly every tradition or superstition that ever existed in this part of the country, and I never heard anything against the bloodstone. It must be some old family legend she's treasuring up, depend upon it. The bloodstone may be of evil omen to the Reece family exclusively. Lend it to me, Miss Wynne; I have a great fancy for defying family tradition."

Before Judith could regain possession of her ring, he had slipped it on his little finger.

"There, now I'm prepared to be the family scapegoat," he said with the same unpleasant laugh as before. "Will you wear my diamond in exchange, or is the diamond a stone of ill-omen to the Wynnes? I would not like to import ill-luck into your family."

He held out his diamond-ring as he spoke. Judith hesitated only one moment, then slipped his big ring on her forefinger. It hung there loosely enough.

"If I lose it, it will be your fault, and, please, I must have my bloodstone back again. It's all but an heirloom," she said laughingly, registering meantime a mental resolve that on the very first opportunity she would endeavour to coax Bryce into telling her the legend of the bloodstone-ring.

As for Mrs. Reece, this exchange of rings between the young people brought a sudden rush of gladness into her old heart. It seemed to her an omen of success to a wish that of late she had begun to cherish.

VII

The opportunity Judith desired came the very next day without any seeking on her part.

She was walking, in the cool of the evening, on the terrace that ran the length of the old house, book in hand, when suddenly she heard Bryce call to her, "Miss Judith! Miss Judith!" in low, hurried tones.

Looking up she saw the old body's mob-cap and wrinkled face peering out at her from among the laurels which half-screened the window of the housekeeper's room.

Judith closed her book. "What is it?" she asked, at the same time making up her mind that if Bryce wanted anything of her she should pay for it with the story of the bloodstone-ring.

She parted the laurels and looked into the small, dark room. It was low-ceiled and oak-wainscoted like every other room in the Grange. From floor to ceiling it was well supplied with the cupboards and shelves supposed to be the indispensable accessories to good housekeeping. On a small table under the window was Bryce's work-basket, containing her knitting-pins and the skein of stocking-yarn unwound still.

"Miss Judith, I want to know a something," reiterated Bryce. "Will you tell me why the master is wearing that ring—the ring that was on your hand yesterday—the ring that'll bring no good to him, nor to any one of us?"

There was something of fierceness, something of terror, in the old woman's voice.

"Now is the time," thought Judith, "for the story." She looked down at the work-basket. "Why, haven't you wound your wool, Bryce? Are you afraid of it because I touched it? Shall I come in and show you how we used to wind our balls in France? My hand is clean now, I dipped it three times in St. Govan's stream just as you told me."

She did not wait for Bryce's invitation to enter, but, as she finished speaking, opened a side door leading into the housekeeper's room, and went in.

Bryce, with a sour face, placed a chair for her, entering her protest meantime against French methods of winding wool, against everything, indeed, that was not purely national and indigenous.

"I never did like foreign ways," she grumbled. "It was all Master Bernard's fondness for foreign parts that brought ill-luck to him."

The mention of the name of this luckless son of the house set Judith's ears tingling. She would a hundred thousand times sooner have heard his history than the legend of the bloodstone-ring!

"Was Master Bernard always fond of travelling?" she asked Jesuitically, trying to give the conversation another turn, and leaning forward with her arms on the table, an expectant listener.

But Bryce was more eager to ask than to answer questions at that particular moment. She gave a succession of brief nods which might be taken for affirmations, or might stand (so Judith thought) for the Welsh equivalent of "Don't bother me with questions when I have something of my own to ask!" Then she laid her bony hand on Judith's arm.

"Tell me, Miss Judith," she persisted, "why you and the master have changed rings. Are you lovers? What does it mean?"

Judith laughed outright.

"Lovers! No, indeed," she answered frankly enough. "I never had a lover in my life. I am expected to wait for my lovers till my father comes home and allows them to me. I have had this notion drilled into my brain ever since I was seven years old—long before I knew what lovers meant."

"Then why did you change rings with him? Why?—why? In Wales, when a man and woman change rings, they mean to marry each other, and do marry, unless one comes between them."

"And so they do in other parts of the world besides Wales—unless they change rings for fun. We only did it for fun."

Bryce shook her head.

"I don't like such fun. It's ill trifling over evil things," she muttered.

"Now, why is that stone evil? You must tell me. It's a beautiful stone."

"It's an evil stone, Miss Judith, with an evil name. It'll bring a curse upon the house, take my word for it."

"Now, if it had been that stone," and here Judith touched the brooch—an onyx with which Bryce had pinned her kerchief, "I could have understood it. The people at St. André had a queer story to tell about onyx brooches, Bryce."

Bryce fidgeted and looked uncomfortable.

"And I don't like my brooch to be called 'evil' without rhyme or reason, Miss Judith."

"And I don't like my ring to be called 'evil' without rhyme or reason," retorted Judith.

"But there is rhyme and reason for it," exclaimed Bryce vehemently.

"Wasn't there a Bernard Reece found lying murdered nigh by the Ffynnon in the wood? He was Master Bernard's grandfather, the first Bernard in the family. Ah, no good ever comes of these outlandish names. All the squires in the old days were ever Owens or Glendowers. It's the three Bernards who brought all the ill-luck."

Bryce's sentence ended in a sigh and another shake of the head. It boded ill for the gratification of Judith's curiosity. She endeavoured once more to lead the old woman back to the ring.

"You've a change of name now in the house," she said. "I should think a Wolfgang has never before been heard of in Wales. Perhaps it was only to the Bernards that the bloodstone brought bad luck."

Bryce shook her head again.

"It's not a change for the better, Miss Judith. It's a more outlandish name than the other. Wolfgang, indeed—heugh!"

Now Bryce's "Heugh!" Welsh guttural though it was, was suggestive, and easily understood. It stood mid-way between a shudder and an imprecation.

Judith met it as she would an argument in the mouth of an adversary.

"But for all that," she persisted, "it is possible that a Wolfgang may wear without any risk a ring that a Bernard shouldn't look at."

"Not that ring!" exclaimed Bryce with an almost savage vehemence. "No Reece can wear that ring without bringing a murderer across his path. There, Miss Judith, I've told it you now! For the love of Heaven get the master to give you back your ring, and you drop it into the blessed stream where that other was dropped."

"What other? The one the murdered man wore?"

"Aye, and that his mother after him wore, too. Listen, Miss Judith. It doesn't follow because the master is wearing it that he'll be the one murdered; but as sure as he's a Reece he'll bring a murderer into the house. That's what he'll do."

"How did a bloodstone ever get into the house, Bryce? Tell me that," pleaded Judith.

"This way, Miss Judith. The first Bernard—our Master Bernard's grandfather—married a Scotch lady, a tall, bony, evil-looking woman, I've heard my mother say. She was very poor, and very proud, and had to give up a lover of her own in Scotland to marry the Welsh squire. She was very silent, very high to the poor people, and never spoke a word to living soul if she could help it. They said she and her husband's mother—who lived in the house—hated each other like poison. She always wore a big bloodstone-ring, which some people said her first lover had given her. Anyhow, her husband hated to see her wearing it, and ordered her to give it to him. There were words over it, and she was obliged to give in. She flung it in his face, and cursed him in her own Scotch tongue, telling him the ring would bring a curse to him and to his children after him, and that sooner or later a murderer would cross his path. Her words were only too soon fulfilled. Within a month from that day Squire Bernard was found lying dead in the wood, stabbed and thamefully beaten about. His wife went back immediately to her own people in Scotland, and did not so much as put on black for him. Then Madame Reece—Squire Bernard's mother—took the ring which the murdered man had worn, put it on her own finger, and remembering the words of the wicked woman's curse, prayed that it might bring her son's murderer across her path. And one night, as she lay in bed—in the very room you are sleeping in now, Miss Judith—there came to her bedside the evil Scotch lady, who told her how she couldn't rest in peace because of her sins; that she herself had first drugged and then murdered her husband in the wood, in order that she might go back to her first lover. Madame Reece sat up in bed, and called her a bitter name, and tried to catch her by the sleeve, but her hand seemed only to go through and through her. Then she made up her mind she had seen the wicked woman's wraith, and she rang the bell, and roused the house, and told them all about it. And, sure enough, when they sent to the Scotch lady's people, they found that she and her lover had been drowned while out boating on a lake. There, Miss Judith, there's the story of the bloodstone, as my mother told it me; and a dismal enough story it is!"

It was a dismal story, and told in that damp, dark room, in Bryce's creaking tones, its dismalness became doubled.

Judith suddenly awoke to the consciousness that the sun had set, that the frogs were croaking drearily, that the evening was getting damp and chill.

"I think I'll say good-night, Bryce; it must be almost time for prayers," she said. "So Madame Reece dropped the ring into the stream when she had done with it. I think I should have kept it. It did, you see, as much good as harm, after all; it told the poor lady the truth about her son's fate. Good-night, Bryce. Some day, perhaps, you'll tell me something about your Master Bernard. I should like to hear his story."

CATHERINE LOUISA PIRKIS

"Miss Judith," pleaded Bryce, catching at the young girl's arm, "you'll get the master to give you back the ring? For all that things are not exactly what one would have; I wouldn't like worse to come to the house."

The last sentence was muttered in an undertone, and was evidently not intended for Judith's ears.

So Judith shut them, and went her way, wondering much over this old body's deep devotion to the Reece family, joined as it so oddly was with evident enmity to the present head of the house.

Nevertheless, somehow the talk she had with Bryce had made her feel a little ashamed of the prejudices she had cherished against her. After all, there might be some foundation—slight or mistaken, perhaps—for the old servant's present discontent, though what that foundation was, she was utterly at a loss to imagine.

VIII

W hen Judith went to bed that night, her thoughts were full of the story of the bloodstone-ring.

"It would make a grand poem," she thought to herself, as she stood in her bedroom window-recess, slowly unplaiting her long dark hair, and picturing to herself the murdered man lying beside the stream in the lonely wood, and the evil wife looking her farewell to him from the other side.

"Or a wonderful picture," her thoughts went on; "if I could paint, it would be the sort of story I should delight in. I think I should choose the moment when the old mother lay awake in bed—that bed, no doubt"—here she nodded at the old-fashioned, heavily-curtained four-poster, which formed her own couch—"thinking of her murdered son, and the dead wife's wraith came and stood by her side. Yes, it would make a wonderful picture. Why, the greatest artist who ever painted might find a wraith beyond him. Dante might perhaps have done it if he had been a painter instead of a poet. Fancy being able to paint a soul! To put all the regret, and sorrow, and pain into one look, and print the look on air!"

Here she let fall her heavy plaits, unlocked her casemented window, and leaned out into the still, night air.

It was early yet, barely ten o'clock, but everything round and about the Grange was as quiet as though it had been midnight. The moon was bright, but not at its highest; the gardens below Judith's window lay in the deepest shadow; the wood beyond caught the white beams on the tops of the highest trees only, but the blue mountains, which towered in the near distance, were literally steeped in the white light. Every jutting crag and fantastic point stood distinctly outlined in all its weird whimsicality against the limpid sky.

Odd thoughts began to shape themselves in Judith's brain. If those rocks could for an instant take to themselves a human voice what strange stories they might tell of wandering prince or dying chieftain, heroic martyr, or feeble anchorite! What secrets some of those dark hollows must hold, what terrible scenes of violence, marauding, and perhaps murder, those sharp, overhanging crags must have looked down upon!

The whole scene, in all its wild desolateness, had a strange fascination for her. She found it difficult to tear herself away from it to complete

CATHERINE LOUISA PIRKIS

her toilette for the night. She closed her window with a sigh, but left the blind and curtains widely withdrawn, so that even from her bed she could see the beautiful, shadowless night-sky, and the grand curves and castle-like turrets of the darkblue rocks.

The moonlight and the rocks, as might be expected, filled her dreams. In fancy she crossed the dark wood in the dead of night, and stood alone at the foot of the mountains looking up at the round summer's moon. It poured its light full upon the earth at her feet; every tiny weed, every branchlet of moss, was outlined in unerring distinctness, and moment by moment the light that fell upon them seemed to grow clearer and stronger. But, strange to say, every ray that fell upon the earth seemed to leave the moon by so much the darker; it seemed absolutely emptying itself of its light, literally pouring it out upon the earth ray by ray, silently, slowly, ceaselessly, till it hung a great, dark, empty orb in the midst of the heavens.

In her dream Judith felt a great awe steal over her. The sky above seemed a great, dull, heavy blank; the earth, which lay at her feet, too bright and dazzling for human steps to tread. A terror took possession of her. This harsh, glittering white light, what horrors and secrets all round would it not lay bare to her eye! A prayer rose to her lips, "Lord, keep Thy great pure light for the heaven of heavens, on earth let shadow and darkness encompass us still." And then she drew a long breath and awoke.

What was it that had awakened her? she asked herself as she sat upright in bed, and listened intently for the repetition of some noise which had distinctly crossed her dreams. It could not have been the striking of the clock, for at that moment the one in the hall below sounded the hour, three distinct bells. She had been asleep, then, longer than she thought, four or five hours, and it had seemed only like a five minutes' doze. Hark! and she held in her breath and strained her ears to listen—there it was again. A footfall at her door, a rustling out in the corridor, it seemed to be. For a moment the blood rushed from her heart to her brain. A deadly coldness seized her. What if some poor, lost, restless soul were to come and stand by her bedside, as once before one had stood on the self-same spot, confessing a terrible crime. She stretched out her hand, almost expecting it to be seized in some damp, clammy touch, pushing aside the chintz curtains of her bed, so as to get a clear view of her room. The moonlight was flooding every corner of it now. The commonplace tables and chairs had a weird poetic appearance, which in the garish light of day they utterly lacked. Some new furniture had been placed in it to supplement the old, half worn-out articles, and in broad daylight the room wore an air of jauntiness, of semi-renovation, of I-would-if-I-couldness, which belied its past history. All this, however, had vanished in the mystic light of the moon, the very air of the room seemed poetised, ethe-realised. Its past days of uncannyness seemed to have crept back upon it. A whole army of restless, antiquated spirits trooping in and out of the corners, opening and shutting the high cupboard-doors, peering and gleaming here, there, everywhere, would in no wise have seemed out of place amid these eerie surroundings.

Judith felt herself growing colder and colder. She strove, by a strong exercise of will, to get back her courage.

"It's all fancy, I know," she said, speaking out as loudly and bravely as she dared; "my ears must have deceived me. I will just open my door, and make sure no one is there, then I'll light a candle and read myself to sleep again."

She slipped out of bed, with bare feet made her way to the door, and softly turning the handle, looked out.

Not a soul was to be seen, not a sound was to be heard. In the corridor was deepest, blackest night, broken only by a thin, white stream of moonlight, which the opening of her door had let out into it. Something glittered in this stream of light on the floor at her feet, and, stooping down, Judith picked up what seemed to her an antiquated shawl-pin, made in the shape of an arrow, and either of gold or gilt brass. It was very odd. Some one, then, had been down that corridor in the dead of the night. Who could it have been? Well, anyhow, she would take possession of the pin, and speak to Mrs. Reece on the matter the next morning.

She was about to return to her room, when at this moment another sound fell upon her ear. It was a groan, or rather moan, as of someone in a fainting-fit or breathing heavily. A quick terror entered her mind. Had robbers broken into the house and half murdered someone, perhaps one of the servants, perhaps Wolf, who was always wandering about the house late at night?

She snatched her dark, thick dressing-gown, which lay on a chair near the door, tossing the old gold-pin on a small table standing by, and with swift, silent steps made her way along the corridor, pausing once at the head of the staircase to listen whence the sound came.

She could hear nothing, however; everything seemed still and vault-like below; but leaning over the oak balustrade, she could see a narrow thread of light showing under one of the many doors which opened into the hall. She rightly guessed it came from the library, and with still the one thought in her mind of someone lying wounded and injured, she ran down the stairs, and groped her way to this door. On the threshold she paused in a thrill of horror, for there, white and motionless, lay Wolf on the floor, almost at her feet. His chair—Bernard Reece's chair—lay overturned by his side, and there was an ugly bruise on his forehead, made possibly by the sharp edge of the table as he fell.

A candle burned feebly on the high mantelpiece. In other respects the room was exactly as when she had last seen it, dust and damp clinging everywhere, and the frank, handsome face of Bernard Reece smiling down upon it all.

She felt certain now that Wolf had been attacked and wounded by someone attempting to enter the house. She kneeled down by his side, raised his head, pillowing it on some heavy folios which lay at hand, and was about to cross the room to ring for help, when he suddenly opened his eyes, caught the hem of her dress, and held her tightly.

Then he began to talk rapidly, and, it seemed to Judith, deliriously, as one not knowing what he said.

"Whoever you are, don't leave me," he implored: "for Christ's sake don't leave me! He had pity even for murderers! I'm not that—no, not that. I tell you I will have nothing to do with blood-shedding. I am a man of God—do you hear, a man of God?" Here he raised himself on his elbow, and looked wildly around him, still holding the affrighted girl by her gown. "I prayed to God as I have prayed here, night after night, I tell you. I vowed to Him I would not touch one penny of the gold more than was absolutely needed, that I did it for them not for myself, that I would give it all up by-and-by, and I prayed to God to let me keep it all for a time. I say for a time. And I prayed Him tonight, just as I have prayed on other nights, to let the dead man's soul come back and speak one word to me. Then out of the mist and darkness something came—a shadow, a shape. It drew nearer—nearer. 'He comes at last,' I thought; 'if he knows what I have suffered his words will be peace and blessing, not a curse.' It stood by my side I could have touched it as I sat. I looked up in its face. Oh God! It was my own; white—white—white was the face, but the hands were red with blood!"

His words ended in a gasp, he sank back on the floor, loosing his hold of Judith's dress; his eyes closed once more, and the heavy breathing recommenced.

Judith felt herself shaking from head to foot. What was to be done? She dared not rouse the household to see their master in this condition; to say truth, she trembled for the next words he might utter. Yet help of some sort she felt he must have. There would surely be some water in the dining-room, and wine or brandy in the cellaret. This she herself could easily procure. She took the candle from the mantelpiece, made her way quickly across the hall, and returned with both water and brandy. Then again kneeling by Wolf's side, she bathed his bruised forehead, and, slightly raising his head, held the brandy to his lips. Little by little, she contrived to get him to swallow some; consciousness slowly returned; he opened his eyes and now recognised her.

"You here, Judith?" he exclaimed—it was the first time he had ever called her by her Christian name—"how is this? Surely it is the middle of the night. Did I call out? I must have fainted, I suppose." Again he raised himself on his elbow; a shudder passed over him. He caught Judith's hand. "Is anyone else here?" he asked. "Tell me, have I been talking? How did you find out I had fallen?" He spoke vehemently, rapidly, his voice growing stronger and more natural in tone.

Judith felt nervous, distressed, and compassionate all in one. How her heart ached for this man in his hopelessness and misery!

"Please drink some more brandy," she entreated. "No one is here but I. I heard you fall, I suppose, and came down thinking thieves were in the house. Oh, you talked nonsense, nothing more; people often ramble when they lose their senses in a fit, don't you know. Shall I ring for Bryce, or Davies"—Davies was the man who combined the offices of butler and coachman in the Reeces' establishment.

Wolf sat upright on the floor.

"No, don't ring," he said; "I shall get up and be all right again in a minute. Yes, I was only talking nonsense, as you say, I don't suppose you could remember a word of what I said, if you tried?"

"No, no, no," answered Judith, trying to put it all out of her thoughts; "at least," she added, correcting herself, "I could not repeat it if I tried ever so hard."

Wolf looked at her keenly.

"Put that chair, please, close to my hand. No, thanks; you are not strong enough to help me up. So—thank you!" With something of an

CATHERINE LOUISA PIRKIS

effort he struggled to his feet again, still keeping his eye almost sternly fixed on the white, trembling girl. "Now, will you kindly try, Miss Wynne, to repeat to me, word for word, what I did say, as nearly as you can remember it? I shall be infinitely obliged to you if you will make the effort;" this was added in his usual hard tone.

Judith could scarcely keep the tears from her eyes, and spite of effort they would make themselves heard in her voice.

"Oh, please do not ask me," she implored; "whatever you said I shall try to forget; and oh, do be sure it will be sacred to me—no word of it will ever pass my lips to living soul!"

Wolf looked down into her white face for a moment.

"I believe you," he said below his breath; "I can trust you. I see truth itself in your eyes. Poor child!" he added pityingly, "how frightened you look! Come, let me take you back to your room. Think of it all as some nightmare you have had. I give you my word of honour it shall never occur again."

He drew Judith's unresisting hand within his own arm as he finished speaking. He was perfectly calm and self-possessed now, she tremulous and ill at ease. Nothing more was said till they reached her bedroom door, when, with the briefest and coldest of good-nights, they parted.

Judith almost staggered into her room, and sank down into the first chair she came to, trying to collect her thoughts. What a bewildering night it had been! What months seemed to have passed since she had lain down to rest on that moonlighted bed! Her dream had been strange and oppressive enough, but what had followed had been so doubly, trebly strange as almost to have swept that from her memory.

What did it all, could it all mean?

In the first place, who could have been outside her door in the dark corridor? That, in any case, could not have been Wolf, for he would not have been likely to carry about with him antique shawl-pins, and drop them as he went along.

Well, she had possession of that pin, at any rate, and would take good care of it. Sooner or later it might lead to the identification of the midnight wanderer.

Mechanically she stretched out her hand, feeling for the pin on the little table where she had placed it, so as to have one more look at it. Felt for it, groped for it in the dark; but mystery upon mystery!—it was no longer there? She lighted her candle; she searched for it till a candle was no longer necessary, for the daylight that came streaming in at the windows; but with no result.

The conclusion was unavoidable. Someone must have entered her room while she was absent, and regained possession of it. Someone, perhaps, who had dogged her footsteps about the house, and listened to Wolf's wild ravings as he lay on the floor. It was too dreadful to think of. Judith felt her brain going round, and her limbs beginning to fail her.

This was the final stroke to the night's bewilderment and terror. She threw herself on her bed, closed her eyes, and tried to silence the whirl of thought that came sweeping down on her; tried to make believe, as Wolf had suggested she should, that the whole thing, from beginning to end, was only a weird, wild nightmare, that had teased and tortured her poor brain with its grim phantasies.

IX

The birds sang loud and louder, the sun rose high and higher in the heavens, yet still Judith lay upon her bed, wide awake, her head aching, her very eyeballs feeling scorched and strained with the effort to solve the mystery, or, failing that, to believe that it was no mystery at all.

Over and over again she said to herself:

"No doubt it all admits of the simplest of explanations if I had but the commonsense to lay my finger on it."

But, even as she said this, "commonsense" suggested that in this case the simplest explanation would be the least satisfactory to accept, for it would prove Wolf to be a man with a burdened, guilty conscience, and would establish the fact that this small household included in its number a spy, or possibly a plotter, who chose to wander about on some uncanny errand in the dead of the night.

The prayer-bell clanged through the house before she had roused herself from her bewildering thoughts to begin her morning toilette. She answered it with a counter-bell, desiring the maid to ask Mr. Reece not to wait for her appearance that morning.

Even as she was speaking to the girl, there came a sudden sharp sound against the window-panes of her room, as of the rattling of small pebbles, followed by a long, low succession of whistles, distinctly imitative of a skylark's song as it rises in the air.

Judith looked at the servant in amazement.

"Why, surely," she exclaimed, "that must be Mr. Oscar in the garden. He used to wake me in that way every morning."

The girl nodded and smiled, and explained, half in Welsh, half in English, that Mr. Oscar had arrived at about seven o'clock that morning, having been travelling all through the night from London.

Judith got through her dressing with marvellous rapidity, and was seated at the breakfast-table almost as soon as the others.

It was a relief to see Oscar's bright, happy, handsome face again. It seemed to bring with it an atmosphere of everydayness, of common life from the outer world. That hearty grip of his hand, that semi-schoolboy slang in which he chose to indulge, did more to disperse the phantasms of over-night than any amount of hard-headed logic would have done.

He made open, undisguised love to her all through breakfast. More than once he got hold of her hand, and asked her when she meant to marry him. To which query Judith replied successively, "When you have done growing," "When your education is finished," and finally, the more effectually to silence him, "When you have taken a double-first at Oxford."

She scarcely dared to look at Wolf, as they sat facing each other at table. Yet once or twice he seemed pointedly to address her, as though he wished their eyes to meet. His voice seemed to her to be drier and harder than ever. Or was it, perhaps, that she had fuller opportunity for noting its inflections? It might have been in honour of Oscar's sudden advent, but certain it was that since Judith's coming to the Grange he had never been so communicative at mealtimes before.

"We are quite a cheerful party this morning," said Mrs. Reece, rejoicing in the unaccustomed flow of talk that supplemented the rattling of the coffee-cups.

"Cheerful, do you call this?" laughed Oscar. "I wonder what you would call our breakfasts at The Retreat before Dean Swift makes his appearance; he's always a little late in showing, but makes up for lost time when he does come, I assure you."

The Retreat was the abode at Richmond, where Oscar was being "coached" for matriculation. Dean Swift was the master of it, and the respected "coach" of some half-dozen scatter-brained young fellows. He had been so nicknamed from the double fact of his owning to the patronymic of Martin, and to a portly person and slow lumbering tread.

"Yes, I can imagine you young fellows make a fine racket," said Mrs. Reece. "Now, which is the noisiest and wildest of you all—that Theo you write so much about?"

"It was Theo who pushed you into the river, and left you to struggle out the best way you could, wasn't it?" queried Judith.

"And I suppose it's Theo who borrows your umbrellas and hats," pursued Mrs. Reece, "and forgets to return them? For the number of these articles you've got through this past two months has been something wonderful."

"And uncommonly nice she looks in my hats, too," said Oscar. "Not one of her Sunday-going bonnets suits her half so well as my old deer-stalker."

"Her!" exclaimed Mrs. Reece.

"Her!" echoed Judith, and even Wolf looked up with amazement written on his face.

"Her? Yes, of course," said Oscar, calmly. "I can't say 'suits she' can I?"

"But—but," stammered Judith, "we thought from your letters that Theo was a boy. She certainly plays boyish tricks."

"And so she is a boy—as veritable a tom-boy as ever lived, but for all that a dear little soul," answered Oscar.

"I suppose she is Mr. Martin's daughter?" questioned Mrs. Reece. "Why, Wolf, you told me that there were no girls in the household at The Retreat."

"Mr. Martin told me that his youngest daughter was still in the schoolroom, his eldest daughter in Germany at a 'finishing' school, and that the household was presided over by an elderly maiden sister," answered Wolf.

"Ah, the elderly maiden sister is there safe enough," explained Oscar. "Theo is still in the schoolroom, in the sense of being always out of it, and Miss Leila returned from Strasburg about ten days or a fortnight ago."

"And what is Miss Leila like?" asked Judith, for her quick ear had caught an inflection in Oscar's tone as he pronounced the name, which roused her curiosity as to the young lady's personality.

"Oh, she's—she's—Oh, I can't tell you what she's like. I'm never good at describing girls," answered Oscar with a transparent attempt at indifference. "Give me the coffee-pot, Wolf. Ah, I beg your pardon, Judith; I forgot you 'presided,' as the novelists say, at the tea-tray now. In the old days, Wolf and I used to hawk the thing round the table as we wanted it."

"It's wonderful," soliloquised Mrs. Reece, "what a number of girls there are everywhere! With the best wishes in the world to keep one's sons out of their way, it's almost an impossibility. If they go up to London and take rooms, and the landlady is as ugly as you could wish, there always turns up a landlady's daughter in a day or two who is a good deal prettier than you could wish; if you let them go and stay with an aunt, a cousin is safe to make an appearance from some unexpected quarter; if you establish them in a respectable clergyman's family with only an elderly maiden sister to look after him, young giddy daughters spring up miraculously, like mushrooms after a wet night, full-grown, ready for anything. No, there's no escaping the girls, do what one will."

"Or they come sailing over from France," laughed Judith, "begging a home of you for two whole years, because they have no—"

But here Oscar put his hand over her mouth, and forcibly prevented the finish of her sentence.

"If Theo had dared speak like that," he said, "I would have—no I wouldn't have taken her out on the river for a month, nor bought her 'sweeties' for a year. But one doesn't know how to punish you, Judith. Now I can always make Theo cry with trying."

"And then, I suppose, you kiss and make it up again! Oscar, I think I should like to see this Theo. You seem such good friends with her and the other young lady her sister," said Judith.

"And I should like you to see them also," said Oscar, growing suddenly serious. "Mother, that was one of the things that brought me home in such a hurry. I wanted to ask you if you would invite the young ladies down here for a few days. Dean Swift is going away on business for a week or so; all the fellows are off shooting or fishing: there is house-cleaning going on from top to bottom, and only the maiden aunt to keep us cheerful. Of course I bolted home here, and the girls said they wished they could bolt too."

"Invite them, mother; why not?" said Wolf, "It will be a little society for Miss Wynne. I am sure she must be dull enough sometimes."

"'Miss Wynne,'" thought Judith. "It was 'Judith' last night." Then aloud she said: "I am never dull. I could never be dull in the summer in the country; but I should like immensely to see and know these two young ladies for Oscar's sake."

This added with a side-glance at his slightly reddening face.

Oscar jumped up all energy.

"And, Wolf, you really must get the old place furbished up a little before they come. Oh, you've no idea how grandly atheistic—no, æsthetic—we all are at Richmond! Anything but a sage-green wall or a blue-tiled fireplace would be voted Philistinish in the extreme."

"There's green enough here of all shades to choose from," said Wolf, moodily, rising from the table to avoid a discussion that had no attraction for him.

But Oscar was not to be silenced.

"You'll let the place go to ruin—utter ruin. Think what the next-of-kin would say if he were any other than your respected and much-snubbed younger brother," he exclaimed, heedless what argument he employed so long as Wolf's eyes were opened to the deplorable condition of the Grange, and the absolute necessity that existed for repairs and renovation.

Wolf, in the act of leaving the room, turned and faced his brother.

"Get that notion out of your head at once and for ever, Oscar," he said sternly. "The place is not going to utter ruin as you call it, and I do not intend that, under my rule, it shall. Walls, roof, and flooring are all sound, and in good condition, and all necessary repairs are and shall be carried out. But what you would advocate in the way of decoration would mean simply outlay, year by year, that would bring in no return to living soul. Who would be the better for a half-dozen or so of extra servants in the house, cleaning, polishing, and spending money in every direction; or say, as many gardeners, hoeing, weeding, planting, watering one year, to unplant and rearrange the next? Talk about what you understand, but do not interfere with me in my management of the Grange."

As he said the last word he left the room.

It was a long speech for the usually curt, taciturn Wolf to make, and it was made with an undernote of meaning which two at least of his hearers failed to catch.

Oscar gave a long, low, whistle as the door closed on his brother.

"All the same, old man," he said, "I shall go at you again at the very first opportunity on the very same matter. Don't shake your head, mother. Wolf needs a little crossing and thwarting now and then. He's a born autocrat, you know; and I represent Parliament and the rights of the people. Come along, Judith, let's have the old greys out, and go for a spin somewhere or other. I've no notion of getting the blues on the very first day of my holidays."

X

O scar spoke truly when he described Wolf as "a born autocrat." It was a fact patent to all.

Judith found no difficulty in crediting Mrs. Reece's statement that even in his first curacy, with a stipend of one hundred pounds a year, he had his middle-aged vicar, and more than middle-aged churchwardens, completely under his thumb. He was emphatically a man born to wield a bâton rather than to wear a yoke. His simplest requests seemed to take the form of an order. The words "If you please," or "Be so kind," on his lips had the ring of a command in them.

After that one night of mystery and terror, Judith, with her powers of observation strangely quickened, fancied that his imperiousness grew upon him hourly; that, in fact, it had resigned its previously passive form for one purely active and aggressive. His manner to her became increasingly abrupt, and more than once, as their eyes met at table, and on one occasion as he rose from his knees at morning prayer, there was an angry challenging look in his which seemed to say as plainly as words could: "If you think evil of me in your heart, say it right out at once. Tell everyone far and near, what manner of man I am. I can face it out."

Judith felt instinctively that this could be but a mood with him, that by-and-by it would pass, the inevitable reaction would set in, and his old gloomy indifference to men, women, and things about him would return with redoubled force. Every day, nay, almost every hour of every day, she found herself wondering over him, his sorrows, and his secrets. She longed to raise up help for him in some quarter; more than once she felt tempted to rouse Mrs. Reece into energy on the matter, to bid her awake to the fact that her eldest son was having his heart burned to cinders with some concealed sorrow; but resisted the temptation, her better judgment telling her that such interference on her part would be deeply resented by Wolf, and little likely to lead to good results. Besides, she felt in a measure pledged to secrecy, not only as regarded the events of that one mysterious night, but also as to the facts which her own powers of observation had revealed to her. She felt the solemn promise she had given to Wolf in the library in the dead of night covered a good deal of ground, and she must religiously keep it. She could only wonder over the obtuseness of mother and brother, who could sit at the same table with him three times in the day, be in his company some six hours out of the twelve, and not hear the under-note of pain in his voice, nor catch the dreariness of his every movement and action. Beyond a casual "Poor Wolf! I think he has a lot of business worries pressing on him just now," Oscar paid not the slightest heed to his brother's gloomy taciturnity.

"Is Oscar, like me, afraid of betraying his brother?" thought Judith; "or has he nothing but fishing-rods, guns, and dogs on his brain?"

It was all very puzzling, very distressing. With the best wishes in the world to stretch out a hand to help this man, she found it an impossibility. Her hands were tied, doubly tied; first, by the promise she had made him; secondly, and with a yet stronger knot, by the consciousness that she had surprised his sorrow; stolen, as it were, the knowledge of it, not had it communicated to her.

She went about the house feeling downcast and almost guiltily miserable. The thought that some one else beside herself had possession of Wolf's secret, or at least a part of it, added not a little to her distress. She shrank, in a way she could not account for even to herself, from taking Mrs. Reece into her confidence on this matter, though the thought pressed upon her night and day: "Who was this person? What was he or she doing about the house in the middle of the night?"

Rightly or wrongly, somehow her suspicions settled upon old Bryce, who, for some unexplained reason, she felt confident bore no good-will to the master of the house.

Now anything more unlike to the gliding, supple motion of a Hindoo, than the hobbling, jerky gait of an ancient Welsh-woman could scarcely be imagined, yet somehow Judith never caught sight of the rugged face, the lean hand, the cavernous eyes of the old housekeeper, without recalling a certain native servant of her father's, a man who eventually had been tried for and convicted of murder. It had all happened in her very young days, when, as a small child, she had gone with a black nurse for change of air to the hills with this man (a syce) in attendance. An English officer, a friend of Colonel Wynne's, had in some way offended him, and the Hindoo had waited and watched for his opportunity, and eventually had succeeded in shooting the officer through the heart. Judith, as a tiny child of seven, playing unperceived in a corner, had seen the Hindoo creep into the room, coil himself like a snake in his lair, watching for his chance.

It was odd all this should come into her head now, after having lain forgotten for so many years. It was odd, and it was unpleasant, but nevertheless so it was.

On the morning after that mysterious, troubled night, she daringly essayed to question Bryce as to the night she herself had passed, shaking Oscar off her arm, and going boldly into the housekeeper's room to do so.

Bryce answered with a roulade of sibilant Welsh, to which Judith returned fire with a round of easy French, informing the old body it was not polite to speak to people in an unknown tongue. Bryce replied with such a cannonade of consonants that Judith felt convinced they must be nothing less than anathemas, and in her turn she sent back a succession of short, jerky Scotch phrases picked up from aunt Maggie, in reality a string of Gaelic gutturals, intended to express such commonplaces as "The weather is fine," and "Hay at a discount."

Then they took breath, and looked at each other.

Bryce laid down her keys, and rested her chin in her lean, brown hand.

"It's grand to have so many languages at the tip of one's tongue," she said with a sarcasm that would have more than passed muster on the floor of the House of Commons, where a little of the commodity is made to go a great way. "How many more do you keep in stock, Miss Judith?"

"Only one, Hindoostanee," answered Judith dolefully, "and I shall bring that out next time you speak to me in Welsh."

"I've neither time to listen or speak Welsh or English this morning, miss," said the old body, taking up her keys again. "What with those girls so lazy over their work, and Mr. Oscar coming upon us so sudden, I've enough to fill up two mornings instead of one."

"Oh," said Judith, essaying a bold stroke, "it's a wonder since you have so very much to do all day long that you do not sleep better at night. I should have thought you would have slept right off till at least six o'clock in the morning."

"And who can say that I do not sleep right off till the morning, Miss Judith?" said the woman defiantly, leaning her elbows on the table that stood before her, and staring the young girl full in the face.

Judith laughed and fenced.

"Depend upon it, Bryce, it's all that wicked onyx brooch you will persist in wearing. Do you know," and here she lowered her voice to a mysterious whisper, "that the people at St. André say there is a wicked spirit shut up in the onyx stone, and that every evening at sunset it comes out and worries the people who wear it all through the night with bad dreams."

Bryce was startled, her deep-set eyes flashed a sudden interest.

"Is that true, Miss Judith—real truth?" she questioned. "Does a spirit come out and stand before you? A real spirit that you could ask questions of?"

She seemed to quiver with intense anxiety as she waited for her answer. Even her hands, resting on the table, showed her nervous tremor.

"So the people at St. André used to say," answered Judith, delighted to have produced an impression, and watching the old woman narrowly. "Of course now you will throw it away at once into the blessed St. Govan's stream, after the bloodstone-ring. You won't run the risk, I am sure, of seeing an evil spirit stand by your bedside in the dead of night?"

"Miss Judith," exclaimed Bryce with a desperate eagerness, "I would have the Evil one himself stand by my side in the dead of night if he would only answer one question I'm wanting to ask. Yes, the Evil one himself," she repeated, raising her voice to an almost hysteric pitch; "if I might ask him one question, I would lay down my life to have answered."

"Ask it of me, Bryce," said Judith quietly, feeling herself on the edge of another mystery now; "you know ladies are taught a great many things which poor people never have time to learn. It is possible I might be able, in part, at any rate, to answer the question that is troubling you so much."

Bryce looked all round her furtively, nervously, as one might who had some guilty, treacherous deed on hand. She shut down the one window of the room, and coming close to Judith's side, bent low and whispered into her ear:

"Miss Judith, what I want to know is, why haven't the rooks come back? Look there" and she pointed to a clump of tall elms which, towering high above the smaller firs and limes, were hung at irregular intervals with the pretty plaited basket-homes of the rooks, now, alas! deserted and tenantless. "Look there, Miss Judith, once those trees were shaking and noisy with the stir and flutter in them; now they are silent as the yews in the graveyard themselves. On the last day of January, this year, they flew away. It was snowing hard, the sky was low and black, and one and all they went away silently without a caw among them. Now, why haven't they come back? If the house had its right master—"

There came at this moment a rattle of sharp raps against the window-panes, which made the rotten old frame quake again.

"Judith, Judith! what are you doing all this time?" cried Oscar's voice from without. "You might as well be interred in a catacomb at once, as drone away the morning in that dreary old den. I have a hundred and one things I want you to do for me."

Bryce started away from Judith like some guilty thing. Judith went regretfully out into the garden sunshine to talk nonsense with Oscar for the remainder of the morning.

XI

The hundred and one things Oscar expected Judith to accomplish for him finally resolved themselves into two, the first of which was that she would get Wolf to buy him a hunter to take back with him to Richmond, "a superb creature he had heard of through a friend, that was literally going begging—could be had, in fact, for a mere song!"

"My dear boy," laughed Judith, "why not ask for yourself? He is your brother, not mine. You would be just as likely to get what you want for yourself as I should for you."

Oscar shook his head.

"It's just this, Judith. I've got as much out of Wolf, one way or another, as I can reasonably expect for another month or six weeks. He's given me a boat of my own to keep at Richmond; he's given his consent—which means, he will supply the needful—to my going to Switzerland with the Martins this autumn, and to Rome with them in the winter; and he has more than half promised that my allowance shall be increased next year. Now, I'll confess I'm not a particularly modest individual, but I ask you, how is it possible, in the face of all this, to go up to him and say: 'I say, old fellow, I want something more out of you now—a nice, jolly hunter.'"

"No, I should say it was utterly impossible, and therefore I should give up the idea at once, for of course it comes to much the same thing whether you or I ask him," answered Judith, conscious of a strong repugnance to ask any favour at Wolf's hands, whether small or great, or, indeed, make any attempt to establish a familiar, easy intercourse between them.

"Oh, it would not be at all the same thing," protested Oscar vehemently. "You have such a nice, gentle way of doing things, I'd defy any man living to refuse you what you wanted. But if I went to Wolf, and begged it as the greatest favour he could grant me, it wouldn't move him one atom. He'd simply say: 'Not to be thought of for a moment; you'd begin with neglecting your studies, you'd end with breaking your neck.'"

"Well, I agree with Wolf; that is exactly what you would do. No, I decline the hunter affair altogether."

Oscar began to growl.

"I can scarcely believe it of you, Judith. You always gave yourself out to be an amiable young woman. Now, if you call this amiability, let me tell you are very much mistaken."

"No, I won't call it amiability, but obstinacy if you like it better. At any rate, I mean to be obstinate. I will have nothing to do with the breakneck business."

"As if my neck were not my own, to break or otherwise as I see fit! Well, I suppose, as you scout the idea of amiability this afternoon, you'll say 'No' to my other request. Such a small one, too—a thing most girls would jump at doing for a fellow, and say: 'Oscar dear, give me something else to do for you; that's not worth calling a favour!'"

"Tell me what it is, and see whether I can 'jump at' doing it for you."

"Well, it's just this, Judith," and here Oscar broke off a big, fan-like bough of laurestinus which overshadowed the path, and handed it to Judith for an impromptu sun-umbrella: "I don't want you to give yourself a mountain of trouble in the matter, but I shall be very glad if you yourself will see that the rooms are clean and fit for young ladies to sleep in, supposing I can get the two Miss Martins down here on a week's visit. My mother will just give old Bryce an order or two, which she will carry out or not as she thinks fit; and of course, as my mother has not her sight, she is obliged to trust entirely to the old cat. So I ask you, will you be so condescending as to take a survey of the rooms yourself, and see that everything is 'just so?'"

"Yes, I think I will condescend so far. But, mind, I shall expect a great deal of gratitude, and you mustn't trouble me often with such tremendous requests."

"And will you please bear in mind, when you make your survey, that in Richmond we live in a land of paper dados and beaten brasses, of sage-green plush and terra-cotta mantelpieces?"

"Ah no; I shall try to forget all about that. The thought of so much grandeur would paralyse my simple efforts at cleanliness and brightness. Fancy, paper dados and sage-green plush at Plas-y-Coed!"

Judith, as she spoke, looked up at the grim, lichen-shaded old structure, and made one step as though she were going into the house.

Oscar put himself in front of her.

"Don't go in yet, Judith; there's something else I want you to do for me. Not now, but by-and-by, when I give you a nudge. I have been speaking to my mother already on the matter, and later on, when I speak to Wolf, I shall get you to back me up in what I want. The idea has come into my head lately that my going in for Oxford is great nonsense after all. Don't start in that absurd manner as though something had stung you. Supposing by great good-fortune I should manage to creep into college say in a year and a half's time. I suppose I must stay there at least three years if I want to cut any sort of a figure. Well, there's a good four and a half years gone smash, and all for nothing at all. I shall be twenty-four and a half years old, and not have earned one penny for myself. Think of that!"

Judith tried to keep down her astonishment.

"There are many men," she said, "who have never all their lives long earned one penny for themselves."

"Ah, but then they step into fortunes ready made for them, lucky dogs! But just think, Judith, how late in life it would be to begin earning one's bread at four-and-twenty. It would take at least ten years to make any sort of income, no matter what I took up with. Why, I should be quite an old man before I should be able to settle down and marry!"

"Settle down and marry!" echoed Judith, in her surprise standing still in the middle of the path, surveying Oscar from head to foot.

Oscar's fair face flushed a deep red.

"Well, I suppose there's nothing very unreasonable in a man wanting to settle down and marry some time or other?" he asked irritably.

"Some time or other, yes," said Judith, beginning to recover herself; "but your 'some time or other' ought to be such a long way ahead that it wouldn't be worth while thinking of it for—oh, let us say fifteen or twenty years to come!" She broke off for a moment, then a sudden merry light shone in her eyes. "It's Theo!" she cried; "I'm positive it's Theo! Now don't get so red, Oscar, and you needn't cut down all those carnations so spitefully with that stick. I don't ask you to say whether I'm right or wrong, but I'm convinced it's Theo."

Oscar's face took a yet deeper shade.

"You're wrong, as usual, Miss Judith Wiseacre!" he cried. "Theo is a dear good child, as I've always said, but Theo is a regular tomboy, and it is not Theo!"

"Then it's Miss Leila," said Judith with great decision; "I'm positive I'm right this time, and if you deny it ever so much I sha'n't believe you. Only tell me what she is like—do, there's a good fellow. Is she little, and brown, and sallow, like me?"

"She is not little, and brown, and sallow."

"Well, then, is she tall, and large, and fair, like Martha, who brings the milk every morning?"

"She is not in the least like Martha, the milkmaid."

"Then who and what is she like? Oh, dear, dear Oscar!" and here Judith laid her hand pleadingly on the young man's arm, "do—do describe her to me—or try, at any rate."

"Judith, God, in all His making, never made anything more beautiful than Leila Martin," answered Oscar gravely, almost solemnly. Then he shook himself free from Judith's hand and went straight into the house.

XII

Oscar's trepidation lest the Misses Martin should not be properly housed during their short visit, could scarcely be a matter for surprise to anyone acquainted with the normal condition of the unused sleeping apartments at the old Grange. A more desolate, forlorn, and shabby succession of rooms could scarcely be imagined. So at least thought Judith as—having first obtained Mrs. Reece's permission—she made the round of them with Bryce at her heels.

The keys creaked in the rusty locks one after the other; Bryce threw back each door with an air half-defiant, half-contemptuous, as of one who would say: "No doubt you, with your modern fastidious ways, would decline to sleep in them, and yet better people than you have lain in those beds." She looked up in Judith's face as she surveyed the faded chintzes, the carpets absolutely tattered in parts, the dirt-begrimed walls and ceilings, ready to take up arms in defence of each piece of forlorn shabbiness.

But Judith made no remark whatsoever; she looked in silence at some ten or twelve bedrooms, going down odd-looking winding passages to get to them, and ascending odd-looking winding stairs. So Bryce essayed a remark which was intended to show she was ready for any attack upon her late master's domestic arrangements.

"Th' old squire," she said with a little grin on her old face, "was not fond of visitors after Madam Reece died."

"No," acquiesced Judith negatively.

"And Master Bernard was always away in foreign parts, both before and after his father's death."

"Yes," acquiesced Judith affirmatively.

Bryce shrugged her shoulders, with her hand on the last lock.

"It's to be hoped the young ladies who are coming are not fond of smart rooms with muslin and ribbons decked about, and easy-chairs, and sofas, and foot-stools, and such like, for they won't get them here," she grumbled.

"Evidently," was Judith's brief reply. Then, seeing that Bryce had not yet unlocked this, the last uninspected room, she asked: "Is this a bedroom, Bryce—can I go in here?"

"It's the tapestry-room," answered Bryce, letting her voice fall a little. "You may go in if you like, Miss Judith; I would rather stay outside."

Judith went in. This was a larger room than any she had yet seen, though, like the others, its ceiling was low. Its four square walls were hung with tapestry, whose subject and colour time, with damp, ruthless hand, had almost obliterated. Here and there from out a grey-brown background of cross-stitch loomed a russet-coloured Titanic face with that sardonic smile on its lips which only cross-stitch knows how to impart. Judith, by straining her eyes and imagination alike, could fancy she could trace the outline of gigantic tree-boughs and enormous chariot-wheels, and now and again a small, childish, cherub head. She longed to have the history of it all.

"Why don't you come in and tell me all about this room, Bryce?" she called to the old woman, who remained obstinately on the other side of the threshold.

Bryce shook her head.

"You'd best come out, Miss Judith; it's the room where the old squire died, and"—this added in a low, reverential whisper—"as he lay dying he said to me, 'Bryce,' he said, 'if ever anything troubles me after I'm gone, and I can come back, this is where you may look to see me.' They were almost the last words he said, Miss Judith, as he lay dying on that bed."

Judith's eyes naturally turned towards the bed which stood at the far end, and in the darkest corner of the room. It was a massive piece of furniture, square, with four enormous pillars and heavy cornice of carved oak. It was hung with full, wide curtains of tapestry, which matched in greyness and grimness the other hangings of the room. They were closely drawn together, so that not a vestige of bed-covering or pillow was to be seen.

Judith had never before set eyes on a bedstead which presented so close a resemblance to a sarcophagus.

"Which way does this room look?" she asked, going towards the window, anxious for an excuse to throw back the half-closed shutters, so as to get a better view of the dreary antiquated relics, which she felt sure must fill every corner.

"Let the windows be, Miss Judith," cried Bryce; "you'll only see the bleak-side of the mountains from there. Come out and let me lock the door again. It's ill prying into dead men's rooms."

Judith's answer was a loud exclamation of surprise.

"Why—why, what is this?" she cried in a tone of alarm, standing still and gazing at an object which at that minute caught her eye.

CATHERINE LOUISA PIRKIS

From where she stood in the dim light, it looked like a narrow veil of black crape or gauze hanging from the ceiling in front of and some inches below the high oaken mantelpiece. She made one step towards it, and then laughed outright. It was simply and literally a veil of black cobwebs, nothing more, spun by the generations of house-spiders who had carried on a peaceful existence there since the old squire's death. Judith's merriment excited Bryce's wrath.

"Miss Judith," she said grimly, "it's ill to laugh where most people would weep. Come out of the room before something dreadful happens. If you raise your eyes a little higher you'll see something you won't laugh at, I'll be bound."

Judith did raise her eyes a little higher, till, in fact, they rested on the mantelpiece, upon which stood one single ornament—a huge clock of strange device in beaten brass and bronze. The design was that of a monument, and in place of inscription was the round figured face of the dial. Beside it lay an overturned bell, over which leaned a gaunt skeleton, hammer in hand, prepared to strike the hour. Beneath him, in quaint characters, was written the legend: "I wasted time, and now doth time waste me." Seen through the black veil of cobwebs, it certainly bore a grim and somewhat spectral appearance.

Judith felt suddenly chilled.

"You are right, Bryce," she said; "laughter is as much out of place here as it would be in a church."

She turned to leave the room as she spoke, but as she neared the door, her foot catching in a hole in the carpet, she fell forward nearly on to her face, barely recovering her balance.

The old flooring creaked, and there seemed to come the faint vibrating sound of the bell, as of the old clock striking.

"Oh, Miss Judith, Miss Judith!" cried Bryce, her face white, her hands quaking, "what have you done? Don't you know there's ill luck in store for them who set the dead man's clock going? Come out, come out!" and she clutched at Judith's wrist, literally dragged her out of the room, shutting and locking the door behind her.

Judith felt a little disturbed with her morning's adventure. She loved old-world stories and mysteries as she loved her dreams, the scent of flowers, the memory of a song. But she loved them to be fresh, sweet, holy poems with the ring of some blessed truth in them, not shadowed, as the traditions of this house appeared to be, with a grim weirdness that suggested evil and pain. She told the story of the tapestry-room to

Mrs. Reece, as they sat together in the heat of the afternoon under the shadow of the slouching yews.

"I did not know there was such a room in the house," said Mrs. Reece; then she in turn handed on the story to Wolf, who was coming slowly along their path at this moment, evidently bent on passing them if he could do so without positive discourtesy.

He listened with a deep attention, standing silent and motionless in front of them as they sat, the bright August sun lighting up a very wan, haggard face under a broad beaver-hat. He made no reply to his mother's remark that the room ought to be opened and cleaned, and the ghosts turned out of it.

"Did you look at the other rooms?" he asked, turning to Judith. "Is it possible, do you think, to make them fit for two young ladies in a few days' time? You know better than I do what is a young lady's ideal in the way of a bedroom."

Judith knew what her ideal of a bedroom was clearly enough, and the bedrooms at Villa Rosa exactly expressed it. She answered frankly and to the point:

"I don't think they could be made fit for any one to sleep in in a few days' time, unless you had an upholsterer down from London—"

She stopped abruptly, recollecting all in a moment Wolf's evident disinclination to spend money on the house, and the large outlay the having an upholsterer from London might involve.

Wolf seemed to read her hesitation.

"That would mean more money than I am prepared to spend," he said with brusque decision. "I must think it over, and see what can be done."

A sudden idea struck Judith.

"Why not let the girls have my room? I dare say they won't mind sleeping together," she exclaimed. "My room has been made so nice and comfortable, I'm sure they would like it. I could sleep in any of the other rooms without any fuss of doing up. Except, perhaps in the tapestry-room."

The last sentence was added *sotto voce*, and as though she were somewhat ashamed of the admission.

A sudden idea seemed to strike Wolf also.

"They shall have my room," he said; "it can easily be arranged to suit them. Will you speak to Bryce, mother, about it? Tell her also, please, that I will meantime go into the tapestry-room. I don't want

CATHERINE LOUISA PIRKIS

it turned out, and that sort of thing, just opened and aired—nothing more."

Judith gazed at him round-eyed and silent. Mrs. Reece found a voice and poured forth a volley of objections.

"Of course I don't believe in haunted rooms and rubbish of that sort," she cried, "but the room must be damp and close, and ought to have a month's airing at least before it's slept in. You will catch your death some day with your mad freaks."

But Wolf was not to be lightly turned from his purpose, and though Bryce raised such a storm of objections and forebodings that Mrs. Reece's were by comparison with them "as moonlight unto sunlight and as water unto wine," the room was made ready for him, and a week later found him duly installed therein.

XIII

It was pleasant to think that the walls of the old Grange were so soon to throw back the echo of young, merry voices, the tread and spring of young, merry footsteps. Judith felt her heart go up at a bound at the thought of possible long walks in the early morning up the rough, misty, mountain-sides, of lazy, twilight talks in the dim, cooing wood with two girls of her own age, and—she hoped—possessing her own capacity for long country walks morning, noon, or night.

To say truth the silence and dreariness of the old Grange was beginning just now to make themselves felt to her. If only dear Uncle Pierre, soft-voiced, always striving to give pleasure, always successful in his endeavour, could but have crossed the threshold, bringing with him the atmosphere of Villa Rosa, the atmosphere which dear Aunt Maggie had compounded of blithe order and decorous abandon for her own and everybody else's delectation, what a magical change would have been wrought at Plas-y-Coed!

Judith's heart in those days was always going back aching and quaking to the happy old time at Villa Rosa. None who knew this girl slightly as did these new friends at Plas-y-Coed, and noted her quiet, even walk through the monotony of life there, her intense delight in simple country pleasures, her unfeigned interest in the most commonplace affairs of a most commonplace world, could have guessed of what strong, deep passions she was capable. Wolf, on the day of her arrival, had described her to his mother as looking pale and wan. "Possibly," he had suggested, "from her long, tiring journey." He did not know—how could he?—that the paleness and wanness were the result of that desperate rebellion, that most futile of all battles into which the youngest and least skilled in warfare are most prone to plunge—a battle against the laws of God which wrench from our clinging grasp our nearest and dearest before we have learnt to walk without them.

Judith had inherited, with other English traits, that thorough-going English habit of shutting the door upon everything in the shape of strong, deep feeling. Her passionate, loving heart she could not get rid of—there it was, and there it must be; but no one, however prying, should know it was there. Her long years of French training had not sufficed to root out this English instinct of hers. Many good things, no doubt, she had brought away with her from France, but not one good thing, essentially English, had she left behind.

"Why, you told me she was half a French girl," exclaimed Theo Martin bluntly to Oscar, as she took a steady survey of Judith from head to foot; "but if it were not for her finikin boots, her big collars, and mounted-up hair, she would be as English as I am."

It was said under Judith's very eyelids. Oscar grew crimson and uncomfortable.

"Hush-sh! We are not at The Retreat now, remember," he said, in a tone of remonstrance.

Judith laughed.

"And I am as English as you," she aid. "At Villa Rosa we spoke and read quite as much English as we do here at the Grange. We spoke French, just as they do Welsh here, only to the servants."

Theo gave her opinion of everybody and everything about her with the same delightful frankness. She was a large, fair, bouncing girl of sixteen, with very short petticoats and very thick ankles. Her features were good, with the exception of her mouth, which was wide and large, without being full-lipped. Her eyes—the best part of her face—were of a dark blue-grey, and were fringed with long black lashes.

Her glad, hearty ways won Judith's heart at once. Somehow she seemed the counterpart of Oscar in her blitheness, her boyishness, and thorough determination to take life pleasantly.

To the elder sister Judith did not feel so drawn, in spite of her rare beauty and grace of manner. Leila's was simply a perfect face, the complexion of a pure pallor, tinged with colour as delicate as the lining of a cameo-shell; the nose straight, with finely-cut nostrils; the mouth full, with coral-red lips. Her eyes were "deeply, darkly, gloriously blue," fringed, like Theo's, with long black lashes; her forehead low and wide; her eyebrows delicately pencilled; her hair, a dark chestnut-brown, fell in one long plait below her waist; her figure was tall and stately, a little inclined to plumpness, perhaps, and her hands and feet were, perhaps, a little larger than she herself would have chosen; but, on the whole, a more glorious creature to look at never walked the earth.

Judith could have sat gazing at her hour after hour, as she would have gazed at a beautiful statue or picture, could the laws of courtesy have permitted it. By Leila's side she felt herself grow small, sallow, and insignificant. With the impress of this grand woman upon her eyes she went up to her own room, and surveyed herself from head to foot in the modern cheval-glass which had been placed there for her. She saw reflected in it a small, slight girl, with tiny hands and feet, a colourless complexion, small indeterminate features, dark hazel eyes—unripe hazel, be it noted—and brown hair, untinged with the faintest suspicion of gold. A lady's face it was, a pure, true, gentle face too, which knew well how to express every shade of tender feeling, and which might, under strong pressure, express passion, poetry, tragedy all in one, but for all that not a beautiful face, not one that would have arrested a second glance from a passer-by—nor even a first had Leila Martin's shone beside it.

Judith almost laughed aloud, as she thought of the contrast. No wonder that poor Oscar, at his susceptible age, had fallen victim to such rich and rare attractions. Then there stole another thought into her heart, a thought that seemed to bring with it a twinge of some sort, slight as a needle-prick, yet as distinct. What would Wolf think of this dainty young beauty? Would his eyes be as veiled to her loveliness as they seemed to be to everything under heaven, lovely or unlovely alike; or would he succumb to her many charms as thoroughly and rapidly as Oscar had done?

Theo made very merry over Oscar's devotion to the fair Leila.

"He thinks he's in love with her," she said, throwing her nine-stone weight on Judith's knees, and putting a heavy fat arm round her slender throat; "but, bless you, he isn't. He'll get out of it in a fortnight's time, when another new pupil comes, and he sees Leila making eyes at him—so," here Theo manoeuvred with her own dark lashes, and gave a Leila-like glance from beneath them. "It's the greatest fun in the world to see them"—*i.e.* the pupils—"all knocked over, one after the other, like nine-pins, and then have to pick themselves up again. Sometimes, however, it gets a little too strong to be funny, at least pa thinks so, and then he packs Leila off to Germany for a month or so, to a school where there are no masters. She's always being sent off in that way. Came back only three weeks ago, and knocked Oscar over like winking. She asked him to cut the 'Cornhill' for her, and he did it on his knees by her side. I knew it was all up with him then, and it was. Heavy, do you say? You feel crushed! Why, what a poor little sparrow you must be, not to be able to stand my light weight!"

Judith could only hope and trust that Oscar would get over his love-sickness as easily as Theo prognosticated. She feared greatly, however, that the malady had taken too strong a hold him to be lightly shaken off. At first it seemed to her laughable to see Oscar so deeply steeped in this midsummer madness, but later on, as the depth and intensity of his passion became manifest to her, it seemed to her far from laughable, only pathetic and terrible. She longed to warn him as an elder sister might, to go to him and say, "Look at this lovely woman as long as you will, gaze at her as you would at the glittering stars of heaven, or some glorious purple sunset, but for all that, never dream of winning her. The stars of heaven, or the sunset sky itself, may be yours before she will."

But Judith's attention was before long to be drawn from Oscar and his headlong, eager adoration to another quarter.

At the third meal at which they had all assembled after the arrival of these young ladies, it was forced upon her notice that Wolf was awakening to the fact that an extremely beautiful young woman was seated at table with him. It was luncheon, which, with Theo and Oscar seated side by side, threatened to be a distinctly lively, not to say uproarious meal.

Theo had begun well by collecting every spoon within reach—salt, table, dessert spoons, and making a packet of them, had presented them to Oscar.

"I know it's sending coals to Newcastle, but no doubt you'll have continued use for them," she had said saucily.

"That's one to you, Miss Theo," Oscar had answered, adjusting a tablespoon in his buttonhole; "but I'm much obliged to you all the same, and I'll pay you back with compound interest at the earliest opportunity."

"What is it—what is it?" asked Mrs. Reece, hearing the clatter of the silver, and wondering what it meant.

"We are giving sweets to the sweet, and spoons to the spoony," began the irrepressible Theo.

"Thistles to the foolish, a long rope to those who want to hang themselves," continued Oscar.

Judith looking up from her plate of salad at this moment, to see what effect this flow of young folly had upon Wolf, was surprised to find his eyes fixed not upon these noisy ones, but on the calmly sedate Leila, who was seated sideways to him and half-way down the table. It was a gaze half of wonder, half of admiration, such as she had never seen on his face before, and which seemed to her fancy to say: "Why did no one tell me what a beautiful creature you are? Why have I been left to find it out for myself?"

Psychologists, in these days, tell us many things formerly supposed to be beyond their ken, but they have never yet been able to explain the magnetic power of a beautiful face. Men and women will disagree in their ideals of beauty—will deny its existence where it really is, and put forth claims for it where it is not; but let a beautiful man or woman enter the room, and every eye, consciously or unconsciously, willingly or unwillingly, will pay the homage due to the face so fair to look upon.

Wolf's eyes had seemed to Judith hitherto veiled to anything and everything that went on around him, a beautiful woman comes and sits down at table with him, and lo! he gazes and gazes as though he had never seen a woman's face before.

Leila bore his steadfast look tranquilly enough, keeping her full white lids downcast to the damask tablecloth. For one thing, she was accustomed to have men's eyes fixed on her; for another thing, she rather liked it than otherwise. She made a rule never to interrupt a gaze of that sort; she liked men, as it were, to look their utmost, and to take a full catalogue of her many perfections. It made them more conscious of her power, and better able to appreciate her smiles and favours when she chose to distribute them. So Wolf looked and looked at her from one side, and Oscar looked and looked at her from the other, and this young woman, fully conscious that two pairs of eyes were fixed upon her, bore the four-fold gaze with the serenity of a queen of beauty gathering in her tribute-money from her subjects and captives.

At last, when she considered that Wolf's eyes had almost drunk their fill—she did not wish them to be surfeited, be it noted—she lifted her eyelids, and said in that slow, low tone she generally affected:

"I am charmed with your home, Mr. Reece. The country is beyond anything lovely. I should so like one afternoon to make that little excursion to Llanrhaiadr Oscar was speaking about."

"You shall make it this afternoon if you like," answered Wolf, rising promptly from his chair to give the order that the old greys should at once be made ready for action.

Needle-prick number two in Judith's heart. Whence it came or wherefore she would have found it difficult to explain, but there it was unmistakably. Sharp, sudden, in and out, bringing no blood this time, just the merest beginning of a scratch, but, nevertheless, a suggestion of a possible wound in the days to come, deeper, wider, more difficult to heal.

CATHERINE LOUISA PIRKIS

XIV

How you mean to entertain these young ladies for ten days at a stretch," grumbled Mrs. Reece, "is more than I can imagine. After you have shown them the church, the mountains (from the bottom), the woods, the waterfall, you'll simply be at your wits' ends how to get through the days. My dears, I think it would have been far wiser for you all to have gone in a body and stayed at their home, and done the London sights at the same time, than have had them down here where there is nothing to see and no one to speak to."

"Oh, Wolf has taken the matter into his own hands," Oscar grumbled back in return, "and, so far as I can see, is providing ample amusement for them—for one of them, at any rate."

"What do you mean?" asked Mrs. Reece briskly. "Are you going to tell me that Wolf has fallen in love with one of these young ladies at first sight?"

"Can't say, I'm sure. I only know that he is making himself deucedly agreeable to them, and instead of shutting himself up in the library writing sermons all day long, he is either walking with them about the woods or taking them long, dusty drives to some outlandish place or other."

"Where is Judith? Judith, are you in the room?" called the old lady. "Come, you always speak the truth; you can't help it. Tell me, do you think Wolf has fallen in love at last? With the soft-voiced young lady of course it must be, for the little hoyden has not yet learnt how to attract men, whatever she may do for the women."

Judith looked up a little nervously from her book.

"I cannot tell—I do not know," she answered hesitatingly. "You see, I know so little about falling in love, it has never happened to come in my way."

"Anyone could see that," said Oscar, speaking as he so often did the first thing that came uppermost, words that he would be safe to unsay in ten minutes' time. "I am sure you are born to be an old maid. Not one of those nasty, sour old cats who do everything in their power to make people miserable, but one of those sweet, darling little creatures who never have any love-affairs of their own, and throw themselves heart and soul into the love-making of other people."

Judith, with eyes bent once more on her book, saw the lines describe all sorts of curious curves and zig-zags.

Never to have any love-affairs of her own! It was a hard sentence to pass on a girl not yet twenty.

"My dear," said Mrs. Reece in a dry, quiet tone, "a young lady of Judith's attractions, and with her large fortune, is not likely to lack lovers."

"Oh, I forgot all about her large fortune," said Oscar, paying unintentionally a compliment that would have done credit to a Chesterfield. "You see she makes us forget it. She never gives herself any airs over it. Ah, there they go again! Off for another walk, I suppose;" this, as the shadows of Leila and Wolf fell athwart the windows, and then followed their owners adown the weedy drive towards the gate.

Later on, when Mrs. Reece had left the room, Oscar grumbled out his sorrows to Judith in a yet stronger strain.

"It's a confounded shame, Judith—that's what it is," he said, going to the window and resting his elbows on the sill. "Why can't he leave her alone? Why does he want her all to himself, morning, noon, and night? What business has he to steal her from me, I should like to know?"

"Steal her from you! Oh, Oscar!" protested Judith, trying to convince herself as much as the boy-lover that Wolf's attentions to Leila involved no covert idea of robbery. "Why, they are only taking a stroll together. I don't suppose they are more than half-a-dozen yards from the garden-gate."

"And what does he want to stroll with her for if he isn't in love with her? And why does he sit and stare at her in the way he does if he doesn't mean anything?"

Judith remained silent. Oscar went on:

"And what did he mean by taking her off to Llanrhaiadr the other day all by themselves?"

"All by themselves! Why, Oscar, you went also!"

"Yes, but I had to stay with the horses while he went into the church to show her the brasses and monuments. Why couldn't he have let me have done it?"

"But, Oscar, you most likely couldn't have acted cicerone as Wolf did. It strikes me if you had taken her into the church you would simply have done as you did when you took me—nodded pleasantly to the monuments, and said: 'Now there they all are, choose for yourself which you like best.'"

"And what if I had!" said Oscar almost fiercely. "Does she care two

CATHERINE LOUISA PIRKIS

straws for monuments or brasses, or anything of that sort? I tell you she cares no more for them than—than she does for me, and she couldn't well care less for anything under the sun!"

His fierceness was rapidly blazing itself out. There was an undernote of pain now in his tone which cut Judith to the heart. She longed to lift up a warning voice.

"My poor Oscar," she said, going over to his side and laying her hand upon his arm, "if you are so positive she does not care for you, why don't you try to get the thought of her out of your heart? Why go on loving her in the way you do when you know you haven't the least chance in the world of winning her?"

"Why—why!" reiterated Oscar, turning round and facing Judith with renewed fierceness; "why do you love the stars, the sun, the flowers—everything that is bright and beautiful in the world? They don't care a brass farthing for you, do they?"

"Possibly not, Oscar; at any rate, they do me no harm. But if the sun suddenly took it into his head to smite me with brain-fever, or the flowers exhaled poison instead of fragrance—well, I should, to say the least, keep out of their way."

"Would you?" doubted Oscar, giving her one long, searching look, which brought to and then banished from her face the quick red blood. "I very much doubt if you'd do anything of the kind. It strikes me, Judith, when once you fall in love, it will be something more than ankle-deep. Headforemost, neck-or-nothing, you'll go, and no matter what sort the fellow may turn out, you'll stick to him like grim death itself. Wait till your own time comes, Judith."

Judith's hand fell to her side. She made one irresolute step as though to leave the room, came back again, seemed to be gathering her courage together, and a little falteringly touched him lightly on the shoulder.

"Oscar," she said in the lowest of low tones, "if it be really as you think—I mean, supposing Wolf truly loves this girl as you imagine—you will not begrudge him his happiness, will you?"

It was said hesitatingly, lovingly, pleadingly. Oscar's face grew very white. It was at least a minute before he answered, and then his words came thick and slow.

"No, Judith, I won't begrudge him his happiness. I'll stand out of his way; I promise you that. Wolf deserves to be happy—Heaven knows, he has done more than ever I have towards earning happiness."

There was a long pause. It was a scorchingly hot August morning; from outside there came the faint scent of honeysuckle and jasmine, and the deep, droning sound of a big humming-bee.

"Thank you, Oscar," said Judith softly, speaking as though he had granted her a personal favour.

"Yes," Oscar went on, as though he had not heard her; "Wolf has had misery and discomfort enough in his time. Compared with his, my life has been all sunshine. He bore the brunt of all our poverty and troubles in London, working like a galley-slave for the poor people all the time. Judith, did I ever tell you what he did in the fever that raged five years ago, when my father died, when the sick nurses even refused to come and nurse the people, and the undertakers had to be paid double to bury them? Why, he sold every mortal thing he could call his own— his books, his watch, some jewellery that had been left him in a will; sent away my mother and me into the country, and literally lived with the poor people himself. Aye; ate, drank, slept with them; prayed with them; nursed them night and day; was one of them till the fever came to an end, and they got their courage back."

Oscar said all this slowly, dwelling on his words as though by thus recounting one by one his brother's good deeds, he were dealing so many successive blows to his own jealous passion.

Judith listened, holding in her breath as one does in the presence of some grand and beautiful thing.

This was the man whom she had believed to be laden with a guilty secret!

Oscar went on, half to himself, half to Judith:

"No, I'm not ungrateful. I don't forget how he starved and stinted himself to give me proper clothes and schooling. Begrudge him his happiness! No. I would double it if I could; but, great Heavens, at what a cost!" And here the poor lad bowed his head on the window-ledge and burst into tears.

Judith put her small arm round his broad shoulders, and did her best to comfort him.

"I know what a fool I am; let me alone in my folly, Judith," he said savagely. "But sometimes I feel as though our coming here to The Grange had brought a curse upon us. Oh, we were all much happier in our poverty in London."

"The happy times will come back, Oscar; I feel sure they will come back!"

CATHERINE LOUISA PIRKIS

"Will they? I don't feel so sure. Oh, what fools we all were to rejoice as we did when the news of our good fortune came! How bright and happy Wolf seemed! Why, he really laughed in those days. Then, when we got here, everything seemed to change all of a sudden, like a sun going down in mid-day. He dismissed all the work-people he had engaged, reduced the servants by one half, and settled down into the gloomy, miserable man he is now. It seemed as though a curse fell upon him as he crossed the threshold of the house. At the very gates he met a child singing, he bade 'God bless her,' gave her the last shilling he had in his pocket, and told her to go and make some one happy with it, entered this house, went up into his room, read his letters, and came downstairs a changed being. Judith, it's my belief there's something wrong about this place—something evil has been done here, and we, who know nothing about it, are paying the penalty for it."

There came a flutter and scramble along the gravel-path at this moment, and Theo, with one of Oscar's wideawakes on her head, made her appearance outside. Her dress was dusty and disarranged, here and there a bramble clung to it.

Judith envied Oscar the facility with which he smoothed out the muscles of his face, and effaced all signs of deep feeling.

"Well," said Theo, standing in the midst of a flower-bed, and leaning in at the window so that her nose almost touched Oscar's, "you are a pair of duffers and no mistake, not to be out of doors this glorious morning. I've been bird-nesting up among the yews; have I brought back a churchyardy smell with me?"

"Bird-nesting in August! I like that?" said Oscar contemptuously.

"And I like it, too!" retorted Theo. "Don't you see, Mr. Wiseacre, one must have an object in life before one can put forth one's best energies. I must have an object before I can make up my mind to climb a tree even. I say to myself, 'I'll get as high as that nest, and put a stone in it,' and I do—that's all. Good gracious, Judith, how dismal you look! Have you been crying? What's the matter?"

"Judith has been reading the lives of the saints, about St. Francis or one of the mfrizzling, and it has distressed her," answered Oscar readily.

"Well, why shouldn't saints frizzle if they like it? I'm sure I feel more than half-grilled at the present moment with this scorching sun pouring down. I say, Oscar, can't you open your window a little higher? I'm sure I could scramble in if you'll stand back."

And while Theo made her entry through the window, Judith made her exit through the door, and escaped to her own room for a little quiet.

Her head was hot and aching. She threw open wide her window. "Fresh air brings fresh thought," Aunt Maggie had been wont to say, and Judith had caught from her the love of open windows, and long breezy walks. She leaned out, looking mountain-wards, and wondering over many things, losing herself in the past history and present love-stories of Oscar and Wolf, when suddenly there came a gentle tapping at her door, and in response to her "Come in," much to her surprise Leila entered the room.

She had still her hat on, as though she had just come in from her walk.

"May I come in?" she asked, standing well in the middle of the room. "I know you have a cheval-glass here; there isn't one in my room, and I haven't looked at myself properly since I left home. I'm not sure about the way this dust-cloak hangs at the back."

As she spoke she advanced towards the glass, stood for one moment looking at her full face, then, half-twisting her neck, tried to get a survey of the back plaits of her robe and long-flowing cloak.

"Certainly," was Judith's brief reply; then accusing herself of lack of courtesy, she added, "Can I help you at all?" and endeavoured to adjust the side-screws of the glass, so as to give Leila a better view of herself.

A lovely picture that looking-glass framed, full of lights and shadows, sharp contrasts and sweet harmonies. A young woman, gloriously, sensuously beautiful; a goddess in her face, and an empress in her gait; a pale dark face, a little in the shadows behind, whose only loveliness lay in fulness of expression and subtle suggestions of spirituality.

Judith felt the contrast between herself and this young beauty in all its keenness, yet she looked and looked into the mirror as though the sight were a pleasant one to her. "No wonder," she thought, "that men should go mad over her," and yet somehow she had fancied this man was not one to be dazzled with a woman's face.

Leila also seemed to take a pleasure in surveying this lifelike picture.

"I wish," she said after a long, steady look, "I had a sister like you, just your age and size, and everything; it would be so nice going out together."

"Ah, nice for the one who got the benefit of the contrast, not for the other," said Judith bluntly, yet without the faintest stirring of that envy in her heart which only narrow intellects can harbour.

CATHERINE LOUISA PIRKIS

"You see," Leila went on, "Theo is not the most companionable person in the world to begin with, and her appearance, though not so bad, if she would study it and bring out its best points, is not one to set mine off to advantage, don't you know."

The frank selfishness of this young woman, could it have been collected and parcelled out, would have sufficed to arm and protect a whole battalion of beauties in their first season.

"Theo is a very kind, good-natured girl, and will possibly win love where others only win admiration," was Judith's significant reply.

"I hope she will, I am sure, for her own sake, since she has no chance of getting anything else," said Leila calmly; "but I hope it won't be love and penury. I always have an idea, somehow, that Theo will be a little reckless in her love-affairs. However, it will be no business of mine."

"No business of hers," thought Judith. "Only two sisters, and the love-making of one to be of no concern to the other!" However, she did not speak her thoughts. As well, she instinctively felt, might she argue with a soulless marble statue, as with this exquisitely wrought piece of humanity, on whose exterior nature had been so lavish of her pains that she had left herself no time to bestow the crowning gift of a tender human heart.

Leila finished her survey, walking a little backward from the glass to get a farewell look.

"I wouldn't have put this thing on, only I thought Mr. Reece was going to drive me this morning. In the oddest manner possible, at the last moment, he altered his mind and proposed a walk. Do you think he's mad, or going mad?"

It was all said in the most even, unemotional of voices, just as if she were saying: "Do you think he has a long nose, or is going to grow a moustache?"

Judith shivered. This was putting into plain words a dread which had more than once made itself felt in her heart. Again and again had she wrestled with the terrible suspicion. She did not mean to succumb to it now on the mere suggestion of this unsympathetic young person.

"No, I do not think so—I will not think so. What can make you have such a terrible idea in your mind? You ought to think twice before you say such dreadful things," she answered with a vehemence that made Leila lift her white lids a good quarter-inch higher than they generally went, and her pencilled eyebrows correspondingly.

"I was not aware you took such a strong interest in the matter. I'm sure I beg your pardon," she said, with a little, meaning smile that was excessively disagreeable, and tended to ruffle Judith still more.

"How would it be possible not to take an interest in such a matter?" she asked vehemently. "Think, if it were true, what it would be to his mother and to his brother. Why, all the happiness would be gone out of their lives for ever."

"I suppose they would feel it; it would make them talked about a good deal. But why does he act so strangely—sit and stare at one? Now, I am accustomed to be stared at," she added naïvely enough, "but not like that. It doesn't altogether seem admiration."

"Would it be possible to look at you without admiration?" asked Judith frankly, anxious to lead the talk away from a subject that chilled and frightened her.

"I suppose it would not," said Leila, taking the compliment as a matter of course, and giving one more look at the graceful reflection which still confronted her. "But one thing I must say. If Mr. Reece is not mad, he is the oddest specimen of sanity I ever saw. Why, he actually told me, not half an hour ago, that his first and only thought in life was his mother and brother. Now, for a man at his age to make such a statement is—well, to say the least, highly eccentric. Hark! there is the luncheon-bell. Thank you for letting me come in. I must go now."

Judith, left alone, came to the unavoidable conclusion that, whatever might be the infatuation of Wolf or Oscar for the beautiful Leila, not the faintest breath of passion stirred her heart for either the one or the other.

XV

Certainly, judged by the rules which ordinarily govern men's actions, Wolf's conduct at this time seemed strangely erratic and incomprehensible, destitute of motive, and following no precedent. His kith and kin had grown accustomed to the transformation of the earnest, hard-working clergyman into the taciturn, indifferent, unoccupied dreamer, had accepted the change, and almost ceased to wonder at it; then lo! suddenly another change had set in, gloom and taciturnity were once more laid on one side, something of cheerfulness (a wry, wintry sort of thing) took possession of him. Meals, that had been of late eaten in all but silence, were enlivened by an interchange of words, if not of ideas. The library, which had been his immediate refuge after every gloomy breakfast or dinner, saw nothing of him; it was, in fact, thrown open to the use of the household generally, and a housemaid had been allowed to enter and remove some of the overlaying dust.

Judith, who remembered the stern, hard look of the man, and the way in which he had handed her out of this sanctum sanctorum on the one occasion on which she had dared to penetrate its mysteries, could only hold in her breath and wonder as she saw broom and brush doing their much-needed work.

Mrs. Reece seemed to feel that changes were rife in the air, though she could scarcely realise their nature and extent.

"It seems to me, my dear," she said to Judith one day as the young girl came into the morning-room to read to her as usual after breakfast, "that Oscar talks less than he ever did in his life, and Wolf more—more, at any rate, than he has for the past three or four months. And it also strikes me that he is showing this Miss Leila Martin a great deal of attention; they leave the room together, and I hear them constantly talking in the garden together. Now, my dear, isn't it so?"

Judith, driven into a corner, was forced to admit that Wolf was showing Miss Martin a great deal of attention.

"Well, my dear," the old lady went on, "she's not exactly the one I should have chosen for Wolf had I been consulted on the matter, and I must say I am a little surprised at his choice. Of course, I'm bound to take what you all say for granted, that she is a very beautiful girl, but I did not imagine that Wolf was one to be fascinated by mere beauty. Now tell me honestly, did you, my dear?"

Judith, driven into another corner, was forced to admit that she had not thought Wolf was one to be fascinated by mere beauty.

"Poor boy!" the garrulous old lady went on. "I suppose it's just this: he has been thrown so little into the society of young ladies, that he falls a victim to the first one who makes a dead set at him. Of course she did make a dead set at him?" this interrogatively.

Judith, however, had no mind to be driven into a third corner. She took up her book hastily.

"I have brought down a poem to read today," she said. "I hope you will like it. I picked it up in London at the railway-station while I was waiting for my train."

"My dear," answered Mrs. Reece, "I fear I have lost my taste for poetry, just as I have for tarts and jellies, which young people can eat and enjoy, and never get enough of. But never mind, you may read it to me. If it doesn't interest me it won't disturb my thoughts, and, in any case, I like to hear your soft, clear voice. It sounds so fresh and young, it brings back young thoughts to me. Read on."

Judith read on.

The poem was a simple one, told by one who had done no great thing in poetic art, save this; and this, though simple, was a great poem. A poem that might have enabled the author to ride straight to fame and fortune had it chanced to tickle the "one long ear" of that "famous beast," the British reading public. However, it had not succeeded in performing this notable office, so it remained the first and last poem the writer ever achieved, or at any rate ever published.

It told in language, destitute alike of veneer or any poetic artifice, "the story of a broken life."

The form of the poem was biographic, and commenced at the period when the man, whose history was recorded, and who had led a dissipated, evil life in foreign lands, was seized with a sudden penitence, and resolved to retrace his whole life, step by step, repairing the evil he had wrought, and making amends to every soul he had injured.

"A building that had been overthrown," he argued with himself, "could be rebuilt exactly in its original form if people gave but the patience, the time, the thought to the work." Well, with infinite patience, and time, and thought, he would rebuild his ruined life, doing, one by one, exactly those things which he ought to have done but had neglected, and undoing every wrong he had ever done to his fellow-men.

CATHERINE LOUISA PIRKIS

In pursuance of this idea, he collected together all the money he had at command, and travelled back to his native village over the exact track he had followed on quitting it.

His first attempt at reparation was to try and bring two lovers together whom he had separated. He found, however, that the man had turned soldier, and had fallen in battle; the girl had married a man for whom she had no love, and who treated her harshly and cruelly.

His second attempt at reparation was to seek out a young brother whom he had thrown upon the world, because his dependence was a trouble and an impediment to him. The young brother, in penury and desperation, had joined the Paris Communists, and had been last seen throwing petroleum on the walls of the Tuileries.

With a sinking heart the man resolved he would stop no more on his road, but get back to his native village as quickly as possible, lest even there Fate might have forestalled him.

He will, he thinks, shower his gold on his aged father and mother, marry the girl who loved him, and who nearly broke her heart when he left her to roam the world over.

He arrives at his village late in the summer twilight. Meeting an old villager in the streets, he asks him of his father, mother, and former sweetheart. For all answer, the old villager leads him to the churchyard, and shows him three graves side by side. The man stands horror-stricken looking down on them. Then he bursts into one passionate appeal to Heaven. Why were things thus ordained? Why was not the remaking of a life as easy as its unmaking? Why could one pull to pieces, yet never be able to put together again? Why could one without an effort, with a wave of the hand, or the breath of a moment, undo a whole structure of good, and yet with hard toil and infinite endeavour never be able to build it up again?—Why? Why?

And the old man standing by his side with bowed head and folded hands, echoed the question—Why? Why?

There the poem ended.

Judith's voice trembled a little as she said the concluding "Why?" She had read the poem at the London railway-station while she waited for her train; then it had seemed to her a simple, touching story, nothing more.

Somehow, read now, in the gloom and seclusion of the Grange, it seemed to sound an undernote of pain and pathos so deep as to be almost prophetic.

"Thank you, my dear," said Mrs. Reece briskly, sounding her own cheery note above every other. "It's a pretty story. I lost part of it here and there, through counting my stitches; but I don't suppose it mattered much; in poetry, you know, there is always a great deal one might leave out and never miss. As I was saying, it's a pretty story, but it seems to me it was a great pity the young man didn't think of going back to his friends a year or two sooner, then he wouldn't have had to stand at their graves, and ask so many Whys."

"The man was a selfish hound," said another voice—a masculine one; and Judith, looking up, saw Wolf and Leila Martin standing at the opened window. "We have been listening here for the last five minutes," he explained. "I repeat, the man was a selfish hound, and his 'Why? why?' nothing more than the whine of a whipped cur. He sinned for himself (not for others), and he gets the punishment in himself, in his own soul. Depend upon it, his people were much better off without him."

"No, no, no, my dear," interrupted Mrs. Reece, buckling to for an argument; "that's too hard a thing to say No parents can be better off without their children, no matter what those children may be, or may do. Depend upon it, this poor father and mother broke their hearts fretting for his return."

"Better break their own hearts than have them broken for them," said Wolf with a laugh that was not pleasant to hear. "They would have had an equivalent for their breaking hearts, depend upon it, if he had stayed in his home and brought shame and dishonour within their doors. No, I repeat," and here his voice grew loud and defiant, "if a man brings disgrace upon his kith and kin, the kindest thing he can do is to take himself and his disgrace as far away from the old roof-tree as possible."

Judith could keep silence no longer.

"I should call that the most cowardly not the kindest thing he could do," she said, speaking up bravely. "Surely it would be far nobler to stand in one's own place, face the evil one has done, and endeavour to repair it, than to run away and hide oneself for safety round a corner."

"Two questions, Miss Wynne," said Wolf, turning his deep-set eyes on her. "Might not the running away under certain conditions, require more courage than the standing in one's own place? And, must the running away of necessity be dictated by selfish motives? Might it not be done from suggestions of Christian charity and regard for the welfare of others?"

CATHERINE LOUISA PIRKIS

He threw a depth of meaning into his question which startled her.

It was positively a relief to hear Leila Martin's voice chime in at this moment with the calmly matter-of-fact question:

"But why read such melancholy stories at all? There are so many pretty, light poems now to be had. I'm sure every month in the magazines one sees such interesting verses—nice things that would set delightfully to music."

"Exactly," said Wolf with the slightest touch of sarcasm in his tone; "why should we listen to anything horrible and distressing, when life is so evidently intended to be easy, and pleasant, and enjoyable?"

"That's just what I meant," agreed Leila, whose ear was not quick to detect subtle shades of voice or speech. "Life, of course, was given us to enjoy; why should we make ourselves miserable with reading about other people's troubles that we have no power to prevent? It's always marvellous to me how people can take up a newspaper, and deliberately set themselves to read all the horrible things that go on in the world."

"Ah," interrupted Mrs. Reece. "We used to hear enough of horrors in the old days, didn't we, Wolf? At one time I remember an epidemic of horrors seemed to set in, one thing followed the other so rapidly. Well, we were used to it then, I suppose, and we did our best under it, but I must say I shouldn't like to have to go through it all again. Poor people are very worrying; they like to tell their horrible stories over and over again, for the pleasure of seeing your flesh creep, I suppose. No, I shouldn't like those old days to come back again."

"Wouldn't you, mother?" asked Wolf in an earnest, startled tone, as though some sudden idea had occurred to him. "Would you not for any consideration go through all those old days of poverty and hardship, with the perpetual sense of squalor and misery about one, and the perpetual necessity for hopeless, hard work?"

Oscar, coming into the room at this moment, heard the question.

"Well, my dear," answered Mrs. Reece, "that is rather a difficult question to answer. I won't say I wouldn't for any consideration go back to the old days, but I am really and truly thankful no such necessity exists. I verily believe six weeks of the East of London would send me to my grave after this peaceful, happy life and pure country air. And of the two, I honestly think the grave would be the better place for an old body like me."

A change swept over Wolf's face; the eager earnestness died out of it. He turned to Oscar.

"What do you say?" he asked; "do you think the grave would be a better place than the East End of London in the height or depth of its wretchedness?"

Oscar hesitated a moment. He looked at Judith, remembering his words of the previous day in praise of their old life. He had meant them as he said them. Seen from a distance, those old days might "loom into the perfect star," but let them come but by half an inch nearer, and they would show as the miserable prison-house they in reality were.

"I don't know about the grave," he answered slowly, "one doesn't care about ending life before it is well begun, but I know this—that sooner than go back to the old, hard-working, poverty-stricken life, I would go and break stones in the quarry on the other side of those mountains."

Wolf turned away from the window without another word.

Leila looked at Judith and gave a little shrug of her shoulders, which was intended to say: "Did I not tell you he was on the verge of madness? Would anyone in possession of all his faculties walk away in that abrupt fashion when he might have had the benefit of my society for another half-hour before luncheon?"

XVI

Wolf still retained possession of Judith's bloodstone, and wore it on the little finger of his left hand. Judith would have liked to ask for its return, but somehow could never find the opportunity. There had seemed to grow up between them of late a something of chilliness and reserve which she did not care to attempt to bridge over. Once or twice, it is true, she had caught his eyes fixed upon her with the same earnest, appealing look she had surprised in them in the first days of their acquaintance, but they as often as not wandered from her face to Leila's, and there they would rest, evidently without the smallest compunction, for five or ten minutes at a time.

"He is putting us side by side, and measuring the distance between us," thought Judith a little bitterly. This was exactly what he was doing, although not precisely in the manner nor with the result she imagined.

Wolf's diamond-ring she had been compelled to put on one side; it was too large for any one of her fingers, and she was afraid of losing it. She let it lie in her drawer till she should have the opportunity of returning it, and asking for her own. Wolf did not seem to notice its absence from her finger, or at any rate made no remark upon the matter. Bryce did, however, with a scowl and a frown—those keen old eyes of hers saw a great deal more than people thought.

"Have you lost it—the master's ring, I mean?" she asked on the first morning that Judith made her appearance without it.

"No," answered Judith; "it was too large, that was all, and would keep slipping off my finger."

Bryce shook her head, and went away grumbling, the only words which reached Judith's ear, as her footsteps died away in the distance, being, "It's ill giving a slipping ring," or something of the sort.

Poor old Bryce seemed always frowning and scowling in those days; she went about the house with a perpetual sense of the approach of some direful calamity weighing her down. The episode of the bloodstone-ring had been bad enough, but the unlocking and occupying of the tapestry-room was as much beyond that as the blue mountains that looked down on them were beyond the dark wood. To her fancy this room was as sacred as the consecrated church in the vale of Llanrhaiadr, or the vault in its churchyard, where lay some generations of the Reece family.

None but Master Bernard, or Master Bernard's son, should have dared to give the order for the unlocking and occupying of this room; failing these, it should have been kept sacred to the memory of the old squire, who, with dim, fixing eyes, had said to her:

"Bryce, if ever anything troubles me, and I can come back to you, look for me here."

Did "the master"—in this way she invariably spoke and thought of Wolf—"really wish to bring the old squire's ghost from the grave that he dared the traditions of the house in this way? Well, those who lived the longest would see the most, but it was ill to put the axe to the root of one's own tree," and so forth—and so forth.

Wolf's defiance of the family traditions set her mind ruminating on other possibilities. Now that all known precedent was being so ruthlessly set on one side, what might not be her own fate in the years to come?

She confronted Wolf one day in one of the narrow corridors, barring his progress with a peremptory question.

"I'm wanting to know," she said in her old, creaking voice, "where you mean to bury me? Now all the Bryces have for generations been laid just behind the Reece vault in graves six feet deep do you see? and there's room left for one more—is that where you mean me to lie?"

Wolf stared at her vacantly. It was full a minute and a half before her meaning dawned upon him.

"My good soul," he said at length, "arrange for your own burying where, when, and how you please. Put it all down in your will, and then no one will make any mistake on the matter, or arrange it all with the rector of Llanrhaiadr, if that will suit you better."

The old body's question brought back to his memory sundry similar matters he had arranged for the poor people during his East London ministrations.

By a coincidence the rector of Llanrhaiadr came over that afternoon to the Grange to ask Wolf to perform the service for him on the following Sunday.

It was not often that he paid a visit to Mrs. Reece or her son. The reason was not difficult to find. He was old and stout, and his cob was old and stout; they each preferred a quiet half-hour's jog-trot along the shady lanes which begirt the Vale of Llanrhaiadr, to the seven miles steep road with which a ride to the Grange made them acquainted.

The rector came upon Judith first in the garden. He was white-haired and venerable in appearance, his manners were kindly, his questions irrepressible, his exclamations excessive.

"Dear me, dear me!" he exclaimed as he shook hands with her. "What a wilderness of a place this has run into! Are they going away? Don't they care for the Grange? I know the old squire didn't keep it up as it ought to have been kept up. Great pity! Pretty place! Might be made very comfortable. I know, too, the old man left all the money he could away from the family, but still he couldn't leave it all to the infirmary. A very good income goes with the estate. It's a great pity to let a place go to rack and ruin in this way."

To Judith's immense relief Wolf appeared upon the scene at this moment, and she was able to make her escape from further questioning.

"Who says I let the place go to rack and ruin?" he asked in an angry tone as he shook hands with the rector; "I beg you to observe there is neither rack nor ruin anywhere. I do not keep a gardener—that is all. But one gardener would be of no possible use, it would require five at least to keep these grounds even neat, and, as I do not choose to go to that expense, I let the garden alone. It is the same in the house; it would require some extra ten servants to make the house look smart and trim. I do not choose to go to that expense, so I let the house alone. I beg you to observe that all you are pleased to call rack and ruin is a lack of purely superficial renovation—purely superficial, I repeat. The dilapidation is entirely on the surface."

The rector looked and felt "sat upon." The long-windedness of the explanation amazed him. He hastened to agree with Wolf that the repairs needed were "purely superficial" ones, and then he dashed into his request, "Would Mr. Reece undertake the service for him next Sunday? An old friend in a distant part of the country had sent him an invitation he much wished to accept."

Wolf frowned, and shook his head.

"My Welsh would not be up to the mark," he said.

"It's the English Sunday," answered the rector, "and even if it were not, you might make it so for once. I assure you all the people about Llanrhaiadr understand English perfectly, even if they cannot speak it."

Again Wolf shook his head.

"I could not possibly undertake it," he said curtly.

"It would be a real kindness," pleaded the rector; "and," he added kindly, "you would in this way introduce yourself to your neighbours on the other side of Llanrhaiadr. I assure you they have been talking a good deal about you. You know there are the Howells and the Madoxes, Lord and Lady Ruthlyn, and some half-dozen others."

"I have not the slightest wish to make the acquaintance of the Howells or the Madoxes, or Lord and Lady Ruthlyn, or some half-dozen others."

The rector stared at him blankly for a moment; then he recovered his powers of speech.

"As a purely personal favour I ask it, my young friend," he said gently.

"I regret I must refuse it," answered Wolf coldly; and to this resolution he adhered, and the good rector went away convinced in his own mind that the new master of Plas-y-Coed was not only one of the worst-mannered men he had ever met, but a most eccentric individual into the bargain.

XVII

No tennis-ground; a piano so hopelessly out of tune that no one with an ear for music would essay a chord on it; no saddle-horses, no river, and, direst calamity of all, neither visiting nor visitable neighbours, and the difficulty of entertaining two somewhat buoyant young ladies in a lonely country-house in the blithest time of year may be imagined.

Each day's programme was of necessity as unalterable as the course of the sun itself. There was the inevitable early breakfast, and the inevitable morning walk afterwards; the one o'clock luncheon, the three o'clock drive, the six o'clock dinner, coffee in some arbour or bowery corner of the garden, prayers at nine o'clock, and all in bed by ten.

And on this meagre diet two young ladies accustomed to the movement and excitement of a lively suburban coterie—the outside ring of the London vortex, as it were—were expected to thrive and be content.

Leila's yawns at night-time were so frequent and prolonged as to threaten dislocation of the jaw.

"It's all very well for you, Theo," she grumbled, "who like to tear about the country, climbing five-barred gates, and doing all sorts of wonderful things—showing your ankles, which, by the way, might be made to look a little more respectable—such boots the other day! But for me—Oh!—ah-h-h!" And here the muscles of her pretty mouth relaxed into a genuine, unaffected yawn of which few would have supposed Leila, the refined, the poetic, capable.

"It's better than Sophonisba!" said Theo with a grin.

Now, Sophonisba was Dr. Martin's elderly spinster sister, so-called by the schoolboy wits of The Retreat from the fact of her avowed admiration for the genius of the poet Thomson. It may be remarked in passing that the said admiration was duly exhibited by her selecting on every Sunday afternoon "The Seasons" to fall asleep over on the drawing-room couch.

"Yes, it's better than Sophonisba," acquiesced Leila, "or else we shouldn't be here; but a great deal worse than a great many other things we might have done. Think how delightful a fortnight at Scarborough would have been just now!"

Theo gave a long whistle.

"And who would pay the piper, I should like to know?" she asked. "You see, pa only said 'Yes' to our coming here because there was nothing but our railway-fares to come out of his pocket."

"Theo, you get more and more vulgar every day you live," interrupted Leila sharply. "What you'll be in another year I don't know!"

"Ah, nobody knows what they'll be in another year. Dust and ashes, it might be," answered Theo, thinking only of emphasis, and regardless of grammar. "But I know what I'd like to be"—this with a malicious upward look into Leila's face—"and that's as near like Judith Wynne as possible. She's about the only girl in my life I've never wanted to have a shindy with. One might be in the same house with her from year's end to year's end, and never have a squabble."

"I don't admire your taste, and I think it's a question whether Judith Wynne would take your admiration for a compliment," said Leila, a decided sneer disfiguring her chiselled mouth. "But I do think that, without following your model too slavishly, you would certainly improve your own style if you would copy a little of her silence and reserve of manner. Not that I believe in it altogether. Your quiet, reserved girls are generally the sly, clever manœuvrers. I've no doubt in my own mind that Mdlle. Parolles has a lover of her own, left behind in France—see what huge packets of letters she gets—and that's why she's so contented in this humdrum old house."

Now the nickname "Mdlle. Parolles," be it noted, was not an original conception of Miss Leila's, but was imitated from one she had heard applied to a silent fellow-student by the schoolboy scamps at The Retreat.

Leila did not understand the Shaksperian allusion—shoemakers' wives and daughters are proverbially the worst shod. Of English literature she and Theo knew next to nothing, their intellects having been nourished upon modern novels of various shades of weakness and frivolity.

Theo flashed into indignation at the charges brought against Judith.

"She sly! Why, she's as open as the day itself. The foreign letters all come from her old uncle in France. She told me so, and if she doesn't speak the truth—well, I never met anybody who did, that's all."

"Oh!—ah-h!" yawned Leila again. "I see no necessity for prolonging the discussion. Good night."

And at this very moment Judith, in her own room at the other side of the house, was seated at her open window, with a packet of

CATHERINE LOUISA PIRKIS

the aforesaid foreign letters on her knee. They were not all from Uncle Pierre this time. One was from Manon, the house-servant at Villa Rosa, thanking mademoiselle for the little parcel of English stuffs and ribbons she had duly received. Another was from the old gardener, sending his grateful thanks for mademoiselle's kind present of English stockings. A third was from a little village girl whom Judith had taught to read and write, telling "Mademoiselle Judeethe" that she could never forget her goodness, and that night and day she besought *"Le bon Dieu de lui accorder sa douce bénédiction."*

The fourth was from Uncle Pierre. This Judith kept till the last to read. It was brief, and almost apostolic in its fervour. The English in parts was quaint and individual.

> "I to you send, dear child," he wrote, "the first flowers that
> have flourished on Aunt Maggie's grave—mignonette
> and amaranth. Let them take to you from me, from her, a
> message of sweetness and peace. Never forget how we prayed
> for you that God Himself would keep you when you lay
> down and slept, when you rose up and went your way. Dear
> child, always remember, in darkness and light, in sorrow and
> in joy, good angels are about your path, to keep your feet
> from slipping, to guard your head with their outstretched
> wings.—*Adieu, chérie.*
>
> Your father in heart,
> OLD UNCLE PIERRE

Judith with her tears watered the half-faded flowers. Her letter lay upon her knee: she clasped her hands across her eyes, and leaning back in her chair, wandered in spirit to Villa Rosa once more.

Phantom after phantom, with solemn, silent feet, trooped past, came back again, and vanished once more. The servants of the neat, trim household, the quaint, old-world villagers, a weird army headed always by dear Aunt Maggie, tall, stately, in her dark satins and lace, and dear Uncle Pierre in his priest's dress, white-haired, with stooping shoulders, and eyes as blue as the forget-me-nots which grew among the rushes on the river's bank.

Ah me! what sweet, blessed days those were! Rich in love, full of peace and every simple pleasure! Why did they ever come to an end? Why had they not been allowed to go on till duty had ended them, and she had been called by her father to fill another niche in life? Why had she not been allowed to stay and comfort dear Uncle Pierre in his loneliness and sorrow? That would have been a work worth doing. Why had she been thrust here among strangers with whom she could have no common bond, where no useful, no definite work of any sort or kind could be given her save that of patient endurance of the dreary months and weeks as they crept by?

Surely, if her father could personally have taken a bird's-eye view of these two households which in turn were her home, he could not by any possibility have wished her to exchange one for the other. There, all had been peacefulness, love, and calm enjoyment; here everything seemed disjointed, troubled and misruled. The very air seemed full of mystery; distrust and suspicion seemed on every side. Do what she would, she could not divest herself of a sense of coming evil—of some hidden terror hanging over the heads of the household.

She would not let herself dwell on a certain dull pain in the depths of her heart which of late had made itself felt, but, all the same, she knew it was there, and it doubtless added its quota to her sense of loneliness and desolation.

While she had been sitting thus reading her letters and dreaming over her past and present, time had slipped on; the moon had sunk behind the mountains; the midnight sky showed black, starless, forlorn. A chill breeze swept into the room; the old yews beneath her window tossed their ancient, creaking arms; a nightbird flew past with a plaintive cry.

It was all very desolate and forlorn. The old Grange was dreary enough in full noonday sunlight, but here, with this midnight blackness falling over it like a pall, it seemed gruesome and eerie to the last degree. Her very room seemed full of ghost-like shadows; her one candle only sufficed to throw a feeble ring of light around the small table on which it stood, and as she looked hither and thither up and down the big and scantily-furnished room, from every corner she could conjure grim phantoms of goblin shapes.

"Dear child, always remember, in darkness and in light, good angels are about your path to guard your head with their outstretched wings!"

The words seemed spoken right into Judith's ear, as with distinct human utterance.

It was as though some strong, authoritative voice had said, "Down!" to the evil fancies and phantoms, as one would speak to a turbulent, troublesome dog.

Eeriness, gruesomeness, and dark corners all vanished together, and in their stead came a sense of peace, of safety, of quiet confidence.

She closed her eyes, leaned back in her chair in the darkness. Even the chill night breeze, which swept in at the opened window across her face, seemed to her like the cold wings of the blessed angels themselves fanning her to sleep.

XVIII

id she really fall asleep, and if so, how many minutes had she sat there unconscious, before there seemed to sound a voice in her ear saying piteously, passionately:

"Help me—help me!"

Judith passed her hand over her forehead. Whence did the voice come? What did it mean? Her room was in total darkness now, for the candle had burned itself out, and not the faintest grey of dawn had as yet lightened the ink-black of the night sky. A soft, cold wind still came in at the open window, a shadowy bat flitted past.

Judith leaned out, peering down into the damp, vault-like darkness of the garden below. Had the voice come from there? Was there some living, suffering soul down there sending up a petition for help? She held her breath and listened.

There came up to her the creaking of the old yew-boughs, the slow, low rush of the breeze, the faraway sound of falling water in the woods. Nothing more.

She closed her window. Could it have been her fancy after all: or had the voice called from within the house? She looked all round her. The big ancient furniture of her room loomed gaunt and drear out of the darkness. The corners filled, emptied themselves of, and re-filled with shadows.

"Help me, help me!" sounded the voice, piteously and imploringly as before.

It was as the voice of some troubled dreamer, who thinks he is shouting with his utmost strength, but whose cry is in reality little above that of a wailing child; and it was the voice of Wolf Reece.

Judith felt her blood grow chill, and her limbs tremble beneath her. But she would not wait for another appeal. Along the darkness, groping her way, she went, dreading she knew not what.

Her room was at the end of a long narrow corridor, which, interrupted and crossed by small passages, ran round the house, and into which all the bedrooms on that floor opened.

Mrs. Reece's room and that of the Martin girls were at the other end of this corridor, Oscar's on the floor above. Right and left of her were two unoccupied rooms; immediately facing her door was a narrow passage which led to the servants' quarters, and a little to the right of

CATHERINE LOUISA PIRKIS

this was a short flight of five stairs which led up to the tapestry room, now occupied by Wolf.

Along this corridor, as Judith opened her door, the darkness seemed to lie in thick folds, which a feeble stream of light straggling down the small flight of five stairs tried in vain to pierce.

Judith, straining her eyes, could barely trace the outline of a man's figure on the topmost stair. She could just see that he leaned against the wall with his head on his arm face downwards; but she knew in a moment that those broad shoulders, that bowed head, were Wolf Reece's. None other.

"Help me!" he moaned again piteously, prayerfully. "God send help to me of some sort!" And Judith crossed the corridor, came and stood by his side, and touched his arm.

He raised his head slowly, and looked at her for a moment, without the slightest gleam of recognition. His face was white and haggard, his forehead was knotted into a heavy frown, one large vein protruding like a massive cord.

"I have come to help you if I can," said Judith softly, wondering whether her voice would recall his scattered senses.

He clutched at her arm.

"You—you!" he cried, surveying her with lack-lustre eyes.

Then, right and left, up and down, and around, his gaze wandered, as though seeking in the darkness for something he knew was there, yet could not see.

Judith followed his gaze.

"What is it?" she asked, determined, if possible, to search out this matter to the depths.

His hand, still on her arm, grew tremulous.

"Do you see anyone—anything?" he asked in a hoarse scared whisper.

Judith shook her head.

"One cannot see even the darkness," she answered, trying purposely to assume a careless matter-of-fact tone; "but if you will lend me your candle I will go along the corridor and see if anyone is there."

He scarcely seemed to hear her.

"It went that way—that way," he muttered.

Then he passed his hand across his eyes as though to shut out some dread sight, and Judith could see that he trembled from head to foot as one might who had suddenly been confronted with an embodiment of the terrors of the grave stripped of its conventionalities and comelinesses.

It was terrible to Judith to see this strong man so palsied and shaken.

"What is it?" she asked; "tell me. I may be able to see what you have seen if you will describe it to me."

"I pray God no!" the words seemed to come from the very bottom of his heart, strong and clear. Then he went on passionately: "Child, child, why do you trouble about me? Why do you not leave me to my fate? Why do you torture yourself with the sight of a misery you cannot help? Let me alone, and forget what you have seen tonight."

"I cannot do that. I would rather stay here and help you if possible."

Wolf looked at her with a sad, puzzled expression.

"Why should you wish to help me—why—why?" he asked.

"Because I see you are ill and suffering, and my heart aches for you."

It was said in low quiet tones, but their depth of meaning, was unmistakable.

"Child, child, have you no fear, no terror? What if it were given to you to see the thing that I saw a moment ago? Could you look upon it and live?" he asked.

"I have no fear, no terror, of the sort you mean; and if you tell me what you have seen, I would tell you whether I could bear the sight of it," answered Judith, strong in her recovered faith in her angel guardians.

Wolf looked at her fixedly for a moment or two.

"I know I may trust you," he said in low tones, as though he were communing with his own thoughts. "This is the second time you have stood by me in a moment of torture." He broke off, and then resumed in a more ordinary voice: "Tell me, Judith. Your conscience is pure, and young, and clear; but supposing it grew suddenly clouded: supposing in one miserable, fatal moment, you did a deed impossible to undo— mind, I say impossible to undo—a thing which, if told, would bring ignominy, disgrace, and absolute beggary on you and yours. What would you do?—what would be your refuge? Suicide or prayer?"

The last three words were spoken in a tone more than half cynical, altogether despairing.

"Prayer," answered Judith promptly. "I should tell it to God before I told it to living soul. But," she added suddenly, looking up in his face with those calm, ruth-speaking eyes of hers, "I should make very sure that it could not by any possibility be undone. I would die in my efforts to make amends for my sin."

Wolf stamped his foot passionately.

"Child, I said could not be undone. Do you not understand?" he cried vehemently. "There are things in life that cannot be undone—are there not?"

"Yes, many. In that case I would pray that I might be shown how I could atone for my sin, though it might cost me my life."

"And supposing your atonement would bring pain, and infamy, and beggary on those you loved best—what then?" asked Wolf in a voice that seemed to jangle and vibrate with the restraint he put on it.

Judith's eyes drooped. For a moment she made no reply. Wolf went on:

"You loved your Aunt Maggie, your Uncle Pierre, deeply, truly—was it not so? Very well, then. Supposing you knew your atonement would bring down chastisement on their heads, and send them broken-hearted to their graves—what then?"

Judith's eyes filled with passionate tears.

"Oh, why are things so?" she cried vehemently. "Why cannot we each one suffer alone for the deeds that we do? Oh, I would pray night and day that I might be shown a way of repentance, a way by which I alone might suffer for the deed I had done, and they might go free!"

Out of Wolf's face faded the shadow of a gleam of hope which a moment ago had shone there. He grew white, haggard, stern.

"And supposing you did this?" he asked. "Supposing you knelt and prayed night and day, night and day; supposing you grew strong and bold in your prayers and craved a sign, a message, and there came—" Here he broke off abruptly, laid his hand upon her wrist. "Come here," he said, and led her up the small flight of stairs to the door of his room.

Evil and weird enough it looked in the light of the one candle that burned upon the toilet-table. The tapestry hung grim and grey upon the walls, seraph's heads and giant's hands alike obliterated in the heavy shadows cast by the massive, ancient furniture. Out of their midst, gaunt and drear, loomed the sarcophagus-like bed on which the old squire had died.

Wolf stood beside her at the door, pointing to it.

"Supposing," he went on, "you knelt there praying instead of sleeping, not one night but night after night—praying for a message, a sign, and for all answer there came to you"—here his voice sank to a hoarse whisper—"an awful shape, near, nearer, till you felt its coldness touching your cheek, your hand; supposing when it stood close to you—close, mind, I say—you saw that its hands were red with blood: supposing when you looked up into its face you saw that it was your own! Ah, God!" he broke off with a groan, "it is there again. Help me! help me!"

he cried in the same piteous, passionate tones Judith had heard before. "Oh, it comes nearer! Now it stands before the light, and shuts it out! Ah, Heaven have mercy!" His face grew livid with terror, his eyes were wild and fixed, his strong frame quivered.

Judith, straining her eyes into the shadows of the room, could see nothing. She took his hand gently:

"Come away from this room," she said. "It is full of dreary shadows. Come out into the fresh air. See, day is beginning to break;" and she pointed to the grey shreds of light beginning to creep through the farthest window. "You will lose your senses if you stay here."

He let her lead him like a little child down the stairs and along the corridor, walking dumbly, unresistingly, as one might under the influence of some heavy drug.

Something dark just within the narrow passage leading off the corridor to the servants' quarters caught Judith's eye as she passed along. It was only a pair of strong, large country shoes—nothing more.

Down the large staircase she led him, thence across the first and second halls out on to the stretch of lawn that fronted the house. The air blew fresh and chill. Here and there the night sky was rent asunder, and the grey of dawn as from a prison-house was finding its way in threads and narrow streaks. The mountains were beginning to show their giant forms and fantastic crags from out the mists, the wood to loom forth in its dun greenness.

Judith felt as one might feel, escaped from a cavernous vault or dismal dungeon. Out here she could breathe and think once more.

Wolf drew a long breath, and passed his hand over his ashen face.

"Thank you," was all he said—all indeed he seemed capable of saying. Even out there in the fresh air he staggered, and would have fallen had it not been for the trunk of a tree at hand.

Judith brought him one of the garden-chairs. He sank into it without a word.

"Shall I fetch you water or wine?" she asked.

"No, thank you; leave me now. I shall soon be all right again. By breakfast-time I shall be quite myself," he answered with a feeble attempt at a smile.

Judith went back to the house, and straight up to her own room, disturbed and tremulous.

As she passed the narrow passage leading off the corridor she looked in vain for the pair of large country shoes. They had disappeared.

XIX

Judith felt how white and haggard she must have looked that morning at breakfast, when she saw Leila's dark, brilliant eyes fixed upon her. Theo openly expressed her opinion of her personal appearance.

"Why, you look as if you had been seeing ghosts all night, Judith," she exclaimed, making a random shot that went very near to hitting the mark.

"Ah, tell us what it was like," cried Oscar, looking up from his plate; "we only want a ghost to make our house the most respectably dismal one in all Wales."

Wolf did not make his appearance at breakfast. Judith was late in coming down that morning, and the information came to her through Mrs. Reece that Wolf had been down, read prayers as usual, and had coffee taken to him in his study, as he had many letters to read and to write.

Leila was a little silent and absent, her head was turned often towards the door, with a half-puzzled, half-expectant look in her eyes. It was the last morning the sisters were to spend at the Grange. To her it seemed a monstrous and incomprehensible thing that an avowed and devoted admirer should not make the most of, get all the honey he could out of, the last few golden half-hours she had to bestow on him.

Oscar was to escort the young ladies to London, where they were to spend a night or two with some near relatives. He, poor lad, had not been included in this invitation, and was making wry faces at the thought of the three or four meals he would have to eat alone with the delectable maiden-aunt, before Dr. Martin's return would enable the whole party to start on their Swiss tour.

"I'm sure she'll kiss you," said Theo consolingly. "Aunt Sophonisba always gets sugary over young men when there is only one left behind. She hates them in the lump—she adores them in morsels."

"Aunt Sophonisba! What an unusual name," murmured Mrs. Reece.

"Why are you not more exact in the terms you use, Theo? You should say she hates them in the abstract, and adores them in the concrete," said Oscar correctingly.

"Bother abstract and concrete!" replied Theo. "Pass my cup for some more coffee;" and so on and so on, until the meal, which seemed to Judith the longest she had ever sat through, came to an end.

As they rose from the table, Oscar pulled at her sleeve, and got her into a corner.

"Is Wolf going to drive us to the station, do you know?" he asked, with something like a gleam of hope in his face.

Judith shook her head.

"How can I know? Why don't you send up and ask?" she answered point-blank.

"Oh, it was only this—I thought if by any chance Wolf did not mean to drive us, you might come, don't you see, and—and take Theo off my hands."

"Ah, Oscar," cried Judith with a sudden impulse, "why haven't you set your mind on Theo instead of on that other? She has three times more heart."

"Hush-sh! that's sacrilege," said Oscar gravely.

Then he sent up a message to Wolf, was he going to drive them to the station that morning or not?

The answer came back brief enough, and barely polite. He had so much to get through; Oscar must drive himself and the ladies, and send back the horses by Davies.

"Now, you'll come, Judith, won't you?" cried Oscar. "Farmer Jones will take down the luggage for us in his cart, and Davies can go with him. It will do those fat greys a world of good to have an extra hundred pounds to carry. Come along, get ready."

And Judith was weak enough to consent thus to facilitate a farewell *tete-à-tete* between Oscar and the lady of his heart, all the time with the feeling strong in her own that it would have been far wiser and kinder, had it been possible, to have built up barriers and mountains between these two, than have thus lessened by so much as half an inch their distance one from the other.

"You will have so many *tete-à-tetes* on your Swiss tour," she grumbled, making one final feeble objection.

"You forget Sophonisba is going," replied Oscar with a look that spoke volumes. "Come along, there's a good girl."

After all, the brisk drive along the country lanes did Judith good, and sent her back stronger in heart to face the mysteries of Plas-y-Coed.

Theo was full of joyous fun, and accomplished with ease seven miles of incessant chatter. Oscar, seated beside Leila on the box, looked radiant as old Sol himself at thus having secured an hour of his goddess's undivided attention; the said goddess, so it seemed to Judith, taking ample revenge for Wolf's cold handshaking and curt farewell, by showering extra smiles and sweetness on the poor befooled boy. Her words were very "soft, gentle, and low," none heard them but he, and her eyes spoke sideways to him under her long lashes.

Possibly Theo noticed the alternate looks of indignation and pain that went sweeping over Judith's face, for she gave her a violent nudge with her elbow and said in a loud whisper:

"Now, don't put yourself out about it, it's her way with them all. Bless you, he'll be sure to find her out sooner or later, and have a row with her, and tell her to go and make eyes at someone else. They all do, one after the other, sure as possible!"

It was poor comfort, but there was none other to be had. Judith could only hope the "finding out" would be "sooner," not later, and that Oscar would take his discovery as calmly as the other young men of Dr. Martin's establishment had taken theirs, if Theo's statements were to be credited.

Yet she could have cried over him as he waved a bright good-bye to her from the window of the train. His heart was made of too good and true stuff, so it seemed to her, to be played tennis with, let the hand that held the racket be never so fair and shapely.

"I shall write to you every other day," screamed Theo, as the train moved off, "and you'll come and stay with us, won't you, and show me how to scratch up my hair at the back and pile it up on top of my head in the way you do?"

"You little stupid," said Leila to her, *sotto voce*, as she honoured Judith with a formal bow of farewell. "Why, of course she mounts her hair up that fashion to get five or six inches more height! you are gawky enough already, Heaven knows!"

Judith had a long letter from her father to read on her way back. The Indian mail had come in that morning, and she had slipped her letter into her pocket till she could secure a quiet five minutes in which to read it. It was full of kindly solicitude for her comfort, not untinged with a certain amount of anxiety lest by any chance he had made a mistake in his selection of her home. Someone had been throwing out hints to him that it was whispered that the establishment at Plas-y-Coed was conducted on rigidly economic principles; that, in fact, it was scarcely the kind of home in which a young lady could expect to have her whims and wishes gratified.

"Now, my dear," wrote the father, "I ask you to deal candidly with me, and if things are with you other than you have a right to expect, tell me, and I will make different arrangements for you. Of course you know it is my wish to have myself the pleasure of introducing you to society, so I will ask you not to ground any objections you may have to your present home on its solitariness or quietude. At the same time understand that I wish you to have every luxury and comfort that money can command. A horse, if the Reeces can't give you a mount, a piano, if theirs does not suit you, and whatever else you may require in the way of maids, or jewellery, or dresses. I have placed another thousand pounds to your account at my banker's, and as you want money, all you will have to do will be to apply, as before, to my London agent and lawyer; but understand, once for all, that I wish you to want for nothing. In about a year and a half's time from now I shall hope to have sufficiently arranged matters to be on my way home to England, and shall look forward to the happiest of old ages in surrounding my darling child with the comforts and pleasures she has a right to demand at my hands."

It was a tender loving letter enough. Judith read it through with a thrill of gratitude, yet with something of a sigh for the distance, the want of sympathy, the strangeness, so to speak, which she felt existed between her father and herself. For a hundred times a day that her thoughts flew to Uncle Pierre, they flew but once to him. As she read the loving words there was no tremulous longing for the touch of the loving hand that had penned them, no terrible, half-silenced dread lest death or disaster might step in between them, and the year and a half fail of its promise. All this, no doubt, was but the natural, inevitable result of their long years of separation, but it was none the less grievous to her, and at that particular moment seemed specially to accentuate the sense of loneliness and heart-emptiness of which she was conscious.

"If he really wished me to be happy, why did he not let me stay with dear Uncle Pierre?" she thought, as she folded and put her letter in her pocket.

Then, somehow, she began instinctively to read between its lines, and made the discovery that it was rather in his own way than in hers that he would have her to be happy. This, possibly, in the years to come, she would have to find out.

It was not a pleasant notion to get into her head. The drive was a long one, but she had food for thought down every shady lane, along every rocky roadway.

She did not get back to the Grange till nearly four o'clock in the afternoon. Mrs. Reece was feeling the heat, and had gone to lie down in her own room—so Bryce informed her—but luncheon had been laid for her in the dining-room, if she would please to walk in.

Now, luncheon alone in that big, dark room had not a very tempting sound to Judith's ear.

"No, thank you," she said; "I would rather have some tea in my own room, if you'll send it up."

Bryce began to grumble.

"In my young days," she muttered, "gentlefolks weren't half so fond of tea as they are now. They didn't say 'no' to good food when it was set before them. But things have changed since then."

Judith turned upon her brightly enough.

"Why, of course they have changed! Everything is different even since I was a girl, so how you can expect forty or fifty years to make no difference I can't imagine. Now, please don't talk Welsh at me, but get me my tea as quickly as you can."

As Bryce went away to order the tea, Judith could not help giving a glance at the old body's shoes. They were large country ones, it is true, but there was nothing in them to specially identify them with the pair she had seen in the narrow passage over-night.

As she went along the hall, Wolf came out of his study to meet her.

"I have been listening for you," he said, coming forward and taking her hand. "Are you very tired? Come into the dining-room and have something to eat."

It was a more genial greeting than he had ever before accorded her. Also there was a look in his eyes as he took her hand which, although she might have found difficult to translate into words, set her thrilling and flushing.

Yet she answered formally enough:

"No, thank you; I am tired, and am going to my own room."

He did not move on one side to let her pass.

"When you have rested, will you come downstairs—into the garden perhaps? I am wishing so much to have a little talk with you."

It was said diffidently—shyly almost; certainly not in the imperious fashion in which he usually commanded a favour.

But Judith grew colder and colder in manner.

"It must not be today," she said with decision. "I have letters to write to save the mail."

"Is the mail in?" he asked eagerly. "Did you get your Indian letters today?"

Judith, a little surprised, answered in the affirmative.

He drew what seemed to her a long breath of relief. Then he reiterated his petition for a few minutes' talk with her.

"You are even too tired to come out for five minutes into the garden now?" he asked.

"I am," was her reply, so unmistakably formal and decisive that Wolf, with a puzzled, pained look on his face, drew back at once, and allowed her in silence to pass up the stairs.

Judith said to herself, over and over again, as she pulled off her dusty cloak and hat, and let down her long hair for a brush, that she was sure she had done right in thus refusing Wolf's request. There was an uncomfortable feeling rankling in her heart, the sense of having twice in the dead of night surprised this man's secrets, taking to a certain extent his confidences by storm, and proffered to him the most unconventional sympathy and assistance. Was he building upon this the notion that he was bound still further to accord his confidences? The idea was intolerable. He might think her cold and stony-hearted if he pleased, but she would take care he should get that notion out of his head.

As well as another, even more intolerable than that! One which made her flush crimson to the very roots of her hair, and stamp her foot at herself for so much as casting a side-glance at it, the idea that possibly her willing offers of help and sympathy had been attributed to deeper feelings than those of mere kindly charity. No, she wouldn't let that thought creep into her brain. It was intolerable—not to be thought of! She wouldn't, she wouldn't—he shouldn't—he shouldn't—Well, he should see that she, at any rate, was not such an one as Leila Martin, to be taken up and laid on one side just as the fancy seized him.

Bryce, coming with her tea-pot at that moment, interrupted the current of her thoughts.

"There's one comfort," said the old body, putting down the cup and saucer with a clatter: "the tapestry-room is to be locked up again, and the master goes back to his own room tonight. It's ill to trouble the dead in their graves, no good comes of it."

Judith was in no mood for Bryce's gossip just then. She knew a ready method of silencing her.

"Ne me parley plus de cette chambre lugubre," she cried. "Vous m'ennuyez avec votre, 'pas de bon! pas de bon!' Alley, babiller avec les pies, et leur demander quand reviendront les grolles."

Bryce flung one sharp, furious look at the young girl, put her fingers in her ears, and backed out of the room, firing a volley of Welsh as she went. All down the staircase and along the passages echoed consonants and gutturals, ending finally with the emphatic bang of the door of her *sanctum sanctorum* below.

XX

At first it had seemed strange to have the walls of the old Grange echoing to the sound of young voices, now it seemed equally strange to have the young voices banished. Everybody missed Theo's hearty laughter and practical joking, and although Oscar had been, for him, unusually subdued and silent, yet so long as he was in the house Judith never lacked a companion.

True, the absence of Leila's big, cold eyes and unblushing flirtations was a thing to rejoice and be glad over, but on the whole the breakfast-room had a dreary, forlorn look after the three young people had departed, and Judith found her thoughts more than once wandering back, as of old, to the bright, cheerful morning-room at Villa Rosa, and the pleasant talk that used to "go" so well with the coffee and hot rolls.

Mrs. Reece, with the weight of some four extra decades of years to stoop her shoulders and lower her vision, naturally saw things from another point of view. She had no special need of young people's society, nor special liking for their voices. To say truth, even Oscar, "the child of her old age," as she was occasionally pleased to call him, was a little too much for her at times.

"We're a small party today," she said cheerfully, as she took her place at table and adjusted her glasses as though they were of real use to her. "I suppose it's the creeping on of old age makes me think so, but really I am beginning to feel that small parties suit me best. Now these young ladies, no doubt, were everything that young ladies ought to be, but really it seemed to me that the voice of the younger of the two was uncommonly loud. Now, Judith, you know more of young ladies than I do, don't you think it was uncommonly loud?"

And Judith, the truth-telling, thus appealed to, was compelled to admit that Theo's voice was uncommonly loud.

"Exactly," Mrs. Reece went on with a little air of triumph, as of one who had compelled an unwilling admission; "her voice was loud in speaking, and, worse still, was loud in laughing. Now, to my way of thinking, a loud laugh in a woman is about the worst thing she can be guilty of—in manners, I mean. She may use her voice in talking, she must use it in coughing, but for laughing she needs only to employ two organs—her eyes and her mouth; her voice should be silent. Of course you'll tell me I'm prim and old-fashioned in my notions, I'm prepared for that—"

"Falstaff had a battle this morning with a shepherd's dog," interrupted Judith, intent on effecting a diversion from Theo and her idiosyncrasies.

"But," the old lady went on, not so much as hearing the interruption, "for all that, I liked her better than her sister. In spite of her noisy boisterous manner, I preferred her to Miss Leila, who—begging your pardon, Wolf—struck me as being a little sly and underhand." ("There," thought the old lady, "I've said it now! He may take it any way he pleases, but it may help to open his eyes.")

"Mother," exclaimed Wolf earnestly, bending across the table towards her, "why should you beg my pardon? How can your criticism of Miss Martin in any way affect me?"

"How—how?" repeated Mrs. Reece not a little astonished. "Why, my dear, you seemed to be taking a very great interest in the young lady, and I did not think it would come to an end the very minute she was out of the house."

"It has come to an end, then, let me assure you, and is never likely to be renewed," said Wolf coldly; and as he spoke, he rose from the table and left the room.

"Well," exclaimed Mrs. Reece, rightly concluding that Judith remained in her place, "I am to live to see strange things, it seems; but if anyone had told me that Wolf would turn out a flirt, I should have said he was just as likely to turn out a monkey. Now, Judith, be honest—do you see anything of the flirt in my eldest son? Anything of the fool, I might say, for the two things nearly always go together?"

Judith, writhing under this cross-examination, was forced to admit that she could see "nothing of the flirt" in Mrs. Reece's eldest son.

"Well, then," insisted the old lady, putting into words the very question that was uppermost in Judith's thoughts at the moment, "how do you account for his conduct with Leila Martin? Why was he always running after her, walking with her, driving her here, there, everywhere?"

Judith confessed it was out of her power to account for these things.

"Exactly," said Mrs. Reece with the same triumphant air as before; "out of your power and out of mine to account for this and a great many other things that are going on at the present moment. It seems to me, my dear, as though both my sons just now were acting in a most unaccountable manner. There was Oscar as heavy as lead all the time those two girls were in the house Now we are prepared for a little gloominess in Wolf;

it's his way, and he has had a lot to go through, which somehow seems to weigh him down still, though I cannot imagine why he could not do duty at Llanrhaiadr the other day, and let the rector have a holiday; but as I was saying—ah, what was I saying?" Here she paused, trying to get back the thread of her talk, which had somehow slipped through her fingers. "Oh, I was saying, so many unaccountable things are happening just now. Only think, last night after you had gone upstairs, Wolf suddenly asked me if I didn't think Oscar had better give up the idea of matriculating next year, and make a start in life at once. And this, after all the trouble he has taken in choosing his college, and getting someone to coach him. It's really incomprehensible!"

"Do you think Oscar has spoken to him on the matter?" asked Judith, recollecting Oscar's appeal to her.

"I am certain he has not. Wolf was so relieved when I told him that Oscar wished the same thing, and said at once he would see about getting him a nomination or something or other for some Government billet. It's all very well talking, but it seems to me that neither of my sons just now quite knows what he is doing. Their conduct, to say the least, is remarkable."

Judith hailed with delight the entrance of Bryce at this moment to receive her housekeeping orders for the day, and made her escape from the room.

Outside the door Wolf met her, and laid his hand upon her arm:

"Come out on the terrace for five minutes," he said; "I have a question to ask you."

There was no getting out of it this time, his hand was firm as his voice; go she must. The question brought the colour to her cheeks.

"Did you think," he asked when they were well out on the weedy path with no listeners save the whispering laurels and yews, "that I took a special interest in Leila Martin?—tell me."

Now if Judith Wynne had been like most other young ladies, she would have tossed her head, and said with a little frown: "I have never thought at all upon the matter, it was no concern of mine." But not being at all like other young ladies, and being utterly unskilled in the art of prevarication, she answered simply enough:

"Yes: who could help thinking so?"

Wolf made a sharp movement of annoyance.

"How can I explain? How is it possible for me to make you understand that I was but making an experiment?" he cried.

"An experiment!" repeated Judith, looking at him gravely.

"Aye, an experiment. You are shocked, your eyes tell me that you do not think experiments on girls' hearts are lawful and right. But what if this girl had no heart, and the experiment was made on mine, not hers?"

He paused, waiting for a reply. Getting none, he went on:

"Will you then think so hardly of me? Will you utterly condemn a poor wretch who, suffering tortures, stretches out his hand to take anything and everything in the shape of a drug that is offered to him! Nay, more, who goes out of his way, as it were, to test whether this or that thing will act as an opiate and lull his pain? Do you understand—do I make my meaning plain?"

"Yes, I understand perfectly. But why say these things to me?—why attempt any painful explanations?" she asked gently, anxious to make him understand that though she would gladly and heartily help him at any moment in the extremity of his misery, yet in cold blood she could not and would not thrust herself into his confidence.

"Why, why!" he repeated vehemently, and for the moment he lost control over himself; "because I value your opinion more than that of any other living soul; because, from the very first day you set foot in this house, I read your truth and goodness in your face, and knew I could trust you as I could none other; because," and here his voice sank to a low passionate whisper, "vile as I am, and vile as you must think me, I would not have you lay to my charge sins which I have not committed, though they be such trivial ones as coxcombry and flirtation."

Judith was strangely moved. For the moment she had no words at command.

Wolf went on. "Heaven knows," he said bitterly, "I have no wish to make myself out a saint. That would be a useless task enough after what you have seen with your own eyes."

Judith could have no doubt as to what he alluded. "All that is to me as if it had not been," she said, quietly.

"As if it had not been!" he echoed slowly; "can that be possible? Will you tell me you have driven out of your mind the words I used in the horror that fell on me? Great Heavens! Nothing—no power in this world, nor any other, will ever sear from my brain the awfulness of those nights."

His eyes fixed themselves on distant space for a moment, then turned right and left of him with a hurried, scared look.

Judith feared lest his fancy might once more conjure up the evil thing that pursued him.

She laid her hand gently on his arm.

"You do not quite understand me," she said: "I meant to say what I saw and heard I should consider sacred, and would not allow myself even in thought to dwell upon. Unless, indeed," she added a little wistfully, "by so doing I could in any way be of service to you."

He turned round upon her, his face alight with gratitude.

"You—you say this?" he exclaimed.

"Yes; why not?" she said, gathering courage now from her own boldness. "I told you the other night how gladly I would help you if I could."

"Child, what you told me the other night I did not hear; my brain was dazed and simply incapable of thought. But I hear you now! Do you mean you would go out of your way—really out of your way—to help me?"

"Out of my way, of course, gladly. Who would not?"

Wolf shook his head sadly enough.

"Many would not. How could it be expected of them? What have I done for my fellow-men, that any should step out of his way to give me a helping hand?"

"What have you done?" exclaimed Judith; "oh, ever so many things for other people, when you were working in London. Oscar has told me, your mother has told me over and over again, all you used to do for the poor people."

His face brightened. It was pleasant to him to think that this girl with the clear, shining eyes should have before her fancy a better likeness of him than the one he now presented to her view.

"Yes," he said, rejoicing inwardly over the Wolf of the past, just as middle-aged people like sometimes to look at their young photographs, and think "this once was I." "Yes, I did work in those days. It was a hard life, but it was a blessed one—" He broke off abruptly; a mist seemed rising before his eyes; he laid his hand tremulously on the young girl's arm. "Judith," he said, sadly, humbly, "God only knows, but it seems to me if you had been by my side then, I should not have brought down this heavy judgment upon my own head."

Even as he finished speaking he suddenly turned round and left her.

Judith stood still, looking after him, blankly, wonderingly. For a moment creation seemed to stand still and hold in its breath, the birds' singing ceased, only the roar and tumble of the cataract in the woods come suddenly close under the garden wall seemed to sound in her ears.

For but one brief moment—no more; the next she had bowed her head and gone swiftly into the house.

All in a flash the knowledge had come to her that pity for this man had deepened into a tenderer, stronger feeling, and that henceforth to the end of her life, come storm, come sunshine, come fair weather, or foul, creation held but one man for her, and that man was Wolf Reece.

END OF VOLUME I

VOLUME II

I

If, as the poet sings, "variety is the spice of life," existence at the old Grange must have been singularly flavourless during the last four months of that year.

Wolf went about the house silent, reserved, gloomy as usual, shutting himself much in his own room, and shunning every possible chance of a *tête-à-tête* with Judith.

Judith went about the house also much the same as of yore, by a shade possibly less sunny and serene, getting possibly one tithe less of enjoyment out of the long hours she spent in reading before a big fire, or in thinking her own thoughts in the solitude of her room.

And Mrs. Reece went about the house much the same as heretofore, save that a rheumatic stiffness in one knee had made itself felt, and she was compelled to use a stick. The equable manner in which this lady bore her misfortunes, small or great, was a thing to be wondered over. Let her but be convinced that this sorrow or that annoyance was inevitable and irremediable, she at once accepted the situation of affairs, and endeavoured to adapt herself to it. Yet one could scarcely describe her's as the patience of Job; it had a something which the patriarch's lacked, and which could perhaps best be described as a cheery stoicism; and it had not a something which the patriarch's had—a full, deep chord of underlying faith and hope.

Of course it might be that these deep chords in her nature had been sounded till they had cracked and given out no more music, in the days when her children and her husband had been taken from her, and she herself had been smitten with blindness; that was a matter that lay between herself and her Maker. What the world saw and noted was a cheerful garrulity, which talked the bitterness out of most troubles so soon as they made their appearance; an active, practical rendering of that well-worn byword, "Where's the use of crying over spilt milk?" Thus, when this old lady saw that henceforth, to the end of her life, a stick, in all probability, would be her daily companion, all she said was, "You'll be sure to buy me a nice, strong, elderly-looking thing, Wolf, with a good stout handle, that I can have well-padded;" and, getting this, she concluded the matter to be at an end.

It is possible, after all, that of these three, Mrs. Reece got the most out of life just then? A comfortable armchair beside a bright fire, her mastiff at her feet, a weekly letter from Oscar, and a daily hour of reading from Judith, seemed to be all she asked or expected in the way of enjoyment, and getting this she was content. The thing that troubled her most was Wolf's steady refusal to assist the vicar in any of the services at Llanrhaiadr. Every day she bemoaned, as cheerfully as she could bemoan, the fact that not Lord and Lady Ruthlyn, nor the Howells, nor the Madoxes, had as yet heard her son speak from the pulpit.

"My dear," she would say to Judith, "if you heard him but once I'm sure you would never forget him. I have seen the people positively shiver—the ostrich-feather that bootmaker's daughter would persist in wearing used to quake like an aspen leaf—as he put before them the terrors of the last day. Now everyone says Lord Ruthlyn is a hard landlord—a scare once a week or so might do him a world of good. Don't you think so?"

Judith assented, at the same time feeling sure in her own mind that if Lord Ruthlyn had to wait for his "world of good" till it came to him through Wolf's energetic preaching, he must be content to do without it till the end of time.

For, with eyes strengthened and quickened by love's magic power, she looked on this man now, and it seemed to her that, as the slow winter days went creeping by, the energy was dying out of him, his bodily and mental strength seemed daily dwindling, his hair was whitening, his shoulders rounding, his footsteps slackening into the gait of premature old age.

How her heart ached over him! How she longed to go to him and say, "Trust me all in all, or trust me not at all. Give me at least one half of your burthen to bear, let it be what weight it may." One such bitter, helpless cry as she had heard on the staircase in the dead of night, one such look of dumb, hopeless misery as she had seen in his eyes that August morning on the terrace, would have brought her to his side with these words on her lips. But as neither the scene on the staircase nor that on the terrace was re-enacted, the words remained unspoken. Wolf went his way, getting through the days as best he could; she went hers, conscious of his misery, her own heart wrung by it, yet unable by so much as a feather's-weight to lighten its load.

As Christmas drew near, Mrs. Reece seemed suddenly to wake up to the notion that things were not altogether as they ought to be.

"When we were in London," she said, "Christmas was always the busiest time of year. There were the trees to be dressed for the Sunday-school treats, the teas for the mothers and fathers, the clothing-club gifts, and a world of other things beside. Wolf," here she suddenly turned her chair to face the corner whence her son's voice had last come to her, "don't you think we ought to have some sort of a distribution here? I don't suppose, from what I hear, that the old Squire was at all famed for his liberality to the poor; but, really, I think something will be expected of us in our position. Coals, or blankets, or a Christmas dinner to the aged poor."

"Mother, I have no money for such things," said Wolf, quietly, "and couldn't manage it if you wished it ever so much."

"No money!" repeated Mrs. Reece, blankly. "I thought, my dear, when we came here there was to be no lack of anything. Are you sure, Wolf," this said in a mysterious, confidential whisper, "that old man Maurice hands you over your income properly—doesn't keep back anything, I mean? Now, you know, he and the old Squire used to have terrible disputes sometimes, they might have been about money matters."

"Mr. Maurice is above suspicion; he accounts for every penny he receives," answered Wolf, with decision; "but I have had heavy calls upon me of late."

Judith thought of her thousand pounds lying idle at her father's bankers, but did not know how she dared offer it for Wolf's acceptance.

She made the attempt, however.

"My father sends me home so much more money than I can possibly get through; if it would be of any good—" she began, hesitatingly.

"Child, it is for your own use, and must not be touched by any hand but yours," said Wolf, in a tone that admitted of no appeal.

So Judith gave in, and Christmas passed away at the old Grange, silently, drearily, like the other days, unmarked by the festivities or bounties supposed of necessity to accompany the recollection of the manger at Bethlehem. The old year was clanged out, the new year was clanged in, by the peal of weird old bells at Llanrhaiadr that had done similar clanging for the past two hundred years; the woods grew hoary with January frost; the little stream, sacred to the memory of St. Govan the Good, shut itself in an ice prison of its own making; the peaks and crags of the blue mountains looked kingly and desolate with their crowns of snow, as no doubt they had looked some decades of centuries before the eye of man had gazed on them, or foot of man had trodden them; and Judith, crouching, kneeling, or sitting before a large fire in her own room or in Mrs. Reece's little morning-room, was compelled to confess to herself that never before in her experience had short winter days spun themselves out to such an unconscionable length; never before had it been her good or evil fortune to welcome with such eagerness the long winter nights of sleep and oblivion.

Perhaps if Oscar had come home for the vacation things might have been a little more cheery. But Oscar did not take his Christmas holiday that year; he had availed himself of Wolf's permission to give up the idea of college with a will, and had placed himself under one of the masters at Dr. Martin's establishment to be prepared for the civil service examination. As heretofore, he never mentioned Leila's name in any one of his letters, but Judith felt she knew what was in the boy's heart, what wild hopes he was fostering, what crazy possibilities in the future he was looking forward to, that he set to work in such mad earnest to shorten the road to independence, if not to fortune.

Theo, however, in her long, rambling letters, written in bold, schoolboyish hand, spoke freely of her sister and her malpractices.

"I am thankful to say," she wrote, "Leila has been packed off to Strasbourg at last. She carried on abominably all the time we were in Switzerland—Oscar was in despair, and threatened to break his neck down a precipice two or three times, only I persuaded him out of it—and came home with the full intention of making everybody as wretched as she could all through the winter. It was only a vet.'s son, too, who was going in for surgery at Guy's, and not a particularly handsome fellow—huge hands and feet—a sort of Bob Sawyer-looking individual. Anyhow, Oscar thrashed him one evening in Richmond Park—he ought to have thrashed Leila instead, and I told him so—and then pa thought it was time Leila was packed off again, so he started her the next day for Strasbourg, and I don't believe will have her back till after Easter."

This was good news to Judith. It pained her to think of the daily torture this boy-lover must have gone through with his heart in such cruel keeping. Once she had hinted to Mrs. Reece her fears for Oscar, and had suggested the desirability of finding another home for him than Dr. Martin's. Mrs. Reece had carried her hints and suggestions to Wolf, herself endorsing them. But Wolf had scouted both.

"If it be as you say," he had said, "he will live out this fancy—at his age it can be nothing more—better on the spot where he formed it than anywhere else. He will meet many such girls as Leila Martin before he is many years older. Is he to run away from his work every time they cross his path?"

So the suggestion came to nothing, but, nevertheless, Judith heard with not a little delight that the dangerous beauty had been removed from Oscar's orbit, thereby freeing the lad from a few of his many daily heart-twinges.

II

The dreary winter came to an end at last, as all things good, bad or indifferent must come to an end in this rickety, scene-shifting world of ours. January's snows disappeared, February's sunshine fled away in tears before the bluff boisterousness of lusty March, who in his turn suffered himself to be taken captive and led forth in chains, by balmy-breathed soft-handed April. The whole earth seemed charged with promise; one could hear it in the swinging tree-tops, as the jays and linnets fluttered in and out, saying pretty things to each other about sweethearting and nest-making; one could see it in the growing greenness of the grass beneath one's feet, in the deepening blue of the sky overhead, and the fleecy whiteness of the sailing clouds; one could scent it in every passing breeze which brought back tales of violets in wooded hollows, of primroses yellowing the furzy hillside.

Emphatically a time for promises, no matter where, when, and how they are to be paid; for weaving dreams and building castles, no matter how quickly they may melt into air, or crumble into dust; for rejoicing in the mere fact of one's youth and gladness, no matter how soon one may be called upon with folded hands and numbed hearts to chant the *Nunc dimittis* and say good-bye to both. All hail! The tourney is before us, the pageant is to the fore; never mind the wrung sinews, the crushed limbs, the dead bodies, which sooner or later will fill the arena. "Those about to die salute thee!" But the time for dying has not yet come. Let us cry while we can with whole heart, "All hail!"

It can scarcely be wondered if Judith, in company with all creation, felt the rush of spring—joy, and gladness in her heart. On the wrong side of forty, it is easy enough to shut one's door in the face of hope and bright suggestions of future possible or impossible happiness; but on the right side of twenty, it is more difficult. The door has a knack of swinging back again on its easy hinges so fast as it is shut; indeed, of the two, it is far harder to keep it shut than open.

At least so Judith found it, as with the birds, and the flowers, and the dormice she woke up to the sense of spring regnant once more, and went forth with all the glad young things to snuff the sweet fresh air and build her castles as she listed.

If she had looked the matter steadily in the face, she might possibly have seen on what narrow foundations those castles were built, how their very erection was due as much to an instinct called forth by the glad spring summons as the nest-building of the jays and linnets. But she did not so look the matter in the face; she only said to herself, as she fastened her nosegay of daffodils in her bodice and took her packet of morning's letters to read in the mossy old garden:

"My opportunity to help him must come sooner or later, and, ah, how I will jump at it! Dear Uncle Pierre!"

And here she gave a good kiss to the thin foreign envelope addressed in the tremulous old writing, which she held in her hand.

But, alas! tears, not kisses, were to greet the contents of the letter when, the seal broken, she had seated herself on a garden-chair to devour them.

The letter was dated from Marseilles, and announced the fact that Uncle Pierre was *en route* for the north of China to join the Jesuits' mission there. It was, in fact, a letter of farewell to her. Judith felt, so far as she was concerned, it was an eternal farewell. She covered her face with her hands, struggling with her tears.

Ah me! what a different letter to the one she had expected—full of all the news she loved best to hear, of her dear old friends at St. André!

A voice sounded at her side. It was Wolf's.

"Judith, what is it?" he asked. "I was at my study-window, and saw you drop your letter. Tell me, child, what is the matter? Is it bad news of your father?"

Judith withdrew her hands from her face.

"Read it," she said, pointing to her letter. "It is from Uncle Pierre."

Wolf read it. It was a pathetic letter enough—the cry of a man whose house-hold gods were shattered, and therefore he would sweep away the niche that had held them.

"I did not write to you before, my child," he wrote, "for I felt you would have flown to me to say adieu, and your soul is too young to bear the shock of so dolorous a parting—mine too old. I have laid for you a wreath of amaranth on Aunt Maggie's grave. Pray for her, my child, pray for me as I pray for you, for her. Let our prayers go up one essence to our Father's throne, that they may return to us again a dew of peace and benediction. All good angels keep thee, my Judith, with their outstretched wings! Adieu!"

Wolf sighed as he looked at the date of the letter.

"If it had come one day sooner, you might have telegraphed a good-bye to him. Oh, Judith, do not cry so bitterly; I cannot, cannot bear it. What can I say to comfort you?"

Judith made no reply; her voice, indeed, was beyond her control.

"What can I say to you?" Wolf went on, in hopeless, weary fashion. "I used at one time to know how to comfort people, but somehow I have no words now. Oh, child—child, do not grieve in this way; I cannot bear to see your tears."

And this was all he could say, seated there by her side among the laurels, and holding her hand firmly in his own—"Child, child, do not grieve; I cannot, cannot bear to see your tears."

Judith found her voice at last, and tried to smile up at him, but it was a very wan little smile.

"I must seem so foolish, but I know it is a good-bye for ever, and I did so love him!" was all she could say, and then the tears flowed afresh.

"Foolish?" cried Wolf. "Ah, your folly is wiser than most men's wisdom. But I would to heaven I could bear this sorrow for you—every sorrow to your life's end. Ah, why must those who have done no sin be made to shed tears like the guilty and hard-hearted? Oh, Judith, be comforted; I cannot, cannot bear to see your grief."

And this from one whom she knew had a sorrow to endure beside which hers must seem as a pin-prick to a sabre's cut! She dried her eyes and folded her letter. Wolf drew a long sigh of relief.

"I'm such a bad comforter," he said; "it was not always so with me. I ought to have been able to say a word you could fix in your mind and carry away with you." His thoughts were evidently going back to the days of his ministry among those poor, squalid ones in London. His face looked dreary and haggard in the sunshine, his voice had a piteous, hopeless ring in it.

Her heart ached with its load of unuttered sympathy—words rushed to her lips.

"Yes," she said, struggling hard to keep the tears out of her voice, "you would like to deal out sympathy and kindness all round—to bear everyone's sorrows for them. But you would keep your own locked up in your heart, and let no one stretch out a hand to help you."

She spoke rapidly, impetuously, not weighing her words, scarcely knowing what she had said till they were spoken; they were in very truth the overflowings of a full heart. Wolf dropped the hand he held suddenly, as though it had stung him. He looked sorely troubled.

"What if no outstretched hand, however kindly, would be of any use?" he asked, after a moment's pause.

"How can you tell that if you put them all on one side?" retorted Judith, speaking with the same earnest vehemence. "Hands that look weak and foolish may yet do some good work if it be given them."

She was not prepared for the sudden sharp cry with which he sprang to his feet and confronted her.

"Judith, Judith," he cried, "what would you have of me? Leave me alone, I implore you. Why do you tempt me in this way? Would you have me shift my wretchedness from my own heart to someone else's."

"Yes, I would," she answered, boldly she had overstepped the bounds now, and was determined not to be driven back till she had done her work, "if that other heart is willing to be burdened with it. Oh, Wolf, Wolf," she cried, calling him now for the first time by his Christian name with trembling lips, and eyes that pleaded with her voice, "if you will not trust me with your sorrow, is there none other in the whole world who could help you? Your mother—dear Oscar?"

"Child, what if it be not sorrow but sin that I keep unspoken?"

The question fell like a sudden frost across her burning, passionate words. She grew deathly white; for a moment her heart felt benumbed.

"If it be sin," she whispered falteringly, "surely you have sorrowed over it, and can believe it will be—may be—pardoned to you?"

"Child, what if it be sin, deliberately and intentionally persisted in?" he asked in the same heart-wrung voice as before.

Judith fell back in her seat, putting her hand before her eyes as though she would shut out some sudden horror.

"Oh no, no!" she cried; "I will not believe it—I cannot believe it of you. You are bewildered, mistaken."

"Ah, Judith," he went on, scarcely heeding that she had spoken, "you would not dare ask to share such a burthen as that. You will not beg of me my secret, now that you know it is a guilty one."

Judith drew her hand from her face; her calmness had come back to her. She rose from her chair, and stood by his side, pale and tranquil.

"Wolf," she said, laying one small hand on his arm, "though your secret be a guilty one, I ask you to let me share it. Not that I may help you to hug it in your own heart, but that I may help you to get rid of it, as one would a plague spot or leprosy."

A mist came before Wolf's eyes; he looked down wonderingly into the pale face uplifted to his own. His lips parted irresolutely, and closed again. He bent low, as though about to whisper in her ear.

There came a sound of footsteps along the gravel-path at this moment. He sprang from her side like some guilty, startled thing.

Davies, the one man-servant the house could boast, came slowly towards them, with a bit of pasteboard in his hand, which he presented to Wolf.

"A lady has come, sir, and wishes to see you," he said. "She has driven straight from the station, and has a portmanteau with her, as though she meant to stay. She told me to give you her card, and you would know all about her."

Wolf took the card. On it was written, "Miss Delphine Pierpoint, Mount Edgecumbe, Canada."

He staggered into the seat he had just quitted, as though he had been suddenly struck with cold steel.

"Go," he said to the man, "tell her I am coming."

Then when Davies was out of sight, he turned desperate, imploring eyes on Judith.

"Judith," he said, speaking slowly and with difficulty, as one might speak who had the beak of an eagle in his heart, draining his life's blood, "a moment ago you offered me help of any sort or kind I needed. Are you willing to give me that help now?"

Judith stood before him calm as before; a shade paler—that was all.

"Yes, to the very utmost of my power. What can I do?" she asked, speaking scarcely above her breath.

"One thing I implore you not to do, that is, leave me—leave this house," he answered in the same restrained voice. Then, suddenly springing to his feet, he seized both her hands, passionately, imploringly. "Oh, Judith—Judith," he cried, "I could never need your help more than I shall need it now. Keep by my side, I beg of you; do not leave me, do not give me up. Swear to me that you will not go away from me, come what will, no matter who may try to drive or draw you away."

Judith suffered her hands to remain in his tightening yet ice-cold clasp. She lifted her eyes to the deep blue sky above them, as though to call it to witness her solemn words.

CATHERINE LOUISA PIRKIS

"I will not leave you, nor give you up, till you say to me, 'Judith, go,'" she answered in low, clear tones.

East winds, blight, snow, frost, set in sometimes without warning in the blithest of spring-tides. The promise of this spring was gone for ever now.

III

As Judith passed the low drawing-room windows, half opened to let in the sweet spring sunshine, she heard a female voice speaking in high-pitched, somewhat shrill, but nevertheless, not unmusical, tones.

"I hope you are glad to see me, Mr. Reece," it was saying. "I have crossed the Atlantic on purpose to bring you news. Bertha is dead—her lungs were always weak, you know—but the boy still lives—a poor, puny little creature!"

Wolf's reply did not reach Judith's ear, for, with almost the swiftness of the wind itself, she sped along the terrace, anxious only to get into some dark, quiet corner, to beat down the tumult in her heart and arrange the incoherence of her thoughts.

Had she parted the bushes, and looked in through the window, she would have seen a young lady standing in the middle of the room, looking up with much earnestness right into the eyes of stalwart, blank-faced Wolf. She was elegantly attired in grey fur mantle, grey fur hat, with just a coquettish peeping out here and there of delicate pink. She was small and slight in figure—as small and as slight as Judith herself. Her complexion was of a rich cream tint, deepening almost to a bronze on her throat and towards the roots of her crisp dark hair. A faint flush of colour tinged each cheek. Her eyes were dark as her hair, and had that excess of brilliancy which suggests, somewhere among the toilet accessories, a bottle of belladonna. They were much given to sudden upliftings, rapid down-droopings, and all sorts of dartings and piercings, as Wolf was soon to find out to his cost. Her teeth were pearly white, small, and childish-looking; her lips were coral-red, pretty when parted in the act of speaking, but a little given to a resolute tightening—a shutting-with-a-snap sort of look—when, the speech ended, she awaited her answer. They were thus tightened, and the effect was not pleasant, as she stood in the middle of the room, waiting for Wolf's reply to her question:

"I hope you are glad to see me?"

But answer she got none.

"You should have written to prepare me for your coming," was what he said, in a tone that would have frozen anyone less frost-proof than Miss Delphine Pierpoint.

"What need?" she said, laughing lightly, a low, odd, but nevertheless musical laugh. "Pleasure is doubled when it comes as a surprise. Now confess you would not have been half so glad to see me if you had been expecting me, say for the last month or six weeks, saying to yourself, 'Will she come? will she not?' like any poor lover waiting for his lady under a trysting tree! Ah, the suspense would have been beyond bearing by this time. Now, confess, Mr. Wolf!" And again she laughed a long, low, rippling laugh—a laugh, however, that had not one vestige of mirth in it.

So at least thought Judith when, about half an hour later, she made Miss Delphine Pierpoint's acquaintance at the luncheon-table, and heard her give one low, long laugh at a remark poor Mrs. Reece was making as she entered the room.

"More girls!" the old lady was saying; "did you say another young lady, my dear? Dear me, dear me! where do they all come from? They seem like the loaves and fishes, miraculously increasing, and they more than meet our wants. Now tell me what this one is like."

There was no time even to say "Hush!" Miss Pierpoint was well into the room, and heard distinctly every word. Then she had given her long, rippling laugh.

Judith looked up at her. What was that laugh like? It wasn't exactly the sort of laugh heard sometimes in a lunatic asylum, when a man gets up and tells you he is a laid-out corpse ready for interment, and then laughs in your face. Not quite, though it seemed to recall it. Judith racked her brains, and suddenly there flashed into them an old Rhine legend describing the laugh of the trolls and gnomes underground, when they found a man careering about their treasure-caves, and shut their gold and diamond doors upon him. "We have caught a man and caged him," their laugh seemed to say, and Judith, in fancy, could hear the same refrain in Miss Pierpoint's musical ripple.

Wolf introduced the young lady to his mother simply as "an old friend of my cousin Bernard's."

Mrs. Reece, from her place at table, held out her hands in welcome.

"Any friend of Bernard Reece is, and ought to be, most welcome here. Of course you will sit down to luncheon with us, and I hope will be able to spend a few days," she said pleasantly.

"In which case may I be allowed to remove my furs?" said Miss Pierpoint with an engaging frankness, at the same time bending an inquisitorial look on Judith, which seemed to say: "Now who and what are you—relative, friend, or 'nearer and dearer one' still? It is my business to find out."

Wolf made no attempt at an introduction. Judith, looking up in his face, saw that a change had passed over it since they had parted in the garden. Then it had looked white and haggard enough, Heaven knows, but it was, at any rate, the face of a man responsive to sympathy, mobile with passionate suffering; now, though white and haggard still, it was hard and inexpressive as the rough mountain side itself; responsiveness and mobility were gone; it was granitic in its effacement of all human feeling. Only his eyes, which burned and glowed beneath his bent brows with carbuncle-like fierceness, told that a human soul was housed within him still.

There came a momentary, awkward pause, which Judith abbreviated by coming forward and offering to assist Miss Pierpoint in removing her fur-cloak.

"Thanks," said the young lady, "it's awfully heavy, and this room is awfully hot," and she slipped the weighty garment into Judith's arms. "No, thanks, I'll keep my hat on, at any rate till you show me up to my room. Is this where I'm to sit?" taking the fourth place at the table, as she spoke, easily and naturally as though she had taken it every day of her life from babyhood upwards.

"She is a stranger to Mrs. Reece evidently; is she as much a stranger to Wolf?" wondered Judith, a vague, uneasy feeling taking possession of her.

"Negus—very hot please," said Miss Pierpoint, pushing aside her glass of sherry. "I'm just a little nipped with my long drive. Do you know this is my first—my very first visit to England," this to Mrs. Reece, "and I'm sure you'll take it as a compliment—a very great compliment—when I tell you that I only stayed one night in London, just to rest myself, so anxious was I to see Bernard's old home and Bernard's only relatives."

"A very great compliment, my dear," answered Mrs. Reece politely—she called Miss Pierpoint "my dear," conjecturing that so young a voice in speaking and aughing must of necessity belong to a girlish owner. "Are you Bermudian?" added the old lady after a moment's pause.

"No; Canadian—that is to say, my father was an Irishman, and my mother a Frenchwoman; therefore, I must be a Canadian," laughed the lady.

"Was it in Canada you first made Bernard's acquaintance?" queried Mrs. Reece, adding, by way of making the conversation general: "There is a young lady seated opposite who would give a great deal to hear

Bernard Reece's history after he left England—I mean during the three or four years that he lived abroad after his father's death. She is always teasing me with questions about it."

Wolf turned sharply round upon Judith.

"Why—why, what possible interest can it have for you?" he asked with an almost fierce eagerness.

"The interest of the romantic and the mysterious," answered Miss Pierpoint, intercepting Judith's reply; "those three or four years abroad were, possibly, the most romantic portion of a most romantic career. Now, the question is," and she darted a side-long, smiling glance right up into Wolf's face from beneath the brim of her grey beaver, "what did he do with himself during those years? With whom did he pass the greater part of this time?"

No wonder she had chosen to retain this grey beaver during luncheon; its easy curves not only set off the most piquant of profiles, but its bent brim afforded ample covert beneath which to carry on any amount of sideway fire.

Wolf was unequivocally disturbed. Mrs. Reece, who could not see his face, calmly continued the conversation.

"Well, my dear, if you ask me what he did those two or three years, I should say a great many things; and, if you ask me with whom he passed his time, I would venture to say with a larger number of people than you would attempt to count upon the fingers of both your hands."

"Then you would be quite wrong in both your replies," answered Miss Pierpoint, keeping her eyes steadily fixed on Wolf's face, as though she were watching for the effect of her words on him. "In the first place, he did but one thing during those years—cruised about in his yacht from port to port; in the second place, his time was passed entirely in the society of but two persons. I speak from positive, actual experience, for those two persons were my sister and myself!"

Wolf jumped up from table.

"Mother, we have all finished lunch this ten minutes; don't you think the drawing-room would be a lighter, pleasanter room than this?" he queried, impatiently.

"Excuse me, Mr. Wolf," said Miss Pierpoint, with a little echo of her usual laugh, "I have not yet concluded my midday repast. I wind up every meal with a glass of dry sherry and a plain biscuit—milk-biscuit, if you have such a thing in the house—I cultivated the taste with great diligence during my yachting period; it made me so thoroughly independent of bad cooks or bad hosts. Let a dinner or luncheon be what it will, give me a glass of dry sherry and a biscuit to finish up with, and I'm content."

Wolf, in silence, handed the young lady her biscuit, and poured out, with a somewhat unsteady hand, her glass of dry sherry.

Mrs. Reece looked as she felt, a little bewildered.

"Well," she said frankly enough, "things have changed since I was a girl! The longer I live the more convinced I am of it!" Then she went back to their former topic of conversation. "And so Bernard Reece was fond of yachting! I suppose that's how so much of his money went. But I don't think he took to it till his father died. The people here—old Maurice and the others—seem to have heard nothing about a yacht."

"I dare say not. When the old man died, young Mr. Bernard went straight to New York; there it was the yacht was built for him. A beautiful thing it was too—the Kestrel it was christened. I think I have a photograph of it I can show you, somewhere among my things. My sister and I had the honour of going with Mr. Bernard on its first cruise—rather a longish one too—to Bermuda."

"My dear," queried Mrs. Reece anxiously, for her ideas of propriety were at that moment being subjected to volcanic action, "I sincerely hope that you and your sister had some elderly person to accompany you—to act as chaperon, I mean?"

"Oh, of course!" replied the young lady; "we had an old horror of that sort on board. Thank Heaven! she's dead now, the nasty old gryphon, and won't worry anybody any more."

Mrs. Reece grew suddenly grave.

"In my young days," she said with dignified emphasis, "young people used to treat their elders, if not with reverence, at least with respect."

Miss Pierpoint shot a mischievous glance at Judith through the branches of the silver épergne which, filled with spring blossoms, decorated the centre of the table.

"Ah, that sort of thing went out with the patches, and curtsies, and the 'sirs,' and 'madams,' of our great-grandmothers," she began.

"So much the worse for the young people," interrupted Mrs. Reece, who was evidently beginning to lose her temper.

"And, instead of respect and reverence," pursued the young lady, pushing her chair back from the table, "we give them adoration. Now middle-age is delightful, so far as it goes," here brilliant side-firing at

Wolf, lost upon him, however, for, with hand pressed upon his eyes, he leaned back in his chair, moody and unobservant; "but, unfortunately, it does not go far enough! Only when it reaches old age does it become adorable!"

Here, with a sudden graceful movement, she flung herself on her knees beside Mrs. Reece's chair, and, raising the old lady's hand to her lips, kissed it once, twice, and again.

It was gracefully, winningly done, yet on one at least of the spectators it failed of its effect. The idea somehow came into Judith's mind that this young lady had more than once gone through this or a similar performance, and before a larger and more public audience; it brought a curious succession of ideas in its train.

Mrs. Reece looked more than ever bewildered, yet withal slightly mollified. Judith thought it best to attempt a diversion. This young lady's conversation and demeanour evidently jarred not a little upon Wolf; she was altogether a new experience to his mother.

"Shall I take Miss Pierpoint up to my room to remove her hat?" she asked of Mrs. Reece. "Will you come?" this, turning to the young lady, who, having risen from her knees, was standing close to the window surveying the ill-kept garden, the luxuriance of the shrubs, the weedy condition of lawn and borders.

Wolf at this moment, with a sharp, sudden movement, faced his mother.

"Mother," he said, in an odd, unpleasant, jarring voice, "Miss Pierpoint has taken a long journey to see us. I am sure you will be delighted if she will make our house her home during the remainder of her stay in England?"

If Eve, after the fall, had been in a position to offer the old serpent a bower in Paradise, she might have done it in much such a tone.

Mrs. Reece with difficulty got her breath together to exclaim "Wha-at!"

Then she strove to gain time for herself.

"Are you making a long stay, Miss Pierpoint? Have you many friends in England?" she asked, weighing meantime in her own mind the probability of a large circle of friends contending each in turn for the privilege of Miss Pierpoint's society.

"My length of stay depends entirely upon circumstances. I don't know a soul in England besides yourselves. I shall be delighted to accept your most kind invitation," was the gracious response. Then, after a moment's pause, as though an idea were pressing on her brain to which she must give utterance, she exclaimed: "What a beautiful place this might be made with a little time and a lot of money spent upon it! But, oh dear, what a mistake to let those big trees grow right up to the windows: they ought to be cut down—every one of them. Yes, I'm quite ready," this to Judith, who stood with her hand on the door, mutely regarding her.

As she passed out of the room she gave Wolf, not a sideway passing glance, but one bold, unmitigated stare—a look at once critical, appraising, measuring, as though she were taking the standard of the man, his mental and physical capabilities.

"Ah," she said to Judith as the door closed behind them, "he would make a magnificent Lear. Of course he would have to straighten out his round shoulders a bit before he would be 'every inch a king;' but he would do to perfection—I can see it in his face—the 'Kill, kill, kill, kill, kill, kill!'"

At each repetition of the word she raised her voice a tone or two, till the last, given with clear, far-reaching emphasis, seemed to fill the old hall where they stood, ring along the corridors, and echo up the staircase to the roof itself.

The servants heard it as they sat at their mid-day meal, and laid down their knives and forks, and came creeping up the kitchen-stairs to peep and listen. Bryce heard it as she stood counting her jam-jars, and she left off her counting, and came glaring, yet quaking, along the corridor. Mrs. Reece heard it as she sat in the dining-room mildly discussing the oddities of the new comer. Wolf heard it, and jumped to his feet, flung open the door of the room, and asked in his deep and always tragedy tones:

"What is it? What, in Heaven's name, are you doing?"

"Doing!" repeated Miss Pierpoint, resuming her usual, pretty, child-like inflection of voice. "I am only quoting Shakespeare: don't you know the part?" Then turning to Judith, she whispered into her ear: "And he would do even better the howl, don't you know?" And now she raised her voice again into "Howl, howl, howl, howl!" till the final "howl" made the old roof ring again.

Then she flung her arm round Judith's waist.

"Come along, show me your room. I dare say we've nearly frightened the old lady out of her senses by this time. Up the stairs, did you say? You're a nice, good-looking girl;" this with a pretty elder-sister sort of air; "and you're not a Reece, are you? No! I'm glad of that. And you're not in love with that thunderous, frowning King Lear, are you, as otherwise we might come to cross anchors? Forgive my nautical phraseology; I caught it out yachting with Bernard Reece. Come along."

IV

Virgo, the Virgin, turning the line into a tight-rope, or dancing a minuet with Taurus, the bull, along the ecliptic, would have been a commonplace person beside Miss Delphine Pierpoint in these early days of her visit to the Grange. Judith, growing strangely quiet, yet keenly observant, as the odd, frolicking time went by, could only hold in her breath and wonder. As for poor Mrs. Reece, she passed incessantly from one fit of astonishment into another, and went about saying to everyone she met, "What does it all mean? Can you tell me, what does it all mean?" A question which no one made the feeblest effort to answer.

Bryce even, to whom it was addressed regularly every morning when she came for her day's orders, was startled out of her usual stony reserve with her mistress, into something approaching a friendly loquacity, and contributed her quota of experiences of the young lady's vagaries.

"She told me only yesterday," she grumbled, "'to go to the devil and shake myself,' only because I asked her if she would have some tea. Then what does she do but grimace right up into Mr. Davies's face when he brings her letters. Now, ma'am, I know Mr. Davies's mouth is drawn down at the right corner, and has been ever since his ague-fit a year and a half ago, and I know, too, his left eye has a cast in it enough to set one shivering; but for all that I will say it's not manners for a lady to make faces at him. Not but what I would rather be grimaced at than served as she served me, not half an hour afterwards, when I took her the newspapers. Up she jumped out of her chair, threw her arms round my neck, and gave me a kiss on both cheeks. 'Bryce,' she said, with one of her odd, wild laughs, 'many's the good kiss I've given your Master Bernard; take it and welcome.' But even that fit didn't last till I could get out of the room. She asks me the next minute if it's going to rain or be dry, and because I tell her I haven't the ordering of the weather, and can't say for certain, she calls me 'an old horror,' tells me my eyes are made of glass; then she hisses at me for all the world as if I were a cat, and orders me to get out of the room as quickly as possible, or she'll throw something at my head. What we're all coming to in these days, is more than I can say?" and so on, and so on, going back to her usual strain of gloomy muttering.

Judith felt the air thickening daily. She noticed that Wolf at this time seemed possessed with a spirit of apprehension and unrest. His absence of mind had vanished; in its stead there had seemed to come a constant uneasiness, a tiger-like watchfulness over Miss Pierpoint and her movements. Let her be in the room, his eyes never lifted from her face, his ears waited for every syllable she uttered; let her be out of it, he seemed always on the alert for her return.

Judith noted all sorts of moods showing themselves in his eyes—bad, black moods at times; sullen and defiant at times; heart-broken and despairing at others. When the heart-brokenness and despair showed in them most he would sometimes suddenly cross the room to Judith's side, make her speak to him by putting some simple question, evidently for the mere pleasure of hearing her voice in reply, would touch her hand, would look round furtively, open his lips as though about to speak, would abruptly shut them, then turn away, and avoid her for the rest of the day. When the black, bad mood was on him he never went near her from morning till night, and his eyes would rest on Miss Delphine with an expression not pleasant to look upon.

As for Miss Delphine, her voice, look, and manner by turns flung fascination or defiance at him. She called him "Royal Lear" to his face, and carolled to him in quaint melody odd snatches of poor Tom's songs, "Child Rowland to the dark tower came," or "Saint Withold footed thrice the wold." When the frown on his face was at its blackest and worst, she would lean forward with her elbows on the table, and reproduce it on her own; when he seemed listless or moody at meals she would stir him into sudden, uneasy life by some anecdote of Bernard Reece on board his yacht, or some casual allusion to her poor sister Bertha, and her short married life. Like some strong, wild animal caught in a lair, and bound hard and fast, by turns he would chafe and struggle against his bonds, by turns lie down wearily under them. Now his face said to her—or so it seemed to Judith—"Do your worst, I defy you!" anon, "For Heaven's sake, have mercy on me, now that the game is so entirely in your own hands!"

"She is part of his guilty secret," thought Judith, her old heart-ache and pain growing on her tenfold, and one miserable surmise after another taking shape and form in her brain.

She felt herself strong to help this man, if he would but let her; nay, would he or would he not, she would fain have opened the door of his prison-house, could she but have found the right key to fit into the lock.

Weary hours of thought this hunting for the key brought her—weary hours of prayer, sleepless nights, anxious days.

If only dear Uncle Pierre, with his gentle heart and wise head, could have been there, she felt things might have grown plainer to her; right would have been stronger in the house, opportunity for evil less. But there was she, single-handed, trying to fight Goliath!

Over and over again she tried to make Wolf speak to her of himself; she tried to make him understand that she was waiting for his confidence; that she stood there, as of old, ready and willing to stretch out a hand. It had to be done in odd moments, when they chanced to meet in corridor or on staircase, for, whether it was that he was afraid to trust Miss Pierpoint out of his sight, or whether a similar fear possessed this young lady, certain it is that morning, noon, and night found them always in each other's company.

Once, meeting him in the hall on his way from the dining-room to his study, Judith paused, resolutely stopping his way, and laid her hand on his arm.

"You are ill," she said in a low voice. "Can no one help you, or do anything for you?"

He looked down on her with eyes into which there leapt a sudden tenderness, a very passion of yearning.

"Yes, I am ill, Judith," he answered in tones that confirmed his words. "Pray for me, child—pray for me that the end may not come yet. I want just a year or two more—that's all."

> *"St. Withold footed thrice the wold,*
> *He met the night-mare and her nine fold,"*

carolled Delphine's voice through a half-opened door; and Wolf started from Judith's side as though she herself were the black night-mare.

He turned back for one moment.

"Judith," he said hurriedly, looking over his shoulder meantime, "when you write to Oscar, tell him from me he is not to come home this Easter—not to come home, you'll make him understand, on any pretext whatever."

V

O scar, however, as it happened showed not the slightest inclination to come home that Easter. He sent Judith a long letter, which he asked her to read to his mother and Wolf, explaining the why and wherefore of this. It was the sweetest and most solemn letter she had ever had from him—the longest too, it may be added, for it covered nearly two sheets of notepaper, and, strange to say, had not one word in it about fishing-rods or hunters.

It began as usual by giving Judith the latest intelligence of the Retreat. How that a new pupil had come, a young Lord Havers, who was no end of a good fellow, and with whom he had struck up a hard-and-fast friendship. But it went on quickly enough, as Judith knew it would, from a lord to a lady, and that lady Leila Martin, as a matter of course. Here Oscar seemed, somehow, to find his words failing him, for he wrote in odd, broken sentences, as one might whose pen was too heavily charged, or whose hand was too tremulous to hold it.

"I hardly know how to write my next news," so ran the letter, "for the joy that is in my heart. Leila Martin has at last promised to be my wife—promised to wait years for me, if need be—months, if I can make it months. We have been corresponding ever since she went away to Strasbourg, and she has written it all down in her dear writing that she will be mine when I am able to ask for her. Dr. Martin gives his consent conditionally. Leila comes home this Easter. God bless her! I know I am not worthy of her, never can be. I can only hope to prove to her how true my love is—nothing more. This midsummer there will be a heavy exam on; if I pass it I am all right for the Foreign Office. Pass it I will. I mean to show you all how I can work now."

And then the letter came to an abrupt conclusion.

Judith's eyes swam with tears of ready sympathy. Was she glad?— was she sorry? She did not know, she scarcely dared to ask herself. She only felt the letter of congratulation would be very hard to write, that it must of necessity be a very short one—would in all probability consist but of one sentence, such as, "God bless you, dear Oscar, and give you every happiness in the years to come!" nothing more.

She went at once to take the letter to Mrs. Reece or Wolf. Looking casually through one of the windows she saw the latter walking on the terrace with Delphine—Miss Delphine, be it noted, with a cigarette between her pretty rows of pearls.

"Where can I smoke? Can't do without a whiff after dinner," she had asked Wolf on the day after her arrival.

Wolf had politely suggested the terrace.

"Very well," the young lady had replied, "that will do, as it has set in warm just now. Now, a cigarette, please."

Wolf had confessed himself innocent of cigar-case.

"Bernard Reece invariably carried one for my sole use," replied Miss Delphine with a conquettish upward look into Wolf's face; "and I shall think it very sweet if you will do the same, taking care the cigarettes are machine-made. I abhor those hand-made, weak-in-the-middle things."

And Wolf, oddly enough, had at once taken the young lady's hint, and provided himself with a cigarette-case, showing a special anxiety over the make and substance of its contents.

They were leaning over the stone parapet, side by side, when Judith looked out at them. Wolf shifted a little farther from Delphine as he saw her approaching.

The sun was setting in a blaze of fire behind the mountains; the sharp crags and castle-like turrets were washed in tawny-gold; the wood beneath lay steeped in an amber mist.

Wolf in silence took the letter Judith held out to him.

Miss Delphine for an instant, took her cigarette from between her teeth to indulge in a string of appreciative epithets on mountain, wood, and sky. She was greatly given to ecstatics over scenery, or "scenic effects," as she was apt at times to style the rapid atmospheric changes this vale and mountain range were wont to exhibit.

"In all your life now, did you ever see anything more gorgeous, more surpassingly lovely?" she asked, turning to Judith. "Now, surely you can spare it one little adjective out of your abundance?" This added with a graceful wave of head and hand.

"God made a whole beautiful world, sunrise, sunset, colour and shade, and only called it 'very good.' This is 'very good,'" answered Judith, coldly.

Delphine shrugged her shoulders and went back to her cigarette.

Wolf looked up from the letter. His eyes were a little dimmed, but his voice sounded hard and stern as ever.

"It will come to nothing, of course," he said, "but it will stimulate him in his work. That will be so much to the good for him." Then he turned to Delphine with what seemed to Judith a quite unnecessary explanation that the letter was from his brother; that he was working hard to obtain a Government billet, and had just engaged himself to a very beautiful young lady.

"Ah, I know—Mr. Oscar," said Delphine, promptly. "Now, is he at all like you, in any way?"

"I thank Heaven, no!" answered Wolf, with an earnestness that was startling.

Judith felt herself in the way.

"Shall I read this letter to your mother, or will you?" she asked a little coldly, for his manner repressed and pained her.

"If you will, I shall be glad," was all his answer.

Then he turned to Delphine once more, proffering the cigarette-case.

There came a sudden rush of tears to Judith's eyes. She dashed them back, and said to herself, it was only the glare of the brilliant sunset that had dazzled her, and made her scarcely able to see her way along the dark passage.

Straight into the drawing-room she went, hoping to find Mrs. Reece there. No signs of her, however, and library and breakfast-room were searched with the same result.

"Perhaps she may have gone back to the dining-room," she thought, and accordingly made her way thither.

The dining-room was nearly as dark in broad daylight as the dreary library itself, owing to the proximity of the old yews whose growth Miss Delphine had so much deprecated. Now, with twilight shadows beginning to fall, it was dim almost as any under-sea grotto might be.

"Are you in here, Mrs. Reece?" she asked, merely putting her head inside the door.

"My mother has gone up to her room; she was tired," said a deep voice from one of the window recesses; "come in a moment, I want to speak to you."

Judith started. Wolf, of course it was; but was Delphine with him?

"Where is she?" she asked below her breath, for the dread of Delphine's sudden appearance from an unexpected corner was beginning daily to grow upon her.

"She is upstairs in her own room," answered Wolf with a slightly scornful accentuation of the pronoun. "But I want to ask you something, child. Have you friends or relatives anywhere in England with whom you could stay, for a time at any rate—"

He broke off abruptly; there was a wistful sadness in his voice which cut Judith to the heart.

Her eyes grew burning hot, her voice was choking.

"Are you sending me away?" she cried. "Has it come to that already?"

As she made out his face in the dimness it seemed to her growing whiter and whiter.

"Judith," and his voice was imploring, tear-charged, "do not tempt me to drag down into the mire one whose place is of right among the angels of God. Child, in the years to come, this brief year of life your will be over-lived, forgotten. I want you to begin the over-living and forgetting as quickly as may be."

"It will never be over-lived, never forgotten," she cried passionately, striking her hands together. "This should be my home for at least another year. Why will you drive me out of it? Why—why?"

"Why—Why!" echoed a voice outside on the terrace; and looking up, they saw Delphine standing at the open window with a pleasant smile half parting her pretty lips. "'Still through the hawthorn blows the cold wind,'" she lightly carolled, looking up into Wolf's white, stern face. Then she turned to Judith, and striking her hands together, mimicked with an exactness that could only come from years of trained practice her "Why will you drive me out of it? Why—why?"

Wolf turned upon her fiercely.

"What were you doing there, lurking outside the windows in the dark?" he asked vehemently, furiously.

Delphine laughed her usual gnome-like laugh.

"Is it worse to lurk outside windows in the dark than to lurk inside them, Mr. Wolf?" she said, throwing back question for question. "I left my book on the terrace. I have no maid; I come down to fetch it; I hear your voices; I join in your talk. Voila tout. But, seriously, I repeat Miss Judith's question—why must she be driven out of the house? Why must she leave us without rhyme or reason? Why—why?"

Judith shivered at the mimicry of her own passion, which with literal truthfulness this young lady once more reproduced.

"There is ample reason why she should go," answered Wolf, at bay now, and reckless of consequences; "as ample reason as there could be for any pure-minded girl to leave a place where impurity and unholiness are beginning to flourish; as there could be for a white-robed angel to

CATHERINE LOUISA PIRKIS

spread its wings and set itself free from the devils of hell." He set his teeth over the last words. He had neared the window as he spoke little by little, and now looked down in her face with a light in his eyes that meant danger.

But Delphine only laughed up at him in reply.

"Which of us is angel—which devil?" she asked, showing her double row of pearls.

Judith, all white and tremulous, tottered to his side.

"Am I to go? Do you say I am to go?" she asked in low, quivering tones.

He looked down into her upturned face—looked, looked, looked into the depths of her eyes as though he would look his soul away. His lips moved. A "Yes" seemed to form on them, then died away unspoken. He took her hands for one brief instant, crushing them almost in a fervid clasp, let them go again abruptly, turned on his heel, and strode away from them, down the darkening garden-paths out into the shadows of the fields beyond.

VI

E ventually there was to be war to the knife between Delphine and Judith: but war to the knife with Delphine was to mean one thing, with Judith another.

With Delphine it was to mean the fairest and sweetest of morning greetings and evening "good-nights," an incessant flow of light, amusing talk whenever they two chanced to be alone together, or of subtly insinuated flatteries if a third person were in the room. This to Judith's face. Behind her back it was to mean a few good round curses, hurled after her through open window or half-shut door, a life-like mimicry of her gait, manner of speaking and listening, to any one of the servants who was to be had for an audience, and a half-hour or so of steady gloomy thought when, alone in her own room, she sat unbraiding her hair before retiring for the night.

With Judith it was to mean long hours of thought, of prayer—of weeping, it might be, for her eyes often looked heavy and tired, and, after a time, large, dark purple rings began to encircle them. In Delphine's society it was to mean a coldness and distance of manner, a repressiveness, so to speak, which would have utterly frozen anyone susceptible of the process, though on Delphine it entirely failed of its effect; and an avoidance of that young lady so far as it was possible for one person living in the same house, and sitting down to the same table, to avoid another; the passing of as much of her time as possible in the solitude of her own room, or alone with Mrs. Reece; and the careful shunning of all mention of Miss Delphine's name to any living soul in the house. In old Mrs. Reece's company this, to say the least, was a matter that required skill and determination.

On the night on which Wolf had gone out alone into the darkness, Judith sat up watching for his return till day broke in the eastern sky, and the mountains were aflame with ruddy gold, all sorts of terrors, meantime, filling her heart. Then, just when her body was at its weakest, and her fears at their strongest—when she had begun to feel that the suspense was no longer endurable, and had tied on her hat, resolved to go forth in search of him—she heard the garden-gate swing back, and saw him come slowly along the gravel path, with bent head, lagging footsteps, limp spiritless gait. At the same moment she heard the window of the room over her own opened with a very determined flourish. This was Oscar's room, and for the nonce had been given up to Delphine. Judith knew what would follow now.

First there came a low, mirthless laugh, then the fragment of a song:

"Sleepest or wakest thou, jolly shepherd?"

then a coquettish "Good morning, Mr. Wolf! What an early riser you are! I should have been glad of a morning's walk had I known I could have had a companion."

Judith threw off her hat, and flung herself on her bed, heart-sick and worn out with her night's vigil. Baffled and weary, she pressed her fingers on her hot eye-balls. If she could but have gone out and met him, had but one word out there with him in the open! Now she felt all attempts to see or speak alone with him would and must be futile, for this day, at any rate.

Delphine with her Argus eyes would be here, there, everywhere, or if not here or there in actual bodily presence, the consciousness of her proximity would be in every hole and corner of house and garden (just as the consciousness of the presence of infection in the air spreads itself everywhere when fever is in a house), effectually preventing any exchange of confidences between Wolf and herself.

A sudden thought came to her—a thought so like an inspiration, that she was fain to believe that one of her guardian-angels in passing had breathed it into her ear. Why not write to him? True it might be difficult on paper to express all the pity she had in her heart for him, all her intensity of desire to help him; but so was this difficult to do face to face with him, for words would fail, and her voice would falter; and more than difficult—utterly impossible to accomplish with the shadow of Miss Delphine hovering near, ready to fall upon them at any moment. Yes, she would write, and rising from her bed, she got out her pens and paper, rang her bell for one of the maids, whom she heard stirring about the house, and asked to have her breakfast brought to her in her own room, at the same time sending a message of excuses to Mrs. Reece, together with Oscar's letter, which she thought it possible Wolf might read to her after breakfast.

Not a doubt about it, there never was a letter more difficult to write. It was not that the words would not come, they came, alas! only too thick and fast—fervent passionate words, which as she wrote them brought tears to her eyes, made hand and pen alike tremulous and incapable, and which, when she read afterwards, she tore into a thousand morsels, wondering over her own effrontery in writing them.

Sheet after sheet of note paper shared the same fate. This was too hot, that was too cold. This showed too plainly how her heart ached, and burned, and suffered with his suffering; that was just such a letter as any well-meaning, well-wishing friend might write—a sort of letter that meant no more than "I'll help you if I can, but there are others who could do far more for you."

It was not till the big hall clock had chimed eleven, that her task was done, and even then not in a manner to satisfy herself. Only once did she trust herself to read her letter through before she folded and sealed it.

This was how it ran:

"I have tried and tried in vain to get the opportunity of speaking a few words to you. Much against my will I will I take up my pen to write them. They are words which would have been far better spoken. They will look ugly enough, I know, when I have written them down.

"For they are words of entreaty and of warning. I know it will—it must seem to you the height of presumption that I, little more than a child in years, should presume to entreat, to warn you, a minister of God. But I cannot forget that once, not so very long ago, you called upon me for such help. I cannot forget your cry, 'Judith, help me!' nor my own solemn vow as I stood by your side in the garden that I would never fail you in your time of need. Have you forgotten this?

"I do not wish—nay, I will not force myself upon your confidence, I do not wish to stretch out my hand and say it is the only one that can help you now; but I do say that those other hands stretched out towards you will not help you in your necessity, for they are false hands and evil ones. Do you know to whose hands I am referring? To Miss Pierpoint's—none other's.

"You will say, 'How dare I thus presume to pass judgment on one almost a stranger to me. How can I know whether she is true or false?' I only know what my heart tells me about her. I feel positive—aye, certain as I am of my own existence—that if you yield to her influence you will yield to an influence that will destroy you body, soul, and spirit.

"Pardon me for writing these words to you—pardon me if I repeat once more the vow I made to you in the garden, 'I will never leave you, nor give up the hope of helping you, till you say to me, 'Judith, go!'

JUDITH WYNNE

It would require not a little courage to give this letter to Wolf, to place it in his hand and say, "There, read it when you are alone." Yet this was what she resolved to do. Past eleven o'clock! Yes, he would be sure to be in his study now, engaged with Maurice, the steward, his interminable gossip and business details.

So straight downstairs to the study she went, hiding her letter in the folds of her dress, lest by any chance Miss Delphine might come upon her unawares on the staircase, or in the hall, and snatch it from her hand, a feat that erratic young person would have been quite capable of accomplishing.

"Come in," said a voice she did not expect to hear in response to her knock, and, opening the door, she found Mrs. Reece sole occupant of the room. "Who is it?" asked that lady. "Oh, Judith! I hope your head is better, my dear. Do you want to see Wolf alone? Shall I go away? I'm particularly anxious to have five minutes' talk with him this morning—about Oscar's engagement, I mean. It seems to me someone ought to write to Dr. Martin, and tell him how long Miss Leila will have to wait for her husband. Have you heard that Wolf is going to London to day? No? It seems rather a sudden idea. He wants more ready money, he says, and is going to 'sell out,' or something or other. I don't like to say so, but do you know, my dear, it somehow seems to me that Wolf never has money at command. Now, a large income goes with this property, I know, so I confess I cannot understand it. Can you?"

Here the old lady paused for breath.

"Will Wolf save the next train, or will he travel by the night mail?" asked Judith, pondering how she could get her letter into his hands.

"Oh, he goes by the next train—starts at once, I think. Dear me! I do so wish he would come in. I must have five minutes' talk with him. Miss Pierpoint drives with him to the station. Now, my dear, isn't that an odd thing for a young lady to do—drive to a station to see a young man off, for all the world as if she were engaged to him?"

"For all the world as if she were engaged to him!" brought the hot blood into Judith's face.

A sudden thought came to her about her letter.

"Will you mind giving this to Wolf when he comes in?" she said, putting it into Mrs. Reece's hand, and closing the old lady's fingers tightly over it. "You won't let anyone but Wolf have it, will you? You will give it into his own hands? Please promise me!"

"My dear, with a great deal of pleasure." ("I wonder," she thought, "is Judith making him an offer of marriage, since he seems so shy of doing it himself? I shouldn't have liked to think such a thing of any girl at one time, but, dear me, dear me, all the girls of late have gone so queer, I dare think anything of any of them.") Then, aloud to Judith: "My dear, I will put it into his own hand, and will tell him to read it when he is alone. Will that do?"

Judith thanked her and withdrew.

"I dare say," she thought, "he will read it as he goes up in the train, and will write to me from London. He will be free to use his pen there, at any rate."

Then she went into the drawing-room, thinking that she would keep in the way in case he might wish to say good-bye to her.

Wolf, however, made no effort to do so. She heard his heavy tread more than once along the hall and corridor: she heard also Miss Delphine's voice, here, there, everywhere, carrolling wildly, lightly, like any half-mad skylark who couldn't quite make up its mind which of the clouds should be its concert room; then she saw the old greys brought round to the front door, and Miss Delphine handed into the phaeton. Then Wolf jumped in after her, crack went the whip, and he was gone.

Judith and Mrs. Reece sat down alone to luncheon. The latter descanted loudly and freely on the eccentric behaviour of both her sons at this particular period of their histories.

"If they had only been weak as their father I could have undertaken to manage them and half-a-dozen others like them," she lamented; "but there they are, as incapable as children of five years old, and as obstinate as though they had all their wits about them. There was Wolf when I tried to speak to him, 'Mother, Oscar must choose for himself, just as I must!' and then he sighed as though I were worrying the life out of him. Well, a nice choice they've both of them made of it, that's all I can say, and they'll say so too if they live long enough."

"Did you give Wolf my letter?" Judith ventured to ask, as Mrs. Reece moistened her lips with her sherry. To say truth they were a little dry.

"Gave it him! Yes, my dear," replied the old lady, "and he opened it there and then. It was only a bootmaker's bill. Why, Judith, you should have made such a fuss over giving my son a tradesman's account is more than I can understand."

This was said in a deeply reproachful tone, Mrs. Reece feeling herself specially aggrieved that Judith should have raised hopes in her heart she had no intention of gratifying.

"A bootmaker's bill!" repeated Judith blankly, and for a moment everything seemed misty and indistinct to her.

"Yes, my dear, a bootmaker's bill. What else should it be? There was the man's name on the envelope. Any one might have read it as it lay on my lap. Wolf did and that's why he opened it at once and wondered what I meant when I asked him to read it when he was alone."

"It lay on your lap!" faltered Judith, beginning to see her way through the mystery. "Did no one—are you sure—come into the study before Wolf?"

"Yes, my dear; Miss Pierpoint rustled in, in her satins and bangles, and rustled out again, and rustled in again. She's a restless young woman, as no doubt you've found out by this time. Then she came up to my side, and kissed my hand in her theatrical style—by the way, she is much more of the Frenchwoman than you, Judith—and told me she did not think she could get back to dinner, as she had oceans—yes, that was her word—oceans of things to buy when she got among the darling shops. Ah, I wish she could buy for herself a little common sense and modesty; but these commodities certainly don't seem to be in the market in these days. I suppose there's no demand for them."

Judith asked no more questions. It was clear to her mind that Miss Delphine had exchanged the letter, which had been written with so much careful thought, for one she had no doubt seen lying on the hall table as she rustled about.

When she went up to her own room after lunch, her conjecture was confirmed. On her toilet-table lay a large sealed envelope addressed to herself, which, on opening, she found contained her own letter to Wolf. It was folded in a half-sheet of paper, bearing his crest and monogram, and on this was written in a small, scratchy hand:

"With Miss Delphine Pierpoint's compliments to Miss Wynne, and hearty congratulations on her simple and pathetic style of writing."

After this it was that war to the knife was declared, and carried out between these two.

VII

Wolf was away but three days. Wonderful results attended his return. The old Grange was awakened to sudden life and activity by the tap, tap, of the workman's hammer. In the course of a few weeks a metamorphosis—as complete as that wrought in the sleeping palace by the kiss of the fairy prince, with the magic music in his heart, was accomplished.

Fifty or so of workmen were set to work upon the exterior of the edifice; vans of mediæval furniture dragged their elephantine forms along the rocky roads; and some ten men, with pickaxes, shovels, rakes, and hoes, transformed the weedy, forlorn gardens into as complete a picture of "inverted nature," as soul of gardener could desire.

Whose doing was it? What did it all mean? Again and again did Judith ask herself this question; getting always in reply this answer: "Miss Delphine Pierpoint's." And what it meant was that her influence, for the time being, was paramount—nothing more, nothing less.

Judith could, in no sense of the phrase, be said to have "jumped at" this conclusion, as though it were something beyond her reach, or out of her path. In good truth it was a conclusion lying ready to her hand, and all things considered, somewhat difficult to avoid. When Wolf returned from London, it was on Delphine he fixed his eyes, as he announced the fact of the projected alterations and repairs. In response to which announcement Miss Delphine jumped up from her place at table, clapped her hands, and cried aloud:

"Oh, my prophetic soul! I knew those old yews were doomed! We shall be soon having light enough in this room to tell what we're eating. Now, you'll promise me those miserable old trees shall be among the first rubbish carted away?"

It was Delphine also to whom the architect's plan for certain exterior alterations was submitted, before even Mrs. Reece was asked her opinion on the matter; and it was Delphine who was consulted as to the advisability of clearing out the moat, and re-establishing the drawbridge, or of doing away with the old pretence of fortification altogether, making a wider carriage-sweep, and building a new lodge.

It was Delphine's voice which, when the repairs were really commenced, was to be heard at all corners: here questioning the foreman of the work; there loudly expressing her ideas upon architectural beauty or ugliness. It was Delphine who made the tour of the grounds with the landscape-gardener, inveighed against the number and size of the trees which shut them in, and decided which and how many of the grand old sentinels should be brought to execution.

And finally, it was Delphine, who, when the question of interior decoration and re-garnishing was mooted, laid it down as law that there was only one man in London capable of doing these things to perfection, and that man must of necessity be employed.

Poor Mrs. Reece felt not a little disturbed and bewildered by the suddenness and magnitude of these repairs and alterations. For one thing, her even routine of life was rudely shaken, not to say upset, and evenness of routine is to old people what fresh water is to a fish, pure air to a bird—a something which can be denied them long with but one result. She never knew in which room breakfast was to be laid or dinner eaten, what corner of the garden would be safe from the crash of falling trees, or passing and re-passing of gardener's barrows. A maid had to be told off to be always in readiness to attend to the ring of the little hand-bell she carried about with her; but the maid, being herself of a lively and social turn of mind, and never having had before in her life such unlimited opportunity for gratifying her love for society, was more apt at listening for the sounds of the smart young workmen's voices than that of her mistress's bell. The consequence was that Mrs. Reece would have been not a little neglected and forlorn had it not been for Judith's watchful eye and ready hand to guide her safely from the sounds of hammer and chisel, the rush of mortar, and splash of whitewash.

She did not like to take a despondent view of things, but nevertheless as she said to Judith with the iteration of a church-bell, or eight-day clock, they were a little beyond her just then.

"Now, my dear," she would say at least twice in every twenty-four hours, "is it not extraordinary that one week, as it were, Wolf should be complaining of want of money, and go up to London to 'sell out,' as he calls it, and the next set going such extensive alterations as these?"

Judith could only suggest, each time the question was asked, that it was possible he had "sold out" enough to cover all expenses.

"Then why doesn't he tell me so?" the old lady would rejoin. "Is it unnatural, now, I ask you, Judith, for me to put a few questions as to the wherefore and the how of these things he is doing? No, of course not! Yet he will not so much as allow me to open my mouth on the matter. I only said to him the other day, 'My dear, there is no mortgaging or dealings with the Jews going on, I hope?' when he sighed as though I had been talking the very life out of him, and said, 'Oh, mother, don't worry! For Heaven's sake don't tease me with questions!' and walked out of the room there and then. Now, of course, I haven't seen his face for many a long day past, but it strikes me if I could but get one glimpse of it, I should see he was not looking as he ought to look."

Not looking as he ought to look! If a man at thirty-two years of age ought to look in his prime and at the summit of his manhood, as a tree full of sap and vigour, as the summertide of the year, full of a golden gladness; if to look as he ought meant to look as a man who was doing well his work in life, who was armed so strong in his honesty that he had dread neither of open nor secret foes, then certainly Wolf was not looking as he ought to look.

To Judith's eyes in those days he looked less a man, a breathing, sentient human being, than a piece of mechanism in the figure of a man wound up to go through certain paces or performances, and capable of that, and nothing more.

She looked at him with wonder sometimes, as she conjectured dimly the terrible strain his nature was capable of enduring without word of sympathy from living soul; and she looked at him with awe sometimes, when she thought of the crash and turmoil that must one day convulse that nature, when his soul, awakened and resolute, would shake off its bonds and claim itself for itself. She scarcely dared speak to him; in his presence she felt oppressed with a nameless dread, silenced with the sense of his pain and iron endurance. Their manner each to the other grew daily more and more distant; hers to him would have seemed, to an uninitiated onlooker, a maidenly reserve frozen into arctic coldness; his, to her, a politeness that fell little short of reverence. She made no effort to bridge over the distance between them, she did not attempt to send him a second letter, nor in any way allude to the past. How would it have been possible to do this when, save at mealtimes, they never met; when every moment he could spare from architects and upholsterers was devoted to Miss Delphine, her odd caprices and ceaseless whims?

Her desires seemed endless, her tastes and wishes simply insatiable. She announced, as a rule, some new longing every morning when she came down to breakfast; her night's rest and refrainment having evidently sharpened the edge of her appetite for pretty things.

One morning it would be, "I am longing beyond everything else for a grand piano, it seems twenty years since I last heard a true note;" and

Wolf would look up and say simply, "Do you wish for an Erard or a Broadwood?" and there and then the order for the piano would be given.

Another day it would be, "I am dying for a new novel;" and forthwith a whole packet of books would be written for from London. As for her dresses, every other day at least brought a new costume from some West End dressmaker, which she duly donned, much to the amazement of the simple Welsh house-maidens, before whose eyes so much bravery of plush, and satin, and velvet, had never been displayed before.

Her latest desire, and one that Judith wondered had not been expressed before, seeing how elaborate her thrice-a-day toilets were, seemed most unaccountably to disconcert Wolf.

"I want a maid—I must have a maid; I shall die if I can't get a maid!" she exclaimed suddenly one evening over her glass of dry sherry. This she was agreeably diversifying by dipping therein cherries, which she put to her lips and forthwith handed to Wolf with sidelong, mischievous glances at Mrs. Reece that seemed to say "If you could but see me, old lady, the room wouldn't hold you and me together, I imagine."

Wolf took the cherries, but Judith noticed he did not eat one—let them lie untouched on the edge of his plate.

"Why do you want a maid—" he began, then checked himself, having probably found out from experience that it was useless to question Miss Delphine's wants. "Well, if you do want a maid," he began again, "I should imagine one could easily be found for you at Llanrhaiadr."

"Angels and ministers of grace defend us!" exclaimed Delphine. "A maid from Llanrhaiadr!" and the way in which she rolled the final "r" at him spoke volumes.

"Well, then, send to London for one; there must be plenty of competent maids to be found there," he said, his voice growing yet more troubled.

"My dear Mr. Wolf, I have already sent for one where I knew she was to be had—a little farther off than London, to Mount Edgecumbe, Canada."

Wolf's face grew darker still.

"Why have you done this—" he began, than checked himself again, and said with evident uneasiness: "I hope she will be a nice person—for the sake of the other servants in the house, of course, I mean."

"You shall decide that point for yourself," laughed Delphine. "I will only say I have known her, oh, about twenty years; that is her exact age, I believe; and she is my double, my shadow, my replica, though in marble, in stone, for she is silent where I am noisy—she is grave where I am gay. What would you have more, Mr. Wolf? Now let us go out and see how far they have got on with the smoking-pavilion. And, oh, by-the-bye, it has just come into my head what an improvement it would be to this old house if it were turned hind part before. No, you don't think so? Ah, you haven't thought it over! I mean the back made the front, and *vice-versâ*. Come, I'll show you what I mean from the terrace, and be sure you don't leave your cigar-case behind you as you did last night, keeping me out there ten minutes waiting for my whiff."

"Is she gone, my dear?" asked Mrs. Reece below her breath of Judith, as the door closed. "Turn the old house hind part before, did she say? Ah well, she has turned it upside down already, she can't do much more, try what she will, unless she makes up her mind right out to turn it into a lunatic asylum, which, as things go, seems a not impossible performance!"

VIII

The fatigue of heart through which Judith went at this time was immeasurable. At no little cost was reared the bulwark of coldness and reserve which she had chosen to set up between Wolf and herself, and which, though to all appearance solid as stone masonry itself, needed but a touch to send it quivering to ruin. A look as of old yearning, beseeching, passionate, into the depths of her clear eyes; a cry as of old, half-commanding, half-entreating, of "Judith help me!" would have razed the fine structure in ten minutes, and all in vain would her weak hands have sought to pile it up again.

She knew this, hugged the knowledge to her heart, and kept eyes and ears alike on the alert for his mute or spoken appeal, which sooner or later, she felt sure, must come, in spite of Miss Delphine's exactions and fascinations. And it seemed to her that Wolf must know it also; that clearly as through crystal he must read the sympathy, the anguish, the heart-ache, the passionate longing to be of use to him, which underlay her cold abruptness of speech and manner, her long silences, and short replies.

Bryce, looking from one to the other, with her keen, sunken old eyes, formed her own conclusions on the matter.

"She's well quit of him," mumbled the old body, as she tied a handkerchief over her head and trotted out into the kitchen-garden to pick her mint and marjoram for her mid-day soup; "it's ill to join a foul hand to a clean one. It's a pity Master Bernard didn't light upon her, and go yachting round the world with her instead of that other."

Here Bryce nodded ominously in the direction of the flower-garden, where she could hear the light and literally fantastic tread of Delphine on the gravel path.

"She's a bit cold-blooded, likely enough, and not much to look at is Miss Judith; but for all that, a body feels she's one to be trusted at a pinch."

When a pinch came, as it did later on—and it was a pinch in which Titanic fingers might have delighted—Bryce, as well as one or two others, found that Judith was one to be trusted.

Over the alterations and repairs of the old house Bryce waxed vehement. It was not that she objected to the old place being restored to its ancient glory, but to its being undertaken by unhallowed hands—

by hands that lacked veneration for the traditions of the house, and that swept away ruthlessly everything that impeded the exact carrying out of the modern architect's modern-antique plan.

When the old yews fell, she covered her face with her apron, fled into the house, and wept aloud. Soon she came back, with face as weird and stern as that of any prophetess of olden time, and anathematised one and all of the workmen who had laid axe to their ancient roots. They, worthy souls, being excellent specimens of the British workman, but entirely innocent of all knowledge of the Welsh tongue, listened to her respectfully, waited till she had finished, and then asked her if she hadn't better go in and have some beer after all that.

In her wrath she confronted Wolf, who, with Miss Delphine by his side, was engaged in giving directions to the gardener as to the laying out of a certain portion of the grounds, that was to be converted into a rose garden.

"Do you know what you have done?" she asked, drawing her small figure to its full height, and pointing with a look of horror to the downcast trunks. "Do you know that you have desecrated a grave with your pick and axe? Ages ago, long before the old house was built, a battle was fought on this spot, and the chieftain, Torwerth ap Rhys, fell fighting here with his two brave sons, and here he was buried."

In her excitement she continued to speak in her Welsh tongue.

Wolf could only get at her meaning in snatches.

"Nonsense," he said irritably; "the trees ought never to have been allowed to grow there; they shut out all air and sunshine."

Miss Delphine, a few paces behind him, mimicked Bryce's wrathful gesticulation and tragic mien to the life—for the delectation of the head-gardener, for none other noted her. Bryce tried to calm herself; she had another question to ask, on a matter which lay very near her heart. She put it in English this time.

"And will you tell me," she began, evidently against her will falling into the respectful old-servant tone which was habitual to her, "what is going to be done to the room—the tapestry-room I mean? This morning two of them"—nodding at the workmen—"came spying about upstairs, and asked me for the key of it."

"The tapestry-room," and a change passed over Wolf's face as he said the words; "it will be cleaned and done up in due course when they get to that part of the house, I suppose. I have given no special directions upon the matter."

"Cleaned and done up!" Bryce almost shrieked at him.

Delphine's curiosity was excited.

"Tell me," she asked, "what room is this tapestry-room? It has a nice, mediæval sound. Is there any old needlework in it that would do for chair-covers or piano-backs?"

Bryce looked at her grimly, and pointed her words at her as though they were so many darts.

"It's the room," she said below her breath, "where the old Squire died, Master Bernard's own father, and it's the room where his spirit will show itself to those that trouble its rest."

"A ghost-room!" said Delphine slowly. "No one told me there was a ghost-room in this house." She turned deathly white, and drew the becoming plush hood she was wearing closer and lower over her face. "Why do people talk of such horrors? It makes one think of skeletons and cross-bones at once. That room must be bricked up."

To this resolution, in spite of every remonstrance, she adhered, and like all of her other resolutions, it was eventually carried out to the letter. The old Squire's death-room was bricked up intact, sarcophagus-bedstead, skeleton-clock, and all going into a sealed sepulchre. The filled-in doorway had a handsome oil-painting of Gwynedd Rhys, the founder of the family, life-size, in his steel armour, fitted into the frame, and in due course the tapestry-room was to become a memory in the house—nothing more.

Oscar made no secret of his delight at the renovation of the old place.

"Wolf has come to his senses at last, I am glad to hear," he wrote to Judith. "What a jolly place Plas-y-Coed will be when it's finished; but what a knockabout thing for you and mother to stay in the house with all those workmen about. Of course, I know it can't be finished by then, but I suppose by about midsummer it will be fit for me to bring a young lady into—" and here the lad indulged, according to his wont, in a string—no, skein, they were so entangled—of eulogistic phrases anent the said young lady, her virtues and graces, winding up with a sort of doxology at the prospect of spending a whole month of holidays in her beloved society at Plas-y-Coed when, his threatened examination over, he would be in a position to lay his laurels at her feet, and enjoy a brief period of well-earned idleness.

"For I'm determined to pass, Judith. No fear, I shall get through," so his letter ended. "I'm working like old boots, and mean to work. I think you would hardly know me, I'm beginning to look so interesting and student-like. Pale-face, big rings under my eyes, and all that, but awfully jolly underneath it all. Shall send you a telegram when I know the day of the exam.—sha'n't have time to write—so that you may think of me from morning till night—not with fear and trembling, for not a doubt I shall get through. Whoever's plucked it won't be me!"

Strange to say, about this time Theo's correspondence with Judith suddenly ceased, letter after letter of Judith's remaining unanswered. She naturally questioned Oscar on the matter.

His answers were curiously unsatisfactory. At one time it was: "Theo has grown savage and glum of late. She is always quarrelsome and ill-tempered with Leila and me." At another time it was: "Leila has persuaded her father to send Theo to a finishing-school at Brighton. She sadly needs it, poor child. I'm afraid we've one and all had a finger in the work of spoiling her."

Judith had failed to find in either of these facts a sufficient reason for Theo's silence to her own repeated letters.

Eventually, dated from Brighton, there came a brief missive in Theo's schoolboy hand, with none, however, of Theo's old school-boyish merriment in it; a quaint, prim little note which seemed somehow to Judith's mind to say, under its breath as it were, and between its lines: "They have made up their minds to turn me into something other than I am, so here am I letting them do what they like with me; but for all that my heart aches not a little for the dear old times gone by."

IX

Midsummer came in due course, a hot, blazing St. John's Day; birds too lazy to do aught but twitter in the deep shadows of the woods; flowers drooping and incapable till the thick, soft dews of evening began to fall, and summer lightning flashed in and out across the night sky—lightning so light, so sudden, so fleeting, one could fancy almost it was wind-blown here, there, from one quarter to the other.

It was much such a day as the one on which Judith had made her first acquaintance with Plas-y-Coed. A whole year ago that was, but what a year! To the girl's fancy, in its three hundred and sixty-five days it seemed to enfold centuries. She had left Villa Rosa almost a child in face, in gait, in heart; she was now a woman in all fulness and intensity though but one birthday had passed over her head since she had kissed and bid good-bye to Uncle Pierre; a birthday about which she had said not one word to living soul, preferring to have it slurred over unnoticed rather than to have it marked by any attempt at congratulations and rejoicing, which, after all, would be but a mimicry of the old, hearty good-wishing of the birthdays past and gone.

Moses at exactly one hundred and twenty years old confessed himself just a little incapable of the work set before him to do; Judith Wynne at precisely the same age, less the hundred, began to feel life pressing heavily on her, began to feel heart-sore and ill at ease, as though her youth were somehow being cheated of its due of joy and contentment. She thought a good deal of Uncle Pierre, and wondered over his labours and sufferings in that faraway country. Also she found herself very often, as she sat in the summer twilight alone in the darkening garden, looking up to the hyaline sky, saying: "Aunt Maggie! Aunt Maggie! I wonder when we two shall be side by side again!"

She sat thus lonely and wistful on the evening of this second Midsummer Day she had passed at the Grange. The sky, however, was not clear, but murky, and the light, sudden flashes of lightning showed mountains of clouds gathering together and rolling up from the horizon.

Judith, in addition to her own heartache that day, was feeling not a little disturbed at not having heard from Oscar respecting his and Leila's intended visit. They had a succession of joyous telegrams from him during the week, informing them of the various stages of the examination he was going through, and a final *io pæan* conveying the glad news that he had got through with flying colours, and that in due course they would receive a letter from him saying by what train to expect him and Leila. But post after post had come in and no letter had been received. Wolf had silenced his mother's rising anxieties by remarking that no one could expect a young fellow so deeply in love as Oscar to be guilty of so commonplace a thing as keeping a promise or saving a post.

Judith's fears, however, had not been so easily allayed as Mrs. Reece's, and as she sat in the garden this midsummer evening, they assembled themselves together in troops, and came down upon her with redoubled force.

The repairs and alterations of the house were as yet, of necessity, far from completion. What remained, however, to be done, was mostly out of sight in remoter corners, such as stables and servants' offices. The front of the old Grange, cleared of its moss and lichen, had already begun to wear a spruce, not to say rakish, appearance. Like some old beau who, somewhat late in life, has contrived to squeeze himself into youthful fashionable attire, so to Judith's fancy the old place now wore an air of jaunty coxcombry at once obtrusive and painful.

The garden, also, in its first unpleasant stage of relaying and replanting, showed as odiously smart and trim as the house.

"I wonder," thought Judith, as a first and second flash of lightning bared to her view the rows of small, newly-planted shrubs which had taken the place of the old tangle and wilderness of flowers, "I wonder will Oscar really think the Grange now as 'awfully jolly' as he expects?"

A third flash of lightning revealed to her something she did not expect—the face of a man looking through the new iron bars which had supplemented the old wooden lodge gate—the face of a man, young, yet haggard and drawn, as only age or sorrow can make it—a face familiar, yet somehow strange. Good Heavens! Oscar's! And Judith, as this idea flashed into her mind, sprang to the gate, caught both his hands in hers (hot, trembling hands they were too), and exclaimed:

"Why, why, Oscar, what is it? What can it be? What has happened? Oh tell me quickly! Is Leila ill? Is she—is she dead?"

The last words seemed to force themselves unwittingly from her lips.

Oscar looked down into her face with a smile. Such a smile! As much like the real, soul-expressing thing as a skeleton is like a breathing, sentient human body.

"Dead? Oh no, far from it. Never more full of life and happiness, I should say," he answered, and his voice was as little like his own as his smile. "Possibly, by this time she's married. I'm sure I hope so. She left home some days ago with Lord Havers, one of the best friends I ever had—do you see, Judith?"

"My poor boy, my poor boy!" cried Judith, folding her arms about him.

Then he stooped his hot, dusty face on her small, slight shoulder, and burst into tears.

They were the first he had shed since Leila Martin's letter to him, announcing her flight with Lord Havers, had been put into his hand.

He let Judith lead him to the seat she had just quitted, and they sat down side by side in the twilight.

"My poor, poor boy!" she kept saying, as she smoothed his fair curling hair.

"I'm very tired, Judith," he said piteously, after a time. "I've walked all the way from London. I don't know how long I've been about it, but after I read her letter I felt I must go somewhere—keep on going, going, till I couldn't go any more; and I set off, hardly caring at first which way I went. Then, somehow, I hardly know how, my feet would turn towards home. I'm glad I came here. Yes, I'm glad I came back, instead of rushing away and hiding, as I meant to at first."

He said all this in short, broken sentences, with his head bowed in his hands, his breathing coming thick and fast.

Judith felt she should be glad to get him into the house. It seemed to her that a long illness must follow this terrible strain upon mind and body.

"Will you come indoors, dear?" she said; "you will feel better and stronger when you have had something to eat and drink."

Oscar made no reply. His head was bowed, still resting on his hands, and his breathing was hard and irregular as that of one sinking into a heavy sleep.

"Come, dear," repeated Judith, seeing the necessity for rousing him. She gently drew his hands from his face. Oscar sprang to his feet with a sudden bound.

"Which way have they gone?" he shouted. "Tell me! I'll follow them, though it be to the ends of the earth!"

His eyes gleamed, his brow crimsoned, a wild energy seemed to have taken possession of him. Transient energy, however, for when

CATHERINE LOUISA PIRKIS

Judith drew his arm within her own, he suffered himself to be led into the house like any feeble child.

In the hall they came upon Wolf and Delphine seated in one of the window recesses—the "right period" architect had decided that the hall-windows must be widened and fitted with narrow seats, so widened and fitted with narrow seats they were.

They rose as the two entered.

"Where's 'the little Leila with her orient eyes, and taciturn Asiatic disposition'?" cried Delphine, her eyes wide-opening at Oscar's wild and disordered appearance.

No doubt she thus identified the lady of Oscar's heart with the little ten-year-old maiden of Don Juan instead of with the heroine of the Giaour, less from deliberate choice than because of her own better acquaintance with the former than the latter poem.

Judith looked with appealing eyes at Wolf.

"She has thrown him over," she whispered. "Oh, be gentle with him—see how ill he is."

But Wolf somehow seemed in no mood to be gentle.

"Come, Oscar," he said in his usual curt tones, "be a man, or at least try to be one. This is no harder a blow than others have had to bear before you, and have borne without flinching."

He might have spared his words; there could be but little use in addressing them to one in the first stage of brain-fever.

X

There are some women who so soon as they are born take their place at "the receipt of custom" and exact taxes of every passer by. Their one cry, from their first baby-wail till Death puts his never-to-be-broken seal upon their lips, is that of the horseleech's daughter, "Give, give!" And there are other women who come into the world as it were with both hands outstretched like any distributing angel's; they tighten round but one thing in life—their cornucopia of gentleness, goodness, sympathy, charity, which is at the command of every one "in sorrow, need, sickness, or any other adversity." Does any one weep? theirs is the heart to ache in response; is one in poverty? their money-box is at once unlocked and emptied; is one sick unto death? they don nurse's cap and apron, and share the night-watches till the final hour comes. They are not angels; no, far from it; only "dipt in angel instincts" which serve them in better stead than the philosophy and logic of the men and women about them.

Judith was one of these women; her heart was open to every cry for help, her ear to every tale of sorrow—nay, more, both heart and ear seemed to be on the alert for either. Some one wishing about this time to give as exact a description of Judith as possible described her's as the most listening face he had ever seen. It was a perfect description. Her half-parted lips, her slightly bent head, her upturned, expectant eyes, to even a casual beholder gave the idea of a gracious, sympathetic listener. At St. André she had been a veritable depositary for old people's ailments, children's sorrows, middle-aged persons' necessities. When she came to the Grange, the same story was repeated with but little difference. Mrs. Reece poured her every trouble into her willing ear; Wolf was drawn to her as by magnetic influence; Oscar brought his love joys and love troubles in a bundle to her; and now, poor boy, as he lay weak and fever-stricken on his bed, hers was the only face he recognised in the intervals of his delirium, hers the only hands he would suffer to bathe his hot brow, and bring him his food and medicine.

One of the maids was told off to assist her in the sick-room. There was an abundance of maids now at Plas-y-Coed. Bryce, much against her will, had been called upon to engage a half-dozen or so of Phyllises from the neighbouring hamlet, and now the flutter of a black gown or gleam of white mob-cap might be seen at any corner of the old narrow passages and winding stairs.

Bryce gave an occasional semi-supercilious survey of the sick-room and its arrangements. To her way of thinking, Oscar's illness was as much the outcome of his own folly, as the breakage of an arm or leg might have been after a boyish feat of bird-nesting.

But, for all that, Bryce's assistance in and semi-scornful supervision of the sickroom were not to be scouted. She took care that the "kitchen-physic" was always the best of its kind, and prepared in the best way; she also regulated in a measure Judith's necessary hours of rest from sickroom duties by herself seeing that the maid who assisted was always at her post at the right moment.

Oscar's illness was short and sharp. On the third day after his return home it reached its height. Wolf, white and haggard, shared the night-watches with Judith, in so far as waiting about in corridor or on outside landing, for a half-hourly report, can be said to be a division of labour.

Every time Judith opened the door of the sick-room, there was he standing white, motionless, like any marble statue. She gave him her brief reports, quiet-eyed, numbing the sorrow in her own heart, that she might whisper words of hope to his. He took her bulletin mutely, not trusting himself to speak; transmitted it to his mother, who lay wakeful and moaning in her room below; then came back again to his post on the stairs, a tall, gaunt, despairing figure standing sentinel-wise throughout the long hours of that long, dreary night. Had Death with his scythe passed him on his way to the sick-room, he must have spared him, perforce, as being naught but his own shadow.

Towards morning a change set in. The patient ceased to toss and mutter, the fever lessened, and he fell into a light sleep—at first an uneasy, restless slumber, but deepening into the quiet, restorative sleep of a little child.

Judith, opening the door softly, whispered the glad news to Wolf.

Day had dawned; rosy sunbeams were creeping in at every high, narrow window; the maids were astir below.

"He has slept for more than an hour," whispered Judith, "and his face has its old look coming back into it."

Wolf drew a long breath.

"What words can thank you?" he muttered. "Come for one moment into the fresh air, poor child; you will be worn out." And there came that yearning, compassionate look into his eyes she had not seen in them since he had sat down by her side on the garden-seat, and besought her: "Child, child, do not cry! I cannot—cannot bear it!"

Judith shook her head.

"Bryce is there, but—" she began.

"If Bryce is there, it will be enough," he interrupted. "I will sit with Bryce for an hour while you get some fresh air. Go down into the hall. There is someone waiting to see you there."

He would take no refusal, so Judith, wrapping a warm shawl about her—for she shivered from her night's vigil—went down. In the hall she came upon a muffled-up figure seated in one of the modern-mediæval chairs, sobbing as though her (for the garb was feminine) heart would break. There was no mistaking the sobs, no one but Theo Martin—who did everything from threading a needle to jumping a five-barred gate with a will—could have commanded a sufficiency of breath for them, they were so loud, frequent, and protracted.

She jumped up at Judith's approach.

"Oh, Judith," she cried, and her words, like her sobs, came in a torrent, "he won't die, will he? Only tell me he won't die! Don't—don't send me away; I've come to help you nurse him. I've run away from that horrid school at Brighton on purpose to come to him; had hardly enough money to get here, took the wrong train yesterday, and found myself in Carmarthen. How I've got here I scarcely know; but you will let me see him, won't you? And he won't die, Judith—only say he won't die!"

Judith told her of the blessed change that had set in that morning, and how they hoped for the best now. Then she took the poor tired child into the dining-room, made her take off her hat and wraps, and have something to eat.

"I only heard it yesterday," said Theo, "and rushed away at once in the first train I saw at the station; I did not care where it took me so long as I got away. Anywhere out of Brighton I was nearer to him. It happened to be going to London, so that was right enough; then I took a cab and drove to Euston, and then—and then—oh, I don't know where I went; I took two wrong trains, and one right one, I suppose, for here I am. And oh, Judith, you will let me see him directly he wakes, won't you?"

"That depends," said Judith quietly, feeding Theo meantime with morsels of biscuit and milk.

"I knew how it would be from the very first," Theo went on between her morsels of food; "directly Leila heard that Lord Havers had come as pa's pupil she made up her mind to marry him. The thing was how to get home to make eyes at him, for she was away at Strasbourg at the time. So she sets to work and writes to Oscar a sort of half love-letter, making out she's very miserable; Oscar falls into the trap and makes her another offer, which she accepts at once, knowing that then there will be a chance of her getting back to Richmond, for pa would think she was going to settle down as an engaged young lady, and Oscar would be safe to talk pa over into sending for her. Of course everything turned out as Leila wished (she never makes any mistake in her reckoning). Directly she got home she set to work to make a fool of Lord Havers, throwing dust into Oscar's eyes by making extra love to him all the time. Then she gets me sent away for fear I should spoil her sport, and one fine morning off she goes with Lord Havers, gets married in London, and then goes on to Paris. Of course he was a wretch, too, but she was a wretcher!" concluded Theo, heedless of grammar, and becoming inventive in her vehemence.

It took all Judith's hour of release from the sick-room to calm and soothe the girl, to convince her that she could not possibly be allowed to see Oscar for many days to come, and then only when—the news of her coming gently broken to him—he should express a wish to see her. Also Theo had to be reminded that her father must be written to and informed of her whereabouts, and Mrs. Reece's permission asked before she could establish herself as a guest in the house.

Theo sighed wearily.

"There's such a lot of botheration over everything," she complained. "Half of life seems made up of botherations;" which was Theo's method of expressing the fact that the conventionalities of life were a pain and weariness to her. "There's one thing," she concluded cheerfully; "here I am, and here I'll stay, no matter what pa may write, at any rate till one of you takes me by the shoulders and turns me out."

XI

O nce round the corner, Oscar's return to health was rapid. A few days later saw him seated in an easy-chair in his own room; again a few days, and he was tottering round the garden, leaning now on Judith's arm, now on Theo's.

Wolf had decided that Theo's coming was not to be kept a secret from him.

"It will be impossible for him to forget the past," he argued. "The sooner he accustoms himself to look it in the face the better."

Theo's devotion to the invalid was touching. Little by little she ousted Judith from her small attentions to the now convalescent patient, taking upon herself the reading of light, pleasant books to him, the bringing to him his between-meals of milk or beef-tea, and finally the offering of her round, strong arm for his support in his first attempts at breathing the fresh air in the place of Judith's small and slender one.

There had been a brisk correspondence between Theo and Dr. Martin, in which the latter eventually succumbed to the young lady's determination and persistence, and consented to her spending a fortnight at Plas-y-Coed, on condition of her quiet return to her Brighton school at the close of the autumn holidays.

"Of course I shall make it three weeks," said Theo frankly; "and of course I haven't the least intention of going back to that old curmudgeon at Brighton. When I do go home to Richmond—which won't be till Oscar is quite, quite himself again, let pa growl as he will—I shall just choose a nice school for myself, where the pupils go in for athletics, not dancing, and lead pa and Sophonisba 'a life' till they let me go there."

The first day of Oscar's coming downstairs was a sort of family festival. Theo outraged every feeling the newly-employed gardener possessed by clearing the garden of every bud and blossom within her reach, and decorating every article of furniture she could lay hands upon, regardless of all laws of decorative art. Bryce even she insisted upon adorning with a huge bouquet of wild thyme and marigolds, pinning it to the back seams of the old body's gown as she sat at her dinner, creeping down into the servants'-hall expressly to perform the feat. Oscar, white and wan though he was, could not refrain from a smile as the old servant flitted past him all unconscious of her rearward adorning.

CATHERINE LOUISA PIRKIS

But the best part of the day to Judith's mind, next, of course, to the fact of Oscar being once more amongst them, was the coming downstairs to luncheon, and finding Delphine's place at table vacant. She could scarcely believe her eyes, and stood staring for a moment at the empty chair, much as Macbeth at his memorable banquet might have stared after the ghost had disappeared.

Wolf followed her gaze.

"I have driven Miss Pierpoint to the station; she has gone to London to meet her maid and to do some shopping—they return tomorrow," he explained.

"You don't mean to say so!" exclaimed Mrs. Reece blithely. "Dear me, dear me; perhaps she may meet some friends in London who will ask her to spend part of her time in England with them."

Wolf sighed wearily.

"I wonder," thought Judith, "will he be more his own self—the first self I can remember—now that the shadow is lifted for a day?"

No! His sun was evidently sunk too far below its horizon for passing shadows to affect its vanishing light. His usual mechanical, weary way of doing, speaking, moving, clung to him still. In vain Mrs. Reece started topic after topic of conversation; in vain Judith seconded her efforts with a will; in vain Theo racked her brain, and turned out of them every conceivable joke or comicality they were capable of holding; in vain even Oscar essayed a question or two as to the house decoration and repairs; taciturn, gloomy, and self-absorbed he remained to the finish of the meal.

Theo, the good-natured, felt oppressed; Judith rose from table with the usual weight at her heart; Mrs. Reece, the unconscious, chirruped her grace, and said blandly:

"Well, my dears, this has been the happiest meal I have had for many a long day past. I am 'truly thankful' for more than my luncheon today. Don't you think, Wolf, we ought to have some sort of special thanksgiving service for Oscar's recovery, just as we did in London after I got well from that attack of typhoid? Dear, dear; how long ago it seems! All go to church together and make a special thank-offering for the poor? Next Sunday, or possibly the Sunday after, when Oscar will be a little stronger?"

Oscar rose hastily from his chair.

"Mother," he said bitterly, "I will have no thanksgiving on my account. I am not thankful for being given back to a life of misery. I would I were lying in my coffin now!"

He strode out through the open window—unencumbered with dark yew-boughs now—on to the sunshiny lawn beyond. He looked thin, forlorn, a mere stripling in stature and strength, standing there in the open with uncovered head.

Theo's eyes filled with tears; she looked at Judith much as a big Newfoundland looks up at his master to know what to do. Judith's eyes said: "Do nothing at all; just let him alone, poor boy!" So she sat still where she was, looking wretched.

"Alas, alas!" moaned Mrs. Reece, "if he did but know how young he is!"

But alas, alas! this is exactly what these young people love-troubled never do know, till youth is past, love-troubles forgotten.

Wolf went over to Judith's side.

"What shall we do with him? What ought to be done?" he asked, looking after Oscar, still standing silent and motionless on the sunlit lawn.

It seemed just as natural for this almost middle-aged man to go to this young girl for counsel as it did for the untrained school-girl, or any other wild, romping child.

"He ought to go away somewhere, don't you think?" answered Judith; "a long voyage might do him good." Then a bright thought came to her. "How would it be to send him out to India to my father? I'm sure he would be glad to see him," she exclaimed.

"Ah! thank you. But no, it would not be quite what he needs. He ought to have good, steady, hard work, something regular, impossible to lay on one side. I might be able to get him into the Indian civil service— yes, I think that might be done."

He was talking more to himself than Judith now. He left the room hastily, as though to put into execution some plan already formed. At the door he met a servant bringing a telegram. It was from Miss Pierpoint, and ran as follows:

"I know you will be grieved to hear I cannot get my purchases completed till late tonight, consequently shall not be able to return till the afternoon of Monday. Olivette, my maid, has arrived, and is as charming as ever."

Wolf, with a brief "Give this to your mistress," went on his way. Judith was called upon to read the message, which Mrs. Reece received with folded hands and pious exclamations of thankfulness.

"Well, my dears, it's a reprieve, at any rate, and that I suppose you'll admit. I know I'm old-fashioned—antediluvian, if you like, in my notions of how a gentlewoman should be brought up, but really, if the young people I see now live to be old women, well, they'll be examples—that's all. Now, there's Miss Theo Martin—"

Theo looked up, startled and crimson.

Judith laid her hand on Mrs. Reece's arm.

"Theo is in the room," she said, feeling that nothing but plain-speaking would serve in such an extremity as this.

"Oh, she's in the room, is she?" continued the old lady, in no wise disconcerted. "Well, now she shall hear to her face what I was going to say behind her back, and that is, if she doesn't divest herself of her loud talking, and laughing, and sobbing, and crying—I could hear your sobs, my dear, the other day across the hall and up two flights of stairs—I was saying, if she doesn't soon get rid of her loud voice in talking, laughing, and crying, she'll find, in a year or two, that it'll have become so much a part of herself that she'll be no more able to get rid of it than she will her flesh from her bones. There, my dear, that was all I was going to say, and you must take it in good part from an old woman like me."

Theo had gone from red to white, from white to red, while Mrs. Reece was speaking. When she had ended she rose from her chair, went across the room, and knelt by the old lady's side. She had stumbled over a footstool, and swept down a chair with her dress to get there.

"Dear Mrs. Reece," she said, kissing the old lady's hand, "I am very much obliged to you for what you've said, and I promise you I'll do my very best. But one thing you must promise me, and that is, not to bracket me with Miss Delphine Pierpoint. I do hope and trust you don't think we are birds of the same feather."

"No—o—ah, not exactly; of the two I certainly prefer your manners to hers; but, my dear, if you go on as you are going now, people, whether you like it or not, will bracket you with her, and a hundred others like her."

"Oh no, no, no!" interrupted Judith vehemently.

"Oh yes, yes, yes, Judith!" said Mrs. Reece with decision. "However, we won't argue the point. We shall have three days—today is Friday, isn't it?—clear of Miss Delphine, and I mean to rejoice and be glad in them, and I think it would be very nice if we all, every one of us, went to church next Sunday, and if we mayn't call it a thanksgiving service for Oscar's recovery, it can just as well be a thanks-giving for something else—say Miss Delphine's three days' visit to London, We've always something to be grateful for, whether it be a great or a small mercy. Now it strikes me, if you young ladies use your powers of persuasion as only young ladies can, you'll get Oscar to shake off this black cloud which is creeping over him, and come as a baptized Christian ought, to say his prayers with us next Sunday, even if he won't join in our thanksgiving."

XII

Whether it was that Judith and Theo did use their powers of persuasion "as only young ladies can," or whether it was that no such vehement persuasion were needed, Oscar formed one of the party that drove to Llanrhaiadr on the following Sunday.

Wolf at first excused himself, as he had so frequently of late, from accompanying them.

Then a sudden idea seemed to strike him, and he started up from the breakfast-table, announcing his intention of walking to the church. He needed a good walk; he had been cramped up indoors a good deal of late, and so forth.

"Something to be thankful for," thought Judith as they set off. "Not once since Delphine's coming has he crossed the threshold of a church. The first Sunday she is absent, his feet turn back, as it were, to the church-door."

Llanrhaiadr church, or, more correctly, Llanrhaiadr (the church of the waterfall), nestled in a wooded vale, through which swept a sparkling stream, mountain-born and mountain-bound. In stormy weather, this stream, rushing down the steeps, would frequently outsound the voice of the preacher or the hymns of the small congregation which, Sunday after Sunday, assembled there. An odd little, three-cornered edifice it was, built with the greyest of grey stone, and now, from roof to basement, greened over with moss and lichen of every shade and hue. But, though insignificant in dimensions, the church had a history and a lineage of its own to boast of. It was built on ground where a boisterous battle had been fought between one of the King Davids of North Wales and his unruly chieftains. On the spot where the king's brother had fallen, the first walls of this old church had been reared. Subsequently there had been attached to it a monastery and chapel, dedicated to the blessed St. Govan. An underground passage still ran from the church to the ruins of the monastery, and a steel gauntlet, hanging on the walls of the vestry, was shown to the curious as part of the armour of the soldier-saint himself, rescued from the reliquary when it and the monastery were ravaged by Cromwell's army.

The effigy of many a knight and lady found niches alongside the comparatively modern oak pews, and a huge altar-tomb, belonging to the Ruthlyn family, occupied nearly the whole of the north side.

In addition to the past history of Llanrhaiadr, its present was far from discreditable. This was, *par excellence*, the church for the gentry of the neighbourhood, and had been so for generations. Let the tradespeople and the townspeople swell as they might the congregations of the followers of John Wesley, Llanrhaiadr could always boast of its well-filled family-pews, its small regiment of liveried servants, and, on Sunday mornings, its black-silk equipped cooks and housekeepers. There, in a row, beneath their altar-tomb, sat Lord and Lady Ruthlyn, in full-blown county dignity, their son and heir, their somewhat faded daughters and daughter-in-law. A little to their right, seated sideways to them, was a whole pew-full of Howels—large and small, middle-sized and minute. In front of these sat the ruddy-faced Lord Lieutenant of the county, and his fragile-looking wife—known in London society as "The Orchid," from the meagre diet on which she apparently subsisted and flourished.

Immediately under the pulpit, in square curtained pew, sat a whole army of Madoxes, grand in lineage, grand in deportment—not one of them stood less than six feet in his or her boots—and connected by ramifications with every other ancient family in this and the adjoining county.

Exactly in the centre of the church, square and red-curtained like the others, was the pew of the Reece family. No matter what iniquities of rapine and injustice they might perpetrate in other quarters, the Reeces had always been staunch upholders of Church and State. A Reece—masculine—had, from time immemorial, supplied the smaller matters of church furniture, such as chalices or alms-basins, and a Reece—feminine—had never been wanting to work altar-cloths or pulpit-cushions. A Reece had presented to the church that tremendous achievement in painted glass, which shut out sunlight from the eastern window, and although the three Bernards lay entombed in the huge, square vault in the churchyard outside with a score or so of their own kith and kin, the effigy of a bishop, crozier in hand, and mitre on head, crowned a nook in the chancel, dedicated to the memory of a Rhys of a yet earlier period.

The good rector of the church, himself a Pryce, delighted to call attention to the fact that he was connected in some sort with this remote Rhys. An assertion no one was in a position to deny. He was a kind-hearted, cheery old man, this rector, and one who loved to hold out the right hand of fellowship to every member of his congregation. A marvellous man, too, in one respect, for he had not only found out that the surest way of winning the affection of his flock was by preaching—on hot Sundays especially—the shortest of short sermons, but he had also profited by the knowledge, and reduced it to practice.

Coming in from the bright sunshine and glare of the limestone road, Judith did not at first see that good Mr. Pryce was not in his usual place in the reading-desk. A stranger occupied it, a man short and lean in figure, but with a grand head; a massive forehead, that is, with a thick wave of white hair pushed back from it; arched brows, full blue eyes, the nose of a Napoleon, but a mouth with soft and curved lips that a woman might have envied. It might have been the head of an Elijah, of a Luther, or a Wagner.

Wolf was in his place when Judith and the rest of the party entered; he made way for them, coming out of the pew to do so; then went back, and deliberately seated himself by Judith's side.

What could be his motive in doing this? Could it be that, freed for a few brief hours from his tormentor and tyrant, he sought to give up one of them to a delirious phantasy, a delusion as dangerous as it was wild—sought to cheat himself into the belief that his enchainment was a thing of the past, and that his hour of liberty, his moment of deliverance, had arrived?

As for Judith, a strange, sudden resolution had come into her heart as she knelt in her corner of the pew, and drew, as she loved to, the crimson curtains at every point, effectually shielding herself from prying eyes. She said to herself as she knelt, disdaining hassock, on the bare floor: "If prayer mean anything at all, I will find it out today! If it be a power at all, it shall be a power in my hands this day! If all its force be as the scientists assert, an electric force, that electric force I will wield this day! If it be, as some sweet saints think, a sending of a message to their guardian angels to go here, to go there, to do this thing or that, that message shall my guardian angels hear this day! From me with their sheltering wings will I drive them to that suffering, stricken soul by my side, nor will I take my mandate from off them until they have done my will. I will pray that man's sin out of his heart this day, though I pray it into my own!"

So she knelt and prayed and prayed throughout the whole service, with head bowed in her hands, silent, motionless, scarcely the flutter of a breath showing that she was a living, breathing soul.

Theo and Oscar, side by side at the other corner of the pew, looked at her more than once.

"Poor Judith!" thought Oscar; "she is worn out with her broken nights, and has fallen asleep as she kneels."

"It's her Catholic way of saying her prayers," thought Theo. "I remember now she has a crucifix and a Madonna in her room."

And Wolf turned to look at her, wondering. What could she find to pray about? Had she so many necessities that hours, not minutes, must serve for her prayers? And then, somehow, as he looked at her, still silent as any marble saint in carved niche, his heart began to feel troubled, his eyes grew dim, he knelt and bowed his head by her side.

"'Repent ye, for the kingdom of Heaven is at hand,'" said the voice of the preacher loud and clear over all their heads, and Wolf started from his knees, and resumed his place in the corner of the pew. "Brethren," the preacher went on, "I came here this morning intending to preach from another text, from notes which I hold in my hand at this moment. Somehow, however, the words I have just repeated to you have come into my mind; I feel I have something to say to you about them, so I will say it if you will be good enough to listen."

This was the preamble to the sermon. Then the preacher repeated his text, and began his discourse. It was the sort of sermon a good, earnest-minded general might have preached to his soldiers on the eve of a battle—a captain to his sailors amid the raging of a storm. Not one person in that small church but felt the preacher was pointing his words at him, not at his neighbour. His intent on this particular morning seemed to be less to bring before his hearers the sweet words of Christian promise, than to show them the hatefulness and horribleness of the sins which, spite of Christian promise, still clung to Christian believers. He catalogued them briefly, he described them with encyclopædic fulness; held up the mirror unflinchingly, and cried out, "Come ye one by one, look therein, and say each one for him or herself, 'this is I.'"

Lord Ruthlyn fidgeted in his seat, coughed, opened and shut his gilt-clasped bible; Lady Ruthlyn let her veil fall over her face, rearranged and fastened it back again. The Howels to a child sat with staring eyes fixed upon the preacher; the Madoxes, small and great, looked at each other and arched their brows; the Lord Lieutenant of the county took a pinch of snuff, once, twice, three times; and Wolf sat motionless in the corner of his pew, with head bowed upon his chest, and eyes fixed upon the ground, till there came a brief pause in the preacher's discourse, when, heedless of the eyes fixed upon him, he abruptly rose from his seat and quitted the church.

CATHERINE LOUISA PIRKIS

Judith looked after him and rose from her knees. She felt as though her prayers were answered. She noted his unsteady gait, his bowed head, and it seemed to her that his hour of deliverance had come. If she had defied conventions, had followed him out of the church, had gone to his side and said, "Here am I! Hand-in-hand let us shake off this devil's yoke!" the man might, there and then, have been saved.

As it was, she sat still in her place, thankful, hopeful, rejoicing over her work done, when in good truth it was but scarce begun.

He, meantime, went walking towards home along the limestone roads and rocky lanes, his head still bent, his breast heaving, his steps unsteady, short broken sentences forcing themselves to his lips:

"I will go back to the path I have left; living man nor living woman shall stop me. I will get back my soul for myself. I will trample my sin in the dust beneath my feet. Judith, help me!"

So he went muttering half to himself, half into the clear summer air, along the miles of steep roadway.

Here and there a peasant met him and saluted him, but he seemed to see him not; a lark rose singing and soaring from a field of cut hay, but he heard it not; over and over again he kept on repeating, as a man might repeat over the beads of his rosary, "Judith, Judith! stand by me, and help me!"

He said it as he made the last turn of the road which brought the old Grange into view; he said it as he swung back the iron gate and made his way along the laurel-lined path to the house; he said it as he sprang up the few steps to the terrace, and then stopped abruptly, chilled, stricken, mute. For, sweeping along the grey flags, in trailing black lace, looped back here and there with a blood-red rose, a lady advanced to meet him, with arms gracefully, but theatrically, extended in greeting.

"Oh, my royal Lear!" she exclaimed, "I knew how unhappy you would be at my long absence—though you hadn't the politeness to reply to my telegram—so I altered my mind at the last minute. Olivette did the packing in a twinkling. We started by the night mail, breakfasted at the station hotel this morning, and here I am. Now let me hear you say you are glad to see me!"

It was Miss Delphine Pierpoint.

XIII

The long sermon over, and the service ended, Mrs. Reece, still full of thankfulness for her mercies, great and small, proposed they should make a circuit, and drive home by a longer road. It would do Oscar worlds of good after sitting so long in the hot church, she felt sure—would freshen them all up, in fact, and send them home ravenous to luncheon.

So the longer drive home was undertaken, the mountain-air was rejoiced in, Oscar, invalid-wise, falling asleep under its soothing influence, and Judith, in the corner opposite, scarce knowing whether it was the fresh, strong breeze blowing in her face, or the quiet gladness filling her heart, which made her feel so brave, and vigorous, and young once more.

As they entered the house, however, courage, vigour, youth, and gladness all vanished together, for, floating along the hall from the opened drawing-room door, came the notes of a wild Spanish ditty, accompanied by chords struck with a will on the grand piano. And the voice was none other than that of Miss Delphine Pierpoint.

This young lady had a great idea of being always "in character." Costumed, as she was, *à l'Espagnole*, she must, perforce, sing Spanish songs. If she had taken it into her head to dress as a gravedigger, she would have gone forth into the nearest churchyard to dig up a skull; if as Minerva, she would have gone about the house with a live screech-owl perched upon one shoulder.

Mrs. Reece, as she heard the ringing, silvery notes, stopped short, with her arm drawn through Judith's, on the top step. Theo, a little behind, stopped also, her lips apart, forming a round O.

"Well, she won't eat us, I suppose," said Oscar a little irritably.

Poor boy! irritability was the order of the day with him just then.

"No; she'll keep us lively—just," answered Theo, and Mrs. Reece sighed in acquiescence.

As for Judith, she felt frozen, benumbed, as one might who, on a smiling summer sea, feels bearing down upon him a sudden iceberg. Her card-castle lay shattered at her feet once more. It seemed to matter little whether it were founded on girlish, human hope and love, or Heaven-given faith and prayer. All one! There it lay, racked and ruined. Let those who would try to build it up again.

With a succession of loud chords, the Spanish song came to an end.

With another sigh, this time one of resignation, Mrs. Reece made her way into the drawing-room, still leaning on Judith's arm, the others following.

Wolf was standing at a farther window as they entered, his face turned from the door. Delphine rose from the music-stool, and came forward to shake hands.

She had arranged some black lace mantilla-wise around her face, looping it back with a red rose. Possibly thence she expected to draw extra inspiration for her Spanish love-ditty.

She looked arch, brilliant, radiant. She carolled once more the concluding line of her song, stooped over Mrs. Reece's hands and kissed them, actually went right up to Judith, and, before the girl knew what she was going to do, had kissed her on both cheeks.

"A Judas kiss," thought Judith, and when, afterwards, she had made her escape to her room, she bathed and bathed her face in pure water, trying to do away with the treacherous touch.

In her effusiveness Delphine disarranged her head-dress, and the red rose, placed coquettishly over one ear, fell to the ground. Wolf mechanically picked it up and gave it to her.

"*Permettez*," she exclaimed, and stretching upwards, fastened it, with arched glances, into his button-hole.

Judith felt herself growing cold, colder. Delphine's next words sent a sudden rush of blood to her face.

"My Wolf," said that young lady as, having adjusted the rose to her satisfaction, she shrank back to her normal stature, "now that the whole family is assembled, shall we tell them?"

"As you please," was all Wolf's reply.

"Good. Then I will, please. Did you wonder, any of you, at my sudden departure for London? Did you marvel at my anxiety to meet my maid—my Olivette? That was only half my reason for going; the other half was to order—to set going, that is, for it is a tremendous affair—my trousseau."

Mrs. Reece felt ready to jump for joy. "Deliverance at last!" she thought.

"So you are going to be married, my dear. Well, I'm delighted to hear it," she exclaimed. "All young people ought to be married; I've always said it. Yes, I'm delighted to congratulate you."

Delphine turned to Judith, who stood statuelike, with eyes riveted on Wolf.

"And you, Miss Judith, will you not congratulate me also," she said, "or are you reserving your congratulations for the bridegroom-elect, for I see you have already guessed who he is?"

Had Delphine been a man, there can be little doubt but what she would have selected experimental physiology for her profession in life, and would have turned herself out the finest vivisector the age has yet seen.

A drear silence followed this remark. Mrs. Reece trembled violently.

"I don't quite understand," she faltered.

Delphine laughed her long, low laugh.

"Is it so difficult to understand?" she asked. "Your son, Mr. Wolf, asks me to marry him; I say 'yes'—that is all."

Another drear silence followed.

Outside one could hear the chirrup of grasshoppers on the lawn; the hum of the honey-bee, as it travelled back, heavily weighted, to its hive; the twittering of sleepy midday thrushes in the beeches and elms. Within, four people looked into each other's blank faces and said never a word.

Delphine laughed again.

"Is this a funeral, at which we are assisting?" she asked. "Or, is there here a bride-elect waiting to be congratulated on her good fortune?"

Mrs. Reece did not seem to hear her. She turned her sad old face in the direction of the piano, whence had last come to her the sound of Wolf's voice.

"Is this true, Wolf?" she asked in a low, quivering tone.

"It is true," he answered, in a voice that might have been ground out of a coffee-mill, so dry was it and destitute of human feeling.

She turned to Judith.

"Help me to my room, Judith," she said piteously; "I have heard enough for one day."

Silently, one after the other, each one left the room—Oscar going out by one door, Theo by another; Mrs. Reece and Judith, arm-in-arm, by a third.

Delphine turned with a gay laugh to Wolf.

"Come, my Wolf, let us have a *bravura* together. Your family have not received me too graciously, I will say that for them. Perhaps it is because I have not been too gracious to them. Well, we must do better in the days to come. What, you cannot sing—*alors, écoutez, mon ami!*"

CATHERINE LOUISA PIRKIS

And clang, clang, went the small white hands on the piano again, and one wild carol after another rang through the house, blithe and cheery, or jovial and frolicing, as though the singer had not a care in her heart, or—more perfect simile still—had not a heart to have a care in.

XIV

O h, I cannot—cannot bear it!" moaned Judith, pressing her hot brow with her ice-cold hands. "I cannot—cannot bear it!" And, dry-eyed, she flung herself on the floor, burying head and hands in the cushions of her window-seat, worn out with the "riot of feeling and tumult of passion" she had that day gone through; and with the weight of the iron restraint she had put upon herself, that both should lie hidden in her innermost heart.

Was this—so she asked herself, crouching there in her window-recess— to be indeed the end of all? Was this to be the only result to her prayers, her heart-aches, her piteous strivings, her passionate love for this man, that he should calmly and without a word of warning betroth himself to a woman for whom he could not have one spark of love—nay, more, not even the shadow of respect? If he had loved her, it would have been bad enough; if she had befooled and fascinated him with her arts and blandishments, it would have been, though grievous, in some sort comprehensible; but that he should do this in cold blood, that he should walk into this snare in broad daylight, with his eyes neither dazzled nor blindfolded, was the thing that galled and pained her, and made her feel that her life, under its present conditions, at any rate, was impossible to endure.

It was a grey summer's evening; through her opened window the south wind brought in the floating strains of Delphine's gay voice, carolling still her wild, reckless melodies in the drawing-room below. Would she never leave off singing? She had sung thus wildly, ceaselessly, till the luncheon-bell rang, and again after luncheon till the dinner-bell clanged through the house. Immediately after dinner she had gone back to the piano, and there she was at it still. Now it was a Spanish song, anon Italian, then again Spanish, and then an attempt at a German melody.

Judith was confident that, one and all, they were bad, reckless, evil ditties. The expression Delphine threw into the words convinced her of that, although she was not sufficiently versed in these foreign tongues to catch their exact meaning.

Could this in very truth be the evening of that blessed morning they had spent at Llanrhaiadr? she asked herself. Was this a fit ending to those blessed hopes and prayers which had filled her heart, oh! not so many hours ago?

CATHERINE LOUISA PIRKIS

Then once more rose up the passionate cry, "Oh, I cannot—cannot bear it!" and the cold hands beat themselves together, and the dry eyes closed wearily.

In good truth the strain laid upon this young girl throughout the day had been heavy and hard to bear. Mrs. Reece had remained shut in her own room, denying herself to Judith even. The others had assembled, as in duty bound, to cheerless meals, eating them in silence, and in silence departing, each to his or her own devices.

Even Delphine, strange to say, had shown a marked disinclination for general conversation, being either absorbed in her own secret thoughts, or else intent upon reserving her vocal powers for musical efforts in Spanish and other languages.

High and higher rose the shrill, gay voice through the still evening air, out-sounding the soft notes of blackbird and thrush as they trilled their good-nights to each other in the tall elms. Higher and higher, sharper and shriller. Could a gryphon on its winged course, in pursuit of some luckless wight, have chosen to trill a song of triumph, it must surely have been in much such an ear-piercing key as this.

Suddenly a man's voice, cold, harsh, stern, fell athwart the wild notes.

"Good Heavens, woman!" it said, "what is this that you have done? How dared you attempt such iniquity as this under my roof?"

The voice was Wolf's. The song ceased. Judith lifted up her white face, startled, terrified. What piece of wickedness had Delphine on hand now?

He went on again, speaking impetuously, passionately. Judith could fancy the fire that flashed from his eyes under their bent brows as he spoke the words: "My hands are clean—I say my hands are clean! and clean they shall remain, from blood-shedding, at any rate!"

It was like the echo of the words she had heard him exclaim so piteously in the dead of night, as he had shrunk away from that haunting, pursuing shadow of himself with the blood-stained hands.

Then came Delphine's long, low laugh.

"Oh, my Wolf!" she said in soft, deprecating tones, "why do you disturb yourself about trifles? Your hands are clean. I'm delighted to hear it! So are not mine, for your English maids when they dust a piano, dust every part but the one that wants it most, the ivory keys; those they leave untouched."

But Wolf's voice only seemed to grow harder and sterner under her light talk.

"I will not have my question put by. I ask you how dared you do it; how dared you attempt such devilry as this in my house?"

"How dared you do it—how dared you attempt such devilry as this in my house?" mimicked Delphine, exactly reproducing Wolf's voice and manner. "My Wolf, there was no devilry in my heart when I laid this little plan. I thought only of making everyone happy—ah, so happy! I said to myself, 'My Wolf will be so pleased to know and love the child I have cherished so long; the little one will gladden and brighten the sad old home. And I!—oh, I shall then always have with me the darling I vowed to my dying sister to love and care for as my own child.'"

Wolf groaned aloud.

"Take the child away," he moaned; "I cannot bear to look upon it."

And Judith, raising herself on her knees, so as to look over her cushioned window-seat, saw two figures disappearing round the bend of the gravel path.

One was that of a slight young girl, dressed in the neatest and primmest of black dresses, with the neatest and primmest of black hats on her head, and a thick coil of dark hair showing beneath. The other figure was that of a tiny child, richly dressed in velvets and laces, with a shower of bright golden hair falling in profusion over his shoulders.

Neither Delphine nor Wolf could she see; they were evidently standing immediately beneath the parapet of her window.

Delphine's high-pitched voice rose up to her again.

"Oh, my Wolf, why send the child away? My own nephew—my darling Bertha's only child! When I wrote to Olivette, I said to her, 'Bring my darling without fail. My Wolf will adopt him and treat him as his own child. When he dies—as die he must, some day, though Heaven grant he may outlive me—he will make this boy his heir.' Do you see, I said, 'he will, no doubt, make this boy his heir.' Now say, have I not done wisely?"

But Wolf's voice came harder than ever again:

"Did you mean this? Will you tell me, before Heaven, that you meant the words you said? No matter what I may do, was this the meaning, the thought in your heart?"

Judith rose and shut her window softly. Deeply, intensely as she longed to know more of Delphine's plot—for that this was a plot she felt convinced—she could not bring herself to play eavesdropper any longer.

There came a knock at her door at this moment, and old Bryce's voice asked if she might come in.

CATHERINE LOUISA PIRKIS

"I've brought up your coffee, Miss Judith," she said as she entered with a small tray. "I thought you would sooner have it up here in peace than downstairs with that racket on the piano going on. No wonder the mistress keeps upstairs out of it all. I must say that things are coming to a pretty pass in the house just now!" And, with not a little clatter, she put down her tray on a small table at Judith's elbow.

But evidently bringing the coffee was but a pretence, for, going close up to Judith, she bent over her and whispered in her ear:

"Have you seen the child, Miss Judith? The one, I mean, that came with that foreign-looking maid, and has been kept shut up all day in her bedroom."

Judith's heart was beating fast, but she answered quietly enough:

"Only through the window, Bryce. I saw him walking in the garden with the maid a moment ago."

"Ah, I've seen him face to face, Miss Judith, and I've had him in my arms, and I've kissed his little lips, for, Miss Judith, he has Master Bernard's own beautiful eyes and lovely golden hair."

Judith started. She began to see the child in a new light now.

"Look there, Miss Judith, will you, and tell me what that means?" she whispered below her breath once more, right into Judith's ear, pointing with her lean brown finger across the grey sky.

Judith looked up. The sky was leaden, opaque in the distance, with heavy masses of neutral-tinted clouds hanging low over the mountains. One could see them falling in slanting streams on the distant peaks, while here and there in the foreground the lower crags were steeped in sunlight.

Now, while everyone knows how to admire the gorgeous reds, and yellows, and blues of sunrise or sunset, but few, by comparison, appreciate the grandeur and gloom of a "set grey" sky.

Judith wondered at Bryce's eye for beauty.

"Yes, it is grand," she began a little absently.

"You don't see, Miss Judith. Look again—just above the elms," said Bryce impatiently.

Judith looked again, and saw now a long, low flight of dark birds, flapping heavy, ragged wings between the dun-green of the elms and the dun-grey of the sky.

"Don't you see them—don't you see them, Miss Judith?" reiterated Bryce with increasing impatience. "The rooks have come home at last!"

XV

Mrs. Reece's practical philosophy, which appeared to have deserted her for twenty-four hours, came back to her aid on the following day. She came down to breakfast with her everyday expression on her face, eat with her everyday appetite, talked in her everyday voice. The line of reasoning which had led her to this terminus was straight and plain, destitute of curves or subtleties, and ran somewhat as follows: "This is certainly a heavy blow, but then I have had heavy blows before, and never yet have I found heavy blows made lighter by resistance or complainings. If Wolf is minded to marry this girl, marry her he will, though all the world said him nay. He evidently thinks a great deal of her—witness how he used to consult her about the repairs and decorations—it is possible he has seen something in her which I have failed to discover. Well, of course, in the long run we shall see who has formed the right estimate of her, he or I. If he is right, no doubt they will marry and have a large family. If I am right, then she will serve him as Leila Martin has served Oscar, and throw him over. In that case things will, no doubt, speedily arrange themselves: Wolf will be as supremely miserable as Oscar is at the present moment, and most likely for a far longer period. Afterwards, in all probability, each will mend his life with some plain and desirable young woman. After all, all things considered, it doesn't do to fret one's life out over the doings of one's bachelor sons."

So on Monday morning the old lady put her key-basket on her arm and trudged downstairs as usual, taking her customary place at table, and making her usual remarks about the weather and the health of her big mastiff, which had of late begun to show signs of the creepings on of old age.

"Yet," pursued the old lady cheerfully, "although his teeth are going and his hair is coming off in patches, his scent is marvellous. The hubbub and scratching he kept up in my room last night was wonderful; all the afternoon, too, he was in a state of fidget to find out what stranger was in the house. It must have been your new maid, I suppose, my dear," turning to Delphine as she said this.

Delphine assented.

"My new maid it might have been, and possibly my little nephew also."

This with a sidelong look at Wolf.

"Your little nephew?"

"Yes; Wolf was good enough to tell me I might have him over from Canada on a visit."

Wolf started. Delphine went on calmly enough:

"He is my only sister's child. On her death-bed she gave him into my charge."

"My dear, did she give any more into your charge?" asked Mrs. Reece dryly.

But though she said this with the view of preparing herself for possible emergencies, in her secret heart she was not displeased at the thought of a little child in the house. She had not had children about her knees since her own bright-haired darlings had been taken away from her, now some twenty years since; the memory of them with their "baby fingers and waxen touches" had kept her heart ever open and sympathetic to the sound of childish prattle and laughter.

She longed to have the little one by her side, to smooth its soft curls, and hear its baby chatter.

"If you don't mind, my dear, I should much like to have the little fellow down and introduced to us all. Now why couldn't he come in here and have his breakfast with us?" she asked.

Wolf's face was growing more and more sombre.

"Mother, we should scare such a small child; we haven't had any children among us so long, we shouldn't know their ways," he said in a troubled voice.

"Fiddlesticks! my dear, speak for yourself," retorted Mrs. Reece; "if I don't know children's ways I should like to know who does? Kindly ring, someone, and have the little fellow brought in. He might just as well have sat down to breakfast with us as not."

"He is oh, so shy!" interposed Delphine. "He is better upstairs with Olivette than anywhere else. He is used to her, but he might make a scene in here; however," here she rose from her chair as though struck by a sudden thought, "if you all wish to see him so much, I will go myself and tell Olivette to bring him down;" and she left the room as she finished speaking.

Wolf abruptly pushed back his chair from the table, and went out by another door. They could hear his quick, heavy tread along the corridor, and the shutting of his study door.

"Wolf grows every day more morose," said Mrs. Reece. "Fancy running away like that because a little child was coming into the room. Why, the sooner he gets used to children the better."

"I wonder what the maid is like," whispered Theo to Judith; "I'm dying to see her. Olivette! Such a nice scriptural-sounding name! She ought to be something of a cross between a Ruth and a Rachel."

At this moment the door opened, and Delphine came in bearing the little boy in her arms.

A lovely picture they two made standing in the doorway with Olivette a little in the rear. The little boy's tiny arms were clasped round Delphine's neck; his fair, pale face was pressed against her dark, cream-tinted one; his golden, soft curls set off the raven crispness of her wavy coils; even his dress of rich violet velvet contrasted deliciously with her pale yellow robe and satin knots of ribbon of the same shade.

She put him down in the middle of the room.

"Now run, and make friends all round," she said, giving him a little push towards Mrs. Reece, "and then Olivette will take you upstairs to play again."

The child cast his eyes round him. Mrs. Reece looked old, and grey, and stern; moreover, she wore blue spectacles, huge things fitted into thick frames. Theo looked fat and unresponsive, Oscar white and miserable; but that pale, dark face, with the clear, wide-open, brown eyes, was the very ideal of a child's fancy. He opened his little arms, ran straight to Judith, and put up his mouth to be kissed. Judith bent over him, took the little fellow on her knee, and folded her arms about him.

Once, some four or five years previously, when standing at the garden-gate of Villa Rosa, a poor little sparrow, pursued by a hook-nosed hawk, had fluttered on to her shoulder, and nestled for safety in her bosom.

The incident somehow flashed into her mind now. She drew the little one closer to her, and made a silent vow, there and then, to give him what she could of refuge and protection.

Poor child! He looked so small, and feeble, and slight: the heart must have been hard indeed that would refuse either to him.

"What is your name, little man?" asked Judith, as the child nestled to her, evidently feeling himself quite at home on her knee.

Delphine's face, as she stood and watched the pair, was not pleasant to look upon.

"Pertie," lisped the little fellow, pushing his hand up Judith's sleeve, and tickling her elbow.

Certainly his shyness, if it had ever existed, had vanished in a most wonderful manner.

"His name really is Ethelbert. My poor sister's name was Ethelbertha. Bertha we used to call her," interposed Delphine. "Come, Bertie; here is another lady who wants to make your acquaintance." And she stretched out her hand to take him.

But Bertie clung to Judith like a bat to a wall.

"My name is Ethelbert Reece," he said, looking up in her face.

"Ethelbert Reece Pierpoint," corrected Delphine. "My poor sister married a cousin, and retained her own name—Pierpoint. Mr. Bernard Reece was good enough to be godfather to their first child, hence the name."

"And how old are you?" pursued Judith, then rising from her chair, she carried the little fellow across the room, and placed him on Mrs. Reece's expectant knees.

Whether it was from the suddenness of the movement, or whether it was that the child's ideas were exhausted, he looked sadly disturbed, shook his small head, and put his tiny white fist into his mouth.

"He is three and a half years old, as nearly as possible," said Delphine. "Come, Bertie, look up and give this lady a kiss."

In speaking to the child, somehow, her voice and manner lost all their silvery tone and silken softness.

"Come, Bertie," she repeated peremptorily; "turn round at once and give this lady a kiss."

Mrs. Reece essayed to take one, where-upon the small mite grew pugilistic, slapped her face first, then pulled off her blue glasses, and, thirdly, attempted a charge at her cap—a huge, much-trimmed lace erection.

"Naughty, naughty boy!" scolded Delphine, giving the child a smart slap on his arm. "Take him away at once, Olivette, and don't let him come downstairs for the whole week."

Enter Olivette. Dressed to perfection, she was, so far as neatness of attire went. She had on the plainest of black dresses, the whitest and most bibbed and be-frilled of aprons, the biggest and most mob-like of caps; but, alas for Theo's Scriptural ideal, alas for the expected semi-Ruth, semi-Rachel! The dark eyes that flashed, and gleamed, and glanced beneath the whiteness of the cap were as full of mischief, of witchery, of love-making, as Delphine's own; the hair had the same dark crispness and wayward curls; the very mouth seemed made for the same fantastic, bewildering phrasing; the very turn and carriage of the head and neck expressed a coquetry innate and not to be subdued—such as one would think only Delphine and Delphine's double would be capable of.

The very straightness and formality of her dress served but to throw these characteristics one and all into higher relief. One could fancy she had but donned the garb in a moment of freak, or else was rehearsing the part of a *soubrette* for future production at a public theatre.

All struggling the child was transferred from Mrs. Reece's lap to the arms of Olivette.

"Plenty of energy," remarked Mrs. Reece, smoothing her ruffled laces and adjusting her blue glasses. "I should say it was a family characteristic."

Judith noticed with indignation the sharp grip with which Olivette held the child's slender arm and waist.

"Are you afraid he will jump out of your arms?" she asked, fixing her eyes on the impression which Olivette's fingers had made on his small wrists.

"Madam!" was all Olivette's reply as she stretched her neck a little forward, then tossed back her head with the found-fault-with indignant air so common to the waiting-maid of low comedy.

"Miss Wynne is afraid you ill-treat the child," said Delphine, giving one peal of her long, low laugh.

Olivette laughed in response.

The one laugh sounded like the echo of the other. It would have been hard to say where Delphine's ended or Olivette's began.

Oscar, waking up from a love-sick reverie, looked not a little astonished from mistress to maid. Really things were going on very oddly just now.

"Mother," he said querulously, "since the thing will have to be done, wouldn't it be as well to set up a nursery at once?"

Judith felt somehow she had made a false step, but scarcely knew how to retrace it.

"He is so small, so slight, it seems as though the lightest of touches must hurt him," she said, apologetically, turning to Delphine.

Delphine smiled up at her sweetly.

"And your heart is so large, and loving, and tender, my friend!" she said caressingly.

Judith shrank back silenced at once. Delphine's scowls were bad enough, but were nevertheless infinitely preferable to her caresses.

CATHERINE LOUISA PIRKIS

XVI

D r. Martin in person eventually lumbered down to Plas-y-Coed to fetch back his truant daughter. He was a cumbersome, cheery old gentleman, somewhat impressed with the awkwardness of his mission, and naturally intent on making out as good a case as possible for both his daughters.

He elaborated apology after apology, running Leila's misdemeanours into Theo's, and Theo's into Leila's, in "most admired disorder."

"She was so young, could scarcely be expected to have made up her mind for good and all at eighteen; the young fellows made such desperate love to her; the school was, after all, a terribly strict one, the mistress no end of a tyrant; she was naturally of a most impetuous, wayward disposition, but if Mrs. Reece would only take his word for it, as good and kind-hearted a girl as ever breathed," and so on, and so on.

Mrs. Reece received his apologies blandly enough, though, to say truth, she scarcely understood on whose behalf they were put forward, pressed the old gentleman to extend his visit another day, asked cordially after the health of Miss Sophonisba.

The doctor looked up puzzled.

"Miss who?" he repeated, blankly.

Theo, in a distant corner, covered her face with her hands, laughter trickling through her fingers.

"Miss Sophonisba—your sister, the lady who manages your household," insisted Mrs. Reece somewhat tartly.

The old clergyman shook his head.

"I have a sister living with me, who is good enough to look after us all," he replied, "but her name is Lavinia."

Each was too obtuse to see the slender joke.

"Poor old gentleman!" thought Mrs. Reece; "he is getting ashamed of the oddity of the name, and has rechristened her. But young people will out with the truth, and there can be no muzzling a girl like Theo."

And, "Poor old lady!" thought the doctor; "her memory must be beginning to fail her, or possibly she wanders a little at times. After the years of trouble she has had, no wonder."

All in smiles and tears Theo departed with her father.

"You'll ask me to come again soon, won't you, dear Mrs. Reece?" she pleaded, as she kissed the old lady a hundred times over. "And dear, darling Judith," she implored, with her arms clasped tightly round Judith's neck, "you will take care of him, won't you, and write to me every day how he is?"

Of course she, like everyone else who came into close contact with Judith, looked upon her as a sort of petty providence, destitute of necessities of her own, and consequently having always a vast amount of sympathy and energy to spare for the necessities of others.

Oscar brightened up a little at the talk of an Indian appointment.

"I don't think I could go through another exam, just yet," he said wearily; "but if I could slip into something that didn't want a great deal of doing, I should like the voyage out."

Wolf showed himself very tender with Oscar in those days. Possibly his weakness and emaciated condition recalled to him the time, long since past, when he had been called upon to interfere and take Oscar under his protection against the bullies—one or two—of a large public school. Only it was a woman who had struck him now! It is wonderful what hard blows a slender white hand can deal at times!

It ended with Wolf and Oscar going up to London together, Wolf having received, through influence exerted by Dr. Martin, the nomination to an Indian civil appointment, where the work, light at first, would gradually increase in bulk and responsibility. The examination for this would be simply a "walk over," the flying colours Oscar had carried from his previous examination, to a certain extent placing him in front of the other competitors, and guaranteeing his success.

Certain preliminaries had to be gone through which Wolf found could be better accomplished personally than by letter-writing. An under-master at Dr. Martin's establishment, resident in London, offered a home to Oscar, and to assist him with his experience in the matter till the "walk over" was accomplished and the time for sailing had arrived.

"My mother thinks I am coming back to say good-bye," whispered Oscar to Judith on the morning of his departure; "but I sha'n't attempt that—couldn't stand it, in fact. I shall most likely write to her from Southampton. You'll keep up her spirits, won't you, Judith?"

This was a second perfectly natural appeal. Judith's spirits could never by any possibility want keeping up, hence she must have an immense amount of spare energy for keeping up the spirits of others.

So on a bright August morning Wolf and Oscar set off together. Delphine, in the daintiest of costumes and in the gayest of moods, volunteered to drive the two to the station in the village-cart, which, among other "necessities" for which she had been "dying," had been sent down from London for her special use.

"See, I will drive you both to good luck and happiness if you'll only let me keep the reins long enough," she cried, springing lightly to her place, and touching up the ponies with a whip, the adornment of which with rosebuds and the choicest carnations the garden could afford had taken Olivette at least three hours. "Fortune is a huge car, mount who dare! Be crushed under the wheels those who do not dare! *Allez!*" and once more the ponies felt the light touch of the lash.

Judith, with straining eyes, had watched the three depart. She had stood on the hall step saying her adieux to them. Oscar had taken her in his arms and kissed her tenderly and lovingly as any brother might—but rarely does—an elder sister. Wolf had stood in the background, holding in his hand the flower-bedizened whip (which Delphine had just committed to his care, bidding him admire Olivette's skill), looking down upon it much as, in the old evil days of slavery, a poor Georgian slave might have looked down on the terrible scourge which a cruel overseer had put into his hand to hold till the moment of punishment arrived.

He did not even touch Judith's hand as he said a brief good-bye in the driest and hardest of tones, and he took good care that their eyes should not once meet, keeping his own fixed upon the ground as intently as though he were a geologist hunting for fossils in the limestone.

Judith was prepared for this, had steeled herself to bear this, or anything else in the way of torture that might be dealt out to her. At first she had cried aloud in her pain, "I cannot—cannot bear it!" and her impulse had been to rush away from every living soul, anywhere—anywhere to hide herself and her pain together.

But now other thoughts had come to her, not of the practical, philosophic kind such as had established and fortified the heart of poor Mrs. Reece, nor of the "dumb-driven cattle" kind, the "can't be cured, so must be endured" line of reasoning.

Poor little Casabianca on the burning ship holding on to his duty with hopeless, dog-like tenacity, would more fitly have emblematised Judith's attitude and state of mind at that moment than anything else under heaven.

"I may die at my post, I will not quit it," she said to herself. "This woman and I are set face to face against each other now. She may win the game—I cannot tell—but I will not throw up the cards and say, 'It is yours.'"

Thinking these thoughts, she had wandered down the hall steps into the garden, straining her eyes to get a farewell glimpse of the village-cart and its oddly-contrasted occupants.

Strange to say, a man, just outside the garden gate, was doing precisely the same thing, standing still in the sunshine shading his eyes from the glare of the white road, in order to get a better view of the departing travellers.

He was a tall, loosely-made man with bushy black whiskers, searching black eyes, rather small nose, and gleaming white teeth. His garb somewhat resembled that of a sailor in a foreign merchant ship. It was loose and ill-fitting, and his big straw-hat had a slouching, bent-about air, not common to the British seaman's. He lifted his hat respectfully to Judith.

"I should be very grateful for a glass of water, ma'am, if you would give me one," he said; "I have walked close upon seven miles without so much as a drink by the way."

"Certainly," said Judith; "come into the lodge and rest, and have something to eat;" and she forthwith summoned the lodge-keeper to attend to the man and his wants.

This was the way in which they had been wont to receive strangers of all degrees at Villa Rosa. The man went into the lodge and sat down, and Judith forthwith forgot all about him. She read for an hour to Mrs. Reece; she took a walk through the wood with old Falstaff, the mastiff, at her heels; and came hurrying home, fearing she was late for luncheon, when, passing the lodge again, Falstaff drew her attention to the fact that a stranger was there by sniffing under the creeper-twined doorway, and giving short, low growls of warning.

A feeling of uneasiness took possession of her. Through the open casement she could see the man to whom she had before spoken seated at the table, his elbows resting thereon, his face uplifted with an expression of intense, painful interest written upon it.

"Married! you say they are going to be married. By Heaven!" Here he broke off abruptly, becoming conscious of Judith's proximity on the other side of the window.

The lodge-keeper, a widow, strongly recommended for the post by the Rector of Llanrhaiadr, was an inveterate gossip; indeed, one might say, an all-but irresponsible one, so overgrown was the habit of talking with her.

Judith felt convinced she was giving for the benefit of this stranger extracts, and large ones, from the private history of the Reece family.

This seemed natural enough, knowing as she did the woman's propensity; what seemed unnatural and unaccountable was the painful interest the man was showing in the narrative. What could it matter to him which members of the household married, and which departed this life in a state of single blessedness? Also, having had refreshment and about two hours' rest, why did not he go on his way, rejoicing or otherwise?

She put her hand through Falstaff's collar, and pushed open the lodge-door, making as an excuse for so doing enquiries as to what o'clock it was, and whether the luncheon-bell had rung. Then she turned to the man, asking him if he had friends in this part of the world.

"Thought I had, ma'am, but I'm none so sure of it now," he answered. Then after a moment's pause he added: "I'm rather brought down in the world, ma'am, just now, and I'm going about selling a splendid recipe for sick horses, when they've a touch of chest disease. It's a thing that's been well tried. I've practised it myself on English thoroughbreds for the past fifteen years. I only want five shillings for it, cheap at as many pounds." Here he fumbled in a side-pocket, and produced a memorandum case. "Now if you'll let me see your stable-manager or head-groom, ma'am, I'd explain to him in a trice the exact treatment."

"I don't think such a thing is wanted here; but I'll send one of the men down to speak to you," answered Judith, thinking it just as well that one of the men should see this dubious-looking stranger off the premises.

So she went on to the house, and coming upon one of the grooms left the matter in his hands.

Why in her thoughts she should connect this man with Delphine she would have found it difficult to say, yet somehow she did; and when, some two or three hours after, hearing the sound of wheels, she looked out of her window, it did not surprise her one whit that he—not the lodge-keeper—should come out and open the gate for the village-cart which Delphine was trotting in, nor that Delphine should pull up abruptly, and with a white, startled face confront the man, who appeared to be addressing her with some energy.

All this Judith saw and noted; also the nervous, jerky manner in which Delphine pulled at the ponies' heads as she walked them slowly past the house to the stables, and the easy, familiar way in which the man walked alongside the cart with his hand resting upon it.

Judith was reading a characteristic letter from Theo at the time—in fact, had looked up from it to make her observations of Delphine and Delphine's companion. It began, as usual with all Theo's letters, in a boisterous sort of outburst, a "let-out," as it were, of the energy and indignation which always seemed more or less pent up in her heart.

What an abominable shame it was that Oscar should be sent off to India while Leila was allowed in peace and comfort to remain at home eating the fat of the land! Why, it was transporting the wrong person; it was as bad as sending into penal servitude the man who had been robbed instead of the thief. Of course, Leila always got the cream of everything—one expected that; but what fools Lord Havers's people one and all must be, for they had actually received her with open arms, and were fêting her wherever she went. Well, they would find out in time, as everybody else did, what she was made of; but meantime— oh, heigh ho! everything was very wretched. Sophonisba was nagging her from morning till night, pa was glum and sullen as a bear with a sore head, and the house from top to bottom as dull and sombre as a churchyard vault. Well, she supposed sooner or later the world must come to an end—that was one comfort; but meantime, as one must do something, and home had grown so hateful, she had promised pa she would go to school in Paris if he would find her a nice one, and go in for any amount of French polishing.

Then followed a whole catechism of questions respecting Oscar and Oscar's health, well-being, and voyage in prospect, and an imploring postscript beseeching an immediate reply.

Judith sat down there and then, and wrote Theo some three or four sheets, in which Oscar's name occurred between thirty and forty times.

It took some little time to write; she was half afraid she had lost the post through adding a final postscript on the state of old Falstaff's health. Had the post boy called and gone?

She ran upstairs to the second landing, where, from a high window, she could get a good view of the steep, winding road. Ah, there was the old letter-carrier, sure enough, ambling along, his horse a little me as usual, and himself nearly as white with dust as the cobbles he rode over; but—but who were those two walking leisurely, side by side, coming from an opposite direction, and apparently engaged in the most confidential conversation? Who could they be? Were they in very truth

Delphine and the sailor-like individual, with his marvellous cure for sick horses? Yes, none other, in very truth, for surely no living woman save Delphine knew the art of walking with so much grace under such an overplus of draperies and laces, and the swinging, long, lounging gait of the man was a thing which, if once seen, was not easily forgotten.

They must have gone out together through the stable entrance, for certainly they had not passed by the window at which she had sat down to write her letter, now more than an hour ago.

Delphine did not make her appearance at dinner that night. She sent a message by Olivette, excusing herself on the plea of over-fatigue from her long drive.

XVII

Little by little the mysteries of Plas-y-Coed, which had seemed to be daily accumulating one on the other, began to clear themselves to Judith's brain. One thing pieced itself into another as the days went by, till, spread before her like a child's dissected map, lay the whole story of Wolf's sin and the terrible meshes in which Delphine held him. Not on a sudden, not as a revelation, did this knowledge find her out, but slowly, painfully, one by one, did fact link itself with fact, circumstance with circumstance, till a veritable welded chain of narrative was formed, which, once locked together, refused to be disjointed.

It had not required the penetration of a Solomon to discover that Wolf had a burthened conscience; this knowledge had in a manner been forced upon Judith as soon as she had set foot in the Grange, and times without number had her fancy made vain essays to divine the sort and kind of this burthen, till, wing-wearied, it had been fain to give up the quest and wait for time or chance to reveal it.

Delphine's sudden arrival and immediate supreme power over the master of the house seemed proof positive that she, if not an accomplice in his guilt, at least knew of it, and was determined to turn her knowledge to account.

It was also possible (the idea naturally suggested itself) that she had made a good thing out of her knowledge of this guilty secret before her coming to the house, and hence Wolf's inability to supply funds for the proper maintenance of his establishment.

The more she thought over the matter the clearer this latter fact grew to Judith. Oscar, she remembered, had said that Wolf had come to the Grange glad, grateful, and determined to enjoy his prosperity to the full; he had gone to his room, taking with him some letters that were lying waiting for him, and had come out of it a changed being, at once stopping the repairs and decorations which had been set going, dismissing one half the servants, and lapsing into a gloom and moodiness from which he had never shaken himself free. Up to that moment no doubt his conscience had been clear; from that moment it had been murky and troubled. The inference was obvious: one of those letters must have contained news which to keep secret was a criminal action, and Delphine, or whosoever had written it, had demanded a heavy sum for the risk she had run.

Now what could that news have been?

Great Heavens! most probably Bernard Reece's marriage in some distant country—the existence of an heir, and that heir the little Bertie who had come to the house with his father's eyes and smile!

Creation grew very black to Judith at that moment.

No wonder that Wolf had shrunk from the child—no wonder at his daily-increasing gloom and moodiness! Why, this was a crime that the sturdiest of criminals might hesitate to commit—that the merest tyro in the school of morality would know to be a cursed and evil deed—and he a minister of religion, a man who had preached repentance and faith, and had baptised and absolved sinners!

Yet, what a man he must have been in those old days of poverty and hardship! How self-forgetting and self-denying! Why, even the anguish and misery he had so manifestly endured since his lapse into sin was in some sort a testimony to his pureness of heart and hitherto irreproachable life.

This was the brief that Judith's heart made out for the man she loved, arguing with herself that he was worthy of that love, that the soul which had showed so noble and stainless in times of trial gone by, would sooner or later shake itself free from the chains of sin that bound it, and soar on eagle's wings to its old heights.

And she would help him to regain his old freedom, help him to shake off the yoke of this evil woman, who, not content with tempting him into this deadly sin, must needs pursue him with her witcheries and wickedness into the very heart of his home; stand between him and his only chance of repentance; make his chains and manacles to rattle in his ears morning, noon, and night; till in one desperate moment he makes a wild snatch for liberty in the only way that seems to offer—by marrying her, and forcing the fetters from his wrist to hers.

It was not a pleasant picture to look at. It conjured up a whole army of doubts, terrors, and suspicions. Foremost among them the thought, what would be the next move in this evil game? So far, Delphine had wrought her own will to her heart's content. What was there yet remaining for her to do? Was she about to settle down peaceable and contented in her iniquity, or had she some other dark and intricate moves on hand?

The latter supposition seemed the most feasible. If she were only wishing to marry Wolf and secure to herself the Reece possessions, why bring Bernard's child upon the scene at all? Why risk failure by bringing this infant among those who had known the father from babyhood upwards? If, on the other hand, she were about to instal the boy in his rights, why not do so openly and at once by producing legal proof of his father's marriage?

And on the heels of this thought came another, a black, baneful, awful thought, which set her shivering and shaking as though struck by a sudden December frost, in the midst of the August sunshine which beat down upon her bare head, and made a whole gardenful of flowers, birds, and insects glad and rejoicing. A voice seemed to whisper in her ear, clear, loud, distinct as ever spoke human voice: "One or other of these two stands in this woman's way; one or other will be put out of it. Which will it be, the man or the child?"

XVIII

He's a beast, just as much as though he had horns and hoofs! He's a viper, a crawling snake, a loathsome lizard, a vile, gaping toad, a hideous, creeping rat, a trailing, wriggling worm!" and Delphine, reclining on a lounging-chair in front of her mirror, threw away the end of a cigarette into her toilet-tray, lighted another, and puffed away vigorously.

It was the evening of the day on which the sailor-like individual had made his appearance at Plas-y-Coed. Delphine's dinner, sent up to her by her desire, stood waiting on a small table in a farther corner of the room; it had been thus standing for the last half-hour, and she had not so much as lifted a cover. Even her dry sherry and drier biscuit remained neglected and untasted, the small heap of cigarette ashes in her toilette tray testifying on what her energies had been expended.

Olivette, leaning back on a sofa, her hands clasped high on her head, her apron and cap lying in a white muslin mound at her feet, seemed not one whit surprised at her mistress's tirade. She only yawned slightly, kicked off her slippers, and asked:

"How did he find out where you where? That's what I want to know."

"How—how—how?" repeated Delphine fiercely, turning round and facing her. "Why, how do you think he could, except through your stupidity? Not a living soul would ever have traced me, I'll warrant that, for I took care to give only one address everywhere, and that at a grocer's in Sydney, New South Wales. But you—you must needs tell Stephen Geary our exact destination; he writes it down, this fellow comes upon it, and off he goes, buys a sailor's rig-out, works his passage over, and here he is; and—and—there we are, that's all."

"You didn't suppose I wasn't going to let Steve know where I was bound, did you?" asked Olivette calmly.

"Yes, I did. I thought you understood that I undertook to find you a better man than Steve, as you call him, a man to whom Steve couldn't hold a candle."

"I thought you understood that I declined the honour."

"And why—why—why?" shrieked Delphine. "What possesses you to stick to a man who has nothing but a cottage and ten acres of garden-ground to bless himself with?"

"I happen to be rather fond of him."

"Fond of him! You!"

The tone in which these two pronouns were uttered is impossible to express with a pen?

"Yes—I," calmly, coolly, obstinately averred Olivette.

"What, after Michael, and Hiram, and Publius, and the Lord knows who besides?"

"Yes, after Michael, and Hiram, and Publius, and the Lord knows who besides, I am able to say I am rather fond of Stephen Geary, my sister;" and Olivette, so saying, rose from her sofa, went to the toilet-table, and commenced uncoiling her thick plaits of black hair, sticking her hair-pins into the cushion in front of Delphine.

"Well, this is the end of your fondness, that's all," retorted Delphine. "The beast has tracked us down, and here we are as completely caught as though we had been taken in a net."

"You'll be sure to find, a way out for yourself. There never was a trap set yet out of which you didn't wriggle."

"Ah, that may be, but there are no thanks due to those who get me into it! Of course I'm bound to get the better of this creature, otherwise I'm in a bad case indeed, but it'll cost me a good deal more trouble than I bargained for, and will go near to upsetting all my plans, just as they were beginning to run along so smoothly."

"What did he know? What did he think we were doing here, you and I?"

"He knew a little too much to please me. He knew we had the little wretch with us"—here Delphine nodded towards the room, which opened off hers, where the unconscious Bertie lay sleeping—"and he part guessed, part pumped out of the woman at the lodge the rest. Off she goes tomorrow, neck and crop, I'll answer for that."

"Of course he didn't approve of the marrying part of the business?"

"The beast! no! He had the impudence to forbid it, and swore—my word, you should have heard him—that unless I fell in with his views, as he was pleased to call them, he would at once go to the nearest magistrate, state the case to him, and have Bertie installed in his rights."

"And how much the better would he be for that, I should like to know?"

"That is exactly what I asked him, and is the only hold I have on the creature. I said, 'Of course you get me as well as Wolf at once arrested and convicted of fraud and conspiracy, Bertie will have proper guardians set over him, your character in my solicitor's hands will come out beautifully, and one and all we disappear from the scene.'"

"What did he say to that?"

"Oh, he had a plan of his own to propose, of course, and tried to prove to me it was to our mutual advantage that our plans should coalesce. He said: 'Of course, if I betray you, you get nothing; if you fail me, I get nothing. The thing is, we must play into each other's hands, and each fulfil the conditions the other imposes.'"

"And what conditions, I should like to know, does he impose?"

"He! First and foremost that I should keep my promise and marry him—him, the toad, the viper, the curse of my life! I think I see myself!" And Delphine burst into peal after peal of ringing laughter, which, reaching Judith's ears in the room below, made her wonder what new piece of iniquity was on hand.

"And then?"

"And then we were to come forward, he and I, as the guardians of the helpless Bertie. No, that wasn't quite it either. He is to come forward, as a stranger to me, but a friend of Bertha's, who has suddenly discovered that the child I have had charge of so long is really legitimate, Bertha having been properly married at Bermuda. This fact I am supposed to be ignorant of; not a living soul in New York knew I had witnessed Bertha's marriage; I did not sign the registry; the parson who married her is dead, and the only other witnesses, two sailors, are no one knows where by this time. It was a splendid idea, so feasible and natural, I couldn't help applauding it in spite of myself. You see, no one at first believed Bertha was married, and I took good care to let no one know I was present at the ceremony. This wretch, however, has taken the pains to go to Bermuda and ferret it all out, and now he knows as much as we do. Yes, it was a splendid plan, only, unfortunately, I happen to have other ideas of my own to work out now!"

"I can't see that it was such a splendid plan—it would fail altogether on one point. Naturally, when Wolf was accused of defrauding the heir, he would betray your share of the transaction, and would prove the large sums you had received from time to time."

The two women were talking earnestly enough now; their heads were close together, their eyes were looking each into the other's with a piercing, prolonged gaze, which said now and again more than their words.

Delphine turned a dead white.

"Wolf was not to be there to say anything," she whispered.

For a moment they stared at each other, saying never a word. Then Olivette drew a long breath.

"Oh-h-h! That was his plan, was it? What did you say to it?" she asked.

"I agreed; I said, 'Yes, my friend, it is a grand conception. After all, it is better than marrying him. My footsteps are light; I open and shut doors without a sound; I creep into his room in the dead of night; I put under his nostrils a bottle of chloroform which I get him to buy for my sick headaches at a chemist's a day or two previously, and which afterwards, so I swear, he borrows of me for his own. He sleeps, and sleeps, and sleeps, till he sleeps for ever. Then comes forward the friend with the marriage-certificate. Bertie is proclaimed heir; the devoted aunt, out of gratitude, marries the benevolent stranger. They cherish the little heir, and live on his property till they have built and feathered a nest for themselves in a distant land, to which, at the very right moment, they stretch out their wings and take flight, never to return to this dreary England any more. My friend, it is a glorious plot; there is only one man in England beside yourself capable of conceiving it, and that man is Mr. Wilkie Collins!'"

"Did he believe in your admiration for his genius?"

"Not he. He took to threatening again, then to reasoning, then to persuading. I agreed, of course, with him on all points; took my earrings out of my ears (they didn't suit me, so I don't regret them) because he said he had no money left—swore and re-swore my promise to marry him, vowed to go up to London to report progress to him from time to time, and so got rid of him."

"Ah, those were your words, but what were your intentions?"

"Precisely the same as before, only possibly things may have to be hastened on a little bit more than I like, or the man will step in again and spoil everything. Also we shall have to use caution—oh, so much—become extra benevolent to the whole world in general, and the little Bertie in particular, that people will turn up their eyes, and say their doxologies whenever they come upon us in the street."

There came a long pause now. Olivette stood still with her weight of black hair lying in one hand.

"Delphine," she almost whispered, herself growing whiter and whiter as she said the words, "I do believe Phil Munday's plan is a less dangerous one than yours. Don't you see—"

"No, I don't see!" interrupted Delphine furiously, jumping up from her chair, and stamping her feet violently on the ground. "I don't see, and I won't see, and I'm not going to see! I won't even talk the matter over with you."

CATHERINE LOUISA PIRKIS

Olivette stared at her.

"Why, what has come to you now? You don't mean to say—"

"Yes, I do mean to say, and I'm going to say, and I shall say as long as ever I please, that I won't hurt one hair of this man's head, because I happen to be, as you said just now of your Steve, 'rather fond of him.'"

Olivette's smile of incredulity may be pardoned her.

"What!" she cried contemptuously, "after Christophe, and Wallace, and Phil Munday, and the Lord knows who besides!"

"Yes; after Christophe, and Wallace, and Phil Munday, and the Lord knows who besides, I am still able to say I love this man. There, believe it or not, as you please; but I love him—I love him—I love him as I never yet loved living man, and will let him go for no living soul. Have I ever before had such a one as he shrink and shiver before me; have I ever before had a man like him to writhe in his chains, and yet not dare to shake them off? Have I ever before made such a bold, hard spirit as his cower or quail in this way? Great Heavens, what a master he would make, let him but once get the upper hand! I can see it in his eye; how it glares and glowers at me sometimes when I smile so prettily up at him and make him kiss my darling lips; I can feel it in his grip sometimes, when he seizes my arm and says in that grandly dramatic way of his—ah, what the stage has lost in him!—'Woman, how dared you do this,' or 'that.' Do you suppose I don't glory in having such a man as this at my feet? Do you suppose I don't delight in feeling my grip, my hold on him, his body, soul, and spirit? Do you suppose I would throw him over to marry such a one as Phil Munday? Bah! it's sickening to speak of the two men in one breath!"

Delphine, in her excitement, had stretched out her arms, as though she were addressing an audience, and, as she finished speaking, clasped and wrung her hands to give extra emphasis to her words.

Olivette regarded her with a look half sullen, half contemptuous.

"Well, you needn't rant and rave in that style as though you wanted to bring down the house," she said. "I repeat what I said just now: of the two Phil Munday's plan is the safest for us all, not that I'm wanting to shirk my share of the arrangement; but I can see just as far as you, my sister, and a little farther at times, and it seems to me this 'grand man,' as you call him, will sooner or later be stricken with a fit of repentance, and will turn round upon us all and denounce us."

"He stricken with repentance, with me at his elbow!" exclaimed Delphine scornfully.

"Hear me out. I saw him come home from church on the Sunday we came down here. I was behind the laurels as he came in at the gate, and I heard him muttering and muttering as he went along, how that he would get his soul back again—I dare say you know what he meant by that—if Judith, Judith, Judith—I'm sure he said the name over a hundred times as he went along—would only help him. Now it strikes me that this Judith—"

"She!" again interrupted Delphine with withering scorn. "She! a milky-faced, insipid, old-young thing like that to do me a hurt and upset my plans! Child, you don't know what you are talking about. Why, she must have been at least fifty when she was born, and now she's close upon seventy! She! I've no patience. Why, her veins run with water, not blood! The thing she calls a heart is nothing but a little reservoir. Would any but she let a woman come into a house and win her lover away from her side without so much as a struggle?"

"Perhaps she is biding her time. At any rate, I strongly advise you to do nothing till she is out of the house. Her eyes are sharp, her ears are keen; see how quickly she has found out that we neither of us are too fond of the little imp in there."

"Wait till she is out of the house! Why, that will not be till next summer! A Welsh winter to be got through! Impossible."

"There are ways of getting through it. You have a nice pair of ponies to drive about; you can go up and down to London as often as you please. It's I who am to be pitied, left alone to look after the imp."

"Yes, and you must look after him a little more closely, too, otherwise we shall have him making more friends than will be convenient. Only yesterday I found him in that wretched old Bryce's room, mounted on a table eating sugar-plums as fast as the old woman could feed him. And you, I suppose, were upstairs writing to your Steve?"

"Yes, but he won't do it again. He gave her a black eye this morning, and sent her away howling. I've made him believe that both these old women"—that meant Mrs. Reece and Bryce—"eat little children. I showed him the corner of the garden where they were taken to be killed, and another corner where their bones were buried after the old women had picked them. He'll keep clear enough of them now. No, it isn't the child, and it isn't the old women you have to fear; it's that silent girl with her eyes always wide open who'll be the thorn in your side, and if you're wise, you won't make one single move till she's out of the house."

She looked up, expecting another of Delphine's vehement tirades in reply. Delphine, however, did not so much as part her lips. She had gone to a chest of drawers and taken thence a red morocco scent-case which she had unlocked, and now stood silently surveying. It contained three small, glass-stoppered bottles.

XIX

That was an awful inspiration which came to Judith in the bright August sunshine, chilling her blood and freezing her senses. For days afterwards she went about the house feeling sick and tired. She could scarcely eat, drink, or sleep. At one moment she felt as though she must rush abroad, proclaiming everywhere her terrors, warning Wolf and Mrs. Reece of the danger which threatened them; at another, as though she must move heaven and earth to get little Bertie from this evil woman's charge, and hide him away somewhere in safety. Anon she would resolve to make one final passionate appeal to Wolf to shake himself free from this terrible bondage, and again the next moment would make up her mind to plead with Delphine personally, confront her with the evil she had done, call upon her to repent and atone, or threaten to denounce her and her misdoings to the world. She actually, with this intention strong upon her, went up the stairs to Delphine's room, had her hand on the handle of the door, suddenly paused, and crept away noiselessly, like any thief in the night, as the thought flashed into her brain that, if she denounced Delphine, she denounced Wolf. They were companions in crime, and must sink or swim together.

Her fears pressed upon her heavily. At times her eyes would brighten and cheeks flush as though fever held her in its clasp; at others she would shiver and tremble as though stricken with ague. When Wolf first came back from his few days' visit to London, he was struck by the sudden changes in her appearance. He could not keep his eyes off her whenever they chanced to be in the same room. Though this did not occur often— never save at meal-times—it added not a little to her embarrassment, and made her feel the necessity for absolute self-control. She envied the hard wooden mask Wolf's features were capable of turning to the world; she even envied Delphine her arts and coquetries, which, like the flimsiest of veils, were as capable of disguising alike features and feelings as Wolf's wooden mask. She spent as much of her time as possible in her own room, or, if not there, alone with Mrs. Reece, whose lack of eyesight made her just then a most desirable companion.

But the night was her worst time. Sleep came to her only in snatches. The rest of the night was divided between hideous nightmares, in which sometimes Wolf, sometimes little Bertie, lay white, writhing, and dying at her feet, and waking hours scarcely less hideous, in which she sat

CATHERINE LOUISA PIRKIS

at her half-opened bedroom-door, torturing herself with all sorts of imagined and imaginary noises.

When September came in, as it did that year loud and blustering instead of golden and hazy as it comes at times, many was the night she sat through, half-dressed at her chamber-door, transforming the low wind-sighs (which not even modern mediæval glass can exclude) into plaintive, childish wails, or hearing above the boisterous gusts which beat now and again against the casement, Wolf's deep voice calling aloud for help.

Once as she sat thus, chiding herself at times for her nervous fears, yet utterly unable to divest herself of them, she was convinced that she heard a slipperless, muffled tread pass her door and go down the stairs. Barefooted herself she jumped up and instantly prepared to follow. Her door was slightly opened (she never shut it now till morning dawned), she made not a sound getting out of the room, and stood motionless in the corridor outside, listening whence had gone the sounds. There was a young hazy moon, across which the wind hurried the fleecy clouds, and there came to her in snatches just enough of light to show her that the corridor, the staircase, and the hall below held not a living soul. She listened for five minutes intently, as though her life depended on the length of time she could hold her breath. No, not a sound anywhere save the rushing of the wind in the trees, and the occasional rattle of an unlocked window. She turned to go back to her room, trying to persuade herself that her ears had played her false, when, lo! there came a sudden gust of wind, and a sudden following gleam of moonlight sped across the corridor, lighting up the off-passages as it went, and revealing to her gaze in that special narrow passage leading to the servants' quarters, the same pair of strong country shoes which had once before vexed her sight.

To take possession of them, carry them back to her room, and to lock securely her door, was the work of a moment.

"There, Bryce," she said to herself, "I shall have something to confront you with now, and one way or another I will find out what work you have on hand that can only be carried on in secret in the dead of night."

And confront her with the shoes she did the very next morning. She waited only to hear Wolf shut himself in his study, to see Delphine and Olivette with Bertie depart in the little pony-carriage for their morning drive, before she went downstairs to the housekeeper's room, shoes in hand, placed them on the table in front of the old woman, and said:

"Bryce, I have brought your shoes back. Now will you be good enough to tell me what sends you wandering about the house shoeless in the middle of the night?"

Bryce started, looked up with a deep frown wrinkling her old forehead, rose from her chair, closely shut her window, went to the door and locked it, folded her arms on the table where stood the shoes, and said:

"Do you mind telling me, Miss Judith, what keeps you awake and listening half through the night, and why it is your door is never shut now?"

Judith was prepared for this. She had thought the matter well over, had made sure in her own mind how far her sentiments and Bryce's ran alongside of each other in this matter, and where they diverged; she had also decided that the most candid was the best method of dealing with the old woman if she expected to effect a coalition between their diverging ideas.

"I will tell you, Bryce," she answered frankly enough; "two anxieties have kept me sleepless for many a night past; one is for the dear little baby-stranger, the other is for your master. Now, please, answer my question."

Bryce shrugged her shoulders.

"Thoughts for the master don't trouble me, miss," she said; "but as for that dear little boy, I would lay my life down to get him safe and sound out of their clutches and put into his rights."

"Put into his rights! What do you mean?" asked Judith, anxious to see how far the woman's knowledge on the matter extended.

Bryce waved her hand towards the window whence could be seen the groups of tall elms, in which the returned colony of rooks flapped, and fought, and quarrelled, and pecked, as some generations of rooks had done before them.

"What does that mean, Miss Judith?" she asked.

"Nothing more than that the rooks have come back to their nests from which they were driven by the noise and hubbub the workmen made," answered Judith composedly; "I mean the first lot of workmen your master had down from London. Don't you know you said what a noisy set of men they were? Very well, the poor things disturbed naturally take flight; when everything is quiet they as naturally come back again."

Bryce shook her head.

"It's no use telling me that, Miss Judith. God Almighty doesn't give His creatures their instincts for nothing. Do you mean to say that they don't know just as well as you or I do"—here she fixed the keenest glance her old eyes were capable of on Judith's listening face—"that Master Bernard's son has come to his own rightful home?"

There was a moment's pause.

"How do you know he is Master Bernard's son?" questioned Judith at length, after she had borne the old woman's gaze unflinchingly for at least a minute and a half.

"How do I know! Didn't I carry Master Bernard himself in my arms from the time he was a month old? Hasn't this boy his father's hair, his father's eyes, his father's bold, winsome way? How do I know? Why, next you'll be wanting to make me believe I'm as blind and unknowing as you'd make out the rooks to be!"

"Ah, I'm afraid you see a likeness where no one else would, Bryce," said Judith, honestly speaking her own thoughts, for little Bertie's paternity was proved to her mind by other evidence than his hair and eyes. "I'm sure he's not half so much like Mr. Bernard's portrait in the library as Mr. Wolf is, and if you went about saying he was Mr. Bernard's son, no one would believe you."

Her last sentence she emphasised word by word. She wished to find out if this old woman had taken anyone into her confidence; also whether she had any further evidence to produce as to Bertie's heirship.

"I know that, Miss Judith," said Bryce in a slightly injured tone; "and I'm not one to go about saying what I can't prove. Not a soul has heard a word from my lips yet—not a soul shall till I've something more to say than I have now. Then let those look to themselves who have kept him out of his rights—that's all."

Judith's heart beat quickly. This was the point at which she wished to arrive. She went close up to Bryce and took her wrinkled old hand.

"Bryce," she said in a low, earnest tone, "we must join hands now and help each other. We are both striving for the same thing—to restore Master Bertie to his rights; only you would do it one way, I another. Now we must work together, hand-in-hand, as I said, for the same end and in the same way. Will you agree to this?"

Bryce freed her hand uneasily from Judith's clasp.

"I don't know quite what you mean," she said in a troubled tone; "for my part I don't care what way I go to work so long as the wicked get judged and punished, and Master Bernard's son comes into his own."

"But I care very much which way I go to work, and I want you to care too. Supposing that all you say is true—remember we have no proof that it is true—I want this house and lands not to be wrested—dragged with threats, as it were—out of Mr. Wolf's hands. No, I want him, of his own free will, to restore them to the child with as little of publicity as possible—as little of disgrace as possible to the old name of Reece."

She knew this consideration would weigh with the faithful old servant if none other would. Bryce looked still more troubled.

"He'll never give up the house and land of his own free will, Miss Judith," she muttered, "and Heaven only knows how we should make him give it up, for proof would be hard to get from all that way across the sea."

"Exactly," agreed Judith; "proof would be next to impossible for us two women to get without calling lawyers in to help us; and think what a terrible disgrace that would be in the county. Why, the old name of Reece would be tarnished for ever."

Bryce said nothing for a moment. Her heart was at conflict with herself; her love for her nursling's son fought with her love and sense of duty to the whole Reece family, root and branch.

"I wish he were not a Reece, that's all," she muttered at length between her teeth; "he would get little enough of mercy at my hands then."

"Yes, but Mr. Wolf is a Reece to the backbone, so we must try to spare him all we can; must—do you understand, Bryce? You must not say one word of your fancies about this boy to living soul, nor let anybody believe for a moment you think him to be any other than Miss Pierpoint's nephew. Do you understand?"

"Aye, that's easy enough to understand! I'm not so fond of gossiping but what I can hold my tongue when there's a need. That's what I'm not to do, Miss Judith—gossip, I mean. Now what is it you want me to do for Master Bernard's boy? that's the thing I'm thinking most of."

"I want you to help me to take care of him till we can see what can be done for the best. I want you to watch over him at every turn, to keep your eyes and ears always on the alert, and, directly your suspicions are aroused about anything ever so slight, to come and tell me. But I want you, beyond everything else, not to show the slightest affection for the child—not on any account to have him in here, and give him sweets as you did the other day—in fact, to take no notice whatever of him, or else you may be quite sure, before you know where you are, you'll be turned out of the house; and what can I do here alone and single-handed?"

CATHERINE LOUISA PIRKIS

"He wouldn't do that, Miss Judith, surely! He's wicked and hard-hearted enough, God knows; but he wouldn't surely turn an old body like me out of the house after serving his family nigh upon sixty years—aye, and my mother and father doing the same before me?"

"He! Mr. Wolf wouldn't, you may be quite sure; but she—you know whom I mean—would in an instant, if you stood in the way of her plans; and you must remember, Bryce, it is she, not he, who is at the bottom of all the wickedness that goes on in the house, so be cautious before her—pray do! You and I must never be seen talking together, or they will find us out; if you have really anything to say to me that I ought to know, come to me in the middle of the night. My door will never be locked, and I know you are famous at creeping about the house after midnight."

"Miss Judith, you are famous at listening; the only three times in my life I ever did such a thing you found me out."

"And why did you do it those three times, Bryce? It was not a nice thing to do, was it?"

"Why? Because I heard him—the master, I mean—walking up and down, up and down, night after night, night after night. And I said to myself, that man's conscience is evil, he can't rest night or day. Then I crept downstairs, and lay hiding behind the big clock in the hall, and heard him shriek out and fall when the ghost came out of the wall and showed him the red hands. Oh, Miss Judith, it's that blood-stone ring! Why did you bring it into the house? Why does he persist in wearing it on his hand, as he does? Get it back, Miss Judith—for the love of Heaven get it back before we go on from bad to worse!"

"I will get it back if it is possible, and will give it to you, and you shall throw it into the stream after the other, if you'll only promise to do what I've asked you."

"It's little enough you've asked me to do yet, Miss Judith; is there nothing besides can be done? Hark! there's the mistress's bell; she wonders why I haven't been up to her for orders yet. Nothing besides that I can do?" she repeated this wistfully, and not a little sadly.

Judith sighed.

"Nothing, I fear, Bryce. These things are never out of my thoughts, night or day. I shut my eyes and think over them till I can think no more. I pray over them till words fail me, and then I kneel with clasped hands till nearly daybreak, hoping for a ray of light. Yet all I can find to do at the present moment, is to watch and wait—nothing more."

XX

Delphine's fondness for her little nephew about this time became remarkable, not to say excessive. It took a violently demonstrative form; everybody who came into the house was struck with it. The child had toys showered upon him from morning till night, a weekly packet arriving from London containing everything that was new and costly in the way of playthings, matched by a similar packet from a leading confectioner, containing everything that heart of child could desire in the way of sweetmeats. Delphine went about with a pouch full of these suspended from her side, and literally pelted the boy with them every hour in the day. As the little fellow set off for his morning walk with Olivette, a sudden shower of chocolate creams would surprise him from an upper window, and handfuls of comfits and sugared almonds would greet him on his return. Then, too, his clothing, always handsome and costly, became at this time a type of luxury and splendour itself. He shone out bravely in flame-coloured satins and ruby velvets, marigold plushes, and sage-green silks, all of them exquisitely adorned with the rarest of Brussels laces and Spanish guipures. Not a servant in the house but what noted the aunt's tenderness and indulgence to her small nephew.

"He's a lucky one for an orphan," said they, "to fall into such good hands."

Even the old rector of Llanrhaiadr, calling about this time to see Wolf, and finding Delphine and the boy alone in the drawing-room, was struck by the maternal fondness she displayed for the child. She held him on her knee close to her heart the whole time the rector was in the room.

"He is your own, of course, ma'am," said the old gentleman. He had not been introduced to Delphine, but that with him did not make the slightest difference; the introduction could just as well follow as precede a string of friendly interrogatories.

"He is my very own—aren't you, darling?" said Delphine, popping a big pear-drop into Bertie's mouth, which effectually prevented his replying; "he is my only sister's only child, and if that doesn't make him my own, what should?" and she put up her hand to her eyes as though to shut out a sudden, painful memory.

The rector hastened to change the subject.

CATHERINE LOUISA PIRKIS

"You are on a visit here, are you not? Do you make a long stay? I have not had the pleasure yet of seeing you at our church."

Delphine drew an exquisite cross, of Mary-lilies in wrought gold, from the bosom of her dress, and held it up to the clergyman.

"I am a Catholic," she said; "that explains. But Mr. Wolf is doing his best to convert me. Ah, the long talks we have about your churches, your prayers, your hymns. And I say to him, 'Mr. Wolf, I would be Protestant tomorrow if you would but get rid of your ugly hymntunes and sing the delicious melodies we sing in our own churches; and then I sing to him our hymns, so soft, so sweet, so touching, and he stands rapt, enthralled. Ah, shall I sing one to you now?"

The question was asked in her sweetest and most caressing of tones; without waiting for the rector's reply, she went to the piano, Bertie clasped in her arms still, and played the air, at reduced time, of the Spanish love-ditty she had sung with such evil effect on a certain Sunday not so very long ago. Into the words, whatever they were, she threw the whole of expression she had at command, upturning her dark eyes coquettishly to the old clergyman's lack-lustre grey ones.

He looked as he felt—bewildered.

"Yes, yes," he said, "very sweetly sung, but—but—pardon me, is it— can it be a hymn?"

Wolf entering at this moment had the concluding stanza repeated for his special benefit, the brilliant, coquettish eyes being transferred from the rector's face to his own.

A dark, heavy frown was the only acknowledgment he made her, an acknowledgment which Delphine in her turn acknowledged by rising slowly from the piano—Bertie still clinging about her neck— and curtseying so low that it seemed as though she must be sinking through the floor. Then, retreating backwards towards the door, she repeated her reverences once, twice, three times—not an easy thing to do with grace, seeing she had a child of three or four years in her arms, but, nevertheless, with grace she accomplished it, going easily and in leisurely style step by step towards the door, till finally, kissing her hand once to Wolf, once to the rector, she disappeared.

The old clergyman turned to Wolf enquiringly.

"A charming person, no doubt, but—ah, pardon me—a little out of the common."

Wolf, however, was in no mood to discuss either Delphine's charmingness or eccentricities.

"You wished to see me this morning?" he said, with a direct bluntness which brought the rector straight to the object of his visit.

He hastened to explain. A series of revival services were being set on foot by himself and some brother-clergymen in the neighbourhood. Would Wolf, as a clergyman experienced in such work, take part in them?

Wolf shook his head resolutely.

"I am not in tune for that sort of thing," he said coldly. "Also my opinions on many points have undergone a modification of late, and I am not so confident as I once was of the capabilities of Christianity for meeting all mundane ills."

So the worthy rector was forced once more to depart, pained and depressed, also not a little startled by Wolf's frank confession of unorthodoxy.

Whether or not it was owing to the change which had taken place in Wolf's inner convictions, a certain visible outward change in the man might at this period have been noted by a careful and minute observer. Delphine saw it, and exulted over it, laying to her soul the flattering unction that her witcheries were all-potent now, that the man had said to himself, "It is kismet!" and had bowed his head to what he felt powerless to resist. Judith saw it, and mourned over it, connecting it somehow in her own mind with odd volumes of Bentham, Locke, and James Mill, which she had more than once noted, as she passed his half-open study-door, lying among his numerous account-books on his writing-table; and she said in the depths of that aching, overstrained heart of hers:

"He is trying a new opiate now. He is drugging his soul as some men drug their bodies, and will be as hard to waken as any half-drunken sleeper."

It was a bitter thought. She felt as one might feel who, in a sinking ship, where a last chance for life depends upon the skill and courage of the seamen, sees the spirit-cask broken open, and the men, one and all, steeping their brains in drunken incapacity. There was she, watching, praying, striving, straining every mental and physical power she possessed to steer him clear of the rocks which threatened to make shipwreck of him. There was he, within, so to speak, an hour's sail of them, shutting his eyes calmly, and saying:

"Thank you; if it's all the same to you, I would rather not see them, and then it will come to pretty much the same as though they were not there."

Thus, at least, she interpreted the impassiveness, the indifference, with which at this period he surveyed Delphine's wildest vagaries and caprices; the calmly imperturbable manner in which of late he had fulfilled his duties as landlord of a large property and master of a fair-sized household; the utter lack of meaning or emotion in eye or mouth. His old startling restlessness of tone and odd abruptness of manner, which at times and by turns had terrified or pained Judith, were utterly gone. In their stead she noticed an evenness, a dryness, an emptiness of voice, look, manner, which could only belong to a man in whom all spiritual vitality were torpid or extinct.

And she, with heart and brain attuned to their utmost pitch, stood waiting, watching for an opportunity for one final, passionate appeal to his conscience!

After long thought she had decided that this was the one and only thing which lay in her power to do now. Other things, as time went on, might lie ready to her hand; but just now, in this dim light, and with eyes strained by tears and long watching, she could see but this one step to take. So she lay awake at nights wondering and wondering how best it could be taken; from the first thing in the morning when she sat down to the breakfast-table, till, prayers ended and good-nights said, she made her way in silence to her room, but one thought filled her brain—how to secure to herself and Wolf a brief ten minutes for quiet talk.

The thing was beset with difficulties all round. In the first place—there could be no doubt about it—Wolf had of late taken to deliberately avoiding her society whenever it was practicable for him to do so. If she went into a room and he was there alone, or with Delphine, he would at once make some excuse, and there and then disappear. He never offered to walk or drive with her now; did he see her in the garden as he returned to the house, he would at once take another path, or even go in by the servants' entrance—anything, so it seemed, sooner than meet her face to face, eye to eye.

In the second place, had he been most willing—nay, more, most desirous to secure a quiet talk with her, circumstances would have been against him. Every corner alike of house and garden seemed pervaded by Delphine's presence, or by that of her shadow, Olivette. Did one sit down with a book in a quiet corner anywhere, there would come without fail a sudden opening of an unexpected door, and Delphine would flit across the room to re-flit in another five minutes through another door, leaving behind her an uncomfortable, apprehensive feeling of her being somewhere close at hand, ready to appear at any unexpected moment; or, her voice would be heard singing in high-pitched keys adown corridors or across the hall as though she were coming, coming, and would soon appear; or, as one sat at an open window writing a letter, a shadow would fall across the paper—one would look up, and Delphine would be there smiling and sunny, or sullen and cloudy, as the case might be. Did one make a vehement essay for solitude, and seclude oneself with one's thoughts in a summer-house or some shady nook in the garden, there would come a rustling somewhere among the laurels and bays, and Olivette would be seen, sometimes with, sometimes without, her small charge by her side. Did one make an attempt for a quiet moonlight stroll on the terrace before doors and windows were shut for the night, there would surely come the sound of the opening of a casement overhead, and the sopranos of one or other of these restless women would fall athwart one's thoughts; or, it might be, perhaps, without so much as a whispered sound overhead, one would look up and find, with a start, one or perhaps two pairs of handsome, large-pupilled black eyes looking down on one with an expression in them not easy to read.

It was bewildering, it was distressing; the more so as the dreary, windy, winter days came creeping on apace, and Judith was compelled, whether she would or not, to recognise the fact that every one of them brought them all by so much the nearer to the wedding-day of Wolf and Delphine.

This had been at first, by an odd caprice of Delphine's, fixed for Christmas Eve.

"We shall then be far away in dear Paris or Rome," she had said, with her arm twined caressingly round Wolf's neck, and her full, dark eyes looking up into his dulled grey ones, "when your odious plum-puddings and mince-pies are being eaten. Heavens! what men and women can bring themselves to feed upon!"

Wolf had acquiesced in this arrangement, making no effort to free himself from her caressing white hand.

Of a truth, so he said to himself many times in the day now, in the path he had chosen to tread a thorn more or less could matter but little.

He announced the date of the wedding-day in the calmest and driest of voices to his mother the next time they met at table.

"So soon, Wolf?" was all Mrs. Reece's reply, in a tone neither complimentary nor congratulatory. And the thought in her heart as she said this was: "Well, if she is going to throw him over, she'll have to be quick about it. What a fool Wolf is to hurry matters forward so!"

Bryce happened to be in the room at the time the announcement was made, having come in on a mission from the servants' quarters. She came up to Wolf's side with a troubled look on her old face.

"Sir," she said, warningly, "if you must have the wedding-feast on Christmas Eve, you'll mind to have the empty chair put for the missing guest. No Reece for the last hundred years has made a feast on Christmas Eve without it."

"I do not understand," began Wolf in an indifferent tone.

Delphine came forward quivering with curiosity. The one weak point in this young person's composition was superstition. Her belief in ancient myth and legend, in the wildest of old wives' fables, was marvellous. It was possibly the only outlet her manner of life had left her for belief in the unseen and unknown. Her scepticism found continuous vent amid the proprieties and virtues of her fellow-creatures.

"Now what's this—who's the missing guest, I should like to know, and why must an empty chair be put for him?" she exclaimed, hurrying her words out with a forgetfulness of their ordinary accompaniment of arch glances and dimpling smiles unusual to her.

Bryce began to explain.

"It's only when a banquet's made on Christmas Eve. People often forget those who ought to be asked, and those whose hearts are right with their relatives and friends like to leave an empty chair for them, so that if they came in they would see they had been thought of. Once a Reece made a banquet on Christmas Eve, and forgot to put the chair—" She broke off abruptly.

"Well, what happened?" queried Delphine sharply.

"It was a feast given to all the tenants and servants on the estate, and they left out one who ought to have been there, the old toll-keeper of Llanrhaiadr gate," said Bryce, raising her voice to narrative pitch. "He was nearly ninety years of age, and they thought he was too old to get so far. But worst of all, they forgot to put the empty chair, and when in the middle of the feast the old man came in, hobbling and limping, there was no seat for him to be seen. So up he went straight to the squire and said: 'Squire, yesterday at midnight I looked out at my window and saw (for all the gate was shut) a whole procession of mourners and a hearse with black nodding plumes go through. A man followed a long way behind, weeping bitterly. I went up to him and said: "Master, whose corpse is that went through the gate a moment ago?" He turned and looked at me, and said: "The corpse of one who forgets the aged and poor." Squire, I didn't know who he meant till I came here today and found never a place left for me at table.' It all came true," here Bryce's voice dropped to a dismal whisper, "the squire was dead before the end of the week, and his corpse was carried along that very road, the old toll-keeper himself opening the gate to let it pass through."

Delphine had turned very white while the story was being told.

"Oh, you old raven!" she said, shrugging her shoulders, and turning her back on the old body. But, when she found herself once more alone with Wolf it was: "My Wolf, it shall not be Christmas Eve after all, nor any day this year, for on second thoughts it is an uneven number and uneven numbers don't serve me well. We will wait till the bright new year comes in, and then we will not say one word to anybody about it, but will creep up to London together, find out a nice little registry-office, just go in and sign our names, drive away and enjoy the most delicious of champagne lunches, and then off we'll go to the dearest, pleasantest city in the world—darling, diabolical Paris, where if such dreary things as corpses and hearses do exist, people at any rate are too polite to talk about them."

END OF VOLUME II

VOLUME III

I

"All things come to him who waits," said someone once, and Judith one day proved the truth of the saying. The opportunity for which she had watched, and waited, and longed suddenly and unexpectedly presented itself, and, quick as any wild bird darting on its prey, she seized it.

It happened in this wise. The day had been rough and blustering as days towards the end of October are apt to be; sunshine had come in fitful gleams; heavy gusts of wind had by turns dashed hail or rain against the panes. Towards evening, however, the wind fell, the sky cleared, and the hunter's moon rose high and bright over the mountains.

Mrs. Reece had gone straight to her room after dinner, saying she was tired and would have her coffee upstairs; Delphine making the drawing-room unendurable to Judith by incessant and highly melodramatic carolling, she wrapped a warm, thick shawl round her and went out into the garden. Finding Falstaff snuffing about the lawn, it occurred to her how much the old dog would enjoy a ramble in the fields beyond, and, without a thought for the lateness of the hour, she forthwith slipped out at a side gate.

The fields lay steeped in the pure silver light of the moon; beyond, the mountains loomed darkly out of the shadowy clouds. Falstaff went bounding hither and thither, delighted at his unlooked-for treat, giving now and again short, sharp, enquiring barks as he scented here a mole, there a rabbit. Judith, drawing her shawl tightly around her, leaned idly against a rough-barked elm, thinking her own thoughts.

There came the sound of footsteps drawing near—nearer.

"One of those dreadful women," she thought to herself; "inside or outside the house it is all one—there is no peace for them."

No such thing. Not Delphine nor Olivette, had they tied weights to their ankles, could have attained so majestic a tread as this. It was a man's, not a doubt, and there was he coming hurriedly down the gravel path as though he had a mission on hand. It was Wolf, and his mission was to search for Judith and bring her back to the house.

Judith started as he came up to her, but he gave her no time for exclamation.

"Child, what is this?" he cried. "What are you doing out here at this time of night? I was standing at my study window, and saw you go out by the side gate. Come in at once, or you'll be catching your death of cold."

Judith looked up at him drearily enough. Something in his voice at this moment recalled the pleading earnestness with which, as she had wept her heart out over Uncle Pierre's letter, he had cried: "Child, child, you must not give way like this. I cannot—cannot bear it!"

Ah, how far away that day seemed now! Then she had a something of hope in her heart for herself, for him. Now scarce a ghost of it remained.

And no wonder!

Possibly something of her thoughts showed in her face, as she remained silently leaning against the tree, making no effort to do his bidding, for he suddenly laid his hand upon her shoulder, and, looking right down into her white, tired face, exclaimed:

"Child, child, are you ill? Great Heavens! what can have happened to change you in this way? Can this be the Judith who came to the house little more than a year ago to be taken care of and made happy?"

The words seemed, as it were, startled out of him. For one brief moment the bonds of restraint he had laid upon himself were loosened.

Judith answered his look with the clearest and truest that human eyes could give.

"No," she said, in low, distinct tones, "I am not the same Judith who came to your house a little more than a year ago, and nothing will ever make me the same again."

"Child, child, you don't know what you are saying!" he cried, vehemently; "you will go from here to another and brighter life, and all this will be to you as though it had never been. It will pass out of your mind utterly—it must, it will—and you will lead the pure and happy life you deserve to lead. I say it must, it will be so!"

It seemed as though he reiterated the words himself to convince himself.

"So, then, I am shallow-hearted as well as of no use to my fellow-creatures?"

He caught at her words angrily.

"Use, use!" he repeated. "Why are you always wishing to be of use? It seems the one cry of your life. Would you have those who are sinking deep and deeper into the mire catch hold of your little hand to help them out simply because you are good enough to stretch it towards them?"

"I would. And so long as I have life and breath it will remain outstretched."

It was said without variation of voice, in the same low, distinct tones as before, she looking up into his face, he down into hers.

The night breeze swept by; a few yellow leaves fell from the old elm on Judith's thick shawl; the moon looked down upon them, quiet-eyed. She was shining down on many a pair of disconsolate lovers, no doubt—on many a sorrow-stricken, weary soul beside—but nowhere, by hillside or shady avenue, did her pure pale rays light up a face more white and haggard than Judith's, upturned to meet Wolf's, more fiercely forlorn than Wolf's, down-looking to meet Judith's.

But as he looked and looked, the fierceness died utterly out of his face, and only the forlornness remained. Once he opened his lips as though about to speak, then closed them resolutely; his eyes drooped before hers; he turned from her abruptly; made a few hasty strides up and down the moonlit field; came back to her side with face blank, calm, passionless as any masked mummer's might be.

"Come, Judith," he said quietly, "come in at once; we will talk no more of these things. I have succeeded in quieting—what shall we call it?—my soul, my nerves, or that inherited instinct we are pleased to designate conscience; I beg of you not to disturb it, and wrench from me the only chance of peace and quiet I may get to the end of my life. Let me alone, child; it is all I ask of you now—let me alone!"

He had drawn her arm through his while he was speaking, and was leading her now at a somewhat rapid pace towards the house.

Judith felt as though her last opportunity were slipping away from her. Speak now, or never, she must.

"I would wrench from you every chance of peace and quiet," she said, her voice scarcely above a whisper, "till you get the only peace that is real and lasting—the peace that comes from doing right."

He had swung back the iron gate for her to enter. They were now standing in the wide gravel-path that led straight up to the house. It lay steeped in moonlight like the fields outside, tesselated here and there with the shifting shadows of laurel and arbutus leaflets.

He paused with his hand on the gate.

"What is right?" he asked dreamily, absently. Something over eighteen hundred years ago Pilate once asked a similar question, and He, who held the secrets of life in His hand, gave him no answer. Judith showed less reticence.

Words rushed to her lips.

"What is right?" she repeated, her voice ringing out clear and strong. "What is light—what is colour? Not I, nor fifty others might be able to tell you what are the elements of either—what makes each what it is. Yet we know light when we see it, we know colour when we see it. We do not need to be told, this is night, this is morning; this is blue, this is red."

"Ah, you misunderstood my question," said Wolf in the same dreamy, self-absorbed tone. "I did not ask by what faculty in our nature we discern what is right; mine was a practical, not a psychological question. I meant to ask, what is the criterion of a moral act? What, in fact, is the moral standard? What circumstance, if I may so put it, decides an action to be right, and not wrong?"

Judith stared at him for a moment blankly. Had he in very truth so beclouded his moral sense that he was obliged to go to another to be guided in his discernment of good or evil; or was this a genuine, unassumed effort to sift right from wrong, lies from truth?

"Do you mean to tell me," she asked, her brain going round, her eyes wide open, "that you actually do not know truth or justice from falsehood and dishonesty?"

His face was turned from her, so that she could not see it. He brought out his words in the same slow, faraway tone as before.

"Truth! justice!" he repeated; "what are they, after all, but means to an end, and that end, men's happiness? They are not the end themselves. Now, it seems to me, if I can reach that end by a shorter road I am justified in taking it—yes, amply justified."

Judith's heart went beating harder and faster. Was not this mere sophistry? Was it—could it by any possibility be the honest utterance of an honest heart?

She tried to keep the sound of tears out of her voice as she asked a question in return:

"Would you for one instant weigh the happiness of a lifetime against the evildoing of an hour? Would you weigh truth and justice against a lifetime of sorrow and self-denial?"

They were walking along the gravel-path now, towards the house. He, still keeping his face turned from her, continued in the same slow, dreamy tones:

"The infliction of pain and the surrender of pleasure can only be justified by being the means of procuring a greater amount of happiness

CATHERINE LOUISA PIRKIS

than was lost. Now, if I, by a certain course of action, can give to a larger number of persons a greater amount of happiness than they before possessed, I say, let that course of action be painful to me or pleasant, I am perfectly justified in taking it."

Judith stood still in the middle of the moonlit path. She laid her hand upon his arm; look at her he must and should.

"Tell me," she said in a low, tremulous voice, "when you talk of making the happiness of other persons, do you mean good persons or evil persons? For remember, what means pleasure and comfort to the one, means anguish and heartache to the other."

He turned and faced her in the moonlight; he could not help it, for she stood right athwart his path. Surely never living man before wore so troubled and forlorn a look.

"Ah, now you bring us back to our starting-point," he said. "Who are the good persons, who are the evil? What is good—what is evil?"

Judith struck her hands together passionately with a bitter cry.

"Is this night or is this morning? Is the light in which we are stepping now rosy and golden, or is it pure pale white?" she asked vehemently.

The troubled look did not leave his face, though a ghost of a smile—a wan, wintry sort of thing—seemed to flit over it as he answered:

"What if I am colour-blind, Judith, without perception of the difference there is between rosy-yellow and pure pale white?"

"Then yours would be a self-made colour-blindness, for you are not one of those who were born blind," she answered in the same vehement tone as before; "only when the time comes, and Christ passes by, do not sit by the wayside crying, 'Jesus, Master, have mercy on me!' for He will not hear you—I say, He will not—will not hear you."

His troubled eyes met her eager, passionate gaze.

"I am not likely to do that; no, whatever else I do I shall not do that;" and there was that in his voice which told her he meant what he said.

They had reached the terrace now. There came the sound of a window opening overhead, and Delphine's soft voice followed immediately.

"My Wolf," she said caressingly, "I want some sweet-scented flowers to put under my pillow. See, I will drop you my handkerchief; you can fill it with something fragrant, and send it up to me. Ah, Miss Judith is there! You have been having a moonlight walk. Is it not sweet of me not to be jealous? But I know I can trust my Wolf!"

Judith made no reply. She felt suffocating, as though even the power of drawing her breath were being denied her.

She somehow made her way into the house, groping for each step, for her tears were blinding her.

Once in her own room she flung herself on the floor, wringing her hands in her despair. Why, this was worst of all! She had absolutely thrown away her last chance! She had meant to plead, entreat, warn, beseech; instead she had argued, dogmatised, denounced. Heaven help them! How would it all end now?

II

Winter set in early that year, and brought with it a terrible return of rheumatism to poor Mrs. Reece. Stairs became an impossibility to her; she was almost confined to a big easy-chair in her own room with the worthy but somewhat archaic doctor from Llanrhaiadr (everything at Llanrhaiadr was worthy and archaic) in daily attendance.

Wolf, Delphine, and Judith made but a sorry trio downstairs. They ate their meals almost in silence, and separated so soon as they were at an end. If only little Bertie had been allowed to take his place with them at table, his childish prattle might in some sort have lightened the dreary monotony. But no; he was strictly confined to his own quarters, emerging thence only for his morning walk with Olivette, his afternoon drive with Delphine.

Judith spent as much of her time as possible upstairs with Mrs. Reece, declining any and every friendly overture on Delphine's part with a frigid persistence that was unmistakable. Delphine, however, never seemed to feel herself snubbed. She would shrug her shoulders, lift her eyebrows, and repeat her little friendlinesses on every possible occasion. As for Wolf, he had once more drawn a line of demarcation between Judith and himself, which neither he nor she showed the slightest inclination to step over. Save at meals they never met; and when on one or two occasions Delphine was absent in London for a few days, he sent each time a polite message to Judith by the old butler, requesting her not to wait luncheon or dinner for him, as pressure of business compelled him to spend the day in his study.

These visits of Delphine to London increased in frequency as the winter set in. Judith could not say why or wherefore, but somehow in her own thoughts she connected them with the sailor-like individual who had manifested such a surprising interest in Delphine's matrimonial arrangements. Yet Delphine never failed to give an ostensible and very plausible reason for each one of her sudden flights. Sometimes she would appear at the breakfast-table saying:

"Bertie has absolutely nothing to wear. I must run up to London and get him a few things;" and on her return to Plas-y-Coed, Bertie never failed to shine out brilliantly in renewed velvets or satins. Or on another occasion it would be: "My Wolf, I want another pair of ponies;

those creatures of yours have hides, not skins, they will go only when they please, and as they please. Now, I want two thoroughbreds, all fire, all life, all go. There is a sale on at Tattersall's. I must go and see if I can get what I want there."

And this visit to London was followed in due course by the arrival of a pair of small-footed, straight-limbed roans, with fiery eyes and a bright dash of red about the mane and tail.

Judith, while in a measure rejoicing in the quietude the household gained during Delphine's brief absences, could not help a secret feeling of dread as to what they might bring in their train. By this time she had learned to distrust every look of Delphine's, every word she uttered, and, could she have read her thoughts, she would have distrusted them also, feeling sure there would be an under-current even there which would run counter to the upper.

Mrs. Reece, growing irritable and inquisitive, after the manner of elderly persons confined through ill-health to a few square feet of boards, put many questions to Judith about Delphine's repeated journeys.

"Surely she must have friends in London by this time," surmised the old lady, "if she hadn't when she first came. Does she go to an hotel, I wonder, or what can she do with herself careering about all alone? And do you think, my dear," this very earnestly, "that Wolf pays her expenses, and gives her money for all the extravagances she brings back with her? Now those ponies; I should like particularly to know about them. Are they Wolf's or are they this young lady's?—that's what I should like to know."

Judith confessed herself unable to give the required information. Mrs. Reece went off on another tack.

"Well now, there's something else that troubles me, and no one seems able to tell me anything on the matter, though I speak of it to Bryce regularly every morning, when she comes for my keys. That is, what is going to be done with that little child, that bad-tempered little creature who nearly dragged my head off my shoulders—he'll grow up just such another as his aunt, take my word for it, my dear. Now I want to know if he's to be a fixture here as well as the aunt, and what they mean to do with him when they're off on their honeymoon—that is, if there is to be a honeymoon, which, all things considered, I'm rather disposed to doubt. Will they leave him here, with that sullen, bad-tempered maid, whom none of the servants like, she carries her head so high, or will they take him off to Paris with them, or Rome, or wherever they mean to go?"

Again Judith shook her head.

"Why not ask Wolf himself what he means to do with the child?" she suggested.

The words were scarcely off her lips before the door opened and Wolf made his appearance. He had a letter in his hand.

"I have brought you good news from Oscar," he said, his face wearing the nearest approach to gladness of which it was capable. "He has passed the preliminary exam. well, and has been well received by his chief that is to be. Altogether his letter is the brightest we have had from him yet."

Mrs. Reece stretched out her hand for the letter.

"Judith will read it to me presently," she said; "but, Wolf, there is something I am very anxious to ask you about. In fact, it was on my lips just as you came in. What are you going to do with the small child who I hear—for he has tremendous screaming and fighting fits at times—is still in the house? Does he come as part of the aunt's trousseau that we shall have to give permanent house-room to, or has he other relatives who will charge themselves with him?"

It was evident, since Bertie's onslaught on her cap and spectacles, that the old lady's feelings towards him had suffered a slight modification.

Wolf's face grew dark again.

"I ought to have told you," he said. "I intend to adopt Bertie—to treat him as my own child. He will hold the place of a son in the house."

Then he laid down Oscar's letter, and cut short his mother's exclamations by at once leaving the room.

"So," thought Judith, "this is the shorter road he has found to secure to himself and a greater number of persons a greater amount of happiness than has been lost to them."

That same night—or, rather, between two and three o'clock of the following morning—Judith was aroused by old Bryce creeping stealthily into her room, and standing by her bedside.

"What is it?" asked Judith, starting up from a troubled sleep,—all her sleep was troubled in those days. "What has happened?"

"Oh, nothing much; don't alarm yourself," said the old body composedly, shutting tight the door behind her, although she had herself ascertained the fact that every other soul in the house was safe in the arms of Morpheus. "Only, after they—you know who I mean, miss—went up to their rooms tonight, I listened for a time outside their door, and I thought you might like to know what I heard."

"Yes?" This interrogatively.

Delphine had returned from London that afternoon. Judith had dreaded what was coming from the moment she had heard her exclaim in her loudest soprano as she entered the hall:

"Oh, my Wolf, I have had such a glorious visit this time! London seemed at its gayest and best. Ah, what a grand, delicious city it is!"

"It's nothing much I have to tell," Bryce went on; "they spoke in whispers, I could only catch a word or two here and there. Once she said—Miss Delphine, I mean—'He was furious. I had much ado to quiet him; but I managed it after a fashion.' Do you understand what that means, Miss Judith?"

"Yes," answered Judith, after a moment of thought; "I think I can understand to whom she referred."

It seemed to her that the "he" and the "him" in this case must, without a doubt, mean the sailor-like individual whom in thought she had connected with Delphine's visits to London.

"And then they talked and talked—oh, for more than an hour, and I listened, and listened, but could hear nothing, they spoke so low, till at last Miss Delphine gave her long, strange laugh, and said: 'Well, one thing's certain—that business will be over and done with by the end of the year.' What can that mean, Miss Judith?"

What indeed! Judith's brain felt stunned for the moment, then ached dully with the thought of unknown terrors which she dared not put into words.

"Give me time to think, Bryce; it means something terrible, I haven't a doubt. Go away, now; leave me alone," and she pressed her hot eyeballs with her cold hands, vainly trying to shape the indefinable fears that came thronging upon her into something definite and tangible.

Bryce made one step towards the door, retraced it, and came back to the bedside.

"Miss Judith," she said, "you did promise me you would get back that evil ring of yours from Mr. Wolf, if you could. I'm sure we shall none of us know what peace is till it's gone to the bottom of the blessed stream."

"Oh, go away, Bryce—go away—don't torment me; I'm trying to think," moaned Judith.

"Well, Miss Judith, if you won't do it yourself, you might let me try what I can do. If you'd give me his diamond ring I'd take it to him and say you wanted yours back again," contended the old woman.

"Take the diamond, then—it's in that little drawer of the toilette-table—and do what you like. Only go away at once, and leave me to think," insisted Judith.

Bryce victorious departed content.

III

O ver for certain by the end of the year!" The words kept repeating themselves in Judith's brain with the iteration of a minute-bell all that day and the next.

It was a bitter morning. Judith sat in her own room with her feet on the fender, shivering, in spite of a huge, crackling wood-fire.

Outside, a furious east wind beat against the panes; the old trees, creaking and groaning, tossed their bare, brown arms like so many weird, evil prophetesses to a hazy, leaden sky. In the lulls of the blast one could hear the rush and tumble of the cataract in the wood, swollen by late heavy-falling rains into a dashing, swirling flood.

It was dreary enough outside; it was drearier still within; and Judith's thoughts on this particular morning piled up the dreariness tenfold—a thousandfold.

"Over for certain by the end of the year!" There was no getting the dismal words out of her ears, fight against them as she would. Why, who could say what might or might not be over by the end of the year? Health might be gone—fortune, friends, happiness, even life itself. Who could tell? No one, unless they had taken certain measures to produce certain inevitable results.

There came at this moment the sound of a window opening overhead, followed by a smart rattling fall of something on the terrace-flags below. Why, surely not! That could not be Delphine scattering her sweatmeats as usual to welcome little Bertie on his return from his morning walk? No one with a grain of human feeling would have sent out a fragile little child to face this cutting, blustering gale. All-apprehensive, she went to the window, and looked out. There was little Bertie, creeping, not bounding, up the gravel-path, closely followed by Olivette. He looked white and nipped, as well he might, and seemed disinclined to stop to gather up the tempting-looking bon-bons which lay scattered on the stones.

Olivette, however, gathered them together for the child, popping one now and again into his mouth. How ridiculous it was of them to feed the poor child in this way with sugar! Sooner or later it would tell on him. No wonder he looked so white and puny.

"Over for certain by the end of the year." Once more the words seemed to repeat themselves, and Judith, looking down into Bertie's pale, pitiful face, seemed all in a minute to take in their meaning.

What were those sweetmeats? Why did these women force them upon the child when he was so evidently disinclined for them? These and a hundred other questions suggested themselves in a rapid succession, resolving themselves one and all at last into the simple and most practical one of—What was to be done now? What could she do for the best?

Judith was by nature no plotter, and it may very well be doubted whether, under any pressure of circumstances, she could ever have played the part successfully. Only one idea suggested itself to meet the exigency of the moment—to go downstairs to Wolf, now in his study, say to him, "Bertie is ill; you must have a doctor at once."

This she accordingly prepared to do. On the landing outside she met old Dr. Williamson on his way to Mrs. Reece's room; she asked him not to leave the house till she had seen him again, as there was another patient for him; then on she went to Wolf's study, knocked at the door, and asked if she might come in.

"Come in," said Wolf, with a slight accent of surprise, and Judith went in to find him, not as usual at his writing-table, surrounded with account and other books, but in an easy-chair on one side of the wide fireplace, while Delphine, with a leopard-skin thrown gracefully across her knees, reclined in a low chair on the other.

Why—why, what was this? Not five minutes ago this woman had been in her room over Judith's, throwing sweetmeats out of the window! Had she a dual existence, and with one life mounted perpetual guard over Wolf, while with the other she carried out her own evil machinations?

For one moment Judith faltered. Only for one moment, however; the next she had gone quietly up to Wolf, and said:

"I am very sorry to disturb you, but little Bertie is ill, I am sure, and as Dr. Williamson is here, I thought you might like him to see the child."

It was a bold speech to make in the presence of Bertie's aunt, protectress, and guardian.

Wolf, who had risen from his chair as she spoke, stared at her blankly. Delphine's eyes gave one lurid flash, as of lightning out of a dark cloud. She had some Christmas-roses and a few holly-leaves on her lap; she twirled them together into a little bouquet, and tossed them into the clear, blazing fire. Then she laughed:

"Ah! how it crackles and spits fire!" Then she turned to Judith abruptly: "My Bertie ill, did you say—my darling, my treasure? Ah, why has no one said this before to me? Ring the bell, my Wolf—ring the bell, and have the little one in. Ah, if he should die, if he should die, if he should die! Ah, ring the other bell, Miss Judith, and send for the doctor at once. How good and kind you are to every living soul who crosses your path! Young men or maidens, old men or children, it's all one to you, you open your heart to them all!"

Judith turned her back on her. How could Wolf stand there, listening to her, and not feel the marrow frozen in his bones?

"Will you ring the bell, or shall I?" she asked.

Wolf rang the bell mutely, and an order was given for Bertie to be brought and a message to be taken requesting Dr. Williamson's presence in the study.

"We shall never be thankful enough to you, Miss Judith, for your kind, watchful care, shall we, my Wolf?" said Delphine in her sweet, low tones. But her eyes said: "All right, Miss Judith, one to you this time, two to me next."

Bertie, in Olivette's arms, entered the room simultaneously with the doctor.

The little fellow seemed scared by the grave faces he saw gathered about him. He fought the doctor when he tried to take him in his arms; he shrank in positive terror from Wolf's outstretched hand; but he smiled, though somewhat tearfully, as his eyes rested on Judith's face. It ended with Olivette whispering something in his ear, which caused him to stand silent and submissive in the middle of the room, looking round him with a somewhat startled air.

The doctor surveyed the child keenly, remarked that he was not looking as a child of his years should, put many questions to Olivette, which were answered curtly and to the point, a few to Delphine, which elicited a touching little history of her sister's fragile health and early death, and of the remarkable likeness that existed in many respects between Bertie and his dead mother.

The doctor grew inquisitive over the boy's dietary.

"There is no disease that I can detect," he said, after using his stethoscope to his heart's content, "but there are febrile symptoms I do not like, and which possibly arise from gastric disturbance."

Judith came forward.

"I think," she said, fixing her eyes on Delphine, not on the doctor, "Bertie has too many bon-bons."

"Bon-bons!" exclaimed Dr. Williamson; "they must be stopped at once. They lie at the bottom of the half of children's diseases. To some children sweets are simply poison—slow, subtle, but nevertheless sure. I must beg of you, madam," turning to Delphine, "to put your sweets in their proper place—behind the fire. The little fellow will soon get back his roses then."

"Ah, dear Miss Judith, how kind, how thoughtful of you! you put your finger on the weak point at once," murmured Delphine in the same sweet tones as before, as the doctor rose to take his leave. But her eyes once more flashed an odd light, and said: "Two to you this time, Miss Judith: four to me next."

Judith made no reply, but left the room after the doctor.

Bertie was saved this time, she felt, but for how long?

Finding herself watched, detected, thwarted, would Delphine give up her evil designs, or would the wicked spirit that ruled her only suggest more subtle forms of iniquity? Judith much feared the latter. She could not picture to herself Delphine sitting down, quiet and submissive, under any defeat, small or great. She racked her brain, vainly endeavouring to think of extra safeguards for the defenceless little one. She would rouse Mrs. Reece, if possible, to take an interest in the child. She would entreat Wolf to give him a new nurse. Yet, somehow, her heart misgave her as to the success she would be likely to meet with in either endeavour. Mrs. Reece was resolute in her likes and dislikes. She had evidently, since the little fellow had declined the honour of her friendship, shut her heart against him; and this door, once locked, was not easy to open, as Judith had found from experience.

And as for Wolf—ah me! her heart somehow went down like quicksilver on a rainy day as she thought of a certain strange light which had shone in his eyes of late as they had rested on Delphine, and which seemed, to her fancy, to tell the bitter truth that he had listened so long to the voice of the siren, that his senses were absolutely becoming enthralled and spell-bound by it.

That night, Bryce once again stood beside Judith's couch and whispered a brief report.

"I haven't much to tell you, Miss Judith," she said; "they spoke low, as they always do, and she—Miss Delphine, that is—laughed more than ever I heard her before. The only words of sense I could make out of it all was that, next time, she would take care that you were out of the house. Yes, Miss Judith, those were her very words, whatever they may mean!"

IV

S o the old year spun itself out, and Delphine's prophecy remained unfulfilled. So far as anyone at Plas-y-Coed could see, nothing but itself came to an end at midnight on the 31st of December.

Little Bertie, on strictly regulated diet, blossomed out in renewed health, and Dr. Williamson would have ceased his attendance on him had it not been for Delphine's earnest entreaties that he should "interview" him at least every other day in the week.

"For my darling is so fragile, doctor," she pleaded; "an east wind, even, might carry him off. Great Heavens! what I suffer sometimes when I bend over him as he sleeps, and see how terribly like he is to his dear, dead mother. Ah, promise me, doctor, to keep your eye on him all through this bitter winter. What should I do without him, my darling, my treasure, my all?"

Of course Dr. Williamson yielded to her entreaties, and went away thinking to himself how rare it was to find such truly maternal devotion, coupled with attractions so many and varied that most possessors of them would have deemed themselves thereby exonerated from the practice of the minor mundane virtues.

Most people, thrown into close daily contact with Delphine, were compelled, sooner or later, to yield to her eerie fascinations. At first, generally, they were startled by her fantastic unconventionalities; it might be, even terrified by odd caprices of voice, look, manner, which baffled alike experience and reason. Little by little, however, the witchery of her dark, changeful beauty, her trained grace of action, would make itself apprehended, and people who began their acquaintance with her fearfully, wonderingly, would, inch by inch, find their wonder growing into admiration, their bewilderment merging into infatuation.

Hers was a veritable *beauté de diable*. A subtle, maddening, intoxicating kind of thing that set men's brains on fire, dazzled their eyes till they refused perforce to take stock of aught that alloyed or blemished such a combination of loveliness, led them *ignis-fatuus* like over marsh and mire in pursuit, left them stranded and weak at last, incapable alike of following the path they had chosen or returning to that they had left. A man with a clear conscience or with a strong human love holding his heart, might have opposed coat-of-mail to her poisoned arrows, but woe to the poor wight who, destitute of these, dared risk the fray! If he came out of it something less than the remnant of a man, he would only have his own hardihood to thank for it.

Wolf, preoccupied, conscience-palsied, brain-weighted, had taken, as he had mapped out his somewhat troubled course, no count of these deceptive quicksands which lay right athwart his path. Other dangers farther ahead he had noted and sought to avoid, but these at his very feet he had, in his far-sightedness, overlooked. Had anyone, in the early days of his fatal intimacy with Delphine, whispered words of warning, they would have fallen on dulled ears. Strong in his love for Judith, he would have laughed to scorn the idea that in any other eyes than hers he would care to read the light of love.

Later on, as time and circumstance put Judith far and farther out of his reach, he would still have scouted the notion that any other than she could ever enter in and fill that great, empty heart of his. But now, as the desolate winter days went slowly creeping by, somehow he began to find that a soft, vibrating voice saying tenderly, "My Wolf—oh, my Wolf!" had a weird fascination for him, and that a pair of dark, dangerous, changeful black eyes were beginning to chase from his memory the pure, clear light of a certain pair of hazel ones.

Yet, so paradoxical was this man becoming in his moods, when one day old Bryce went to him, bringing back his diamond ring, and asking for Judith's bloodstone in return, he stared at her blankly at first, furiously afterwards, as though she had asked him to pluck out a right eye or cut off a right hand.

"If Miss Judith wants her ring, let her come to me and ask me for it," he thundered; "only to her asking will I give it up."

Then a change swept over his face. He went penitently up to the old woman and took her by the arm.

"Look here, Bryce," he said in a voice that trembled with the restraint he put upon it, "you are old, and I am, I suppose, scarcely yet to be counted with the middle-aged. For all that I haven't the least doubt but what I shall go down into the earth before you. Now I charge you solemnly"—here his hand tightened upon her arm till it gripped her like a vice—"when I lie in my coffin you yourself come to my side, see that this ring is on my finger, and that it goes into the grave with me."

Then he had released her, gone straight into his study, and with Delphine's hand in his, and a Baedecker open before them, had planned out a deliciously enjoyable wedding-tour through the south of Europe.

When the new year dawned, and that "old, antediluvian, Time," set to work winding-up, cleaning, regulating, and starting afresh all his half worn-out clocks, Judith set herself to face steadily two events which every minute that ran out of the aforesaid old clocks brought nearer to her. One was Wolf's marriage with Delphine, the other was her father's return to England and her consequent departure from the Reece household.

Both events she found difficult to realise. Though she said to herself, at least a hundred times a day, "He will soon be wholly hers, body and soul," she could not bring herself to believe the words as she spoke them; she might as well have talked to herself of the great day of judgment, of the sun being turned into darkness, of the moon into blood—as well could she bring before her mind in grand, distorted picturesqueness the one event as the other.

Then, too, as she read her father's kindly, loving letters, his lavish promises of the good things he meant to shower upon her in the days to come, his glowing pictures of a wealthy, peaceful home, where care and sorrow would be barred and bolted out, were equally difficult of realisation. Everything in the future seemed to her blurred, misty, indistinct; only the dreary, living present seemed actual and true. In this she felt her life centred; with it, as it slipped from her view and her grasp, she felt as though her life must depart.

On New Year's Day, a dreary portent for the young year, there came to her a troubled, weary letter from Uncle Pierre. It was dated from Pekin some two months previously:

"My Child," so he wrote

"This will be the last letter I shall send to you from this place. I am ordered by my bishop, who is the head of this mission, to go into retreat, first at Palermo, afterwards at Versailles. So I go. Into silence I go, my child, for my voice as preacher and teacher on this earth will be heard no more. My superiors tell me, and I bow to what they say, that of late I have erred in my teaching, that I have spoken not with the voice of the Church, but with the voice of my own heart. Ah me! that voice seemed so like the voice of God to me, I was forced to give utterance to it! Of late it was so loud, so supreme to me, I could hear no other. So I speak and preach no more. But I pray, my child, I pray none the less for all poor suffering souls, for all poor sorrowing ones, for you, my Judith, my well-beloved child, that soon, face to face in the Father's kingdom, we may clasp hands that will never need to be lifted in prayer again.

Your uncle,
PIERRE

Judith crept away into silence and solitude with her letter to hide her tears.

For the matter of that, however, she might just as well have stayed where she was. None would have uttered a word of remonstrance had she washed away her eyesight with her crying. There was no one to seat himself by her side now and say pitifully: "Child, child, you must not give way like this; I cannot—cannot bear it!"

V

Delphine's trousseau seemed to give her a good deal of trouble about the beginning of the year. She made frequent visits to London, returning from each visit, if possible, more blithe and radiant than before; also, if the truth be spoken, a trifle more exacting of attention from Wolf, a shade more erratic and fantastic in her manner of conducting herself towards the other members of the household. Wolf, so she decreed, was to escort her to the station at Pen Cwellym, she driving her fiery little ponies; Wolf was to meet her when she came back; Wolf was to desert the family dinner-table and dine alone with her on the evening of her return; Wolf was to sit with her in the drawing-room afterwards, or in the rooms she had specially dedicated to the shrine of nicotine, whence in addition to the highly perfumed fragrance of her cigarettes would issue the wildest strains of Spanish canzonets or Italian bravura, or occasionally the most weird and mournful of Swiss or German lullabys. At one time one might fancy a whole troupe of half-mad prima-donnas held wild carnival within; at another that some solitary sea-maiden was mourning, to the time and tune of the waves, her lover's death, or else soothing him to slumber with a siren's lullaby.

Mrs. Reece, imprisoned in her own room, naturally saw and heard but little of all this. She had taken into her head the comfortable belief that sooner or later Delphine would throw Wolf over, and when elderly ladies of resolute temper get sturdy notions into their heads they are somewhat difficult to uproot.

"My dear," she would say to Judith on every occasion of Delphine's visits to London, "do you think she'll come back this time? Has she taken anything extra with her? Does the maid seem to be packing up?"

As for Judith, she felt herself daily shrinking more and more from the society of both Wolf and Delphine. How it would all end not she nor any other living soul could by any possibility have averred. As before, she could not see one hand's breadth in front of her; she only felt that clouds—veritable thunderclouds—were encompassing them all, and that sooner or later they must burst. Her former fatigue of heart had left her now; she no longer mourned even to herself, "We are so tired, my heart and I;" she felt herself ever on the alert, as though her very life were merged in her senses—in those at least of seeing and hearing, for her powers of speech just then appeared to have well-nigh deserted her.

So the winter hours went limping past, haggard, wry-faced, joyless things, every one of them; each, with a terribly strong family likeness to the other; each, if possible, a little more of a laggard than the last. How they all got through that winter Judith never knew. Hopelessly, interminably, it dragged its slow length along, fighting, so it seemed to her, harder and harder for its life, as its days drew towards their end, till at length, in a terrific struggle and out burst of rain, hail, sleet, east wind, and ice, it died hard in the very bosom of spring.

Spring, regnant once more, greening every lane, tree, hedge, field, ditch, brought no promise of hope this year to Judith's heart. It brought but a scanty store also for poor Mrs. Reece, whose rheumatism showed no signs of succumbing to old Dr. Williamson's lotions or unremitting attention. Her health began to suffer from her lack of bodily exercise; with her health, her spirits sank by a degree or two; she became less confident of Delphine's elopement with some unheard-of stranger; she grew fretful and irritable at the mention of the word India, for the double reason that it recalled to her the fact that Oscar would soon be departing thither, and that Colonel Wynne would soon be returning thence and claiming his daughter.

Also, about this time, another circumstance added somewhat to her melancholy; poor old Falstaff, her faithful friend and companion for so many years, overcome by age and infirmities, died at her very feet, his head resting on her footstool.

"The ill-mannered brute!" cried Delphine, when she heard of this, clasping her hands on top of her head and sinking languidly into a rocking-chair; "he should have gone away into a corner to die. No one should have the effrontery to die in public. No living soul shall see me in my death-struggles. I'll answer for that! Fancy some half-dozen people staring down on one, watching one's eyes getting glassy, and one's limbs rigid! No; when I die you shall see me as I am today—you shall look for me tomorrow!" and from this expression of sentiment she glided, according to her wont, into the barcarolle from Masaniello, that, in its turn, giving place to snatches of airs from Don Giovanni, an opera for which she evinced a most marked affection.

Possibly about the best thing the dreary new year had to bring to the Reece family, was continued good tidings of and from Oscar. His letters were little by little going back to their old tone of careless good-nature, and easy bad grammar. Now that he had forced himself to learn the irremediableness of his sorrow, he was evidently setting himself to face and fight it manfully. Life is all paradoxes; the irreparable is most easily repaired, the unconquerable (even death itself) conquered.

Towards the end of winter he had brought himself to talk almost hopefully of his Indian appointment; towards the end of spring he was growing absolutely impatient for the time for sailing. He wrote long (for him, that is) loving letters to his mother, to Wolf, to Judith, and even went so far as to pen a few fragmentary missives to Delphine, whom he was evidently trying to bring himself to look upon as a future member of the family.

Delphine made very merry over these slight epistles in the solitude of her own room; the manifest effort with which they were written amused her, the little final note of sadness, with which some of them concluded, stirred her contempt.

"Here's Narcissus again doing a Niobe," she said, making the latest received into a pellet, and throwing it at Olivette's head.

But Olivette, occupied in reading a letter of her own, accorded her sister but a scanty attention.

"Oh, that's from your Narcissus, I suppose?" Delphine went on, determined to have an audience. "Oh, ah—h, what a much pleasanter world this would be if Narcissuses were extinct."

"Including your own, I suppose?" retorted Olivette derisively.

"My dear, I have no Narcissus, I have no patience with the tribe—a Polypheme, if you like. If you had but seen him this evening, as I sang to him, and he stood just under the lamp—ah, so grey, and wrinkled, and ugly, yet so grand! No, no, you may keep your Narcissus, and enjoy him if you will, my dear; give me a Cyclops—a Cyclops I can chain, and drive half mad, and let go and beckon back again. Ah, that's a sort of thing worth doing," and a low, long laugh trilled forth once more.

Olivette folded her letter and put it by.

"There's something here you'll like to hear," she said a little sullenly, for Delphine's manner of speaking of her lover invariably ruffled her temper.

"Ah, Steve, I suppose, has added another acre to his cottage!" queried Delphine indifferently.

"No such thing, Steve has sold his cottage, and is off to Mexico. He has bought a farm out there for next to nothing. But that wasn't what I thought would interest you, it was something about Phil Munday."

"About Phil Munday! What?" and Delphine suddenly awakened to an unmistakable interest in Olivette's letter.

"He says that Phil is wanted by the police at Montreal. Before he came over to England it seems he was for about three months working as letter-carrier in the town, a number of letters containing money were missed, and—"

"Ah, bravo, *bravissimo!* I knew something would turn up, and it has."

And Delphine, starting from her chair, jumping at least two feet from the ground, alighting on the tips of her toes as only a practised dancer can. Then she went close to her sister, and breathlessly put a whole string of questions.

"When, where, how had this thing happened? How did Steve know of it? Could it certainly be brought home to Phil Munday? When would Steve write again?"

Olivette shook her head in reply to each one. Steve had written on the eve of starting for Mexico; when he would write again she did not know. All he said was he had heard it rumoured that the police were after Phil Munday for robbing the post-bags.

Delphine grew grave, speaking in jerky whispers.

"You must find out the truth for me. If I can but handcuff him now—or threaten to do so, better still—it will keep him quiet. But I must know more. I mustn't try for a grand throw, and spoil my game. No, I will not say one word till I am sure. I must just keep him quiet with promises. I have told him my Wolf and I quarrel so dreadfully, if I made the attempt now I should be at once detected, and I have told him St. Judith must be out of the house before I can do anything—"

"Yes," interrupted Olivette with an air of decision; "St. Judith must be out of the house before you do anything, or she'll spoil your game, not a doubt. When does she go?"

"The father is expected some time in June, not before. Well, this is February. I have four months to keep him quiet; it will be hard work, and will take a lot of spare cash, for he gets more ravenous every time I see him. Ah well, my Wolf is generous. No matter what I ask I always have."

"It seems to me, if you go on at this rate, you'll ruin your Wolf, and have nothing left worth playing for. You mustn't forget between you the two thousand pounds you are to pay me."

"My dear, you are not likely to let me forget. But you must earn it, remember. It strikes me it'll take close upon another two thousand to keep Phil Munday quiet for four months."

"Couldn't the girl some way be got out of the house sooner?"

Delphine shook her head.

"If she went out of the house tomorrow, what could I do till I have my blow ready? Between ourselves, I'm not sorry the sweetmeat business was a failure. I'm not so sure but what at the very last the Beast might have turned rusty, and refused the bribe I meant to offer. He might have been obstinate, and insisted on my marrying him, after all, and—and getting rid of Wolf. But now, if this is only true, I have the whip-hand of him, and he shall know it. Now find out for me, as quickly as possible, all you can, By June—by midsummer, say—I shall be ready; the girl will be gone, the imp disposed of. Ah, how glorious!"

She spoke off abruptly for a moment.

"Hark! Did you hear anything—anyone move outside the door?"

For a few minutes they both listened intently, then their talk fell into whispers.

Bryce, standing by Judith's bedside, aroused her between one and two o'clock that same night.

"I am sure they are sisters, those two," she said, nodding her old head wisely; "and I'm sure they've been on the stage, both of them."

"That does not interest me," said Judith coldly. "I have no wish to know who or what they are. Is there anything else you have to tell me?"

"They've made up their minds to do something—what, I don't know, but they won't attempt it till you are out of the house. They seem more afraid of you than of any mortal soul."

"Yes? Was that all you heard, Bryce?"

"All," sighed Bryce; "they talked so low, and the walls that side are so thick. On the other they are nothing but lath and plaster, and one might hear everything. Ah, if I dared go through the tapestry-room one night and go along the outer passage—"

"What's that?" asked Judith sharply. "Why, Bryce, you know as well as I do that the tapestry-room is bricked up."

Bryce laughed.

"On this side, Miss Judith. They didn't know—not one of the men who did the work here, one half that I could have told them. The tapestry-room has three entrances. There's a door inside one of the cupboards in my room (the housekeeper's room, I mean, miss), which opens on to a flight of stairs that leads right up to a door at the back of the tapestry bed. No one knew of that, Miss Judith, and I wasn't going to tell them. Why should I? It may be, when the right master comes into the house, he won't choose to have his grandfather's room bricked up in that fashion as though it were a tomb."

"Go on, Bryce. That is one entrance to the room; that makes two we know of. Now where is the third, and where does it lead?"

"The third, Miss Judith, is inside a cupboard that is on one side of the fireplace in the tapestry-room; it opens on a narrow passage which runs just outside Miss Delphine's room. Her wall that side is thin—very thin, one could hear a pin fall on the floor."

"Ah-h! Does any one in the house know of these entrances to the tapestry-room but yourself?"

"Not a soul, Miss Judith. All the servants are new, you see, and I'm not one to be gossiping to them," in a tone of ineffable disdain. "Davies may have known of them at one time, but they have been out of use so long, I'm sure he has forgotten them. That passage outside Miss Delphine's room led at one time out through a window on to the leads where Master Bernard kept all his carrier-pigeons. When he went away once the squire had them cleared out and the way on to the leads stopped; the pigeons were for ever tumbling down the chimneys and pecking at the mortar, squire wouldn't be bothered with them. Now, if I dared go through the room and get into that passage—"

"No, no, no, Bryce," exclaimed Judith vehemently; "not to be thought of for a moment. She might hear you if the wall is so thin, and you would spoil everything. Now promise me—promise me—" this most earnestly, "that you won't on any account attempt such a thing."

A sudden idea had come to her, an idea which seemed to her like the opening of a door of hope by an angel hand. It grew and matured in her brain as the weeks and months in slow procession went by.

VI

Never, surely, since the days when Vivien with "woven paces and with waving hands" put to sleep the "gentle wizard" in the hollow oak, was man so befooled, spell-bound, and enthralled by woman as was Wolf Reece by Delphine Pierpoint.

In her presence, or within sound of her voice, he seemed as inert, as "lost to life, and use, and name, and fame," as ever did the sleeping Merlin. Not at a bound was this condition of things attained, but by successive stages—somewhat short and rapid ones it must be owned, but nevertheless easily apprehensible. In the first days of his acquaintance with Delphine he had shrunk from her with a loathing and horror natural to a man brought suddenly face to face with a bold, unscrupulous woman who holds the secret of his life in her hands. Her arts, and blandishments, and beauty, seen in this light had repelled rather than fascinated him. Later on, as he knew her better, and sounded, as he thought, the shallowness of her nature, a feeling of disdain took the place of the shrinking and loathing he had previously felt; he grew to look upon her much as one might look upon a playful, petulant kitten, whom circumstance and chance, not nature, had made poisonous and dangerous.

From disdain to tolerance was but a step, and he took it. From toleration of her arts and caprices he learnt submission to them. Thence the road was easy and downhill into the realms of bewilderment and fascination itself, until at length—with truth it might have been said—no Parthenope, ancient or modern, ever held her enchanted one more securely than Delphine held her Wolf.

Yet the man at times had lucid intervals—short periods of returned consciousness and manhood—times when he loathed less the woman who had ensnared him than himself, the weak, befooled prisoner, when he chafed at the chains which bound him, tried his strength against them, made some wild, desperate struggle for freedom, and then went back sullenly to bondage once more.

These brief periods of vigour and returned reason generally occurred during one or other of Delphine's absences in London, when her wild, thrilling voice no longer woke up the echoes of the old house, and the apprehension of her soft, springing footfall ceased to make itself felt at every turn of the staircase, behind every half-opened door. If the line of demarcation he had chosen to set up between Judith and himself had not

CATHERINE LOUISA PIRKIS

by this time grown to the strength and consistency of iron, it is possible Delphine's dominion would have been rudely shaken if not overthrown. As it was, however, the very reverence he had for Judith, her truth and purity—he said to himself it was reverence, nothing more—kept him apart from her and helped him to lose his own soul a little faster.

Better that, so he said to himself, than taint hers by so much as a finger-print; better his own conscience burdened, scorching, seared beyond remedy, than hers overshadowed by so much as a passing cloud.

Sometimes—and this always when Delphine was away—a sudden terror would seize him lest, after all, some of the infection which, to his fancy, filled every nook and corner of the old place, might light upon Judith and poison her life springs.

Once this feeling came upon him with such overwhelming force that he could not withstand it; it seemed as though his good angel, whom he had shocked, grieved, wounded, warned off, and was now about to put to flight for ever, was whispering a farewell plea to him for the young girl who had been sent into his house to be taken care of and made happy. "Send her away," it seemed to say, "before she grows into such an one as you are—as that other is." Not once, but again and again the voice made itself heard; and at last, one morning, he laid down his pen, closed his banker's-book, and went up and down the house looking for Judith.

It was nearly the middle of June now. Summer, with its glories, was draping the land and painting the skies; the gardens of the old Grange, a little recovered from their late uprooting and replanting, were shining out in summer colours, yielding their souls in summer fragrance, under a cloudless mid-day sun. Coming straight from his one-windowed study, with its odour of musty volumes, and from staring at his rows of figures, Wolf felt owl-like, half blinded; he stood for a few minutes on the terrace, shading his eyes with his hand, wondering whether he would find Judith in any of her favourite shady nooks among the laurels, or whether she had wandered out, book in hand, into the woods beyond.

As he stood thus, a voice, soft, yet clear and trenchant, fell upon his ear. "I have not heard from him by the last mail, Bryce; I cannot say when he is coming," were the words he heard.

It was undoubtedly Judith speaking; she must be in the housekeeper's room, he thought; and a feeling something akin to reproach made itself felt that this young lady should be so destitute of companionship as to have to seek it among the servants of his household.

If he had only been a little more awake to what went on under his very eyelids, he might have known that Judith never under any circumstances found her way into Bryce's *sanctum sanctorum* except during Delphine's absences in London. He went straight into the small, dark room. As he entered, Bryce sharply shut an open cupboard-door near which she was standing, locked it, and put the key into her pocket. It was an odd, unaccountable thing to do; but, then, so many things that this old body did were odd and unaccountable.

He did not heed her; he had something to say to Judith at that moment which absorbed all his thoughts. It did not matter that Bryce should be in the room to hear it. Of the two he rather preferred that a third person should be present, it would prevent the striking of painful chords, the introduction of matter essentially beside the point.

"Miss Wynne," he said, going up to Judith, and making no pretence of prelude to what he had to say, "it has occurred to me that, since your father's return appears likely to be somewhat delayed, a pleasanter house than ours might be found for you to stay in."

It came upon her like a thunderbolt. She started, turning to a deathly pallor.

"Are you saying to me, 'Go'?" she asked in a voice that trembled, vibrated, and died away in a muffled whisper.

Wolf went on as though he had not heard her.

"I have been thinking well over the matter, and it seems to me, that if it suit you, Dr. Martin's house at Richmond would be a bright and happy home for you—at any rate, till you hear from your father and learn what his wishes are."

Judith only stood still, staring at him blankly, and repeating in the same unnatural tone as before:

"Are you saying to me 'Go'?"

It had occurred to her that necessity might arise for her departure; that of her own free will she might leave the house; but not that he would come to her in this dry, apathetic manner and bid her depart.

He gathered together his strength and essayed to answer her.

"Yes, I say 'Go,' because I feel, I see, I know that it will be better for you to do so? How shall I explain? Why do you wish me to explain? Have you not eyesight and understanding of your own?"

For the life of him he could not keep his heart from making itself heard in his voice, just a note or two.

Judith's eyes drooped, but her lips refused to give out a sound. She looked fragile, slender, like some bending white lily, as she stood there silent by his side. She still wore her deep mourning for Aunt Maggie. It added possibly a shade of pallor to her always pale face.

He went on with increasing earnestness.

"I feel sure they would do their best to make you happy at The Retreat. Theo is a good girl; you seemed to get on well together. If you will consent, I will write to Dr. Martin today, and arrange for your going there in a day or two?"

Still no reply from Judith.

He grew impatient, imperious, as his wont was when thwarted. Why did she set herself in this way to make a long matter of what need be such a short one, to stir up feelings which he felt lay only too dangerously near the surface?

"Of course," he went on, trying to make his voice as hard and inflexible as voice could be, "I cannot turn you out of the house if you wish to stay on; but I tell you frankly that it will be an immense relief to me if you will go."

"I will go." It was slowly, resolutely said, but in such low tones as to be scarcely audible.

"Thank you. I felt sure that, if you thought over it, you would see the advisability of your leaving us. Today is Tuesday, will it suit you for me to take you up on Thursday to the Martins? I shall being going up to say my goodbye to Oscar in a day or two, as you know."

"Thank you, I will travel alone," in the same slow, resolute tone as before.

Wolf started. He was scarcely prepared for this. Yet, after all, perhaps it would be better so. Away from Delphine, alone with Judith for hours! The temptation would be hideously great. Yes, undoubtedly it would be a better arrangement.

"Very well," he said coldly, "since you prefer it. What day may I fix for your going? They will naturally wish to know."

Judith thought awhile.

"Thursday, next week, will suit me," she answered, and only a faint quiver of her down-drooped eyelid showed that she had a vestige of feeling on the matter at all.

"Very well, then; Thursday, next week, let it be," said Wolf, and fearful of breaking the thin ice on which he knew he stood, he turned abruptly, and left the room.

VII

Mrs. Reece became by turns indignant, expostulatory, vociferous, and denunciatory, when she heard of Judith's projected departure from Plas-y-Coed.

She catechised Judith ruthlessly on the matter.

"Why, why, why, my dear, what does it all mean? What can be sending you away from us just now, just at the very end of your visit? Has Wolf been particularly discourteous to you? I know he has grown morose, almost beyond bearing, of late, but I don't really think he means anything, certainly does not intend any personal rudeness, and I'm sure, if I spoke to him on the matter, he would at once apologise. He's not a particularly good hand at apologising, but still, I feel sure he would do it if I asked him."

"Oh, no, no," interrupted Judith hastily. "There is nothing whatever for him to apologise to me for, I assure you."

"Then, my dear, why are you going away from us? You surely are not running away from that fast young woman, who has so marvellously succeeded in blinding and fascinating my son? Dear me! dear me! To think that both my sons should have made such a mess of their love-affairs! Now, honestly, my dear, is it on account of this Miss Delphine that you are leaving the house?"

Judith felt that a portion of the truth might possibly succeed better than anything else in silencing the old lady's interrogatories and setting her mind at rest.

"It is on account of Miss Pierpoint that I am going," she answered quietly.

Mrs. Reece's exclamations then took another turn.

"Dear me, dear me, Judith, you surprise me! I took you to be a girl of another sort altogether. I thought your quietness meant strength, resolution, and now I find that after all it means nothing more than any other girl's at nineteen—no, twenty—you are just twenty now, are you not? To think that you should allow a woman of that sort to disturb your peace of mind, and turn you out of the house! My dear, what would you do if you had to face one half the troubles I have had to go through? Would you throw up your hands and run away from them, leaving those behind to do the best they could?"

Judith struggled painfully to keep her composure.

CATHERINE LOUISA PIRKIS

"Dear, dear Mrs. Reece, I feel leaving you—oh, I cannot tell you how deeply," she contrived to say; "you have been goodness and kindness itself to me."

"Then why go, Judith?" asked Mrs. Reece testily. "No one is driving you out of the house. I know the place must seem dreadfully dull and stupid to a girl at your age; but I don't believe you will find Richmond a bit better place to live in. From what Theo tells me, it is horribly suburban, split into cliques and sets, not one of whom will have anything to do with the other. There is the high-church set, and the low-church set, and the middle-church set, and the Catholic set, and a whole army of dissenters, whom no one meets anywhere, but who, nevertheless, do exist!"

"Oh, how can cliques and sets matter to me? You know I shall go nowhere, and see no one, till my father returns."

"Then, my dear, for all I can see to the contrary, you may just as well stay where you are." And then, in another key, she repeated the same song; dwelt pitifully on her increasing age and infirmities; on the pleasure Judith's society had been to her; on her loneliness and desolation in the days to come, with not a soul to speak a kindly, sympathetic word to her. "Here I shall be, my dear," she concluded pathetically, "all alone—for Phoebe doesn't count for much—in my own room, from morning till night. Wolf, somewhere, I suppose, playing at love—for it isn't the real thing—with that fast young woman. Oscar away in India, and you—ah, you!—who might have stayed with me and made my life pleasant to me, miles and miles away, and only an occasional slip of paper to tell me you are in the land of the living at all!"

All this, and a great deal more of remonstrance and reproach Judith had to endure, not once, but a hundred times over, before the day for her departure arrived.

Delphine, returning from what she intended to be her last journey to London before her marriage, heard with not a little surprise of Judith's plans.

"Ah, the fates fight for me!" she cried, clapping her tightly-gloved hands together, and pirouetting for Olivette's benefit round the room.

"Let the fates be! What about Phil Munday?" queried Olivette, always bent on the practical and matter-of-fact.

"Ah, the wretch! the toad! the awkward crab! the sour cabbage! Yes, I quieted him. Promised! Ah, what didn't I promise him? And all the while I had your letter from Steve in my pocket. Oh, if I had shown it him, it would have made him feel for a knife to stab me to the heart!"

"Why didn't you tell him what you knew? Threaten him with the police and be done with him."

"Ah, my dear, things are not finally settled yet; it would set him thinking and planning to thwart me once more. No, I wait till I have played my game and won; I wait till I have got rid of the little imp and married my Polyphemus, before I strike my final blow. See, things are settling themselves now. I give them but a touch and on they go—smoothly, gloriously, like a sleigh down a snow-hill. Next week will be a week of events, my sister. On Monday, my Wolf will go to London, meet Narcissus, and go hand-in-hand with him to Marseilles, where they will make their adieux. On Thursday, departs St. Judith! May blessings follow her every step of the way she treads! On Friday—ah, we will pass over that day, it will be the day we strike our blow. My Wolf out of the way, the Saint gone, what day could happen better? On Saturday, back comes my Wolf by the first train; he will get here by seven in the morning, travelling all night. I tell him what has happened; we mourn together; we search together for the little imp. By-and-by they bring in his body; we mourn again together; we go to the funeral together; and then the day after we go up to London together. We go to a registrar's-office and get married—ah, so quietly! (after such a calamity we must do things quietly, you know); and then we start for Paris—dear, darling wicked Paris! And from Paris I write to the wretch and tell him I have done his bidding!" Here her long low laugh echoed through the room. "I wish him health and happiness to the end of his days. I tell him I know all about the post-bag robberies, and I will set the police on him the very minute he grows troublesome; but that if he keeps quiet, and only if he keeps quiet, there will be a hundred pounds every three months for him to the end of his life, not a sou more, not a sou less. Ah! I am—oh, so tired. I can't say another word!" and thus ending her long speech, Delphine threw herself on the bed and prepared to settle to sleep for the night.

But Olivette had one word more to say.

"Supposing Phil Munday gets suspicious and comes down again to see how things are going on!" she whispered.

"Supposing! Raven! He—ush—sh!" cried Delphine, throwing out her arms at her as though to scare her away. "What should make the wretch suspicious? I was sweet as honey with him all day yesterday."

But Olivette was not to be so easily deterred from her croaking. She went one step nearer the bed.

CATHERINE LOUISA PIRKIS

"And supposing," she whispered, "'my Wolf,' as you call him, does not see fit to go to London and get married, but chooses to set up a hue and cry after the child!"

"He set up a hue and cry, with me at his elbow to swear to him how it all happened, to soothe him, to charm him, implore—threaten him, if need be! Fiddlesticks, my dear! Go tell that story to the marines, not to your sister!"

And with this expression of incredulity, Delphine sank back on her bed once more, and in another minute was sleeping soundly, as though her pillow had been stuffed with benedictions, not feathers.

VIII

W olf set off for London to say his good-byes to Oscar on the Monday before Judith was to leave Plas-y-Coed. The ship in which Oscar had taken passage was to set sail on the succeeding Wednesday from Marseilles. Thus far on his journey Wolf had decided to accompany his brother; he had much to say to him, many farewell counsels to give, many matters of importance to impress upon his mind, notably among them the fact that from henceforth his future must rest entirely in his own hands, for neither yearly allowance nor portion, great or small, was he to expect from the master of Plas-y-Coed.

These and equally weighty matters no doubt filled every corner of Wolf's brain, as he breakfasted with Delphine and Judith on the morning of his departure, for he was singularly—even for him singularly—silent and abstracted throughout the repast.

"From Dr. Martin," he said, handing to Judith a letter.

"Thank you," was all Judith's reply, and she scanned quickly the good doctor's warm, kindly words of welcome to his home, and folded and returned the letter to Wolf with another brief "thank you." These were the only words that passed between them during the short, dreary meal.

Delphine hovered over Wolf incessantly, till the time came for bringing round her ponies, like any gaoler over some notable captive, who, he feared, might escape him before the day for execution came round. She waited on him throughout breakfast; brought him his letters; hung about him as he opened and read them; followed him into his study, and sang her softest and sweetest to him as he finished sorting and arranging his correspondence and business papers there; followed him out again into the garden, and stood side by side with him in the glinting sunlight, talking blithely with arch, frequent upward glances into his absent, weary eyes; went with him even into his mother's room to say good-bye before he started; had her own hat and dust-cloak brought to her there, and equipped herself in front of Mrs. Reece's mirror for driving him to the station. Mrs. Reece meanwhile recited folios of messages to be delivered to Oscar, her love, her disappointment at not seeing him again before he sailed, her earnest prayers for his happiness in the future.

Judith was seated, winding Mrs. Reece's knitting-cotton, when the two entered. She rose immediately to leave the room. Wolf intercepted her at the door.

"I will say good-bye to you now," he said, a little formally, and with a manifest effort. "I am off almost immediately."

"Good-bye," answered Judith, in a tone that seemed the echo of his own. Then their fingers for one second touched, their eyes meantime looking away into the farther corners of the room, and she was gone.

So they parted.

Ten minutes after, Wolf, with Delphine by his side, drove away. Delphine in an altogether ecstatic frame of mind whipping up her fiery little ponies till they went along at an almost incredible speed.

"Ah, I would fly through air with you, my Wolf, as Francesca fled with her Paolo, sooner than say farewell," she whispered, as they sped along the rocky road, with mountain, wood, and fields fleeting past them in wind-like haste.

A silence fell on the house that day—a silence not so much as flawed by Delphine's return in the afternoon.

"May I live upstairs with you now, till I go?" Judith begged of Mrs. Reece. The old lady gave her permission to do so, though, truth to tell, a somewhat ungracious one, for she could scarcely bring herself to regard the young girl's departure from the house in any light save that of a positive personal injury.

So the days went round, till Thursday, the day of more farewells, arrived; Judith keeping so strictly to the upper floor of the house and Mrs. Reece's apartments, that not once during these days did she and Delphine set eyes upon each other—a circumstance for which she scarcely knew how to be adequately grateful. It is possible that Delphine in a measure reciprocated her feelings, for, with a brain webbed and intricate as that of the great Machiavelli himself, she no doubt rejoiced in a freedom from observation which enabled her to put and keep her thoughts in steady train.

On Thursday morning, however, the two met in the hall.

Judith, having said her final good-bye to Mrs. Reece, was standing there in travelling cloak and hat, with all her boxes and belongings about her. Delphine came down the stairs brilliant in the most dainty of morning costumes, with eyes dancing, smiles gleaming.

"Ah, let me drive you, Miss Judith," she said winningly, "as I drove my Wolf the other day. We made the journey in fifteen minutes less than we ever did before."

"Thank you, no. Davies will drive me," answered Judith in unmistakably arctic tones.

"Is there then nothing—nothing I can do for you, my friend?" this with just a pretty shade of mournfulness thrown into her voice and eyes.

Judith turned and looked at her steadily.

"Yes, you can do one thing for me," she said; "you can let me go upstairs and kiss little Bertie before I go."

Delphine started. She was not prepared for such a request as this; yet she speedily recovered her self-control.

"The little Bertie? Ah yes, my friend, go by all means, you were always kind and good to him. You will find him in my dressing-room at play; you know the way to it."

But she took care, however, to follow closely upon Judith's heels.

Bertie was seated on the floor playing with his nine-pins, a wooden ball was in his hand, wherewith to knock them down so soon as they should be set up in rank and file. He was, as usual, richly and daintily dressed. A light Indian-silk tunic set off to advantage the delicate shades of his transparent complexion and the bright gold of his long curls; deep falling Spanish lace shadowed his thin white arms and hid the hollows about his slender throat. He looked up as the door opened, an angry flush swept over his face as his eyes rested for one moment on Delphine, then, lifting his tiny hand with deliberate aim, he flung the wooden ball straight at her head.

"Ah, the little fury!" cried Delphine, dodging away from the ball, but she laughed pleasantly all the time, as though the child's display of temper amused rather than angered her.

Judith went up to the little fellow, and knelt on the floor by his side.

"Bertie dear," she said softly, "look up at me. Will you give me a kiss and say good-bye to me? I am going away."

The child's reply was to fling his arms tightly round her neck, and press his little lips vigorously to her cheek.

"Do you love me, Bertie?" whispered Judith right into the child's ear now.

The answer this time was an embrace so vehement, that her hat was knocked off her head, and fell to the ground.

Delphine picked it up.

"Naughty boy—naughty boy!" she cried; "you will crumple all Miss Judith's beautiful frills and laces;" and she endeavoured to disengage the still clinging boy.

CATHERINE LOUISA PIRKIS

Judith, with difficulty, and a huge pain at her heart, set herself free from the child, replaced her hat and veil, and left the room.

Delphine went with her to the top of the stairs.

"Adieu, my friend," she said sorrowfully; "we shall miss you—oh, so much. My Wolf and I will so often talk of you as we sit together outside on the terrace in the long summer evenings. Ah, my Wolf esteems you so much—so very, very much; I have seen it many, many times in his eyes as they have followed you about the room—here, there, everywhere. Going? yes. I had so much to say to you, but I will tell my Wolf to put it all in his letter when he writes. Adieu again, my friend;" here she extended both her small white hands for a farewell clasp, then recoiled a step, exclaiming: "Why, my friend, surely you are not going away without shaking hands with me!"

Judith paused a moment a few steps below her on the stairs.

"No," she answered, looking steadily up into the brilliant, evil face, "I cannot bring myself to touch your hand," and without another word she went slowly down the stairs into the hall.

Delphine, giving one long, low laugh, which seemed to echo through the house like the pæan of a triumphant fiend, went back to her room.

In the hall Judith found Mr. Maurice, the land-steward, awaiting her.

"Mr. Reece said he wished me to go with you to the station, and see you into your train," he explained, accounting for his unexpected appearance.

Bryce came forward with a huge bouquet of roses as a farewell offering. The old body said little, but she hung her head and looked troubled.

One or two of the maids who had grown to be fond of Judith shed a tear or two; the gardener and gardener's boy, to whom she had lent books, stood at a little distance, touching their hats.

Then crack went the coachman's whip, the old greys—not so fat as they were a year ago—set off at a fair pace, and Judith was whirled away out of sight down the laurel-edged drive.

A yet deeper silence seemed to fall upon the house that day.

Bryce went into her dark little housekeeping room, and gave short answers to everyone who ventured to approach her. Mrs. Reece declined her luncheon and dinner, and desired Phœbe, her maid, not to speak to her unless she was spoken to Delphine also retired into her own quarters, ordering the butler to send, at the regular hours, her meals upstairs, inclusive of dry sherry and cigarettes. Little Bertie was seen going out for and returning with Olivette from his usual morning's walk, and afterwards, as usual, disappeared for the rest of the day. As for Olivette, she had suddenly fallen into a fit of most profound sullenness, from which neither Delphine's raillery nor her petulance sufficed to arouse her.

Not till the whole household had retired to rest for the night, did she find for herself a voice and words. Even then the voice was faint and the words were few. She looked all round her in every corner, as though she feared some lurking listener, and went up to her sister, who half reclined, half lay, in loose muslin *peignoir*, on the bed, laid her hand upon her shoulder, and whispered into her ear:

"Give it up, Delphine; give it up. It's a dangerous game, and will bring you to no good."

Delphine raised herself a little higher on her elbow, stared blankly at her sister for a moment, and then burst into a reckless laugh.

"What, now, at the very last moment, give it up, when everything has fitted itself into my hand and the game is all my own? Thank you, no, my sister! If you are going to turn coward and sneak, you'll have to do it on your own account, not on mine."

"Why not," pursued Olivette, in the same low, hurried voice, "content yourself with marrying Wolf and adopting the child, as he intends?"

"What about Phil Munday, who knows the secret? Is he the man, think you, to let himself be jilted, and lose the opportunity for revenge?"

"You might buy him off; you'll have to do so. That is part of your plan, isn't it?"

"Aye, he'll be bought off, no doubt, when he finds the case is hopeless and there's no better game to play, but not before. I know the man! Besides, so long as the boy lives, there's always the fear of my Wolf turning soft-hearted, and in a sudden fit of penitence giving back everything to him. I've seen him on the verge of it already more than once. I know that man too!"

"Well, I don't care what you know or don't know. I know this is a dangerous game, and I advise you to give it up—that's all."

"Dangerous! where's the danger?" And again she laughed wildly, recklessly. "If there were fifty thousand times more of danger in it, I should do it; if there were anything of risk in it, I should run it. But there's none—none whatever. Now, listen, my child, and I'll tell you exactly how the whole thing will be done from beginning to end, and you shall judge for yourself how much of danger there lies in it. I go out in the afternoon, tomorrow, the little imp with me. I take also an easel and painting materials, and I say to one or other of the servants carelessly, as I pass, that I am going to paint that little bit of open glade Mr. Wolf so much admires, to surprise him on his return. Very well, I go; I plant my easel there; that is all. I leave my painting materials and camp-stool there—that is all, and I go straight back into the woods with the imp—no one ever passes there, no one will see. I take him past the stream, right on to the foot of that grey, rough mountain. I point up the steep, narrow, winding way, and I say to him, 'Little Bertie, your mother is up there; would you like to go find her?' Ah, how he will jump, and caper, and be off like a bird! Then I take him again by the hand, and say, 'Do you see those dark trees, Bertie, far away up the path? Well, your mother is hiding among them. You must go up, up, up, till you get to them; then you must crawl down on your hands and knees, part the boughs, and you'll find her.' Now, my sister, those trees spring out of a sandy hollow at the side of the rock; they branch over the path; they hide the precipice. Let one who doesn't know the road try that way—that's all! I've studied it—ah, I can't tell you how often. Well, Bertie won't get beyond those trees. I wait—I wait at the bottom of the mountain. I go a little way up; I call to him—no answer; I wait till night falls; I go back; I raise the hue and cry; I weep, I say my darling strayed away while I painted in the open glade; I say every man in the place must turn out and search. They go; they find my easel where I put it; they come back without the child, tired to death. In the morning, they say, they will search the mountains. I implore, I command that they go at once with torches. They shake their heads; I rush to the door; they rush too, and pull me back. I faint on the floor, as I know how. Ha, how white I can make my lips when I please! All that is but rehearsal. Tomorrow comes home my Wolf, and I go through it all again to perfection. Now, my child, what risk is there in all this? Tell me. Oh, not one quarter so much as I have gone through before, and thought nothing of. It is a little comedy—nothing more—a little drawing-room piece I go through to a not too clever audience. They will be interested, and pay me compliments. I laugh at them all meantime in my sleeve. What would you have more?"

Olivette, standing in front of Delphine, with folded arms and frowning brows, had listened intently to this long speech. At its end she went close to her sister, leaning over the bed.

"No," she said in low, resolute tones, "I can't go in for this. I shall start for Steve and Mexico tomorrow morning."

"You fail me at the last—coward!"

The words were hissed at Olivette as though they had been darted at her by an adder's tongue.

"Yes, perhaps I am. I've helped you so far, because I promised, but I can't go any farther. You give me one-half your fine jewellery and a hundred pounds down for travelling expenses, and you may be quite sure I won't trouble you any more."

Five minutes of silence between the sisters. Delphine pressed her hand across her forehead; she was evidently thinking deeply.

Olivette went on:

"The whole thing has been too drawn out to please me. Your finessing is too fine for me, and to tell you the truth, I can't do what you'd do in cold blood."

Delphine drew her hand from her eyes.

"After all," she said slowly, as though she were thinking out her plans as she uttered them, "it may be the very best thing that you should go tomorrow morning. You see, if you are here it should be you, not I, who take the boy out for a walk, whereas, if you are gone away suddenly, it follows naturally that I should take him out. Yes, I see it all. You heard from Steve yesterday. Very well, the letter was to say your mother was ill, and wished your return. I naturally, with my kind heart, send you at once. Tomorrow morning, before I have my breakfast even, I will send for that old Gorgon Bryce, and tell her that she must find a nurse for me at once at Llanrhaiadr, or wherever else they are to be had. Ah, *brava*, Delphine, what a brain you have! How well it all fits in! Ah, Olivette, my child, I am very much obliged to you, after all. Yes, you shall have your hundred pounds, I can manage that, and some of my jewellery—that means the things that don't suit me, nothing in the shape of diamonds, don't expect them—but you'll have to sit up all night packing; you'd better begin at once. Don't make too much racket about it, I'm not very much inclined for sleep tonight, and if you stir about and make a clatter, I sha'n't get a wink. Stay! I think I'll take a dose of chloral. The scent-case is at your elbow, there's the key; put me a little in that wine-glass and leave it by my bedside, so that I can take it off the last thing."

Olivette did as she was bidden.

"Does Wolf know that you and Bertha were not really sisters, only sisters in the profession?" she asked, as she drew one cut glass bottle out of the case, and prepared to unstopper it.

"He know! how should he?" answered Delphine. "Why should I tell him? It's no business of his," she broke off abruptly. "Simpleton!" she cried, making a sudden bound from the bed to Olivette's side; "don't you know chloral when you see it? There, give me the bottle! That's—Well, no matter what that is; that's my reserve bottle, in case everything else fails me. That never can fail one in need. Now go, begin your packing, and leave me in peace for the rest of the night."

IX

The day after Judith's departure seemed an odd, blank, disjointed sort of day at Plas-y-Coed. Yet a day of events too. It began with the vehement ringing of Delphine's bell, and the request that Bryce should be sent to her at once. Bryce on entering the room was confronted by Olivette equipped for travel, by corded boxes, umbrellas, and hand-bags. Delphine, with many exclamations and regrets, related the story concocted over-night; asked if Olivette and her baggage could be driven to Pen Cwellyn in time for the early train; and wound up by asking Bryce if she could find a nurse for the little Bertie immediately, as she herself knew nothing of the management of children, and she shuddered at the thought of her darling being neglected in ever so slight a degree. The woman must be staid and careful, clean, good-tempered, capable of washing and dressing a delicate child; in fact, must possess all the cardinal virtues, and not a few of the minor ones.

Bryce's old eyes wandered lovingly to a corner of the room where little Bertie, surrounded with toys, was trying to build himself into a castle of toy-bricks and turrets; a wall behind and before was already set up. It recalled a score or so of bygone reminiscences to her old brain. Tears glistened in her eyes.

"If you would only allow me, ma'am," she said, "I would act as nurse to the child—till you could find a better, at any rate; I would give you my word he should not be neglected."

Delphine was equal even to this emergency.

"Ah, how kind, how good of you!" she cried, going up to the old body, and taking her hand. "The very thing beyond all others, isn't it, Olivette?" Olivette made no reply. "Now I know my darling will be taken care of. Come here, Bertie"—Bertie, with his little frock filled with bricks, came slowly forward—"see here, my child, Bryce has been good enough to offer to be your nurse, for a time, at any rate. Go up to her now, give her your hand, and I dare say she will take you downstairs and give you some breakfast."

Bertie, with the remembrance of Olivette's warnings against the old women of the household floating in his small brain, stood still where he was, eyeing Bryce from top to toe somewhat viciously.

Bryce advanced towards him.

"Come, Master Bertie," she said, holding out her hand.

Bertie's reply was to retreat a step, upheave one of the bricks he held in his frock, and throw it with deliberate aim at the old body's eye. A second, a third, a fourth, a fifth followed in rapid succession.

Bryce made for the door backwards, shielding her face with her hands. Olivette caught the little fellow up in her arms and carried him off kicking and fighting into an adjoining room.

Delphine began to apologise.

"I don't like to say so," she said, turning to Bryce with one of her sweetest smiles; "but I fear he likes only young and pretty faces about him; he has evidently taken the matter into his own hands, and has decided you are not eligible for the office."

Bryce's answer was muttered in the most uncouth of Welsh gutturals as she quitted the room.

Translated into English, it might have run somewhat as follows: "His father, no doubt, loved young and pretty faces to his own hurt. Lord, keep him from a like fate!"

Olivette departed.

Bertie was allowed the run of the house that day under Delphine's supervision. He was taken upstairs on a visit of ceremony to Mrs. Reece, when the little fellow's perversity and troublesomeness were noticeable, and Delphine's forbearance and indulgence were much admired—at least, by Phœbe, for Mrs. Reece was singularly repressive and irresponsive that morning. Bertie was allowed to appear at luncheon also, sitting at Delphine's elbow, and helping himself to any dish he chose.

At the close of the meal, Delphine asked the butler if one of the servants could take her easel and camp-stool to the little open glade at the farther corner of the wood, as she was wishing to make a sketch there that afternoon.

"Mr. Wolf admired that nook, ah, so much last year. She herself thought it would make a grand picture. She only feared she would not be able to satisfy herself with her own productions, but she could but try." And with a "Come, Bertie, get ready for a lovely afternoon of play," she went upstairs to her own room.

Half an hour afterwards she and little Bertie were seen leaving the house together, followed by a man-servant carrying sketching-apparatus and camp-stool. Although she did not expect one single eye to rest on her save that of squirrel or bird, Delphine was as elaborately and daintily dressed as though she were about to stand the levelling at her of a few score of critical eyeglasses in the Row or the Bois de Boulogne. Her dresses were nearly all indescribable, like herself; they seemed to indicate the most graceful of lines and curves, but with a phantasy that was difficult to follow, and an originality that was all her own. The thing she wore this afternoon was deep violet in colour, relieved here and there with a fleck of old-gold, and completed by a hat which matched in colour and material.

Bertie's dress was all of old gold, sombred here and there with touches of violet. Those who saw him go out that afternoon thought how like a little fairy prince he looked in his bright attire, with his ostrich-plumed hat, and golden curls rippling beneath in the light summer breeze.

It was a glorious afternoon, hot, hazy, as became a midsummer's eve, yet, withal, kept fresh and pleasant by a soft south wind blowing off the mountains. The valley seemed full of a light golden haze. A hundred thousand song-birds were twittering in the woods.

Bertie's bright frock made a pretty bit of colour in the landscape as for a moment he paused at the garden-gates, looking up at a certain corner of the house where a pair of noisy martins were fluttering in and out from under the eaves, evidently intent upon building and setting up an establishment.

"Come, Bertie," called Delphine's clear voice a little way ahead; and the little fellow was gone.

X

W olf, whirling home to North Wales in the night-express, looked before and behind him, and asked himself a few questions. What and how much of his past must be sealed and consigned to oblivion? What and how much of his future would be his own, to mould as he would, to do with whatsoever seemed good in his own eyes?

Away from Delphine, the spell of her eyes, the magic of her presence, it was possible for him to put these questions to himself with some chance of getting a rational answer.

A rational and a practical one was what he wanted. It was of no use for his conscience to say to him, "go here," "go there," "do this," "do that," on matters where such going and doing would be impracticable No! Such suggestions, he had long since decided, were not to be listened to, they were futile, and, no doubt, after a time would cease to be whispered in his ear. The matter before him was to decide how to make the best of things as they were, not to attempt to re-cast them in any other mould.

And here he fell to congratulating himself that, after all, things had turned out better than he had any right to expect. The woman he had so dreaded, and whom, out of sheer desperation, as the only means of stopping her rapacity and wresting her sceptre from her, he had promised to marry, was really, after all, less dangerous and far more attractive to his fancy than he would at one time have thought possible.

Then, too, that preposterous deed of hers, the bringing little Bertie upon the scene after he (Wolf) had paid such large sums to keep him away in America, had not turned out such a bad arrangement, after all. A danger under one's eye was certainly less to be dreaded than a danger some thousands of miles away. Besides, it gave him such splendid opportunity for reparation—for more than reparation—for showering upon little Bertie, in the shape of educational and other advantages, far more than ever he had robbed him of.

Now what benefit, so his thoughts ran on, would the knowledge of his parentage and station in life confer upon this boy? He, Wolf, would take care that of not one real advantage that parentage and station could give him, should he be deprived; the knowledge of both could avail him but little. At his own death, no matter what other claims might be upon him, little Bertie should have everything given back to him increased and improved a hundred-fold by his kinsman's brief stewardship.

Who would be the worse for this stewardship? he asked himself fiercely, defiantly. Not Bertie, for he had just sworn that not by a hair's-breadth should he suffer in mind, body, or estate. Not Oscar, for he had gone off to begin a new life, armed cap-à-pie as he never could have been had they all remained in their hideous poverty at the East End of London. Not Mrs. Reece, for was she not now in her old age surrounded by comforts and luxuries which all aged people needed, but which wealth alone could procure?

Why, if anybody had suffered by this deed which he had done, it was himself, and himself only, in sleepless nights and anxious days; no living soul had right to point the finger and say: "This man dragged down our souls to hell with his own."

And here there came a mist before his eyes, which, had he been a weak man and given to emotion, might have passed for tears. As it was, with his heart grown now into something of the substance and density of flint, he said to himself, "It was nothing but weariness and weakness of the eyelids, through midnight travelling and lack of sleep. For what could there be in the thought of any young girl of twenty, least of all such a girl as Judith Wynne, to fill a man's eyes with water or set his heart aching and quaking?"

On this count, more than any other, there was cause for naught but rejoicing and thankfulness. Many men in his place, so he told himself, would have done outright what he so nearly did—have taken advantage of her girlish simplicity, her kindly sympathy, have sought and won her love, and thrown the half of his heavy burthens on her weak shoulders. Ah, thank Heaven, he had stopped short of that! He had not sullied her pure conscience with the guilty whispers of his own—nay, more, he had strength and courage to send her away from his side to a brighter and more suitable home, where, no doubt, among congenial, light-hearted companions she would speedily shake off and forget the gloom and sadness of the past. Yes, thank Heaven! she, no more than the others, would have cause to curse him when the great day of reckoning came. Hideous as his own soul might be, and no doubt was, it had at least kept its hideousness to itself, had not tainted any other soul with its infection. Black and vile it might be to its very core, but others had been the better, not the worse, for its blackness and vileness, and if it so happened that it died at last of its own plague, it would be at least the plague of a canker, a disease self-centred, for which none but itself would suffer.

These and similar ones were the thoughts wherewith he shortened his long journey home. Towards sunrise of that midsummer day he slept a little from sheer eye-weariness and bodily exhaustion. As day dawned fully over the Welsh mountains he aroused once more, and found himself entering the town of Pen Cwellyn.

He had desired that no one should send to meet him from Plas-y-Coed, meaning to take a hired fly from the railway-station. One fly was always in attendance to meet each down train, although there was but seldom a demand for it. Pen Cwellyn was the quietest and least frequented of market-towns, it led nowhere save to Plasy-Coed, and a stranger alighting there was looked upon somewhat as a *rara avis in terris*. However, on this particular morning, as Wolf descended from his railway-carriage and looked about him for further means of transit, he saw that such a *rara avis* had actually alighted before him, and was now making for the one little cab Pen Cwellyn could boast.

He was a stalwart-looking individual, very much muffled up about the throat, and with hat drawn rather low over his brows. As he went rapidly along the narrow footway, Wolf could only discern that he had jet-black whiskers and a noticeable row of gleaming white teeth.

XI

S even o'clock on a midsummer morning; the dew not yet scared by scorching sunbeams from off moss or grassy border; the air faintly troubled by awakening flower-scents and uprising larks; many-leaved beeches and birches rustling together, as though they were telling each to the other their overnight's dreams; long grasses billowing and bending under a light scudding breeze, now flashing back a rich aquamarine, anon "in colour like the satin-s ining palm on sallows in the windy gleams of March," a quaint old house, brightened up coquettishly here and there with modern touches, standing serene and stately in the midst of it all.

In very truth, a fair midsummer picture it made. No touch of tragedy here; one could scarcely bear even to think of a dead sparrow in the glamour of this sunshiny landscape.

Yet if Wolf, as he paused at the door of his own house, had seen inscribed over the lintel those words of doom, "Abandon hope, all ye who enter here," or that mystic handwriting which startled the Assyrian king in the midst of his revels, it might have been better for him—might more fitly have prepared him for that which he was to see and hear when the door opened to receive him.

As it was, he started back, as though he had been met by a volley of musketry as he crossed the threshold. A woman in dark violet robes lay stretched upon the floor of the hall, her hair hanging down dishevelled, like a black silken veil, below her waist, her hands clasped and extended high above her head. Her face was death-like in its pallor, her full white eyelids were closed, and one might have thought she slept, had not piteous moans from time to time broken from her lips. It was Delphine. Thus, in spite of all remonstrance, had she lain throughout the entire night moaning, incessantly, "Oh, my Bertie—my Bertie!" the plaint changing now to "Oh, my Wolf—my Wolf!" as the hall-door opened and she became conscious of Wolf's presence, of his standing over her in amazed silence, of his kneeling down on the floor beside her, and endeavouring to unclasp her cold, rigid hands.

The servants, in twos and threes, were standing at the lower end of the hall talking in whispers.

"She has been like this all the night through," he heard one say to the other.

"What does it all mean?" he asked, and a great fear shook his heart.

"Oh, my Wolf!" she moaned again. "Oh, my Wolf, my Wolf! how shall I tell it to you?"

"Don't try to tell me anything here," he said angrily. "Get up and go to your own room; or, if you feel yourself unable to move, I will carry you."

He put his arms round her waist and lifted her bodily off the floor; then, with the help of one of the maids, little by little, they got her up the two flights of stairs to her own room and laid her on the sofa.

Safely landed here, her grief overcame her once more. She buried her face downwards in the sofa-pillows; she beat her hands frantically together, and moaned again and again:

"Oh, my Wolf, my Wolf! How shall I tell you!"

"Don't keep me any longer in suspense, Delphine," said Wolf in low nervous tones, for he was beginning to feel the strain beyond bearing, "Tell me right out at once. Is my mother all right?"

"Oh, yes! oh, yes!" sobbed Delphine; "she is as well as ever; she doesn't feel it as I do."

"And Judith?" The words seemed wrung from his lips: he hated to mention Judith's name in this beautiful, evil woman's presence, yet perforce he must. The dread of some ill having befallen her, which, lightning-like, had flashed through his brain, was a dread not to be borne voluntarily for more than a second and a half.

Delphine lifted up her white face from the pillows. For one instant there came a steely, baneful look into her dark eyes; for one instant she cursed her own folly, which had let this girl depart from the house unthreatened, uninjured.

"What should I know about her?" she said in sharp, metallic tones. "What would it matter to me what became of her? Should I lie here and weep for her, if she were dead and buried a thousand times over?"

Wolf's face grew hard as iron.

"I dare say not," he said coldly, "but others might." He paused a moment, as though mastering some strong feeling, then went on in a more conciliatory tone: "Well, now, Delphine, that you are calmer, tell me what has happened that I may see what can be done for the best. Why are you lying here in this state?"

Delphine sobbed and moaned again.

"It's my Bertie—my darling Bertie!" she said between her gasps. "He's gone for ever. I shall never—never see him again."

"Bertie!"

The word broke from his lips in sharp, agonised accents. Then he stood motionless, rooted to the spot, all signs of human life dying out of his face.

"Aye, my Bertie!" sobbed Delphine. "He strayed away yesterday; he has been seen by no one; he is lost, or drowned, or dead. I shall never—never see him more!"

He made her no answer. He still stood there, staring at her with stony, lack-lustre eyes, spellbound, as though he had been listening to the sweet notes of Rhiannon's birds.

Delphine grew frightened at her own handiwork. What was going to happen? Were things about to take an awkward turn now?

She lifted herself languidly from the couch. She dragged herself slowly yet gracefully to his side, as one might go who was half worn out with grief and pain.

"Oh, my Wolf!" she said softly, laying her hand upon his arm. "Do not look like that at me. Speak to me one word—one little word. Ah, I did not think you loved the little one so well!"

Her voice, her touch, seemed to break the spell which bound him. He recoiled one step, shaking himself free from her.

"Back!" he said in a voice that sounded like the fall of some mighty hammer on Vulcanic anvil. "Back! Don't touch me—stand where you are. Look in my face, and tell me what you have done with the child."

And Delphine stood where she was, looked up in his face piteously, innocently, and said in plaintive tones:

"Done with the child? Oh, my Wolf, what can you mean? The darling strayed away yesterday while I sketched just outside the wood. I call, I search for him everywhere. I come home, I send the men out to search. They come back; they cannot find him. I know not where to send them next;" and once more she sobbed and moaned, essaying to hide her weeping face on his shoulder.

But he put her from him with iron hand.

"It's a lie!" he said in a voice growing harder with every word he uttered; "a cursed lie! You know where the child is; you have hidden him away somewhere. I will have no trifling now. I command you tell me the truth on this matter, though you lie to me about everything else under heaven."

"Oh, my Wolf, you speak to me so?" and Delphine sank on the floor beside the sofa, hiding her face with her clasped hands.

CATHERINE LOUISA PIRKIS

"Yes, I speak to you so—I, the man whom you have befooled to your heart's content. I speak to you so, and I mean every word I say. I tell you I will have no murder done in my house—no diabolical cruelty practised on this child. I say I will have clean hands! Clean hands—do you hear? not bloodstained ones!"

It was once more the echo of that voice Judith had heard in the corridor in the dead of night.

"Murder! Oh, my Wolf, my Wolf!" sobbed Delphine; "you do not mean to say you think my darling is murdered?"

"I can—I do; and I say more, I dare accuse you of his murder!"

He strode to her side; he took her hands from her face, holding them both in one of his strong ones.

"Look up at me, Delphine," he said. She did so. It was marvellous how she could stand the fire of those fierce, angry eyes. "Look up and see that I mean every word as I utter it," he went on. "I command you to tell me what you have done with the child; where you have hidden him; in what corner of the woods or mountains he is lying now. Do you understand me?"

Delphine's penetration had not deceived her when she had said that this man would make a terrible master if once he got the upper hand.

She felt cowed—a little; not much.

"Alas! my Wolf—" she began.

But Wolf stopped her, laying his other hand upon her lips.

"I want no words from you, except they be answers to my questions. Once more, and it is for the last time, I ask it. What have you done with the child? Where is he?"

Delphine's head drooped upon her bosom.

"Alas! my Wolf, I cannot tell you," she sighed.

Wolf let go her hands, and strode to the fireplace, giving one loud, long pull to the bell.

"Send Mr. Maurice to me at once!" was his order to the scared maid, who came running up, thinking her aid was required by Miss Delphine.

Mr. Maurice, who was in the house, quickly made his appearance.

Wolf addressed the worthy steward with peremptory abruptness.

"I want to know exactly what has been done with regard to the search for the missing boy?" he said.

"Well, sir, considering how short a time has elapsed since the child was lost, I think everything possible has been done," answered Mr. Maurice. "A party was organised directly Miss Pierpoint returned saying the little fellow was missing, and we searched the woods till night fell, from the point where the child must have strayed. We could not attempt the mountains so late—there was no moon—but as soon as day dawned all the men round far and near formed three parties and went up three several ways."

"Well?"

"Two parties have returned, sir, but not the third; they have nothing to report; they came upon nothing unusual anywhere."

"Has the stream been dragged?"

"Not yet, sir, but that can be set about at once. You see it's getting wind in the neighbourhood that the child is lost, and men keep coming from all parts offering their services."

"Very well; accept the services of every man who offers, and let them set about dragging the stream at once. Have the police been informed?"

He asked this question with eyes fixed full on Delphine's bowed face. She did not start nor shrink, however, but upturning her beautiful eyes, said softly:

"Ah, we did not think of that; we were all so shocked and bewildered."

"Well, sir, I thought of it, to tell you the truth," said the steward, "but scarcely liked to take so much upon myself in your absence."

"I will ride at once myself to Pen Cwellyn, and send over an inspector. I may not come back with him, for I shall want to go into the woods to see what the men are doing there; but see yourself that he is shown up here to hear from this lady's own lips exactly how the child was lost."

And with this final order Wolf strode away, and in less than five minutes, break-fastless still, was in the saddle, and setting off at a good rattling pace down the rocky road to Pen Cwellyn.

It was Merlin awaking with a vengeance at last!

XII

The search for the lost boy continued all through that long midsummer day. Wolf having informed the police at Pen Cwellyn, and sent the chief-inspector into Delphine's presence, himself rode off to the woods to superintend the efforts of the searchers. Fruitless, all of them. At noon the head of one party came to him, reporting that the stream of St. Govan had been dragged from bank to bank, and save a few bits of broken fishing-tackle, and an old shoe or two, nothing had been brought to land. Party after party of the men who had been scouring the country round came back with blank, tired faces, and no tidings of any sort. Wolf was always there to receive them, he remained in the saddle the whole day, eating nothing, saying never a word, staring with wild eyes at every man who approached him, as though he would read the news he had to bring before his tongue had time to speak it. From post to post he wandered, his heart, a thousand times that day, torn with wild, impossible hopes, with equally wild, impossible terrors.

At one time he could have sworn he heard afar off a wailing, pitiful cry as of a small child hiding amid the brushwood, and pushing forward to the spot with a terrible eagerness, out would flutter a dismal corncrake, or wild, piping finch. At another his strained eyeballs, discerning the approach of some distant wood-cutters, would picture in their arms the dead body of the little Bertie, with torn blood-stained clothing, and draggled, unkempt hair. In that one long midsummer day he seemed to live a life-time twice told, he passed and repassed from youth, with fiery blood and courage, though middle life to old age; once and again he could feel the life dying out of him inch by inch, the blood thinning in his veins, the spirit within him dwindling and quenched.

Those who saw him, who, not all-absorbed in their work of searching, had time to note his anguish, his fierceness, his despair, pitied him, and sympathised with him as they never had sympathised before. Wolf had not, since his coming to Plas-y-Coed, been a popular man among his neighbours; this sorrow, however, and the way in which he bore it, drew many to him who had hitherto held themselves aloof. The loss of a child touched a chord of some sort in every heart; it was a grief which every man, woman, and child in the community might some day, in some fashion or other, be called upon to endure. It made hearts at one with his, who had hitherto never dreamed such sympathy possible.

The day wore away. Five o'clock found men talking together in twos and threes debating what next could be done. It found Wolf sick and giddy, reeling in his saddle, and thanking a farmer's lad who stood by for a drink of water from a tin can which he held in his hand.

"You'd best go home, sir," said old Davies, who had come out in search of him; "the mistress has been asking for you all day long, and wondering whether you have had aught to eat or drink, and, sir, some of the men who have been searching the mountain have just come in, and have something to say to you."

Wolf turned his horse's head towards home immediately, all sorts of wild surmises fleeting through his brain. Standing just outside the door were some four or five stalwart-looking men, all talking in earnest, low tones to each other in Welsh.

One, who appeared to be acting as chief among them, came forward, fumbling in his waistcoat-pocket. He said he did not know whether what he had found would be of any use in the matter, but thought it as well to bring it to the house. He then produced a small fragment of white Spanish lace.

Wolf shook like an aspen leaf, he could scarcely command his voice to ask where it had been found.

The man explained that he had discovered it caught in some brushwood a little way up the mountain passage which led out of the wood.

This was the least frequented of the three roads leading up the mountains. It was a deceptively dangerous passage, presenting for the first hundred yards or so simply the appearance of a steep pleasant footway—nothing more. Step by step, almost imperceptibly, the dangers grew upon one; here the path suddenly narrowed, and was encumbered by huge boulders and gigantic fragments of rock; there it as suddenly shelved, and with a sharp turn skirted the edge of a deep precipice, from whose sandy sides sprang a few mountain trees which concealed without lessening the danger of the chasm. Just before, however, this precipice was reached, there were a few clumps of stunted furze and broom, and it was in these that the fragment of white lace had been discovered.

Wolf looked at it for a few minutes, then he said a little hoarsely:

"Fetch the inspector here; he had better see this."

The inspector came, and the lace was handed over to him.

"Miss Pierpoint is the only person in the house who can say for certain whether it belonged to the child or not," said Wolf.

CATHERINE LOUISA PIRKIS

The inspector at once offered to take the lace for Miss Pierpoint's inspection.

He returned in a few moments, saying that Miss Pierpoint was certain the lace was little Bertie's, and that the child had worn a frock trimmed with it when he had gone out yesterday. He added that the young lady had been greatly overcome by the sight of it.

"The precipice must be searched at once," said Wolf.

Even as he said this he grew sick and giddy again, almost falling forward on his horse's neck.

Mr. Maurice brought him some brandy.

"Sir, you must give in for today," he said. "You have eaten nothing. You have all day been riding about in this scorching sun. I will give orders about having the precipice thoroughly searched. There are plenty of men here who are only too anxious to be of use, and who will begin the work at once."

Wolf with difficulty got himself out of the saddle, and went into the house. The butler came forward to tell him that refreshments were laid for him in the dining room, but he waved him on one side impatiently. The old man followed him, saying that Mrs. Reece had been sending messages for him all day and was most anxious to see him. But Wolf went past him as though he had heard him not, straight into his own study, shutting the door behind him.

Almost mechanically he took his usual seat at his writing-table, then he fell forward, bowing his head upon it with one heavy groan.

"My God!" he moaned bitterly, "have mercy! My punishment is greater than I can bear."

Self-branded, he sat there with the cry of Cain upon his lips.

For a few moments a mist and blank seemed to fall upon him. His brain felt stupefied, inert, incapable. Little by little, however, it cleared. Thoughts began to form in it, visions of the past to come slowly forth and confront him; spectres of the present to troop forth till they gathered together a goodly company around him.

This, then, was the end to which his sin, step by step, had led him! This was to be the result of his many sleepless nights, his weary, painful days, his strivings against the voice of conscience, his resistance to the pleadings of his good angel, his toilsome building up of philosophic and ethical bulwarks, his resolute determination in so far as in him lay to repair the evil he had wrought by a lifetime's devotion to the one he had wronged. This—this the result, to see all swept and whirled away in a moment like a dry leaf upon the flood, and the awful guilt of blood-shedding brought home to his very door!

One more exceeding bitter cry escaped his lips, and then he bowed his head again and wept passionately.

Not as a child; not the sort of tears that women weep—easy-flowing, heart-lightening; not the summer shower that gives promise of sunshine breaking forth presently from behind the dark cloud. No! Men such as Wolf Reece know not tears of that sort. When they weep it is once for all in a lifetime, and the tears they shed are not healing, nor burden-lifting, but bitter, burning, scorching things, which sear as they fall; which tell a tale of wounds never to be healed, of hope burnt out, and retribution at hand, as sure, as inevitable, as final as death itself.

Thus he wept.

For how long he knew not. The sunbeams slanted, the shadows lengthened; outside, on field and mountain, there lingered enough of light to enable men who knew every square inch of the ground to continue their search for little Bertie, but within the old Grange the grey twilight had deepened into night itself.

There came a gentle knock at Wolf's door, and, though he heeded it not, the handle turned, and Delphine came in. Her entrance was silent and stealthy as that of a moth's flight into a dark room. Not a footfall nor flutter of skirt stirred the air. Wolf did not know of her presence till she stood by his side, twined her arms round his neck, laid her cheek upon his bowed head, and moaned pitifully.

"Oh, my Wolf, my Wolf, you are breaking my heart!"

He started from his chair as though an adder had stung him, recoiling a step from her.

"Go!" he said in a choking voice. "For your own sake, don't come near me, tonight at any rate."

The room was too dark for her to see the wild glitter in his eye.

"For my own sake—oh, my Wolf, what do you mean?" and again she essayed to twine her arms about him.

"Stand back!" he said in a voice of thunder. "What—do you not know a desperate man when you see him?"

Something in his voice cowed her. She stood still and silent for a few seconds surveying him.

In those few seconds she measured her danger, its possibilities, its probabilities. Truly things had turned out other than she had expected. Her fascinations evidently had lost their cunning, or else—more likely—

the material upon which they had been wont to operate had suffered change of substance. Well—easy remedy enough—other forces must be brought to bear upon it.

The clay had been transformed into iron; no use trying to mould that—it must be heated, beaten, forced into "shape and use."

"My Wolf," she said, altering her tone from that of a single string to a trichord, "you speak roughly, rudely; you forget you are talking to a woman."

"Can you wonder if I forget you are a woman? Have you not yourself already forgotten the fact?"

The words were spoken slowly, sternly, incisively. Delphine, as she listened, said to herself that it was high time she buckled on her armour and took her weapons in hand.

"You forget something else beside, my Wolf—you forget the bond there has been—there is between us. You are ungrateful, my friend. Ah, what have I not done for you? and here you are, all in a moment, wanting to forget everything! Once it was not so. You were grateful enough; you gave thousands when I asked for hundreds. I asked for your friendship, you gave me more—your true eternal love. Is this truth, my friend—is this love eternal? Now, what have I done, I ask, that you requite me thus?"

Wolf was at bay now.

"What have you done, do you ask?" he cried in a voice that gall itself might have been wrung out of. "I will tell you what you have done—robbed me of my honour, my truth, my honesty, made me hateful in my own eyes, despicable in the sight of every living human being, dragged my soul down to hell, and would keep it there with your own hands if it were not that the devil himself has got hold of it now and doesn't require your services any longer."

Delphine did not smile at him now, according to her wont; it might be she thought, her smiles might lack their usual power over him in this frame of mind; or it might be she thought, the room was too dark to show them to their best advantage.

So she contented herself with saying quietly and with tightening lips:

"My Wolf, do you defy me?"

"Yes!" was his reply, thrown back at her in fierce, deep-chested tones. "I defy you a hundred times over. You have done your worst—your very worst. What remains to be done—what by any possibility you may do can be but child's play now. You may ruin my reputation. What is that when my honour is gone? You may set men on to prosecute and imprison me for the wickedness I have wrought. What is that when I feel that eternally God's wrath will be upon me, that for me there will be no place for repentance, let me seek it never so earnestly, in this world nor any other."

His words for once made her tremble. Yet, as she stood there facing the man in the rapidly-darkening room, some new, unknown chord in her nature seemed touched; something—could it be a feeling akin to reverence?—flitted through her soul for him, standing thus beaten, baffled, at bay; making one last struggle to free himself from the web of iniquity she had meshed about him.

However, the chord, though touched, had no vibration, but passed quickly "into silence out of sight." She went back rapidly enough to the matter in hand.

"My Wolf," she said, "I have no wish to do any one of these things you speak of. You misunderstand me altogether; you say hard things of me, of yourself, my friend. Now, be reasonable; let us talk quietly. Why should you make all this hue-and-cry about a small child who is nothing in the world to you, whom you were quite content should be put quietly on one side for your interests, whom, should the men searching outside bring back to you alive and well, you would find very much in the way, and would send upstairs to a nursery, to live there, out of sight, a dependent on your bounty?"

"No such thing," broke in Wolf with savage vehemence, and lifting his hand on high. "God is my witness! In the future, to the very end of my life, not one penny of that child's fortune will I touch. I know—you know that repentance of mine now will avail me nothing—you nothing, for God's curse is on us both for the sin we have wrought; but should that boy ever be brought back to us alive, I swear, by all that is holy and righteous, on my knees, before all the world, I would give back to him every penny of which I have robbed him."

He finished his sentence in a loud, passionate ring. What recked he of listeners, a desperate man in a desperate mood? Delphine might well shrink back from him a step or two into the darkness.

The door opened at this moment, softly, lingeringly; it let in a long stream of yellow light from outside lamps, which had been lighted. It cut the dark room in two; it put distance between Wolf and Delphine; they looked across it one into the other's face, she into his fierce, desperate eyes, he into her evil, glittering ones. Then they each turned and faced a dark figure which stood like some silent angel in the midst of the yellow gleam.

It was Judith, with little Bertie clinging tightly round her neck!

XIII

For a moment there was silence among them. Wolf, drawing a long breath, staggered against the wall of the room, and, incapable of speech, with staring, stony eyes, gazed upon the two. Delphine came one step forward, with something of a crouching panther step. She was not pleasant to look upon at that moment, and a poignard might have been a very ugly weapon in her hand.

Judith was the first to speak. Her face was deathlike in its pallor, but her voice calm and passionless as might have been that of one of Guido's saints.

"I have brought back the child whom you plotted to murder," she said, slightly, turning to Delphine.

Then she crossed the room, and stood in the darkness by Wolf's side.

"Here," she said, "is the boy to whom not a moment ago you promised restitution and reparation."

Delphine began to re-muster her forces. Was this to be a final defeat, or simply a rout?

"I plotted to murder!" she exclaimed in accents of surprise. "Oh, Miss Judith, Miss Judith, why do you hate me so? What have I done that you should pursue me in this way with slander and calumny? Is it because I have crossed you in your love-making that you bring these terrible charges against me?"

"Hush!" said Judith peremptorily. "Do not attempt to deny it. Do not add lies to your wickedness. I slept in the house on Thursday night, in the Tapestry Room. In the passage that runs at the back of your bedroom I stood for hours. I heard every word of your shameful plot, and took my own measures to defeat it."

Judith *victrix* at last!

But Delphine was not one to throw up her arms and cry *misericordia* while there remained a ghost of a chance of turning the tide of battle.

She gave the lowest, longest, most mirthless laugh of which she was capable. She even clapped her hands together softly, as one, kid-gloved, might applaud at a theatre.

"A brave story, Miss Judith!" she cried, "a story everyone in all the world would believe! You go into a room that is bricked up and cannot be entered; you hear me speak words I never uttered! It is a delightful mystery, my friend!" and once more her scornful laugh trilled forth.

"It is no mystery at all. Bryce will tell you how I entered that room if you ask her," answered Judith calmly; "it can all be easily explained if you wish for an explanation. On Thursday, when I went away from here, I went only so far as to the next station, returned to Pen Cwellyn at night-fall, and walked back to this house. Then I went straight up to the Tapestry Room by a side staircase, heard your plot, went out again, feeling and finding my way into the woods. There I stayed till day dawned. Then I made my way up the mountain-side."

"A brave story—" began Delphine again.

"Hush—sh!" said Wolf authoritatively, though his voice sounded terribly out of tune and unlike his own. "Go on, Judith," he added, turning to the young girl.

So Delphine contented herself with another, and another of her long, low laughs. Yet even as she laughed her plans were forming.

Judith went on:

"I lay hidden all day long among the brushwood. In the late afternoon came little Bertie up the mountain looking for his mother"—here she turned and faced Delphine. "He found me instead hidden among the gorse, this side of the deep precipice."

"And then?" queried Wolf in the same unnatural tone of voice, drawing almost involuntarily nearer and nearer to where Judith stood.

Bertie had all this time lain quiescent in Judith's arms; as, however, he saw Wolf approaching, though only by a step, he clenched his tiny fist, and tried to aim a blow at his face.

Wolf shrank back; he felt a coward now before the uplifted hand of this small child.

Judith went on:

"I kept him there safe and out of sight till night began to fall; then in the darkness I brought him back to the house." She paused.

"Go on; what then?" said Wolf.

"I brought him back into the Tapestry Room, giving him the food Bryce was good enough to bring up to me. He has been in that room the whole of this day."

"You—you—you did this?" exclaimed Wolf, a terrible twanging harshness making itself heard in his voice.

He was silent a moment, weighing the enormous physical strain that this young girl had endured voluntarily during the past two days; against this he fell to measuring the fearful mental strain he himself had sustained throughout the past twelve hours.

"And all the time I was enduring this awful torture and agony the child was safe with you, and might have been produced at any moment. Judith, Judith, was this well done?" and here his voice rang out sharply, passionately.

"It was well done."

"What, to keep me agonised, tortured, suffering, my brain racked, my senses almost leaving me, my heart well-nigh broken?"

"It was well done, I say," answered Judith loudly, clearly, her voice as decisive as his own in his best days, "and I would do it over again tomorrow if it had to be done. I would rack your brain, I would break your heart a thousand times over sooner than have it hard, stubborn, callous, as it has been in the days gone by."

"You would do this—you?"

"Aye, I would do this. I have done it today; I would do it again tomorrow should the need arise."

Wolf opened his lips as though about to speak, then he caught back his breath with a gasp, saying nothing.

"Hear her! She threatens you, my Wolf!" said Delphine softly.

"I do," said Judith, once more turning round and confronting the woman. "So far as he shows mercy to himself, so far will I have none for him. I will be pitiless so far as he shows himself pity."

"I am not likely to do that now, Judith," said Wolf in low, unnatural tones.

Then, somehow, he pulled himself together, quitted the room with lagging, uncertain steps, crossed the hall, and went out into the warm, hazy darkness.

Delphine for one instant faced Judith.

"Adieu, sweet Miss Judith," she said softly, making her the lowest and most profound of curtseys. "I congratulate you on your day's work. 'It was well done, and fitting for a princess the daughter of so many kings.' But others, perhaps, can do better than well Be warned. 'When clouds are seen wise men put on their cloaks.' Shall I lend you one, Miss Judith? The game isn't quite ended yet. It may be 'double,' it may be 'quits,' between us the next throw. We shall see. Adieu, my sweet young friend. I kiss your hand!"

Then, making another elaborate curtsey, she turned and went out after Wolf into the night.

XIV

O utside in the dark garden the air was hot and still, not the faintest breath of wind stirred leaf or twig. There was no moon; black, murky clouds hung low, as though resting on the very tops of the sombre beeches. The garden seemed literally walled and ceiled by beech and cloud.

Surveyed from the terrace-steps, where Delphine stood for a few moments, it seemed like some dismal cavern, a Dom-Daniel, perhaps, "lying under the roots of the Ocean," and containing all sorts of hideous possibilities and sorceries.

There was evidently a storm coming on. Now, if there were one thing which Delphine dreaded more than any other, it was a thunderstorm. Only next to apparitions and ghosts she ranked the evil things, thunder and lightning.

During a storm, her usual refuge was a dark cupboard or cellar, and one seeking her would have found her, while the tempest lasted, ready and willing to fall down and worship eagle, sea-calf, or laurel—anything, in fact, that ancient or modern wisdom had put upon a pinnacle. Her senses on the matter of thunder and lightning were peculiarly sharpened and intensified, and she was wont to declare she could smell a storm on its road when it was a hundred or so of miles away.

So now, as she stood for a moment locking down the dark avenues and up again at the inky sky, it occurred to her how much nicer and pleasanter it would be if she could get Wolf back into the house, and have her little talk with him between four solid walls of stone masonry, instead of out there, amid the shifting, deepening shadows of the trees.

"Wolf—my Wolf!" she called softly. "Wolf, Wolf—my Wolf!"

But not the faintest vibration stirred the air. Stillness, hot, hazy darkness everywhere—nothing more.

Well, there was no help for it. See him she must and would that night. It was of first and final importance. It meant, in fact, to her all the difference between a safe, leisurely, comfortable retreat and a helter-skelter rout and flight. That was all.

It would be difficult in this grimy darkness to find him, no doubt. He might possibly have gone wandering out into the fields or woods. He was just in the frame of mind to do unpleasant, unheard-of things. Well, if so, all she could do would be to wait at the gate till he returned.

He must come back some time or other. It would be tedious, it would be disagreeable, no doubt, but it was one of those tedious, disagreeable things there was no getting out of: like the paying of bills or the taking of nauseous medicine, it simply must be done. First, however, she would make the round of the garden and shrubberies; he might be hiding himself somewhere among the laurels in the darkness.

Her thoughts came to a sudden ending. Hark! what was that noise somewhere on her right hand? A sob, a groan was it? For a moment she listened intently. It sounded again, though more faintly. Ah, it must be Wolf, and not far away, either. It seemed to come from that huge beech-tree half-way down the gravelled walk. And with something of a gleam of satisfaction—born of the thought that the Fates were still fighting on her side—parting her lips and lighting her eyes, she went softly and slowly down the terrace-steps and out into the laurel-walk beyond, looking right and left as she went along.

A graceful, lissom figure she looked, gliding in and out among the shrubs. Delphine was always scrupulously—daintily-attired, but never more so than on this day of bewildering hopes and fears.

She had taken much pains with her toilette before she had faced Wolf in his study, and not one fold, one ribbon of it was disarranged now. She had on a robe of some soft satiny material, a pale carnation in colour. In make it closely followed the lines of her slender yet well-rounded figure, expressing as well as draping it. Her eyes were very brilliant that night, her colour almost hectic. Seen thus gliding in and out among the dark, shining laurels, pausing a moment to listen for a faint echo of sound, anon calling softly, sadly, "My Wolf—oh, my Wolf!" one might have fancied her a "mournful Ænone, wandering forlorn," and seeking her Paris amid the shadows of Mount Ida, or a love-lorn Dido in quest of her Æneas among Carthaginian groves.

Under the huge beech-tree there had been of late fixed a rustic garden-seat; on this, with head bowed on his clasped hands, Wolf was seated. Just before a bend in the path brought the dark outlines of his figure into sight, Delphine paused, and, taking out the big gold Tuscan pin which fastened up her knot of jet-black hair, let the whole fall *en masse* to her waist like some great silken mat. She shook it out into careless ripples, dishevelling it a little about her ears. It shadowed somewhat the bright carmine in her cheeks, and gave her a forlorn, pathetic appearance, which she knew added another dart to her quiver. Also, it would be likely to impress upon a beholder the fact of her womanhood—of her young womanhood—another and yet more dangerous weapon, she knew.

Her footfall was so light he could not have heard her tread; his instinct alone must have warned him that danger was at hand. He drew his hands from his haggard face and started to his feet.

"What is this? What is this?" he cried in loud, startled tones. "Why do you pursue me? Go at once, in Heaven's name! I have no wish to hurt you."

Delphine's hand was on his arm, her dark, beautiful face uplifted to his in a moment.

"My Wolf," she said sorrowfully, "you bid me go—where am I to go? You turn me out of your house in Heaven's name, but it is not to heaven you would send me. No, better let me stay here, and the police come for me and hang me to please your Judith."

Wolf winced.

"You came from somewhere," he said, but in not quite so firm a tone as before. "Whence you came, thither get you back. No one here will hunt you down."

"No one! Oh, my Wolf!"

"No one, I say—no one!" reiterated Wolf.

"Not even that white-faced, pale-blooded girl who, not five minutes ago, came and stood between us, and threatened you, my Wolf, with vengeance? Do you think she would spare me?"

Wolf made no reply. Delphine went on:

"Now tell me, my Wolf, what think you has made her play the part she has: hide herself in the house, hide herself on the mountain, bring back home a boy whom no one wanted here? Think you it was love for the small boy whom just, once, twice, three times she had seen and kissed? Ah no. It was hatred of me, my Wolf, because I had out-rivalled her and won your love. Only that—nothing else. She has loved you as girls love for the first time in their lives. I have seen it—I saw it in her face the first day I set foot in your house, and I saw it in her face tonight when she came in and stood between us!"

"Stop!" said Wolf with an almost savage vehemence. "I will not have such words as these spoken, even out here in the darkness. Am I altogether cast in iron? Can I stand here listening to your wild talking, and not lose my reason?"

Her words affected him in a way she had not dreamed. It was like showing a drowning man a coil of good rope safely stowed away out of his reach; or like the last glimpse of the garden of Eden which Adam caught betwixt the flaming, shifting swords of the cherubim as he toiled wearily adown the dusty, forlorn footway.

Delphine in an instant saw the mistake she had made, and retrieved it.

"She loves you, my Wolf, and she hates me for winning you. I must say it; it is true. But her love is not the love I have had to give you. No! She would love you, and keep to you so long as you were respectable, so long as you held your place in the county, and did not break any one of the ten commandments. But you turn thief, murderer, villain! Ah, she will shake you off as though you were a viper! 'So far as you show mercy to yourself so far will I have none for you.'" (here she mimicked Judith's voice and manner to the life). "No, my friend, when you turn villain, and are out at elbows, it is to the Delphines, not to the Judiths, you must go!"

Wolf was sorely troubled, he sank down on the seat once more, putting one hand before his eyes. Yet it was not Delphine's voice which wrought all this turmoil and pain in his heart, but rather the echo of Judith's words: "In so far as you show yourself mercy, so far will I have none for you." It was like the sounding of a true, clear note to a man who had once been a lover of music, but who now through physical incapacity could not touch string nor key.

Delphine drew a little nearer to him now with each word she spoke.

"Think you, my Wolf," she went on, "that out of love to you, to save you a pain, that girl would herself do a bad deed? Not she! Would she have dared, as I have, everything—everything for her lover? Ah, my Wolf, she loves in her own way, but not in mine. Your Delphine would risk her soul to give the man she loves a five minutes of pleasure. She has tried to do it and has failed!"

Her words ended in a sort of sob; she sank down on the seat by his side as she uttered them. Her warm breath fanned his cheek, her silk matted hair somehow swept itself over his shoulder.

Wolf lifted up his face in an agony.

"Great Heavens, Delphine!" he exclaimed in a voice of horror, "you don't mean to say you attempted this deed of wickedness for me—for my sake? Great God! what depths of iniquity I have dragged you down into." And he groaned aloud.

"My Wolf, I would do it all over again tomorrow, even though it failed all over again," murmured Delphine, laying her hand softly upon his arm, her head upon his shoulder.

"Hush, hush! You cut me to the heart," groaned Wolf.

In very truth this seemed to the man the hardest, bitterest blow of all. In his fiercest self-accusations it had never for one moment crossed his mind that Delphine's iniquities might in this way be laid at his door.

"My Wolf, I will say it no more! I can speak, and I can be silent. You will see! When she drags me, as she will, before the police, I will say to them, 'Yes, I tried to do it because I wanted the house—the land to be all my own. My Wolf knew nothing of it. He is innocent; I am guilty.' You will see!"

"Now, this is nonsense—sheer, contemptible nonsense!" said Wolf angrily, though his hands were gentle enough as he freed his arm and shoulder from her clinging embrace. "I can stand it no longer, my brains are going. The truth of it is, Delphine, I am too much shaken to contend with you, or even talk the matter over with you. You must simply do as I tell you; get away from here as soon as it is light tomorrow, and never attempt to see or speak to me again. You must understand everything is at an end between us."

"My Wolf, I will never leave you—never give you up!"

"Delphine, you must go!" Slowly, distinctly, and with iron force, he spoke the words.

"My Wolf, if I go, you must go with me!" She whispered the words softly, winningly into his very ear.

Wolf started. A new temptation was to beset him now.

Delphine's long veil of hair somehow swept across his breast. She looked sweetly up into his face.

"My Wolf," she murmured again, "say, what is there to keep you here now? Your house, your land, will be taken away from you; your name made a byword in the county. Think you there will be found bishop bold enough to give you even a living of three hundred a year? Are you meaning to go back to your curacy at the East of London?"

Wolf drew a long breath.

"For Heaven's sake, tempt me no more, Delphine!" he implored in an agonised tone.

"Is it a temptation? It seems to me deliverance I offer you," she said sweetly.

"Let us go away together, my Wolf, this night, before anyone can stop us. Everything is swept away from you here, you have no home—no profession—a tarnished name! Come away with me to Paris, Montreal— where you will. I will show you where to live—how to live. Ah, I know!

I will sing, and act, and get money—ah, ever so much. It will be a life worth living. Come, my Wolf—say you will come!" and once more her head drooped on his shoulder.

"In so far as you show yourself mercy, so far I will have none for you." Judith's voice at that moment seemed to repeat the words in his very ear. Would she, so he asked himself, have counselled him thus to flee from the punishment his own sin had brought upon him? Would she not rather have stood in front of him, and said: "If only by fire your sin can be purged, stand there and endure the hottest of the flames."

He rose to his feet, putting Delphine away from him gently but resolutely.

"I say you must go at daybreak, Delphine, and go you must. I will have no more said on the matter."

At this moment there came a long, low growl of approaching thunder. The mountains echoed it, ekeing out the peal to nearly double its length. There followed a soft rustling among the boughs overhead, as though a breeze had risen up and whispered among the leaves to warn them of a coming storm.

Delphine clung to him in simple abject terror.

"Oh, my Wolf—my Wolf!" she cried; "save me, save me! Ah, the terrible lightning!" And as one brilliant flash played across the sky she hid her face in his breast, trembling from head to foot.

"Come into the house," said Wolf; "there is no danger;" and he tried to draw her along the path towards the house.

But she clung to him, impeding his steps, called him her dear and dearest Wolf, implored him not to leave her; besought him again and again to take care of her. Whom had she in the world but him, her own—her very own? If he forsook and gave her up, where in the wide world could she turn for protection?

And through it all, over it all, flashed the lightning, crashed the thunder, and soughed low over their heads a mournful wind.

XV

One by one the lights in the Grange disappeared. No one knew of Wolf's and Delphine's absence from the house, save Judith, who had seen them depart. Mrs. Reece had been told by her maid (who was herself under that impression) that Mr. Wolf had gone to his room for the night; and though the old lady felt not a little sore at heart that he had not so much as greeted her since his return, she said to herself that, all things considered, perhaps it was for the best. She felt disturbed and agitated after the terrible anxiety the day had brought. He, no doubt, felt the same; and tomorrow would find them all stronger in body, clearer in mind, and better able to look the mystery, or rather succession of mysteries which had occurred, in the face.

For that there was a great deal of mystery behind it all, she was compelled, howsoever unwillingly, to admit.

Of Bertie's heirship to the estate, of his kinship to Wolf, she knew nothing. It seemed to her that Wolf had been most unnaturally disturbed by the loss of the child; she could only trace his anxiety on Bertie's behalf to a deeper, fonder feeling for Delphine than she had accredited him with, and which, to say truth, under the circumstances not a little surprised her. Possibly the greatest mystery in the affair to her mind was Judith's sudden return to the house, and appearance with little Bertie in her arms. From Wolf's study she had gone straight to Mrs. Reece's room, presenting herself without one word of explanation.

In reply to all questions, she had simply said:

"Dear Mrs. Reece, ask me nothing tonight, I implore you. Tomorrow Wolf will tell you everything himself."

Then, as little Bertie steadily refused to be on amicable terms with the old lady, Judith had thought it best to carry him off to her own room, where, laid on her bed, the little fellow very quickly fell fast asleep; and, sitting down by the bedside, she had watched her darling.

To know Judith thoroughly, one must see her with a child in her arms. A love for the weak and helpless among God's creatures was with her at once an instinct and a passion. Now, as she sat watching the little sleeping Bertie, she felt—as any mother might—all in one breath, fierce and watchful, tender and protective. For him she had felt willing to risk her life, and would have done so, had the need arisen, without a second thought on the matter. Saved and rescued now, her feeling was she must devote her life to him. Through good or ill, through difficulty or danger, she would do—well, her utmost for him. And "utmost" with Judith meant, perhaps, a little more than it does with most people.

Then the storm had crashed over the house, and she had gone to the window wondering whether Wolf had come in, and when and how they would meet on the morrow.

There followed another "riot of feeling." The "when" mattered but little; sooner or later the meeting must come; the "how" was the thing that set her heart aching and quaking. How would he face the difficulties that beset him? How would he comport himself? As penitent or as himself the wronged one? In what relationship would he stand now towards Delphine? Was his love for her the true, vital thing that compels a man to stand by a woman through sin and disgrace even till the last hour of his life; or was it after all but the flimsy pretence of love, which dissolves like ice before fire at the first rude shock it receives.

In all this range of thought it will be seen she, herself, occupied but a small space; a space so small indeed as to be almost infinitesimal. Her path was clear, her line of conduct was marked out with lines sharp as flint could mark it. This man had never asked her love, but somehow, without pretence of love-making, he had won it. There it was, his for ever, for time and for eternity. Word of love might never to the end of their lives be spoken between them, it would make no difference; her love had been given once for all, and could never be withdrawn. She looked for no result to this love; she never for one moment expected that she and Wolf would stand side by side as man and wife. No, the only hope her love had given rise to had been the hope of saving him from himself; from the evil consequences of his one departure from the path of right. She would save the thing she loved, not that she might possess and wear it as some precious jewel richly set, but simply and solely because salvation meant all that was holy, beautiful, rare, and worth having to the thing itself, as opposed to all that was worthless, marred, dishonourable, distorted.

All this time the storm was steadily increasing in violence, the wind coming and going in low, sobbing gusts. It was a grand sight. Now and again the sharp turrets and peaks of the grey mountains stood out clear and distinct in livid light, while forest and field below lay steeped in ink-black darkness; anon the mountains showed black and dim, while field and forest were for the moment ablaze with fleeting flame. As she stood thus surveying the all-but-supernatural beauty of the landscape,

CATHERINE LOUISA PIRKIS

there came a sudden terrific flash, which seemed to spend itself on the garden immediately beneath the window, lighting up every bowery corner, every tree, shrub, flower with its scintillating blaze, and showing to Judith's straining eyes a sight she would have given worlds to shut out from them: a tall, dark figure, with stooping shoulders and bare head, standing in the gravelled pathway, midway between the house and the shrubbery, and holding in his arms, and, as it seemed to her, close to his heart, a woman clad in light summer dress, with a long black veil of hair streaming below her waist.

Judith left the window immediately, and went back to Bertie's side. The rest of the night she spent on her knees.

XVI

Had Judith been by Wolf's side at the moment when the lightning revealed him to her, she might have heard him saying to Delphine in peremptory tones:

"Delphine, Delphine, rouse yourself, for Heaven's sake! How am I to get you to the house if you cling to me in this way."

And she might have heard Delphine's low, sobbing reply:

"Oh, my Wolf, my Wolf, who shall I cling to if not to you?"

And then her clinging, her tears, her piteous exclamations, had redoubled.

Wolf looked all round him despairingly. The house was still some hundred yards or so distant. His burthen was not a heavy one, but it was nevertheless a difficult and unmanageable one. Had Delphine lost her senses he might better have succeeded in getting her to the house, simply carrying her with one or two pauses by the way. As it was, however, what with her clingings and exclamations, and the weakness and dizziness he felt slowly creeping over him, the task was beyond him. The terrific strain he had endured throughout the day, his long abstinence from food, was beginning to tell upon him. The man's soul had been rent and torn till it held itself together merely by threads and shreds. His brain seemed whirling; his legs staggered under him; his arms trembled beneath their load.

He looked right and left of him. Midway between the house and where he stood, a little on his right hand, was the smoking-pavilion, over whose decoration and furnishing Delphine had expended such a vast amount of time and thought; thus far, possibly, by making a huge effort, he might contrive to get her. So, half-leading, half-carrying, he made the attempt, and somehow achieved it. He got her under shelter, he laid her on the couch just within the door, and himself stood bareheaded outside, braving the storm. Better a thousand times, so he said to himself, risk all Heaven's thunderbolts, than another half-hour of this brilliant, false woman's fascinations.

Delphine must have fainted as he laid her down, otherwise it is inconceivable that she should have given him even a brief five minutes' respite from her beseechings and allurements.

Little by little the storm ebbed, paler and fainter grew each flash, more distant and muffled each peal. It was not, however, till the

CATHERINE LOUISA PIRKIS

darkness began to lift, and grey dawn to streak the east, that it entirely subsided.

Delphine had lain, white and motionless, on her couch, and Wolf had stood outside the pavilion door throughout the remainder of that short summer night.

If only one of those grand, bright flashes of flame had struck him with death as he stood, he thought, what divine mercy it would have been! Yet, so he asked himself, what right had he to expect mercy, human or divine? And, again, Judith's voice sounded in his ears:

"In so far as you show mercy to yourself, so far will I have none for you."

These were the words beyond any other this man had need to hear. The cries and beseechings of a weak woman praying him to repent and atone, would have fallen unheeded on his ear; but these stern words of condemnation seemed to rouse him from his stupor, shut out all thoughts of self-pity from his heart, showed him what she expected of him—what her ideal of repentance was, whose soul naught but the highest ideals could satisfy.

He watched the great red sun slowly rise from behind the mountains; he watched the grey mists, one by one, creep away like evil ghosts from field and fen; he saw, through a break in the trees which shut the garden in, the deep green valley filling with a soft golden light.

One by one he heard throstle and black bird piping to its fellows in the wood a glad good-morning; then he went into the pavilion, and stooping over Delphine, endeavoured to arouse her.

"It is morning now," he said. "Come, Delphine, rise and go into the house; you must get away from here before people begin to ask questions."

Delphine opened wide her beautiful eyes.

"You send me away! Oh, my Wolf!"

Then she closed them again wearily.

Wolf felt unequal to another struggle. Little by little his life seemed ebbing out of him. Yet one final, huge effort he felt must be made, or he must own himself baffled, defeated.

"Listen, Delphine! I will tell you, so far as I can, what I am going to do, and you shall judge for yourself whether you will go or stay," he said, throwing as much steel into his voice as possible. "First, I am going to have Bertie's parentage and rights here fully recognised. I shall place his mother's marriage-certificate and the other papers you sent me, in the hands of a London lawyer, who will thoroughly go through with the matter. More than that, I intend to throw no veil over the part I have played in keeping him out of his inheritance. Before night falls today every man, woman, and child in the county will know I have been a cheat and a villain. Now, can you stand that?"

"My Wolf!" and Delphine in her amazement raised herself from her recumbent position, and sat upright on the couch.

"Do not attempt to argue the matter with me," he said, his voice increasing in strength as he went on. "My mind is made up. No one could move it—not even Judith!"

He said the last words with a slow precision. He intended them to cut her to the heart. It seemed to him only by a direct blow he could loosen her arms from about his neck.

Delphine looked up at him, cold, white, glittering.

"Not even if she knelt at your feet and hung round your neck, as I did last night?" she asked in scornful tones.

"She is not likely to do it; but if she did entreat it would be for good, not base ends, and one might save one's soul by listening to her."

Delphine laughed—not her usual long, low trill, but a loud clanging, scornful laugh.

"So then you mean to try and save your soul by means of Miss Judith's help? Go then at once, my friend; ask her to finish her good work and marry you. She'll jump at you, no doubt;" and again she laughed.

"I would die inch by inch rather than so insult her," answered Wolf sternly.

"So then what is no insult to me would be an insult to this sweet, pure-minded young lady?" she queried sharply.

Wolf gave her no reply.

For a minute she sat waiting for it. Then she rose, went to his side, and laid her hand upon his arm.

"Come, my Wolf," she said, making an attempt to regain her usual gaiety, "be honest with me. Since when have you held so exalted an opinion of this young lady, that you have looked upon an offer of marriage as an insult to her?"

"Since the very first day I set eyes on her. It will last as long as I have breath left in my body."

Then these two stood for a moment staring at each other with eyes that said as much as their silence. Words failed them. As well be dumb as loud in passion!

Wolf was the first to find a voice.

"Come, Delphine," he said, moving one step towards the door, "be reasonable; take the only road that is open to you now. Come into the house, have what refreshment you need, and take what things you like away with you. The house will soon be stirring; that means gossip beginning; and the sooner you are home again in Canada, among your own people, the better."

Delphine looked round her with dreary, dreamy eyes. Another change was passing over her—real or assumed it would have been impossible to say. To his dying day Wolf was unable to divide what was genuine in this woman from what was false.

"Home!" she repeated, letting her eyes wander here and there absently. She made a movement towards the door, looking out on the fair picture of mountain, forest, and garden which it framed. "This, I thought, was to have been my home—here, I thought, I should live in peace with my Wolf! It is passed—it was a dream." She shaded her eyes with her hands, then resumed in slower, more mournful tones: "I go—I say good-bye to it all! My fair English home that was to have been, Adieu!"

"Would you accept it as a home under its changed conditions?" asked Wolf wearily. In good truth he felt worn to his last extremity now, capable only of making one grand final effort to get this woman away from the house before the hue and cry began.

"What!" she exclaimed with a touch of her old savage petulance; "with Miss Judith preaching piety on one side, and you posing as a penitent on the other" (she gave out her p's as though they were so many raps from a wooden hammer). "Thank you, one or other of us would be under the daisies before a week had passed over our heads." Then she relapsed once more into a mute dreaminess.

"Come, Delphine," urged Wolf again; "according even to your own showing, there is no other way." He spoke as a man might who had taken a narcotic and was beginning to feel its effects creeping over him.

"There is one other way," said Delphine in a low, strange tone.

But at this moment, a sudden look of terror went fleeting over her face. She grew deathly white, even her lips fading into a grey neutral tint, her eyes growing round and staring.

Wolf followed their direction, and saw through the parted boughs of the trees which let in the wild, beautiful glimpse of valley and mountain—a tall, stalwart stranger with slouched hat and muffled throat.

The distance was too great to discern his features, but Wolf thought he recognized the outlines of the stranger who had alighted at Pen Cwellyn Station the day before.

"What frightens you?" he asked Delphine. "He is most likely some passing tourist. See, he is gone! Now come, let me take you back to the house."

She made no further resistance. Her steps faltered somewhat; she leaned heavily on his arm; she let him take her into the dining-room and put food before her, but she put it away untasted, begging only for a glass of wine. This she drank eagerly, asking for another and another. The wine seemed to put a little life into her; she smiled up in his face again.

"Now pledge me, my Wolf," she said gaily, "as I pledge you: 'A happy future to you! A long life and a merry one!' Come, my Wolf, fill your glass!"

But Wolf would as soon have thought of drinking healths at a funeral as at such a repast as this.

"Put down your glass," he said sternly. "Go upstairs and put together what things you mean to take with you—your jewellery, I mean, you may want it—and I'll go and rouse up someone to get a carriage ready for you. You can easily save the first London train if you make haste." And he went out of the room as he spoke to give the necessary orders.

"My Wolf," said Delphine, calling after him in soft, beseeching tones, "you will let me drive my ponies down for the last time? I can tell one of the men at the station to bring them back."

When, about half an hour afterwards, Wolf himself brought the ponies round to the front door (for he would not let the man come out of the stables), Delphine was standing on the terrace waiting for him, ready equipped for her journey.

Brilliantly beautiful she looked! Her eyes were dancing, glancing, flashing, changing as on the first day he had seen her; her cheeks were, perhaps, just a little more flushed than was their wont; her lips as coral-red, and smiling as when on the day of their betrothal she had lifted them up to his and said: "Seal our vows with one little kiss, oh, my Wolf!" She was as elaborately and daintily dressed as though she were starting for a royal garden-party or wedding ête, instead of a journey to London. Her favourite colours of cream and damask-red were blended and divided about her dress and hat with delicate, harmonious effect, her long cream gloves looking more suited to clasp a partner's hand in a valse than to drive a troublesome pair of fiery little ponies down a steep, rocky road.

"Have you all you want—money, everything?" he asked, as he handed her into the carriage.

"Everything but one," she answered gaily; "that you only can give me. Come, my Wolf, give me one kiss before we part for ever!"

Even as she spoke she stooped over the side of the carriage and impressed upon his lips one long, light kiss.

There seemed to Wolf an odd, indescribable odour about her lips.

In another moment she was gone, fleeting along at what seemed to him, a wild, reckless speed, throwing him one bright, laughing, defiant look, as she passed through the gates of the Grange.

Outside, for a second she reined up her ponies. Wolf sprang forward, thinking something possibly had gone wrong with their harness But no; it was only to speak to a man who stood there in low-crowned, slouching hat, and who, to Wolf's intense surprise, swung himself into the carriage alongside of her, and on they went at as wild, wind-like speed as before.

Wolf drew a long weary sigh as they disappeared in the grey distance. Then he went back to the house, up to his own room, and sank down on his bed utterly spent, mentally and physically. One hour at least of sleep he felt he must have, before he could face the work which that day would bring him to do.

As he turned wearily, hiding his face in his pillows, a thrush perched upon his window-sill burst suddenly into a glad, full-throated song.

Somehow it sounded in his tired ears like a *Te Deum Laudamus.*

XVII

Sunday morning. Church-bells sounding over all the land, households by the score gathering themselves together to start for their divers Zions. A family of four assembled in the hall of the old Grange: a blind old lady with a somewhat enquiring, anxious look on her well-featured face, which seemed to say: "Well, I suppose I shall know all in good time; but I shall be uncommonly glad when the good time comes;" a small boy of four or five, fragile, and fair-haired as a gold-winged fairy; a young girl with pale face and dark eyes, that looked weary and wistful; a tall man, deathly white, with rigid muscles and firm-set mouth, which seemed to betoken a task set before him—a something to be done that needed a clear brain, an iron will.

Not a trace of last night's storm remained, save that, if possible, the whole landscape of mountain and glen shone out a little more golden-green than its wont. There was a look of wind-blown clearness about it which threw into bold relief every distant peak or jutting crag.

There seemed, too, to lurk a latent fragrance in the air, as though the scent, beaten out of the flowers by over-night's storm, was left behind to tell the tale of its power and grandeur.

Party after party of church-goers went toiling along the steep road to Llanrhaiadr, saying one to another how terrific the tempest of last night had been, and what a mercy it was that the poor little orphan boy at the Grange had been found and brought home before it broke over the mountains.

All sorts of odd stories, anent the finding of little Bertie, were by this time afloat in the neighbourhood, each person having a theory of his own on the matter, which he affirmed with all the doggedness, and not a little of the exaggerative power, of the Welsh peasant. Of the Reece household servants, not a soul save Bryce knew the real truth, and she was far too wary to commit herself on the matter. The child was saved, that was all she cared about; Miss Judith would, she knew, see that he had his rights, now that wicked aunt of his was off the scene. If Mr. Wolf were wise, he would, of course, leave the house as soon as possible; but there, after all, that was his business, not hers.

Many were the hearty greetings little Bertie had as he drove along to church that Sunday morning, in fact he went bareheaded nearly all the way, and almost kissed the tips of his little fingers off returning the salutations of old, young, and middle-aged.

They mustered a somewhat strong party from the Grange. Wolf had said at breakfast that morning that he wished every soul in the house to be present at the eleven o'clock service, and that he had a particular reason for wishing it. There had consequently been a more vigorous stampede than usual towards the parish church, and a solitary kitchen-maid, and equally lone stable-boy, remained the only representatives of domestic economy at Plasy-y-Coed.

It seemed a long, silent drive to Judith that morning. Mrs. Reece, even, appeared to have lost her ordinary inclination for asking and answering questions. Whether it was the shadow of coming or of past events which had fallen upon her she knew not, but certain it was her usually serene brow was clouded, her usually active lips were at rest.

As for Wolf, not once during the three miles' drive did he open his lips. In silence he handed his mother and Judith into the carriage, then leaned back in his place with frowning, knotted brow, and eyes that looked all absorbed and far away; in silence he handed them out of the carriage and followed them into the church; then, to Judith's surprise, instead of taking his usual place in the pew, he went at once into the vestry.

Here he found the worthy rector already robed and about to enter his reading-desk. He shook hands warmly with Wolf.

"You will hardly believe it," he said, "but I have only this morning heard of the terrible anxiety you have been suffering at Plas-y-Coed. I was away from home all yesterday. I returned too late last night for rumours to reach me. This morning I was told of the loss and the finding of the child in one breath. Otherwise, you may be sure, I should have ridden over to offer my services. You must tell me all about it after service, for all sorts of queer stories are flying about the place."

Wolf thanked him briefly.

"I have a favour to beg of you," he then went on to say. "You have frequently asked me to occupy your pulpit. I shall be very glad if you will allow me to do so this morning."

The rector gladly consented, thinking to himself that possibly Wolf was awakening at last to the responsibilities of his position in the neighbourhood, and was anxious, it might be, to take his place among his neighbours, not only as a rich land-owner, but as an active, zealous clergyman.

When Judith saw Wolf seat himself within the altar-rails, her heart died within her. What did it mean—what could it mean? He could not surely—no, she would not let herself think that. It would be too dreadful! He had some definite reason, no doubt, for what he was doing; he had something to say to the congregation he thought worth saying, some good advice to give—nothing more.

He had something to say to the congregation, and he had no sooner mounted the pulpit and given out his text than she knew what it was, word for word, as though she could read it written in his brain. Self-pilloried he meant to stand there and acknowledge his sin to the world! It was brave, like himself; it was fiercely defiant, like himself; it was, perhaps, the only sort of repentance and atonement a man of his temperament was capable of, a repentance sincere and thorough, no doubt, but withal without so much as one grain of Christian humility in it.

For one moment before he gave out his text Wolf stood silent in the pulpit surveying the congregation. As usual, the small church was well filled. There were Lord and Lady Ruthlyn, with their family, in their places, the lieutenant of the county and his family in theirs, and Madoxes, and Howels, Wynnes, and Williamses might be numbered by the score.

The man's face was ashen grey as that of a corpse, his muscles seemed stiff and rigid as though life had gone out of them; one knotted vein stood out on his forehead; his eyes gleamed with something more than their usual brightness; the high light in which he stood threw into prominence his blanched hair, his furrowed brow, the lines which care, not age, had marked about his mouth. Some of those who saw him that morning in their thoughts might have likened him to a Thomas à Beckett thundering forth a Pope's anathema, but not one to a Paul or a John the Divine.

In the pulpit Wolf had ever had a strong, clear voice, an arresting, an assertive voice—the voice not of a controversialist, a reasoner who is willing to allow that a very fair case may be made out for the other side, but rather that of a dogmatist—a judge, a man given to pronouncing final judgments from which there was no appeal. His voice had never in his best days been firmer or clearer than it was now when he opened his Bible, and read out his text from the fifty-first Psalm: "I acknowledge my offences, and my sin is ever before me."

He read it out once, looking straight in front of him; he read it a second time, looking to his right hand—a third time, turning to his left.

Then without preamble of any sort he began his sermon, or rather what was to stand in guise of sermon to the congregation that day.

"The story of a sinner," it might have been called, for such it was from beginning to end.

"Not to a scriptural sinner, nor yet to an heroic sinner do I wish to direct your attention today," he said in slightly scornful tones, "but to a most commonplace specimen of a commonplace class—the class who for a mess of pottage will sell what little soul they happen to possess, who at the shrine of Mammon are willing to sacrifice honour, honesty, truth, and religion."

And then he went on to tell them in the third person, as though that of a stranger, the story of his own life from those old early days of poverty and hardship onwards to that day, extenuating naught, exaggerating naught, naught omitting, naught slurring over.

It took a long time to tell. He spoke slowly; he made long pauses between his sentences—pauses during which the congregation, looking one at the other, wondered of whom he spoke, scarcely daring, even in their thoughts, to fix the suspicion of the course of crime he detailed on the minister of God who stood there in the pulpit addressing them.

He apologised somewhat for the allusion to his early life of poverty.

"You must not think this is in any sort intended as a palliation of this man's crime later on. I tell you this portion of his history simply because without it I could not give you a perfect picture of the man. If you take it as an extenuation of his later life you will make a mistake. It is not so intended; you must not so take it."

On Delphine's share in the evil-doing, her wiles and temptings, he touched but lightly—as lightly as was consistent with the continuity of the narrative. He spoke of a letter containing an evil offer—an offer of concealing the existence of an heir to property which had lately come to this man, and then dwelt at length and fully on the deliberate manner in which he had closed with it; the deliberate course of concealment and fraud he had pursued even when, later on, the young heir was committed to his care and protection.

And then he hinted at an attempt which had been made to murder this young heir, where and how he did not think it necessary to relate, for it must be fresh in all their minds at that moment, made, as it was, in their very midst, only two days ago.

Here he made a long pause. It might have been that the recollection of those awful hours of suspense nearly overcame him; it might have been, in good truth, that, stupendous as was this man's strength of will and purpose, sheer physical weakness was beginning to sap both.

There came a visible stir and movement among the congregation as he thus paused. The interest in the narration had by this time passed through its preliminary stage of curiosity, and had become painful—intense. Judith felt as though Æons had passed over her head since she had entered that little church not much more than an hour ago. Her heart thrilled with every word he uttered, her throat felt choking, her brain went round, as he thus dealt himself blow after blow, each one harder than the last. She longed to stand up and cry aloud in the congregation that there was a side to this man's character which he had not shown to them, and of which they knew nothing, and that, strong as he had been for evil, so strong was he for good.

And Mrs. Reece, too, felt herself suddenly grow aged, spiritless, incapable, as she sat there listening to these terrible revelations—sat with face as immobile and marble-white as the one that looked out of the pulpit, and with will as iron as Wolf's own, suppressing every sign of emotion even to a quiver of her eyelid, that might show her heart was being stabbed in a thousand places.

Wolf's concluding sentences may be given word for word.

"You will ask me," he said, looking round on the people with an eye that would not have quailed before the sternest there, and in a voice which, spite of its failing force, had a something of defiance in it—"you will ask me, naturally enough, how does this man's history concern us—what has it to do with us? This is how it has to do with you, this is how it concerns you, each one as individuals of a community. A plague-spot has somehow shown itself among you—it must be cleansed away. A fraud and criminal act has been done in your very midst, it must be searched out and punished. One among you stands up a greater criminal than ever had sentence of penal servitude read over his head—he must be brought before a bar of justice. It rests with you, fathers of families, magistrates, and administrators of justice in the county to do this."

"I do not need to tell you who this man is nor where he lives. Nathan-like already your hearts have, I know, turned towards me saying, 'Thou art the man!'"

And then he sat down, and everyone felt the discourse had fitly come to an end, and were right thankful that it had. Each one looked

CATHERINE LOUISA PIRKIS

into another's face, drawing a long, deep breath. The old rector got up from his chair, and in a shaking voice, and with tears running down his cheeks, concluded the service, for Wolf made no attempt to do so. He remained seated in the pulpit till the benediction had been pronounced; then, as the congregation stirred and prepared to depart, he rose, left the pulpit, paused at the foot of the stairs to deposit his surplice in the verger's hands, went through the very midst of the people straight to his own carriage, where Judith and Mrs. Reece were already seated.

One and another looked after him.

"He is callous and stony-hearted," said one.

"He is broken-spirited and half-dazed," said another.

"Let him alone," said a third. "God has judged him. See, he has death written on his face."

In silence, as they had driven to the church, so Wolf and his party drove back along that weary three and a half miles of road. It might have been a funeral-car they sat in, those three, for their white faces, their bowed heads, and weary, strained eyes, to which the blessed balm of tears had not yet been vouchsafed.

At the gates of the Grange, an unaccustomed sight greeted them—a small knot of people gathered together, evidently awaiting their return.

A man came out of the lodge, as they drew up for the gates to be opened, with a strange story to tell.

He was a police-superintendent, and stated that he had come over from Pen Cwellyn, and wished to speak with Mr. Reece.

Wolf jumped out of the carriage. What horror was to greet his ears now?

The man looked at the ladies; Wolf took the hint, and led the way towards the house, the man, in the meantime, telling his story.

A terrible accident had occurred that morning, or rather event, for circumstances attending it showed such evident design and forethought that accident it could scarcely be called. A lady and gentleman had, with carriage and ponies, been precipitated over the Pen Cwellyn falls, a height of some sixty feet or so. Their bodies had been found fearfully mutilated at the base of the jagged rocks, and had been recognised— the lady's as that of a late visitor at the Grange, the man's as that of a stranger who had recently put up at the Pen Cwellyn Inn.

Wolf reeled, sick and faint, against the rough trunk of a big elm-tree near which they stood. This was indeed an awful epilogue to the drama which the past two years had seen played out.

XVIII

Mrs. Reece and Judith saw but little of Wolf that Sunday or the day following. All through that night a light came streaming from his study-window, making a square yellow patch on the lawn beneath, but never a sound came from the room, not so much as the crumpling of paper, or rustling of leaves.

No one dared disturb him in his solitude and sorrow, each one rightly feeling that intrusion at such a time would have been an impertinence. Food was taken to him from time to time, and Mrs. Reece sent one brief message, asking him if he would go to her for a few minutes, to which he wrote back one brief reply:

"Not tonight, mother—tomorrow."

On the morrow things went on much the same way, save that an intimation from the county coroner was received by Wolf, stating that the inquest on the bodies found below Pen Cwellyn falls would take place that day, and requesting his presence as a witness.

This inquest, of necessity a dismal affair, brought to light so many curious circumstances connected with one of the deceased persons that an adjournment was asked for and granted in order that a *post-mortem* examination might be performed. This examination proved beyond doubt that the lady had been so bent on death that she had taken poison before starting on her last reckless drive, and that the poison must have begun to act just before, or at the time she reached Pen Cwellyn falls.

With respect to this drive, some singular facts transpired. The lodge-keeper at the Grange deposed to hearing the sounds of wheels early on Sunday morning, and wondering who could be about at that time, peeped out through the blinds, and saw Mr. Reece opening the gates for Miss Pierpoint to drive through. It struck her as being strange and unusual, and she went into the next room, whose window looked down the road, and saw Miss Pierpoint suddenly pull up, and say something to a man waiting there. He immediately jumped into the carriage beside her, and the two drove away down the Pen Cwellyn road.

Wolf's evidence at this point corroborated the woman's testimony.

Another witness—a lad driving some cattle to a field—deposed that at a turn in a narrow lane the carriage and ponies came suddenly upon him. The cattle were straggling, and obstructed the road, and the lady with not a little difficulty pulled up the ponies, who were going at a very rapid pace. The man who sat next the lady offered to take the reins, in fact, urged upon her to give them up to him, whereupon the lady replied:

"My friend, they wouldn't stand your touch; you would pull at their mouths as you pulled at your ropes on board ship, and they would go mad—just."

The evidence of the last witness, however, was of the most importance. He was a night-keeper on Lord Ruthlyn's preserves, and was going home to his breakfast when he heard a carriage coming along at a tremendous pace down the Pen Cwellyn road. He thought at first that the ponies had taken fright and bolted, but when they came nearer he saw that the lady had them well in hand, and was urging them on with light touches of the whip and a coaxing "So ho! so ho?" To his great surprise, she suddenly and sharply turned them round the corner out of the high road and down a narrow, steep way which led straight to the falls. He was himself standing at the corner of this narrow road, and heard the man who sat with her in the carriage make some remark, to which the lady replied: "My friend, it is a short cut;" and as she spoke she once more touched up the ponies with the whip, and they went like the wind, tearing down the steep lane. The lady looked, he thought, nearly as wild as the ponies, and she laughed a long, low laugh as she spoke which was not pleasant. He was near enough to see that her eyes were very bright and her cheeks very red.

It all struck him as being strange, and he waited at the corner of the turning to see what happened next. The lane was perfectly straight, he could see right down it to where it suddenly overlapped the falls; a narrow footway turning to the left being here the only outlet to the path. On and on went the ponies; he expected to see them slacken, and the lady and gentleman alight to view the falls; instead of that she seemed to be still urging them on, till at last the little creatures were evidently past control, and had bolted. Then he saw the man stand up in the carriage, and snatch at the reins, he saw the horses rear violently on the very edge of the rock, and then in another moment all had disappeared.

He could not bring himself alone to face the terrible sight which he knew must lie at the base of the cliffs, so turned back and went to Pen Cwellyn, and gave notice to the police.

This was all the evidence (with collateral corroboration) needed to prove the identity of the deceased persons, and the cause of their deaths. A suicide and a murder most undoubtedly it was.

Delphine's room and boxes left behind at the Grange were in due course searched, and the scent-case containing three bottles was produced. One of these held chloral, a second a deadly poison, a third a poison not less sure, but slower in its effects. Of this last, no doubt, Delphine, to doubly ensure her own death, had partaken before she set off on her mad quest of vengeance.

Both bodies were buried in Llanrhaiadr churchyard in separate graves. The man's marked only by a grassy mound, Delphine's with a headstone carved with her initials, D. P.; this erected by Wolf's orders. He could not forget that he and this woman had once clasped hands as betrothed lovers.

When the news of this terrible event reached Canada sundry details respecting Delphine and Olivette Pierpoint were brought to light, and published in the public journals there. It may be as well to give them in this place.

Of the early parentage of these women little was known, save that their father was given to frequenting low cafés in the slums of Montreal. Their mother was supposed to be French, for both children spoke their English with a strong French flavour, a flavour which in later years Olivette dropped, but Delphine cultivated and retained. Both these children were of remarkable beauty and great intelligence, and thus attracted the attention of the manager of a low class theatre, who, among other *aliases*, bore that of Phil, or Philip Munday. This man conceived the idea of forming a trio of beautiful children, who should make part of a travelling company, and pose in the interludes as Graces, Fates, or what you will.

One child, a little orphan called Bertha, he had already secured, Delphine and Olivette eventually fell into his clutches, he, no doubt, making it greatly to the father's advantage to hand the children over to him. It did not appear at any time that he treated these children with any special or intentional brutality; they were naturally dragged to his level, which, to say truth, was a low one. As the "Three Graces," afterwards as "The Fates," and last of all as "The Sirens," these girls made the tour of Canada and the States, gaining some little celebrity, and putting not a little money into Munday's pocket. As time went on, however, and the girls grew to womanhood, he began to find them somewhat assertive and unmanageable. They would, strange to say, choose lovers for themselves, also they occasionally accepted engagements without deference to his opinion, and Bertha, the eldest of the three, at last entirely threw over his authority by eloping with Bernard Reece in his yacht, and persuading Delphine to accompany her. The man Munday felt this blow doubly, first in his pocket, for forthwith his travelling company, bereft of these brilliant actresses, collapsed, and secondly in his affections, for of late he had posed as the accepted lover of Delphine. From this time forth he led a downward career, figuring in all sorts of doubtful vocations with a more than doubtful success. As for Delphine, her introduction to the refinements of life on board Bernard's yacht quickly cured her of all taste for Munday's society, and awoke in her a vast ambition to secure for herself some of the good things which were showered with a lavish hand on Bertha. Bernard's early death so quickly followed by Bertha's, their child, being left unprotected and unacknowledged on her hands, gave her the means in some sort of realising her wild schemes.

She came to Europe. Her tale has been told.

XIX

The inquest and funeral in all occupied five days of that eventful week. A wearying, harassing five days they were to all concerned—a five days that seemed to have compressed into them the anxiety, the anguish, the suspense of at least five years. For suspense prolonged, never for one instant lifted, was the one terrible feature of those terrible five days, at least to Judith and Mrs. Reece; what Wolf thought or felt was not easy to get at.

Day after day these two women rose from their beds with one thought in their minds: "What will happen before we lie down here again tonight?"

How far Wolf had made himself amenable to the laws of the land they did not know, nor how far the county magnates might feel inclined to put those laws in force against him. But they never saw messenger coming up the avenue, nor heard the sound of stranger's voice in the hall, without saying to themselves: "It has come now. It is Wolf they are seeking."

Judith began to feel herself growing old in those days; Mrs. Reece laid aside her knitting and took to reading her Bible a great deal. It was one with raised characters, specially procured for her by Wolf.

The county magnates, however, showed no sign of moving in the matter, though no doubt they talked it well over between themselves and said each to the other that it was a crying shame that such a crime as that should go unpunished; the man was a self-confessed criminal, someone ought to interfere for the protection of the child; the bishop ought, at least, to be written to, to inhibit the man; and then, no doubt, they shrugged their shoulders and went home to their dinners, each one saying to himself it wasn't exactly his business, and he didn't care to be the first to move in the matter.

Some or other of these Welsh squires met Wolf almost daily while the inquest was going on; they used to look somewhat askance at him, and no doubt would have shunned him, had it not been something of an impossibility to shun a man who makes no advances to you, who persistently in a room sits as far off from every one as possible, and never opens his lips save when he is pointedly addressed.

What the man himself, during those days, thought, felt, suffered, no one ever knew, for he took no one into his confidence. He rode over to Pen Cwellyn daily to attend the inquest, answering every question put to him in a dry, hard voice, which seemed to those who heard him to betoken either a callous heart or a torpid brain. On one point only did he observe a strict reticence, positively declining to satisfy any one's curiosity. This was with reference to Delphine's attempted murder of Bertie, when incidentally alluded to in the course of the inquest. How it came to his knowledge, who was his informant, he declined to state. No good end could be now served by his supplying information on the matter. The child was safe, the intended murderess had met her doom. So far as he was concerned, the whole thing was a sealed book, and though whispers and rumours were rife in many a household throughout the county, no one gave affirmation or denial to them, and a sealed book it remained.

When Wolf came back from Pen Cwellyn each day late in the afternoon, he used to go straight to his study, and there remain till nightfall, and the rest of the household had gone to their rooms. Judith or Mrs. Reece rarely set eyes on him; no one knew when he rose in the morning, nor when he went to bed at night. His study-door was always shut, and he denied himself to all enquirers. It is true he accorded to his mother the interview she had begged, but it might as well have been refused, for all the gratification she got out of it.

As she said pathetically to Judith afterwards:

"My dear, we were like strangers to each other; we were simply miles apart. He was politeness itself to me, gentle—for him, that is—but I would far sooner have had an ounce or two of his roughness and bad temper, and felt all the time he was my own son. He put all my questions on one side, begged me not to allude to the past, asked me if I wanted anything, said he would send Phœbe to me, and then went away and left me. My own belief is," and here her quavering voice sank to a whisper, "that his brain is failing him—little by little, my dear, but only too surely."

And Judith, thinking over all that this man had gone through, and was enduring now, said to herself:

"What wonder was it if his brain did fail him?"

Surely never since the days when Samson Agonistes laded himself with the gates of the city of Gaza, had living man sought to bear alone and unaided so terrible a burthen!

How would it end? The thought oppressed her beyond endurance morning, noon, and night. Sometimes when she watched him riding away to Pen Cwellyn down the avenue in the bright June sunshine, looking white, forlorn, preoccupied, a terror would rise up in her heart lest he should never come back again. The feeling grew upon her day by day. What plans could he be forming in his brain for the years to come? or was he in very truth so brain-sick, so time-tired, that he lacked power to form plans of any sort, and was going to let himself drift hither, thither, like straw or dead leaf upon a whirling stream?

Again and again did his own words, spoken in that hard, metallic voice of his that terrible morning when he stood self-pilloried in the little parish church, come back to her, and re-reiterate themselves in her brain.

"All that goes to make youth or even middle-life is lacking to this man," he had said. "Hope is dead, faith, too, in God, in man, in himself. He has no eye for the beauty in the world around him; no ear for the music that holy voices, happy voices are for ever making the universe through. He has no brain to give to thought or study; no heart for human love; no soul for prayer or praise. What more can be wanted to complete a picture of cheerless, joyless old age?"

What more, indeed! And the man not yet in the prime of his manhood! It was too awful to think of him seeing himself thus as it were in a clear, faithful mirror, and going his way saying: "It is Kismet—thus it must be."

"There is a time to speak, and a time to keep silence." Judith felt that her time for keeping silence must be drawing to a close, that her lips could not much longer remain sealed, for there was that in her heart which must be put into words.

When the Friday of that week came she watched him riding away to Llanrhaiadr churchyard to attend Delphine's funeral. Others who were there told her afterwards that bare-headed he stood beside the open grave like some marble statue throughout the whole service, but that not once did he bow his head or his lips utter an Amen.

She watched him riding back late in the evening slowly, wearily, like a man whose evening hymn is, "Thank God, my work is over, for there is not left in me strength for another hour of toil." His head was stooped on his breast, the reins lay loosely in one hand, the other occasionally shaded his eyes, or hung limply by his side. He made no effort to guide his horse, he passed the man who stood there

CATHERINE LOUISA PIRKIS

waiting for him to dismount, and let the animal take his own way to the stables. Afterwards she heard him enter the house with his usual slow, flagging step, then almost immediately the study door was shut heavily.

Judith's mind was made up. She went downstairs, ordered wine and food to be brought to her on a tray, and herself took it to Wolf's door, knocking and asking if she might come in.

He knew her voice in an instant, and immediately himself opened the door.

"Why, what is this?" he exclaimed, taking the tray out of her hands and carrying it into the room; "what does it mean, Judith?"

"It means," she replied firmly, "that you must eat and drink, for you have need of food. Sit down, I mean to wait upon you;" and she drew a chair forward for him, and placed the tray in front of him.

He obeyed her like a little child almost, looking about him meantime somewhat absently and dreamily. He put the meat away from him, however, taking only the bread and wine which she offered.

"See Judith," he said, "it is a sacrament to me." And in good truth a sacramental feast it seemed to both in its silence and solemnity.

When he had finished he leaned back in his chair languidly; he looked like a man wearying for sleep and rest, which for some reason he dared not take.

"Why not?" said Judith gently. "Lie down and rest; I am sure you are worn out."

Her voice seemed to recall his drowsy senses. He pulled himself together and rose from his chair, making a visible effort to do so.

"Will you go out with me, Judith, this evening, into the woods, it is not very late? You would not be afraid, would you?" he said.

He made the request humbly, diffidently. Judith mentally compared his manner of asking now with the peremptory "Come into the woods" he was wont at one time to address to her.

She hesitated only a moment.

"Are you fit to go out this evening?" she asked, "after all the fatigue you have been through today?"

His reply was another question: "Are you afraid to trust yourself with me, Judith?" It was spoken humbly, diffidently, as before.

It cut Judith to the heart. It seemed to say, "Now that my infamy is blazoned abroad in the world, a young and innocent girl may well hesitate to be seen in my company."

"Afraid? No! I will fetch my hat at once!" was her indignant rejoinder, and forthwith she departed.

When she came downstairs, Wolf was waiting for her at the hall-door. They went out through the garden, thence into the fields, thence into the woods beyond, almost in silence.

The sun had only just sunk behind the mountains, a shifting, golden haze yet filled the glen, and hung in patches on the mountain-side; but here, in the woods, all was solemn, twilight dimness; green was fading into grey; bird's notes were hushing and ending in low, soft trills. There was a distant cooing of some sleepy wood-pigeon, a far-away sound of burring insect or twilting bat. That was all. As they made their way through the tangle of brushwood, stooping under the low-growing bows of sycamore and birch, the place seemed to Judith solemn, sweet, and holy as the aisle of a church.

Wolf walked on a little ahead, stamping down, here and there, a tall thistle, and carefully clearing her path of bramble and briar, yet, so it seemed to her, with such feeble, languid hands, and eyes so inward and, withal, so far away, one could fancy he was looking at strange sights in another world.

Judith felt somehow spellbound, as though her lips had been touched with an enchanter's wand, and power to part them failed her. On and on in silence she followed him; where he led she felt she must go, though it were to the nethermost gulf to the souls of the lost.

At the edge of St. Govan's stream he paused for the first time. Something had whispered to her that he would lead her here; her thoughts flew to the first walk they had taken together now so long ago, and the desperate eager questions he had put to her about the possibility of an erring soul achieving salvation. Was this also in his thoughts, she wondered, and would he—did he mean in this place to repeat his old vehement questions?

His first words, however, showed that another, not himself, filled his thoughts now.

"Judith," he said in quiet dreamy tones, that had not in them the faintest echo of his old abrupt peremptoriness, "my mother is old and feeble now; I want you to promise me that, in the days to come, you will think of her, and take care of her."

Judith felt greatly troubled, she scarce knew why.

"To the end of my life," she answered with odd catchings of her breath, "she shall be as my own mother."

"Thank you," was all he said in reply. Then on he went once more, turning sharply to his left hand and following now the upward course of the stream.

On she went after him; the sparkling rivulet narrowed and rippled, and widened again, and then dashed itself in a miniature cascade over mossy stones. Quieter and darker grew the woods around them, greyer and dimmer showed the patches of sky here, there, through the arching boughs overhead.

They had now almost reached the foot of the mountains; the steep treacherous path which Delphine had cajoled the little Bertie to mount was about a hundred yards or so in front of them. It was a place of dreary memories. Judith thought with a shudder of the terrible hours she had passed there.

Wolf's voice was even quieter and more weary than before, as he asked a second question:

"I know," he said, "you will take care of little Bertie. I need not ask you to do that; but will you think of Oscar too—sometimes?"

Judith, with an effort, steadied her voice to answer in the lowest of tones:

"Bertie shall be to me as my own child, Oscar, as my own brother."

And for the life of her she could not divest herself of the feeling that she was talking to a man in a trance, who was seeing sights that were veiled from her eye, hearing sounds that her dulled senses could not receive.

Wolf looked up dreamily, wearily, at the beetling mountains, dun-grey now in the fast-fading light.

"I want to be alone, Judith," he said, speaking like a tired child whose powers have been overtaxed with a day of toil. "I think if I went up those mountains I might perhaps be able to—to pray."

He said the last word hesitatingly and almost in a whisper.

Judith started, looking up in his face; it showed ashen and faded as the twilight itself. The words of Christ to His disciples, "Tarry ye here, while I go and pray yonder," came into her head. It might be easier to pray alone on a mountain-side than in a deep wooded glen.

She seated herself on a rough mossy stone.

"I will wait here till you come back," she said quietly, folding her hands in her lap.

He made no reply. He gave her one long, lingering, dreamy look, and then slowly and wearily began to mount the steep path.

Her eyes followed him, step by step, as he went. Faint and fainter sounded his footfall; dim and dimmer showed his black, stooping figure against the grey sky, until at length he rounded the narrow ledge of the upward way where grew those treacherous trees in which Bertie had so nearly met his doom, and disappeared from her sight.

Patiently and with clasped hands she waited his return.

The air began to blow chill and damp, a low breeze began to sigh among the larches. The night-clouds began to creep up from the horizon, a ghostlike mist seemed to hang between the sycamores, and spread itself over the running stream.

And suddenly as with electric force another thought flashed into her brain—of Moses, when he had finished his work and said "good-bye" to his countrymen, going up a solitary mountain-side alone in solemn grandeur to die.

She sprang to her feet, a sudden, awful terror seizing her heart.

"Oh, Wolf, Wolf, Wolf!" she cried passionately, stretching out her arms towards the rough, blue crags. "Come back, come back!"

But only the mountains and forest echoed her wild cry through the gathering gloom: "Wolf, Wolf, come back!"

Then, "at one stride came the dark."

XX

Four new years in succession have been born, have flourished, have died, and been buried by their successors under heaps of snow since Wolf and Judith looked their last at each other at the foot of the Llanniswth mountains, and lo! now a fifth with laggard ancient feet is going to his death-bed, but never a word of Wolf Reece yet!

It is now a thing of the past how Judith and Mrs. Reece had sought him the country through; how they had offered rewards for any scrap of tidings of him if living, of his body if dead; how, from time to time, their hearts had been rent and torn by scares and rumours; how they had been now and again lifted to the pinnacle of false hopes only to be once more dashed to the depths of despair; how Judith had herself scoured the mountains from north to south, how she and Mrs. Reece had together posted from town to town, from village to village, all through North Wales, seeking news of him; how they had joined hands in prayer, praying God to let them know the worst, and end their awful suspense; how they had wept on each other's necks as, this prayer denied them, they had risen up and faced the dreary days once more; how, at length, with bowed head and wan face they had gone about the house trying to stamp out of their hearts alike hope, expectation, or despair.

All this is now a thing of the past; whatever else of good or bad the hours may have in store for them, this, with its intermittent hopes and numbness of despair can never be given them to live through again.

During these five years so nearly run out, time, the great scene-shifter, has done his work nimbly, deftly, as of yore. And death, that silent footed stage-manager, has followed in his wake, changing the dramas, and calling now this actor, now that, from off the stage; dismissing here one who played a chief part, there, one who was little more than a *figurante;* here one who was a very veteran in his art, there one who was scarcely even a *débutante.*

Over to France he went, found out old Uncle Pierre in retreat at Versailles, and cried to him to give up his part for the time, for exit had come. Then back to Plas-y-Coed he footed it, and wrested the play-book from little Bertie's hands before he had well conned his first half-dozen lines. Off to India next, and there he finds Colonel Wynne with all sorts of delightful pre-visions in his heart of a bright, happy, English home, ruled by a bright, happy, English daughter. He touches his hand, he whispers a word in his ear, and lo! the colonel, instead of steaming home along the pleasant ocean highway, with a score or so of other cheery, homeward-bound passengers, sees a great silent ship waiting for him, in which, willy-nilly, he is forced to take passage, and go sailing away to the unknown land.

It was hard on Judith, thus one by one to have her household gods shattered. Her heart seemed to grow very chill, very empty. She was not one of those who fill old shrines with new divinities. No; "let that which God hath made empty so remain; let that which is broken lie broken still," was rather the language of her heart.

Little Bertie's death she probably felt the most of the three. It was more actual to her—it left more gaps and blanks in her everyday life. Uncle Pierre she had wept and bewailed as henceforth dead to her when he went sailing away to China, and she had, to a certain extent, over-lived (though unknowingly to herself) the wrench and pain of that bereavement before the final blow came. For her father's death her grief was even less poignant; years of separation had made a gulf between them which it would have taken years of companionship to bridge over. But with little Bertie it was otherwise. The child had somehow so entwined himself about her heart, she scarce knew which were his fibres, which her own.

After Wolf's disappearance she had constituted herself his guardian, his teacher, his nurse, his playfellow—in a word, his mother. The words on Judith's lips, "He shall be as my own child," meant more than they might on the lips of most young girls. As her own child he was to her during the brief span of life allotted to him, and when, after a winter of sharp lung-disease, he slowly faded, just as spring violets and primroses were coming into bloom, it was as her own child she mourned him.

Old Mr. Maurice, so long administrator to the estate of the Reece family, had been charged with the task of identifying the little Bertie as rightful heir to the property. He naturally preferred a coadjutor in the matter, and selected for the post a much-esteemed lawyer living at Pen Cwellyn. Together they went through Wolf's papers, finding them in a surprising state of order and exactness. In a large sealed envelope in a prominent place they found the marriage certificate of Bertie's father and mother, together with full information of the minister who performed the ceremony, and where he could most likely be heard of. All receipts and expenditures of the estate were made up to date with scrupulous exactness, and Wolf's bank-book showed pitifully with what small sums for personal use he had contented himself, and how insatiable had been Delphine's rapacity.

The details of the inheritance had not under these conditions been difficult to arrange. The Pen Cwellyn lawyer had proposed that Bertie should be made a ward in chancery with Judith nominated as guardian.

This had been scarcely done when symptoms of his mother's fatal disease showed themselves in the child, and he was removed from earthly to heavenly keeping.

Oscar, of course, in the event of Wolf's decease, stood next heir; in his brother's death, however, Oscar steadily refused to believe, and as steadily (for three years, at any rate) refused to take possession of the estate. The story of Wolf's sin, of his repentance, and of his subsequent disappearance had been a terrible blow to Oscar; it had been told him gently but truthfully by Judith in a long, carefully-worded letter. She and Mrs. Reece had rightly judged that it would be wiser and kinder not to keep the truth from him, for there is no land to which rumour, on its swift, strong wing, cannot bear its load of lies.

A sharp, bitter blow it was to the lad that the brother he had so deeply reverenced could thus have erred, but it was a blow nevertheless which seemed in some sort to restore his own mind to its right balance.

It somehow shook out of his heart the ashes of the lost love, the regrets, the self-pity which lay smouldering in it; it seemed to set his feet more firmly in the upward path he had marked out for himself.

Oscar did very well out in India. He made friends rapidly in all directions. Of his own free will he would have remained there, climbing step by step up the ladder, making his own way and fortune in life. His mother's importunities, however, and, of late, Judith's, succeeded at length in bringing him home.

"See, dear Oscar," wrote Judith, "everyone, everything here, needs you. Your mother cannot hope to see many more years. She has had pain and sorrow enough, Heaven knows. Give her what you can of peace, if not of joy, in her later years. Then, too, this place is needing a master sadly. Mr. Maurice is so old he wants to resign, and there is no one here who can appoint his successor. Everything seems getting into almost inextricable confusion for want of a final decision. A variety of small, harassing matters are being daily referred to your mother, with which she really ought not to be troubled. It certainly seems to me your bounden duty to return at once, and take all these things upon your own shoulders. Do not look upon yourself as in any sort an usurper of

Wolf's rights or inheritance. Call yourself his steward, if you will, and hold yourself in readiness to give up the reins at any moment. But, in any case, come, for we all of us feel that you ought to be here."

And then there followed a postscript—much such an one as she had sent him a score or so of times before—how that Theo Martin had been staying once more at the Grange, and how sweet, and gentle, and beautiful she had grown.

And after this a second postscript, the like of which she had never sent him before, and which, strange to say, did not touch him in the manner he had at one time expected such news might. It contained the tidings that Lord Havers was dead, and Leila, consequently, a widow—how that her husband had concluded a most profligate course of living by a death through delirium-tremens, and how that Leila had gone home to her father's house, a mere wreck of the beautiful girl of lang syne.

XXI

Thus things in due course adjusted themselves, and when the fifth year after Wolf's disappearance was preparing to make its exit amid Christmas joys and festivities, Oscar was well-established as master of Plas-y-Coed, and, more than that, was making preparations for the due instalment of a sweet young girl as its mistress.

That young girl was Theo Martin. Judith had taken care that Oscar should find her at the Grange on his return from India, and somehow, though how it came about, no one seemed quite to know, when she went home, after a long visit, it was understood to be only on furlough, to order her trousseau and be married from her father's house.

So Christmastide brought to the old Grange that year not only a train of kindly charities for the poor and needy, but also preparations for a banquet to be given in honour of the return of bride and bridegroom, on as large a scale as anything ever attempted at Plas-y-Coed. Every neighbour, high or low, rich or poor, was to be invited. In the servants'-hall covers were to be laid for upwards of a hundred persons; in the dining-hall above space was to be extended to its utmost limit, so that not one of the tribe of Howell, Madox, or Watkins should be excluded.

Judith herself took the keenest and most active interest in these preparations for the feast. Heavy as had been sorrows through which this young woman had passed, they had not hardened her heart, nor turned her spirit to gall. Possibly she was not of the kind to be hardened or embittered by trouble. The true diamond can stand the touch of the lapidary's chisel, and get increased worth and beauty from the friction it undergoes. There could be but little doubt now of what stuff Judith was made.

As of old, every one, more or less, seemed to depend on her for something. Bryce, still holding the keys of the household in her wiry old fingers, deferred to her in every matter, small and great, from the supply of household damask which the young couple would be supposed to need, to the decoration of the banqueting-hall and table.

Mrs. Reece whispered to her confidentially:

"I don't want to wear your brains out quite, my dear, but I shall be greatly obliged to you if you will take as much as you can off mine."

Oscar, even, took to consulting her as to where the tennis-court should be made, upon various details of stable-management and expenditure, and the "latest sweet thing" in fishing-rods and guns. And as for Theo, the folios of letter-paper Judith received from her while the trousseau was in progress, requesting her opinion on colour, size, and shape of all sorts of garments, definite and indefinite, would have necessitated an extra leathern pouch for the solitary postman of the district had not the one he carried been already of inordinate size.

With hands thus filled, it may be imagined Judith had but little leisure for repining over a sorrowful past, or for tending and watering "that sweet self-pity," which is so emphatically the plant of idle and luxurious hours.

Not that the past ever was or could be dead to her. Not one act of the bitter drama in which they had all played their parts ever was or could be obliterated from her memory. Every word Wolf had ever spoken to her, every look his eyes had ever given her, remained as deeply impressed upon her memory as though graven there with iron tool. Her grief had in no sense of the word gone from black to grey, from grey to colourless white. No; black it was and ever would be to the end of her life—black, dense, irremediable as the darkness that filled any dungeon or churchyard vault. But she thanked Heaven she had door to shut upon it and padlock to put upon the door, and no one to the end of her days need be any the worse for the sad recollections which lay hidden thus under lock and key.

Sometimes it is true—though this always when alone—one by one the spectres of the past would troop forth and confront her with their gaunt faces and lack-lustre eyes, and, for a time earth would seem to her a dreary, beclouded place, and heaven—ah, such a long way off! Sometimes at night, in her own room, the distant mountains, looming out of the blackness, would seem to her dismal giant-ghosts guarding their terrible secret; the very stars would seem to shine with a pitiless glitter for the story they might, but would not, tell; but that did not mean that next day she would go weeping and moaning about the house, or, sour-tempered, shut herself in her own room. No; it meant, possibly, a night spent on her knees, with hidden eyes, a lying, face downwards, on her pillow, with so sharp a sense of pain at her heart as to be real and physical, cheeks a little paler the next day, and eyes a little more weary, and, if possible, a little more of kindness and attention than usual to be shown to Mrs. Reece—nothing more.

Mrs. Reece also was brave in bearing this sorrow as she had been in bearing her other and earlier troubles; possibly, she thought to herself, it was all for so short a time now that nothing could matter very much. Naturally, however, she had suffered physically more than Judith. At her age, long hours of passionate grief leave a more tangible impress than they do on persons some forty years younger; the rheumatism, which before had been intermittent, was now chronic, the labour of mounting stairs could scarcely be undertaken, and, once seated in her chair, no matter where, she was loth to move out of it.

"Put me face towards the mountains," she would say pathetically to the servant, who placed her chair; and face towards the mountains she would sit for hours, her blind eyes, possibly, filled with visions of her eldest son coming back to her the way he had gone.

Oscar's return home with his young bride naturally put a little more of life and circulation into the house. Theo tried to hush her cheery laugh, feeling almost guilty in her new-found happiness, and Oscar made as little parade as possible over his possession of a sweet young wife and mastership of Plas-y-Coed; but for all that there was more stir, more talk, more movement about the old place than there had been for many a day past.

On this particular Christmas Eve, as may be imagined, the stir and movement was increased a thousandfold. The coming and going was incessant, the sound of wheels up and down the avenue as though never coming to an end.

The banquet was to take the form of dinner for the poorer, luncheon for the richer, neighbours; all were to sit down at the same time—one o'clock; an early hour having been chosen out of consideration for those who had long distances to drive along steep roads, rendered yet more difficult by late heavy falls of snow.

It was a severe winter that year, hard frosts had set in at the beginning of December, and the whole country round was ice-bound. The woods looked like fairyland itself, with every fir-spire, every pine-needle marked out in glittering crystal. The mountains, snow-capped, showed grandly desolate against a leaden, storm-threatening sky.

"There'll be a storm before night; we must get away early," said one to another of the expected guests, as they prepared to set out for Plas-y-Coed.

"You'll see that all the fires are well kept up, Davies," said Judith to the butler, for the last time making the rounds of the rooms before she went into the drawing-room to help Theo and Mrs. Reece receive their guests.

Bryce followed her step by step as she went.

"They have forgotten something, Miss Judith, they ought to have remembered," she said, looking discontentedly up and down the long, tastefully-arranged dining-table.

Judith's eye followed hers.

"The table seems to me perfect, Bryce, I can't find fault; you must tell me what they have forgotten," she answered.

"The chair for the missing guest, Miss Judith, that's all," answered Bryce with the air of one who thought the *ultima thule* of human forgetfulness had been reached.

Judith started. There was one guest always missing, so it seemed to her, at every meal to which they sat down.

"Yes," she said sadly, "the chair must be placed. There's one we shall all miss today."

Bryce did not respond to this. In her secret heart she had never quite forgiven Wolf for the part he had played. She began bustling about among the chairs.

"Where shall I place the empty chair, Miss Judith; either side it will make the numbers uneven?" she asked.

Oscar coming in at this moment had to have the situation explained to him. He grew suddenly grave.

"The lists have been gone through carefully," he said; "no one has been forgotten; there can be only one person really missing today, and there can be only one place for him—that of the master of the house."

So the place at the foot of the table was laid and left vacant in memory of one who was Heaven only knew where!

The guests wondered as they came streaming into the dining-hall, Oscar leading the way, with Lady Ruthlyn on his arm, and cast their eyes on this empty chair. Then one began to tell another the tradition of the house, how that no Reece ever made a Christmas feast without leaving a vacant place for a possibly omitted guest, and the dreary story of the old squire whose coffin had been seen to pass through the closed turnpike-gate was told once more.

Mrs. Reece took her usual place at the head of the table, Judith hers at her right hand; Oscar and his bride sat facing each other half-way down.

It was a bright, pleasant scene to look upon. The old hall itself, with its fine carvings, stained glass, and ancestral portraits, was worthy of any painter's pencil; the table, with its load of shining glass and silver, its tastefully-arranged hot house fruit and flowers, looked as inviting as table could to hungry guests who had driven some six or eight miles in keen, frosty air. Handsome, well-featured faces were in the ascendant among the younger guests; good dressing prevailed among the elder, and one and all had that kindly, genial feeling towards each other which alone can make an entertainment of this sort a success.

All these good people were well-pleased to be able to hold out the right hand of fellowship to a neighbour who promised, as Oscar did, to be one of the right sort; all were glad to be able to bury in oblivion the miserable story of his elder brother's life. To have heard their hearty expressions of good-will, their cheery predictions of good-fortune to the young bride and bridegroom, one might have thought that never a cloud had darkened the windows of Plas-y-Coed, never a tragedy had been enacted within a stone's-throw of its gates.

So the wine flowed, jest and merry talk went round; Lord Ruthlyn paid the bride the neatest and prettiest of compliments, which she received with arch incredulity and the softest of blushes and smiles; the lieutenant of the county talked politics with Mrs. Reece, and recalled memories of various members of the Reece family he had known lang syne. A Madox, seated on one side of Judith, talked foxes and hounds to her, while a Howell, who sat opposite, wondered over her beautiful eyes and pale face, and thought how sweet a bride she would make when her time came. And Judith looked straight in front of her through the windows at the snow-crowned mountains, and thought of one who had once made his way up their rough grey sides, and had never come down.

The storm which had threatened all day came creeping on near and nearer. An east wind began to sigh and moan among the beeches; a few slow, sleepy flakes of snow began to fall.

It grew very dark within the house. Oscar gave orders to one of the servants to light the candles, which, in case of need, had been placed on the table. But Bryce stopped the man with a lighted taper in his hand.

"Candles lighted at a wedding feast," she said in a portentous whisper, "means a funeral before the year is out."

"Oh, the old raven!" cried Lady Ruthlyn; "better let us feel for our food, and the way to our mouths, than have such ill-luck as that whispered about."

So the candles were let alone, the room grew dark and darker, the snow-clouds came creeping down apace, and people began uncomfortably to think of the close of the entertainment, and the long, chilly drive that was in store for them.

It might have been this thought, it might have been the darkness which made something of a pause in the midst of the bright talk and laughter.

"I remember," said Lord Ruthlyn, addressing Judith across the table, "much such a Christmas Eve as this, now some forty years ago. Ah, you won't be able to boast of such a stretch of memory as that for many a long year to come."

Judith made no reply, and Lord Ruthlyn, looking up at her, saw a sudden startled expression sweep over her face; her eyes seemed to grow round with terror, her cheeks blanched, her lips, even, became ashen. His eyes naturally followed the direction of hers, and to his intense surprise he saw that the vacant seat at the foot of the table was vacant no longer.

In the semi-darkness, amid the laughter and the talk, one had silently entered the room, and taken possession of it.

XXII

Judith's heart beat wildly. Did her eyes deceive her? Did others see what she saw, or was this but some spectre rising, Banquo-like, to take his place among them for a brief moment before settling to everlasting rest?

At that, the lower end of the hall the shadows were deepest, and an occasional fitful gleam of firelight seemed only to define the semi-gloom. She could make out—yes, there could be no doubt about it—the outline of a massive head, of broad but stooping shoulders. Great Heavens! Did no one see him beside herself? Why was everyone turning round to stare at her, not him?

Was she going mad, and was madness written in her face, that they gazed and gazed at her in this way?

She could bear it no longer. She sprang to her feet, clasping her hands together.

"It is Wolf, Wolf, Wolf!" she cried, with a loud, passionate cry.

And then the guests, one and all, rose tumultuously to their feet.

Mrs. Reece alone sat still, trembling exceedingly.

"What! Who?" she said in a low, quavering voice. "Judith, for the love of Heaven, do not keep me long in suspense!"

But no one was in suspense long, for Oscar, with one loud shout, had jumped up from his chair, had thrown his arms round the stranger's neck, and with one hearty "Thank God, at last!" had burst into a flood of tears. The thoughts of bride, of assembled guests, of mastership over a famous property, all swamped in one deep flood of joy that Wolf, his Wolf—brother, father, guardian to him from his earliest years, was back among them all once more.

"Take me to my son, Judith—where is he?" said Mrs. Reece, making a vain effort to rise from her chair.

There was no need; for Wolf, loosing Oscar's arms from about his neck, rose and went to her side, one and other of the guests falling back and making way for him.

A fuller light fell upon him as he walked the length of that long room. It was Wolf Reece, not a doubt, with his stalwart figure, massive head, and stooping shoulders, yet not altogether the Wolf Reece of five years ago—certainly not the Wolf Reece with whom Judith had parted so sadly at the foot of the Llanniswth Mountains. A change of some sort had passed over the man; there was a something written in his face now which that other man lacked, there was a something lacking in his face which that other man had. True, there was a past, and a sorrowful past, written in every line of feature and brow. It was emphatically a face with a story to tell, no one could mistake it; but the fierce forlornness had died out of his eyes, the hopelessness, the look of desperate struggling, seemed gone; in its stead there seemed to have come a quiet, a restfulness which told of victory gained, an end achieved.

Judith's hands were both outstretched towards him as he kissed and folded his mother in his arms. He took them both, he held them for one moment in his own; their eyes met—nothing more.

There followed a huge amount of handshaking all round. For, somehow, these kindly members of the Welsh squirearchy seemed suddenly to have made up their minds, since the evil-doing of this man could not be undone, it had best be forgotten, or, at any rate, forgiven, as heartily as it had been heartily repented of. Then one and the other began to say, "It was time they said their good-byes, the storm would soon be down upon them; a family-meeting of this sort was not of daily occurrence; how glad they would all be to be alone!" and so forth.

Wolf bowed and thanked them. His manner of somewhat reserved courtesy seemed to have returned to him, the icy-cold abruptness, which for a time had distinguished him, had departed.

"There is one thing I would like to make clear to you, gentlemen, before you go," he said in clear, firm tones, "and that is, that I intend to resign all right and title to this place in favour of my brother Oscar."

Oscar began a loud demur. Judith laid her hand upon his lips "Hush, not now!" she whispered.

And so, with brief adieux, the guests departed, like the gentlemen and ladies that they were, asking no questions, though wondering much among themselves over the strange story Wolf must have to tell.

When the footsteps of the last departing guest had died away, Mrs. Reece laid her tremulous old hand on her elder son's arm. "Tell me," she said, "have you been far away from us all this weary five years?"

"I have been at times in the far North of England, at times in the extreme south, and at times within ten miles of my own door," answered Wolf slowly.

"Within ten miles of your own door!" repeated Mrs. Reece.

"Oh, Wolf!" cried Oscar indignantly, reproachfully. "And our hearts were breaking for you all that time. Did you never think of that?"

"I thought of it, Oscar; it added not a little to my punishment," answered Wolf sadly. "I had broken your hearts before I left you, I knew that; and worse still, had brought shame and dishonour upon you. It seemed to me I could not heal your hearts by staying here with you all, but I could do something to lift the disgrace from the house by hiding it and myself in some unknown corner. But leave me to tell my story my own way, Oscar. You can judge me when it is ended."

So they left him to tell his story his own way, gathering about him in a circle, with eyes fixed intently upon his face (the face they had never expected to gaze upon again in this life, at any rate) with breath held in at times, but never a word escaping their lips.

The story took a long time to tell. It began with that dreary twilight good-bye he had said to Judith at the foot of the Llanniswth mountains, and told how worn-out in mind and body, dazed and incapable, his one thought had been to creep up there, and in solitude to say a prayer and die. How it seemed to him that death could be the only fit ending to his miserable career; how that he felt it must be in very truth at hand when, as he reach the mountain-top, cloud-capped and night-crowned then, he sank down in a heavy stupor or fainting-fit.

Or it might have been a trance. He did not know. He could not say. Nor could he say how long it lasted. He only knew that in the grey dawn of morning a vision came to him. He seemed to be in a garden, shut in with high walls, a carefully-tended, neatly-kept place, filled with luxuriant flowers. He had gardening tools in his hand, but for some reason or other had ceased from his work, and stood looking around him at the beautiful plants.

Suddenly a cool shadow fell on him, and looking up, he saw it was the shadow of an angel with outstretched wings. At the same moment a voice, sweet and solemn as a distant bell, spoke, saying:

"Go, take your tools, and work outside the garden-wall. There are plenty of labourers who will work within."

He awoke, feeling a message had come to him straight from Heaven, and that his life, which in his despair he had accounted forfeited, had been given back to him. His clothes were drenched with the night-dews; his limbs were stiff and all but incapable; but nevertheless he managed to drag himself to his feet, intent only upon obeying what seemed to him a Divine mandate—upon finding out where was "outside the garden-wall," and setting to work there as a labourer.

In very truth this seemed to the man his one only chance of reparation and atonement.

Slowly he dragged his weak, weary limbs adown the mountain, wrapped still in its dawn, mists and dews, and at its very base the question he held in his heart seemed answered. A troop of gipsies, in long, slow, lumbering vans, were going along the steep road, and one of them, walking at the head of the foremost horse, pitying, possibly, his wan, weary looks, pulled up, and offered to give him a lift.

Wolf somehow managed to stumble into the van, and then fell senseless on its floor, overcome utterly now in mind and body.

For weeks he lay in the grasp of fever, unconscious of all that went on about him, but tended by these half-wild, altogether heathenish people, with a rugged kindness and care all their own.

Truth compels the admission, however, that while he lay thus ill and unconscious, they robbed him of every penny he possessed; that was simply their way of earning their livelihood. Also, it may be surmised, that the main motive for their kindly care of him and the indefatigable manner in which they shielded him from prying eyes, lay in the fact that by so doing they thought they were eluding the vigilance of the police.

"Why didn't you set me down by the wayside to die?" Wolf asked their chief one day, when he had so far recovered as to be able to take his turn at the horse's head.

The man shook his head.

"It isn't our way with those we've given shelter to," he answered. "Besides, we guessed by your mutterings and talk in your fever that you were being hunted down by the police (you said a great deal about your hands being stained with blood, and the like); and 'tisn't our fashion to help them in their work—they don't help us in ours."

So for five years Wolf had sojourned with this wandering tribe, an Ishmael among Ishmaelites, learning their trades of basket-making and tinkering, teaching them to read and write, marrying their sons and daughters together, christening their children, preaching to the elders; not as in the old days he had preached to his sinners in his London church; from an immeasurably superior height condescending to their depth, but as one standing on their level, a man who had fallen low as the lowest there, a sinner to sinners.

Wolf Reece's five years among the gipsies may one day be written and given to the world; it may contain a few hints useful to those desirous to work, as he did, "outside the garden-wall."

The best testimony to the success of his work among them lay in the fact that, little by little, the tribe melted into less than half its original numbers, many of the younger men and women betaking themselves to honest trades, and settling down in decent neighbourhoods.

At length the old chief died, leaving neither kith nor kin to step into his shoes. An odd circumstance followed. Wolf with one voice was unanimously elected king in his stead. Possibly he was the first, and may be the last clergyman of the Church of England ever elected a gipsy king.

He accepted the honour conferred upon him, but announced his intention of ruling as an autocrat. His first decree was a strict prohibition of thieving in every shape or form; his second an order that every man should adopt an honest trade. The result was that the remaining half tribe was split into fractions, and eventually altogether dissolved.

What was he to do now that his work had virtually ended itself? Chance answered the question. Chance had brought him in his journeyings to the borders of North Wales; chance placed in his hands the fragment of a newspaper containing the announcement of Oscar's wedding, and his intended return to Plas-y-Coed to receive the congratulations of the county.

But Wolf's voice, clear and steady as it had been throughout his narrative, here suddenly grew husky and threatened to fail him. He threw a troubled look at Judith.

"I thought," he went on, "that two who were very dear to me had joined hands now. I said to myself, 'They are worthy of each other; who am I to grudge them their happiness?' and I prayed harder than ever I had prayed before that my name might become a dead letter to you all. But somehow the prayer seemed useless and vain. I could fancy it was being thrown back in my teeth as I uttered it. My heart yearned and ached for you all. My soul had grown so strong within me now, it would make itself felt, it would carry all before it. Perforce it drove me back to my old home. I said to myself, 'I will creep like a thief into the house, I will read in their faces whether my prayer has been heard, and they have forgotten me.'"

But Judith could keep silence no longer. The room was quite dark now, for the big fire had burned low, and the lamps were not yet lighted. No one could see her face as she rose hurriedly from her chair.

"Ah, cruel, cruel," she cried in low, passionate tones, "to think you could keep your own truth while others lost theirs!"

The words seemed forced from her lips. She turned abruptly, and quitted the room.

Oscar looked up keenly into Wolf's troubled face.

"Is it your pride or your humility which will keep you and Judith apart?" he asked bluntly. "For the life of me I couldn't say which."

It was the first time in his life Oscar had ever turned mentor to his elder brother.

Wolf, with never a word, rose from his chair and left the room.

Without, in the big hall, lamps were lighted, curtains were drawn. Coming out from the dark room, the light was dazzling. Wolf had to shade his eyes with his hand to distinguish Judith at the farther end of the hall, standing at the glass doors which opened on to the terrace.

Outside, the garden lay one pure, unsullied sheet of snow. The storm was over; a clear, full moon went sailing overhead, flooding mountain, wood, and valley with its silver light.

A small, dark figure, standing just outside the doorway, showed wan and ghostlike between the white of the snow at her feet, the white of the moon overhead. Her face was upturned. It had a curious, questioning look on it, born half of patience, half of pain. Truth to tell, she was asking herself much the same question as Oscar had asked of his brother not a minute ago, and had found it every whit as difficult of solution as he.

It was no wonder. In this man Wolf Reece's somewhat complex nature, his pride so frequently masqueraded as humility, his humility as pride, it may be doubted whether he himself was at times quite sure which was which.

There came a strong, kindly voice at her elbow which made her start and tremble.

"Child, child," it asked, much as it had some six or seven years ago, among the laurels in the garden, "what is it that troubles you?"

Even as he asked the question, his arm had somehow crept round her waist; he was drawing her near, nearer to himself, till her head rested on his breast.

Then she turned her pale face to meet his dark one.

"Nothing troubles me now," she said softly.

"Judith, Judith!" he cried passionately—though he held her close and tight to his heart all the time—"do you know what you are doing? You are casting in your lot with one who has a miserable past to redeem, who, to the end of his life, will know nothing of ease or wealth, but will be a toiler—and a good hard toiler, too—'outside the garden-wall.'"

And Judith, with her head still on his breast, answered in the sweet, solemn words of one of old time:

"'Whither thou goest I will go; where thou diest I will die, and there will I be buried.' Naught but death shall part thee and me."

And naught but death can part those two, so firmly clasped are their hands one in the other's, as together they labour "outside the garden-wall."

Not among the gipsies and tramps now, but among a set of poor sinners who, at one time, formed part of Wolf's East London parishioners. Every whit as lawless and squalid as gipsy or tramp are they, and as emphatically "outside the garden-wall" as any herd of Ishmaelites.

THE END

A Note About the Author

Catherine Louisa Pirkis (1839–1910) was a British author known for her detective fiction. Pirkis wrote fourteen novels and contributed to many magazines and journals, sometimes publishing under her initials, C.L. Pirkis, to avoid gender discrimination. Later in her life, Pirkis transitioned away from her writing career to join her husband, Frederick Pirkis, in his fight for animals' rights. Together, the couple founded an activist organization to save animals from cruel conditions. Their organization continues their advocacy today, and now goes by the name "Dogs Trust".

A Note from the Publisher

Spanning many genres, from non-fiction essays to literature classics to children's books and lyric poetry, Mint Edition books showcase the master works of our time in a modern new package. The text is freshly typeset, is clean and easy to read, and features a new note about the author in each volume. Many books also include exclusive new introductory material. Every book boasts a striking new cover, which makes it as appropriate for collecting as it is for gift giving. Mint Edition books are only printed when a reader orders them, so natural resources are not wasted. We're proud that our books are never manufactured in excess and exist only in the exact quantity they need to be read and enjoyed.

Discover more of your favorite classics with Bookfinity™.

- Track your reading with custom book lists.
- Get great book recommendations for your personalized Reader Type.
- Add reviews for your favorite books.
- AND MUCH MORE!

Visit **bookfinity.com** and take the fun Reader Type quiz to get started.

Enjoy our classic and modern companion pairings!